This is David Phillips' first foray into fiction. Born in Australia and living in Melbourne, he has always had lots of ideas and imagination and wanted to put it all together and see what emerged. He enjoys a wide variety of novels, including historical, sci-fi and fantasy. Outside of this journey into fiction, David has worked as a medical researcher and research manager for many years. His other interests are delving into family history, playing golf and jogging to stay active.

See https://calembeena.com.au/books/

Smith

David Phillips

SHAGREEN PRESS

ISBN **978-1-7636502-0-6**

ISBN (eBook) **978-1-7636502-1-3**

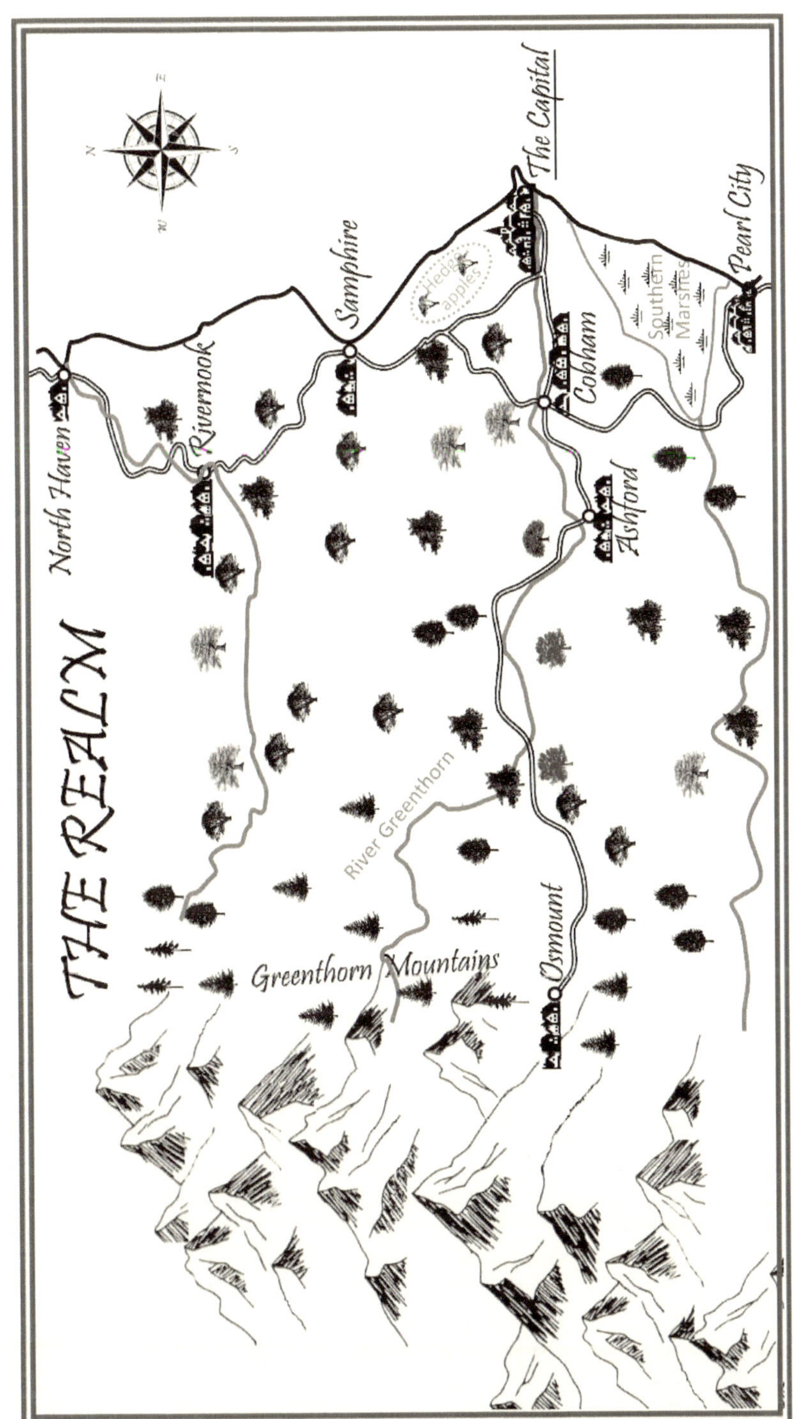

THE REALM
N
E
S
W
North Haven
Rivernook
Samphire
Hedge apples
The Capital
Cobham
Southern Marshes
Pearl City
Ashford
River Greenthorn
Greenthorn Mountains
Osmount

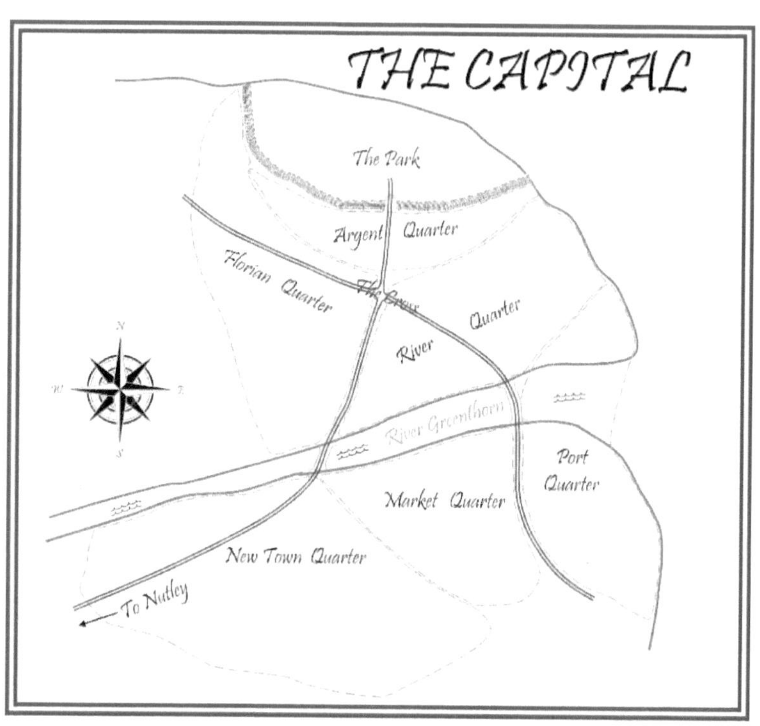

THE CAPITAL
The Park
Argent Quarter
Florian Quarter
The Spur
Quarter
River
River Greenthorn
Port Quarter
Market Quarter
New Town Quarter
To Nutley
N
W
E
S

Parts of a sword or dagger

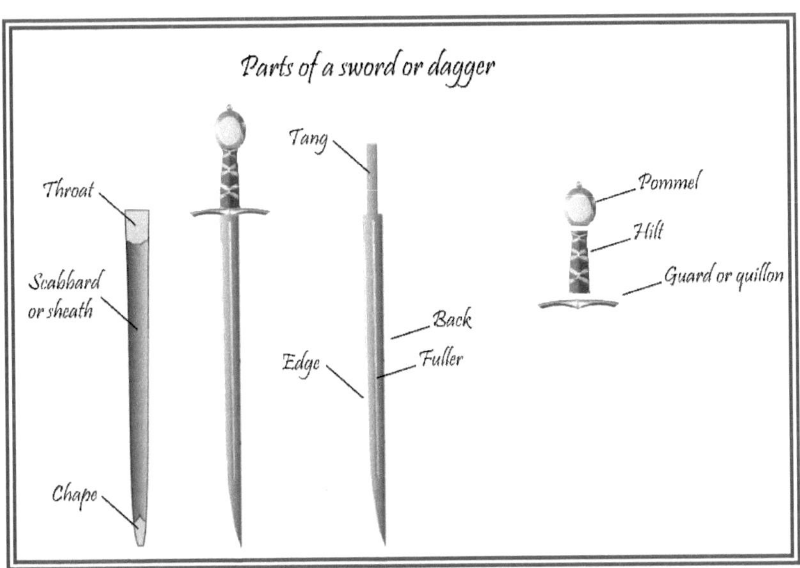

Chapter 1
First Meeting

It was another typical wintery day, with a cloudy sky and the threat of a little rain later on. The street still had puddles from the downpour two days ago and was showing its muddy, well-trodden visage, typical of this part of town.

The smith looked over the totally familiar streetscape without really seeing it and instinctively checked the metal rod heating in the coals of the forge. It was ready again, with the bright yellow shades showing it was the correct temperature to draw down the bar. He pulled it out, transferred it to the anvil and worked the rod flatter with seven consecutive blows. He stopped for a few heartbeats to assess progress and pushed it back into the coals. He would grab the other rod he was working on in a few moments from the forge, maintaining the working rhythm of seven blows, then the equivalent time to work out what was the next step, then the equivalent time corresponding to another seven strikes to ponder on anything else and to get ready for the next cycle. It was an easy and productive routine, as he had been taught and now was second nature to him. He could maintain this for an hour or more, until it was time for a longer break, a drink, meal or a short walk to clear his mind and have a bit of a stretch.

Past experience had shown him that it was very easy to stay in the moment, to immerse himself in the cycle of working the metal, a pause to review, a few quick thoughts, then back to the metal. He would often emerge from this trance after several hours focused on his work. He would realise that the day had shifted on, having no recollection of people passing in the street or normal town noises, or that a potential customer had become increasingly intrusive in trying to distract the smith from his all-consuming work.

About to pull the other rod from the forge, the smith somehow felt there were eyes on him. Still watching the rod, he swiftly scanned from under lowered brows. There was nothing out of place in the shop. No one was approaching the forge, the street was empty, none of the neighbours were about and the alleyway was empty. Wait! He noticed a slight form at the corner of the alleyway, leaning against the side wall of Postlethwaite's shop, gazing at the workshop intently. It was hard to judge exactly who this was: remarkable only that whoever they were appeared clad in rags and were dirt-smeared, with dark, lank and tousled hair.

The seven moments were over and it was time to work on the other rod.

One-two-three-four-five-six-seven blows. Hmm, he thought, it was coming along and almost ready for the next step: to fold in with the other rod. Seven beats to think about something else. The smith looked over to the alleyway and saw nothing. No figure leaning against the wall. A quick glance up the alley and the street: nothing. Perhaps he had imagined it. The town was known to have a number of urchins and other children that drifted in and out. Who knows what they did and where they lived. Presumably they were homeless. The only thing that was a little odd was that intense feeling of the figure watching his every action. You wouldn't forget that in a hurry. Well, back to the cycle and the job at hand.

The smith didn't think further of this strange encounter and completed the ploughshare blade that day and began filing and polishing it up. He was sure that Master Finean would be quite satisfied with it, particularly since he was waiting for this repair to start ploughing ready for spring sowing. Finean had left it far too late to come: his plough had become warped, buckled and was not functioning as it should. The smith tamped down the forge and put away his tools. Another part of the constant ritual was that everything was returned to its place, and it would be a reverse cycle at the start of the new day, setting his tools out where they were quick to hand and to fire up the forge. He whistled tunelessly as he took one last glance out at the sky beginning to darken towards night. The final part of the closing routine was to pull the wooden partitions across the opening to the street and drop the plank into the slots at the back of the partitions to secure them. He grabbed his sack from near the interior door and walked down the short, covered walkway to the back door of the cottage. Today had been a good day's work and he felt content. He might even call in at the Wheatsheaf for an ale before dinner.

The smith wakened the next morning soon after dawn. The weather remained very closed-in and with a steady, penetrating drizzle. One advantage of working in the forge was that the temperature was always warmer than outside. That helped in the cooler months but was a curse in summertime. Also, the roof was doing its job apart from the mysterious leak in the far corner. The tub underneath the leak sufficed until he had the time to climb up onto the shingles and work out exactly where the water was dripping through. That reminded him: he should dedicate the time to look at how the shingles were doing. It was a few years since he had last done that and there were bound to be quite a few that needed to be replaced.

After unbarring the partitions at the street front, firing up the forge and setting out the tools, implements and materials needed, today's main task was to begin putting together the cast-iron gates that the guild hall had commissioned. It had been a significant project just in trying to encapsulate the guildmasters' thoughts. These were all about the importance and gravitas of the guilds to the town and surrounding district, which must, of course, be understood from the symbolism and design incorporated into the gates. And without compromising on functionality and being able to be drawn open and closed shut by the doorkeeper, who was over sixty if he was a day. This would happen if any visiting nobility or other important guests arrived by coach or on horseback. It had taken six return visits to the guild hall and multiple drawings of the gates and the opening mechanism before they were satisfied and approved the design. Still, it was an important piece of work and would continue to build on his reputation as the finest and most well-known smith in the district.

One-two-three-four-five-six-seven, and rest. He was already in the cycle of efficient productivity and would go for another hour before his first break for a drink of cool water and part of a roll filled with meat left over from last night's dinner. During the thought part of the routine, the smith had been mulling over what sort of charcoal would be needed for the next lot of jobs. Each wood gave a different charcoal with various properties in terms of heat produced, residues, effects on the steel derived, and so on. There were so many things to consider, including which yard would be able to provide the best wood, and for a reasonable price. Or should he take a day off and explore into the forest to find any seasoned, deadwood that had dried out? Reflecting further, that was not really a sustainable option: he would spend all his time sourcing and carting back firewood, then converting it into charcoal and wouldn't have any time to do smithing. That said, the last lot of cherrywood charcoal he had got from Forsyth's timber yard had been no good for some of the more finicky projects needing a very flexible steel that could be worked into complicated shapes. It was only when considering whether it might be worth a trip to Cobham, the larger town about half a day's travel away, that the smith could feel the intense gaze on him again. It was from the same place, the figure leaning up against Postlethwaite's in the alleyway; the same unremarkable form, same dirt-encrusted hair and rags, the same intense, yearning stare. Another cycle of blows to the forge-heated iron, checking on its progress and the next steps needed, then time to think and look out. The figure hadn't moved! Perhaps they were waiting for him to get distracted and turn away, before running in and grabbing something. No, it had to be they were interested in what was going on and the steady but somehow intense work within the forge. *Hmmm.*

On an impulse and without even thinking further, the smith put down his tools, straightened up and slowly walked out of the forge. He began crossing the street, not even registering his subconscious navigation between the worst of the puddles and mud. The smith was slightly hunched from years of leaning over the anvil but was still an imposing figure of just under six feet tall. The leather leggings, jerkin and apron did nothing to disguise the corded and defined musculature, particularly in the shoulders and arms, not surprising given the years of striking the anvil and working with materials that had to be cajoled into changing shape or being folded or welded to each other. The face was not unkindly from what could be seen beneath the full beard: blue eyes set in a growing web of wrinkles, a nose with a distinct kink – the result of a long-ago break – and a mouth held in a serious, businesslike pose but which knew how to smile and laugh all the same. Hair of a nondescript dark blond, shoulder-length or so, but tied at the back with a leather thong. The figure watched the smith getting closer and closer, the eyes losing their intense stare that had been following every action in the forge. They began shifting left and right, looking for the safest pathway to flight. The figure tensed and looked ready to bolt.

The smith stopped about ten feet from the figure in the alleyway, which had come erect to a not very imposing height, poised on the balls of their feet. 'This is the second day you have been watching me work. Is there something you want to say to me?'

The figure shuffled a little. The smith felt the same yearning, intense look as the boy resumed his stare. 'I want to learn. I want to do what you do.'

Silence for many heartbeats. 'Hmmm. I'll have to think about that. How about you come over to the forge and watch from there? You'll have a lot better view, and we can chat at the same time.'

It was only a minor change to the smith's normal working routine: seven blows on the anvil, seven moments to assess and plan, and seven moments to talk instead of think. He had upended a firkin sometimes used to hold stakes and which the boy could sit on, out of the way but just behind where he was working. The boy perched on the makeshift seat, when he wasn't craning forward to gaze raptly at the heat, the flame, the sparks, the noise, the smells, everything.

'Do you have a name?'

'Gerant.'

'Gerant. Fair enough. I'm Sveg.' A pause. 'Where do you live, Gerant?'

'Just around.'

'Not at home?'

A negative shake of the head.

Another pause. 'Where do you keep your stuff?'

'Haven't got much. So I just keep it where I'm staying.'

A longer pause. 'How old are you, Gerant?'

'Don't know, for sure. Probably eleven or twelve. Might have lost count.'

Sveg pondered these brief responses. *At least the kid was talking, that was a start. That answers one thing: homeless and living on the street. Might have a little bolthole or just find somewhere out of the way each night. Wonder what brought that about? Parents died? Had he run away from another town or village? Well, that might emerge a little later.* 'Want to ask me anything?'

'Sveg's a funny name.'

'Well, it's not if you're from up north. There up plenty of Svegs up that way, so not surprising my mother named me that.'

'Oh.'

'Can you give those bellows a few turns? We need to keep the coals heated up.'

Gerant quickly jumped off the firkin and grabbed the handles of the bellows.

'Whoa, whoa, back off a little, matey! You need to work them steadily and just for a few steady puffs at a time. We don't want to burn down the forge, do we?' A pause. 'That's the way. Can I leave you to keep an eye on that and do that every couple of times? Good job.'

Another cycle completed. 'Do you know where the guild hall is?'

'That the big place down near the river?'

'That's the one. I'm building a new set of gates for them. It'll take me about a week to finish them. Want to see the design drawings?'

'Sure.'

'Let's take a short break then and I'll show you. We can have a drink as well. Working with the forge is thirsty work.'

Sveg walked into the back where his drafting bench was positioned to catch the best light and grabbed the paper on which he had laid out the drawing of the Guild Hall gates. He showed

Gerant the design and how the pieces they were working on fitted into the gate structure.

'Make sense?'

'Yes. Did you draw this yourself?'

'Sure did. This is another part of being a smith. You need to take the picture that's in your head and what you are trying to make, then be able to put it down in a diagram or drawing so everyone knows what you are going to do.'

The boy made a small soundless 'Oh'. His brow furrowed a little as he continued puzzling through the smith's words. 'I thought all this was about making stuff and hammering it to what you needed. And don't you do things with horses?'

'Ahhh . . . horses. I haven't done fitting up horses with shoes for years. Found it too boring and got engrossed in some of the more interesting design stuff and more advanced skills. So, I was able to give up that stuff: the town is big enough for some other blacksmiths who look after that. Hoskins and Tootling do reasonable work in that line.' Sveg collected his thoughts and continued.

'Working and shaping metal, that's the key part of it, but you also need to be able to design what you are going to make so you know what materials and pieces will make it up, and then be able to put it down on paper or parchment so you can make it again and they all end up the same. That's why my sign outside says, Master Sveg Martinson, metalsmith and artisan. Go on. Go and look. The board is hanging up under the eaves, just between the two posts.'

Gerant walked to the edge of the street and looked up at the sign. It took Sveg a few moments of watching to realise something was not quite right. He also came out to the front of the street and gazed up at the sign with the boy. His hand subconsciously rested on the boy's shoulder. 'You can't read, can you?'

'Nope. Never needed to.'

'Well, you've got plenty of time to rectify that. Let's go back inside and we'll keep working. We'll try to get a good way in and then we can break for lunch.' The smith didn't need to ask whether the boy had any food with him and mentally resigned himself to sharing what Marion had packed him that morning.

Sveg had lots of things to mull over while working on the gates with the boy. *This lad is clearly interested in everything going on, once I have explained it and the reason behind it. He clearly comprehends it and is absorbing it like a sponge. Admittedly, the tasks I have asked him to do are fairly simple and routine, but the speed at which he has picked them up and started to anticipate the next move is really encouraging.*

Sveg continued to cycle through his normal routine in constructing the gates, thinking through the startling idea and having a brief comment or question with the boy every cycle or so. *At least he isn't the sort of kid who keeps on talking and can't shut up. It's more the other way around, although so far he hasn't dodged the occasional question. It's just he is far from expansive in his responses.* That suited Sveg.

So, is it a really crazy idea to even think that this boy might be interested in becoming an apprentice? Is that totally far-fetched? He is clearly enthralled in working in the forge and so far has been quick to pick up the basic concepts and routines. But that's a far cry from it actually working out. Assuming the boy actually wants to become an apprentice, where the hell would he live? Where was he living? Would the guild approve an application? Who would sponsor him and provide a surety? The kid can't read. That's a huge limitation. How would they get around that? If Gerant became an apprentice, would an option be that we set up a bed in the smithy and he can stay there? There is no way that Marion will let him stay in the cottage. I'm not ready to do that either. How to even bring up what has happened today with Marion? She will probably go crazy about it.

All these disjointed bits of thought swirled around Sveg's mind. He surprised himself that, in these unconnected moments of reflection, he was able to work as normal and maintain a calm and measured conversation with the boy. Immersed in all these things, he suddenly looked up and realised that some hours had passed, and it was late afternoon. That was a positive sign: they could clearly work together, even though the boy was only contributing in a very minor way. The gates were also coming together as planned, although there was still at least a day's hard slog to get them close to completion. Well, it was time to shut down the forge and call it a day.

Sveg went through his end-of-day routine with Gerant helping out, putting the tools in their racks and storage spaces, tamping down the forge and sweeping the dirt floor of metal scraps and other offcasts. 'Did you enjoy today, Gerant?'

'It was interesting. I liked it.'

'Well, I appreciate your help. You made a difference. I thought it went well.' Sveg paused, thinking about how he could frame the next question. 'So, you're going to go back to wherever and grab something to eat?'

'Yeah, something like that.'

'Well, the last thing to do is to pull the partitions closed and put the bar across. I'll do that from the inside and then I'll also call it a night.'

Sveg finally decided to risk another thing that he had been mulling over for the last half hour.

'So, will I see you again tomorrow? You're welcome to help out like today.'

'That would be good. Thanks.'

Sveg surprised himself in feeling an enormous sense of relief. 'Have a good evening then, Gerant. We'll see you on the morrow.'

The boy slipped out of the partly closed partitions and disappeared quickly into the growing twilight. Sveg finished pulling the partitions together and dropped the bar into the slots. He grabbed his sack and walked back through the smithy to the connecting passage and the cottage, a thoughtful look on his face as he whistled tunelessly.

Chapter 2
A Proposal

Breakfast was, as usual, an hour or so after dawn and a chance for the three in the family to talk and, well, act as families should do. Bree was bolting down her porridge, alternating between her usual chatty observations and moments of reflection and thought. She was certainly developing into an interesting young lady, sometimes quite childlike, spontaneous and even younger in outlook than her ten years of age; yet, at other times starting to ponder and think through and act as an adult would. She was quite slim and about average height for girls of her age, but with the promise of a growth spurt and filling out in the usual female areas sometime fairly soon. Her strawberry blond hair was plaited halfway to her waist, with a smooth, roundish face and bright blueish-grey eyes. Nonetheless, in particular lights, or when she was serious and thoughtful, her facial features and profile hinted at the woman she would become. She would not be a classical beauty but someone who would cause heads to turn because of a notable presence – people would look twice after an initial, cursory glance.

Her mother was also slim of figure and willowy. The dress Marion wore accentuated her svelte hips and a bustline that was clearly feminine and not top-heavy. Her auburn hair was a little more than shoulder-length and framed her face with gentle ringlets. Her movements were considered, free-flowing and economical: one sensed she was an excellent dancer. She had an was aquiline profile, with a gently curved nose, with some of which you could already see in her daughter's developing profile and features. What was also clear from a few minutes in her presence was that she showed a very caring attitude, coupled with forthright thinking: happy to express herself, yet careful not to say anything out of place. She was someone whose thoughts and opinions should be considered carefully and were often on the mark.

Marion had unconsciously noted that the byplay between Sveg, his daughter and herself was refreshingly bright this morning. Not that her husband was morose or uncommunicative, just that at the breakfast table he was often thinking ahead of what the day's tasks in the smithy would bring.

'You woke up in a good mood, darling. I can't recall the last time you were so perky. Something good going to happen today?', remarked Marion.

'Daddy's excited about the drawing I am going to do today and how well my letters are going.'

'Well, that too, I suppose.'

'Oh?' Marion's eyebrows were arched with expectation.

'Let's just see how the day plays out. If it goes the way I am hoping it will, I will have some news to talk with you tonight. I would value your thoughts ... this is not a decision I want to or could make on my own. You always give me some extra things to consider, that I hadn't thought of.'

'That sounds a little ominous. The guild giving you trouble?'

'Not directly. No, something a bit more immediate that could impact on us as a little family.'

'I await your pronouncements anon, my lord.' Marion gave a deep curtsey with lowered eyes, which set off Bree in a fit of giggles.

After packing away the breakfast plates with Bree, Sveg strolled down the connecting passage to the smithy. Sveg was having mixed thoughts. The evening before, the boy had indicated when he left he would be back, but there was a niggling doubt that maybe had only been pretending to be interested in what Sveg had showed him the previous day. Well, fate would determine what would emerge. The smith put down his sack containing lunch and a couple of other bits and pieces in its usual place, noting that things were as he had left things the night before. He paused briefly before taking off the bar.

'Just get on with it, my lad,' muttered Sveg to himself. He gave a quick nudge to the well-oiled shutters on their tracks, leading to sunlight flooding into the workspace. A figure detached itself from the laneway across the street, walked over and quickly slipped through. The slightly worried expression on Gerant's face quickly changed to relief. Clearly the smith hadn't been the only one with mixed feelings that there had been a change of heart overnight.

'Ah, Gerant. Well met! I thought we could keep working on the gates. How would you like to try your hand at hammering?'

The boy's eyes were almost as big as saucers and all he could do was nod vigorously.

'And after lunch, we might sit down and have a chat about how you've found things so far and what the future might hold . . .' Sveg watched the boy very keenly to see what sort of reaction that brought. After an initial freeze in posture and expression as Gerant took in the words, there seemed to be many thoughts cross the boy's brow, before an almost grudging nod.

'Yeah, that would be good. I was thinking about that in the night and have some things to tell you.'

'Hmmm. It would be good to hear them. But let's put in a good morning's work and then we can sit down and take a bit of time and hear what each other has to say.'

Sveg and Gerant got things ready, with the smith naming the various bits of equipment and tools as they got them out. Gerant softly repeated the names, getting used to the sound of the words. The last step was to work the bellows to make sure the coals were heating and starting to develop a steady, even heat. Sveg put a bar of iron into the centre of the rosy, glowing coals to heat.

'Tell me, are you left-handed or right-handed?'

A look of confusion crossed the boy's face.

'Perhaps I could ask you in a different way. What hand do you normally hold a spoon or fork in when you are eating?'

'Either, but more often my right hand.'

'Well, that makes it a little easier to show you. I'm right-handed as well. You put the hammer in your right hand and the tongs in your left. Depending on the job, I use seven or eight different hammers and five or so types of tongs. But go with this ball-peen and these tongs.' Sveg passed over the tools he had named.

'OK. What do you think you are missing? Think about how I was working when you were sitting behind me yesterday.'

A pause. 'Oh, gloves.'

'And . . .?'

'The apron.'

'Well done. These are going to be way too big for you, but at least you will get the idea. Let's get the bar out of the coals. Normally you would do all this yourself, but I think for the first few times I'll hold the bar on the anvil and you just concentrate on striking it with the hammer.' Sveg, with practiced skill, grabbed the bar from the glowing coals and placed it deftly on the anvil, holding it steady with the tongs. 'Remember, seven strikes to push the iron flatter from the tip to about three inches, where it is glowing that strong yellow colour.'

Gerant had his tongue just peeking out of the side of this mouth as with intense concentration he smashed the hammer down on the bar. After seven strikes the bar was a little flattened in a few places near the tip.

'That's a really good start, Gerant. So, let's put it back in the coals for the next round, and talk about what just happened.' Sveg paused for some moments, wrestling with the way to talk honestly to Gerant about his first try with anvil work, but do it in a way that was not overly critical and didn't totally dishearten him. 'How did you find that?'

'It was harder than I thought. It didn't do what I wanted it to do. You make it look so easy.'

'Well, that's years of practice, but let's talk about how to achieve what you want. You must be at one with the piece of metal you are working on. You must understand it, work with it, hear what is has to say, not fight it. In many ways, it is alive and responds to a firm touch, but will resist you if you don't listen to it and just try to smash it into submission. I suppose I sound a bit crazy, but that was what I was taught and what I have learnt on my own.'

Gerant thought for a moment. 'Is that why your eyes kind of go off into the distance?'

'Exactly. I am trying to work with the bar, not against it. I guess I am having a little bit of a conversation with it in my head.'

Sveg was relieved that what he had said made some sort of sense to Gerant. He did most of this now as second nature. It was a little difficult to put it into words. 'This way of thinking also means you know exactly where you have to strike and how strong and to be able to get the metal to do what you are wanting. It's about your eye seeing and your head being able to tell your hands and arms and body what it needs to do to achieve that.' The smith thought some more. 'Part of the reason, Gerant, why your blows were not quite where they would have been best is because you don't have that skill yet. But we can start working on that. I'll show you how I was shown by the master smith who taught me.'

Sveg looked around. 'See that dagger on the design bench? Can you grab it?'

Mystified, Gerant passed it over.

'Now, watch. See that knot in the wood about a foot from the top of the post over there?'

Gerant looked where Sveg was pointing. Yes, there was a growth whirl in one of the posts supporting the smithy roof, about fifteen feet away.

The smith relaxed his posture, weighing the dagger in his right fist. He then smoothly half-turned, at the same time uncoiling his body a little and quickly flicking his arm at the post. *Thunk.* The dagger buried itself into the post, vibrating and quivering for some moments and then was steady, almost growing at right angles out of the thick timber. Gerant walked over and looked up: the point was roughly an inch below the knot, but in line.

'I practised for hours until I could get a dagger to land almost exactly where I was aiming for. It certainly was a fun way to improve my hand-eye coordination, and it was also a very useful skill to have. You never know when you might need it in to protect yourself, for that matter. Is that something you would be willing to try? Strictly for smithy training, of course,' Sveg said with a broad grin.

Gerant's rapid nodding and a shy grin was response enough.

'I thought as much. There is another old dagger packed away somewhere that has reasonable balance and we can start with that.'

After a lunch break in which Sveg shared his slices of roast beef, cob of bread and mustard, the smith started a conversation that he had been pondering. *It would be interesting to see where it would end up going,* he thought. 'I have been pondering for some time about getting a bit of help in the smithy and also passing on some of my learnings to the right sort of person. Then you showed up and it got me thinking more of that possibility. We have only known each other for a very short while, but I have watched you and you appear to be very interested in the trade. If things worked out, would you like to begin an apprenticeship with me and learn how to be a smith?'

'Umm, I think so. Umm, yes, I would.'

Sveg was hard put to not show his relief. 'Well, that's a good start. But there are many other aspects we need to think through. Tomorrow I could go to the guild and have a meeting with them and see if they are willing to consider you as an apprentice under me. There are quite a few things that I will have to convince them to agree to.'

Gerant nodded slowly as he took in what the smith was offering.

'Another important thing to work out is where you fit in here at the smithy. It would make a lot of sense that you stay here somehow. I've already got some ideas. But first I need to talk to Marion about what might be possible. That's my wife. She is trained as a nurse and spends time at the town infirmary most days. She should be back from there soon.' Sveg paused and watched the lad's face. There was a look that might be shock as he seemed to be dealing with unfamiliar ideas like having a job and somewhere proper to live. *I'm not surprised,* thought Sveg. *At least he isn't rejecting this idea out of hand.* The smith decided to press on.

'I don't want to promise you anything: it may or may not work out. My family may be totally against this sort of arrangement. But let me go to the cottage now and see if she has returned. OK?'

'I'll just wait here,' said Gerant. Sveg wandered off down the passage that Gerant now knew went to the back of the cottage.

Sveg found Marion just arrived back from the infirmary, with a basket of carrots and cabbage which she was putting away on shelves in the kitchen. She offered her cheek for her husband to kiss.

'I thought I'd make a quick stew for tonight with these vegetables, plus some of the potatoes and the leftovers of the beef we had.'

Marion paused. 'Something troubling you, my husband?'

Sveg was clearly wrestling with how to start. 'You remember some time ago that I talked about getting an apprentice to help out? Well, I think I have found someone that has all the signs of going to be really worth putting the time and effort into. I was thinking of going to the guild tomorrow to see if I could get him put on the books.'

'That's very good. You are getting busier and busier now, so it would be helpful for someone to share the load. Is it someone I know?'

'No, very unlikely you do. His name is Gerant. He's a young lad, a little older than Bree.'

'Great. Where does he live? Would he have far to come to the forge?'

'Well, that's the first thing I wanted to talk to you about. I was thinking of setting up a corner of the forge near the storage area as a little place he could sleep. It would be easy to partition it off and put a pallet in there.'

'That is a lot of trouble to go to. Why can't this Gerant stay with his family and come over every day like most people?'

'Well, as far as I have been able to find out, he doesn't have any family and a home to go back to. Looks like he is homeless. He's been a little evasive about this, but he never knew his dad and his mum died when he was very young. He's been on the streets ever since. That's why I thought we could set something up for him at the smithy.'

Marion's mouth fell open in shock. 'Whaaat? Are you thinking straight? It sounds like you know nothing of this boy. How can you trust him? He could steal everything, and you couldn't stop him!'

'I don't think he's like that. He is very interested in what I've already shown him, and my sense is that he is an honest lad and just needs to be given a chance. I hope it would also be possible that he could eat with us, as he has no way to support himself. I know I am asking a lot, but at least let me go and get him and you can meet him.'

Marion's face showed strong disbelief. 'I am not sure what you expect me to say. Everything you have told me so far has not convinced me of anything. I think you have stars in your eyes.'

'Another thing is that he can't read. Not surprising, really.'

'Sveg Martinson! You have rocks in your head. I am now very curious about this lad. Has he bewitched you? Let me meet him and see if he has the same effect on me. Ha!' Marion turned away and continued to put away the vegetables. Sveg sighed quietly and shambled off.

As Sveg walked back to the forge, he mused that he shouldn't have been surprised at Marion's reaction. He had quite a lot of further explaining to do, even if she would even let him get that far.

'Gerant, come and meet Marion. I've explained a few things about you.'

As he approached Marion with Gerant in tow, Sveg watched a series of reactions cross his wife's face. First, there was shock at what she could see of this young lad wearing little more than rags and with face and arms smeared with dirt. Her nostrils then flared as she picked up a distinctive, unpleasant reek – not rotten or sickly – just emanating from someone who hadn't taken a wash in an awfully long time. Then all of her self-control took over and she put on a polite, welcoming smile.

'You must be Gerant. Sveg has just been telling me a little about you. I hear you are interested in becoming Sveg's apprentice?'

The boy nodded hesitantly several times.

'Well, there are a few things I need to discuss with my husband. Very nice to meet you. Would you excuse us while we have a bit of a chat?'

Gerant headed back to the smithy to await the outcome. He poked vaguely at the coals with a set of tongs as he couldn't help but hear the argument erupting.

'What do you see in him? I see a filthy, smelly wretch that I would cross to the other side of the street to avoid. How can you even think it would be possible to have someone like that live nearby, let alone come into our house?'

'Despite appearances, he is a good lad.' A pause. 'We need to give him a chance. If we don't give him a start, who will?'

'He can't read, he has no family, no one to recommend him. How are you going to convince the guild to take him? Who is going to provide the surety for him?'

'Well, I will. There are other apprentices who can hardly read. I have a little bit of money put away that I can use as surety.'

'What sort of example would we be setting for Bree? How can we show her how to behave and be shown good examples, when someone like him is around? Have you thought about that?'

'I have. I think that Bree will enjoy having someone closer to her age around. We can clean him up and it shouldn't be a problem.'

The animated conversation went back and forth for ten minutes or so. A little later, Gerant saw the smith return to the forge. He looked pale and was quite subdued.

'Well, Gerant, we have some work to do. I had to make a number of promises and you will also have to agree to some things as well.' The smith sighed and mentally appeared to resolve himself to a path that he was not looking forward to.

'Before Marion will formally agree, I have to go and visit someone and get his advice, as this person knows quite a bit about the workings of the town. We'll finish early today so I can do a couple of those chores.'

Marion had been very insistent in trying to find out some more about this young lad and Sveg had agreed to find out what Amos Moorhead, the captain of the town guard, knew or was willing to share.

'Just so you know, I will also go to the guild this afternoon or the day after and see if they are willing to take you on. I am hopeful, but it may depend on how well I argue.'

It was all Gerant could do but to nod firmly. This was way out of his experience, and it was enough to digest what was happening, let alone contribute to the conversation. Sveg watched carefully the series of expressions travelling across the boy's face and was reassured.

'OK, let's put in a few good hours' work and then shut up for the day. You can be back here on the morrow, to continue helping, if you like. I hope I will have some firmer news for you about a longer-term arrangement.'

Sveg reached out to ruffle the boy's hair. After an initial shrinking back, Gerant allowed the smith to continue, although clearly a little uncomfortable with this gesture of camaraderie. Sveg realised this was only the beginning of what he hoped was just the start of a firm relationship, and that he had be patient and just take things a step at a time.

Chapter 3
Moving In

Sveg found the captain of the guard at the town's main gate and clasped his hand in a strong grip, happy to see Amos.

'How are things, my friend?' Captain Moorhead chuckled, 'Staying out of trouble?'

Wrinkles around the guard captain's eyes showed that he knew how to laugh even though his position as the head of security for the town was a senior post.

'Oh, you know, Amos, I do my best, but sometimes things happen . . .'

Both men laughed as they knew Sveg was one of the most abiding citizens in the town, consistent with his position as one of the well-known tradesmen and artisans in the district.

'Speaking of potential trouble,' Sveg continued, 'I wonder whether you would be willing to let me know if you've heard anything recently about something I am thinking of pursuing. Over a tankard of ale, of course.'

'Music to my ears.' Amos smiled in anticipation. 'I'll just let the lads know I am off on official business, then I'm yours.' He winked in an exaggerated manner.

At the Wheatsheaf Tavern a few streets away, Sveg brought over the tankards and they clinked before each downed a long draught.

Amos burped contentedly. 'I could get used to this,' he sighed as he gently patted his tunic in response.

Sveg burst out laughing. 'By the look of your gradually expanding torso, you are making this a regular stop!'

Amos affected an expression of hurt feelings. 'Hey, hey there. That's a low blow if I ever saw one. I have a lot of responsibility to keep this town safe and no one should begrudge me if I had the odd soothing ale to calm my nerves.' He clinked his tankard with Sveg's again. They had rapidly slipped back into the teasing and gentle insults of two men who had known each other for several years and were comfortable in each other's presence.

'Actually, Amos, I am in a little bit of a pickle. I have come across a young lad who might have the makings of an apprentice. But we know next to nothing about him, and Marion rightly suggested I talk with you to see if you know anything useful. You see, this lad's name is Gerant but he appears to be homeless. He's not very talkative but he did let admit that until recently he was part of a gang of boys who wander around the town and survive on whatever they can steal or find around the place. Ever run across them?'

The guard captain took another pull of the Wheatsheaf ale and thought for a bit. 'Hmmm, we do occasionally see those lads here and there, although they largely keep to themselves. We have been called to incidents now and again, but they know if they get too obvious we'll come and find them, break them up and move them on. That said, I do recall a few weeks ago there was a bit of a dust up where we came across some of them who had been in a fight. A couple of them were in a bad way and they probably didn't make it through the night. Not much we could do and when we went back the next morning, they had all disappeared.'

Sveg pondered on this news. 'Thanks.' He thought some more as he quietly sipped his ale. 'Would you recognise any of them? The one I mean is about normal height for his age and has dark hair and is pretty scruffy. Ring a bell?'

Amos laughed. 'You are describing half the boys in this town, my friend. No, your lad didn't appear to be one of the gang leaders and certainly wasn't one of the clear troublemakers. Who knows what he's like. He might be a bad egg, but until he has the opportunity to show his worth, you won't know. All the same, if you take him on, you'll just need to keep a keen eye on him until he has shown he can be trusted.'

Sveg shook his head in wonder. 'I must really want this to work. First, I need to convince Marion, though.'

The guard captain also shook his head and smiled ruefully. 'Well, that's your affair, my man. It's not for me to stand in the way of the likes of your Marion. I like and respect her too much to put myself in that sort of danger.'

The next day, Sveg had another frank chat with the young lad, who had appeared from across the street as soon as the smith had opened the shutters at the workshop.

'I had a good long talk with Amos Moorhead, who you might know as the guard captain in this town.'

Gerant nodded with wide eyes.

'No, no, nothing like that.' Sveg could sense that the boy thought he was about to tell him to get out and any arrangement was finished.

'Captain Moorhead knows a little of your circumstances and I talked things over with Marion last night. She is far from comfortable about things as they stand.' Sveg frowned at the young man and then burst out. 'Don't give me any shit, now. Are you still involved with that gang of boys? If you are, then the deal's off.'

Gerant had turned white with this outpouring of emotion and clearly was taking his time to order his thoughts. 'No, there was a fight with another gang about who had the best areas to look after and . . . one of the boss boys got stabbed and I am not sure what happened after that. I wasn't in the fight, and I had been thinking of leaving anyway. I was sick of just wandering around stealing stuff and always being hungry. So I found my own little nook and was just seeing what was around and heard these strange noises and saw this place and it looked interesting. So here I am . . .'

Sveg looked down at the workbench to hide his relief. 'Hmmph. Well, this might work out, but it is strictly on a trial basis. One stuff up or you go back to your old habits, and you are out on your ear. No second chance, mind.' Sveg had his stern face back on.

Gerant quickly nodded furiously. 'I won't let you down, Sveg. I will work hard and whatever it takes, I'll do it.'

The smith's expression relented. 'Well then, let's start as we mean to go on.' He went into some more matter-of-fact aspects he had clearly been thinking about. 'I can set up a pallet just over there.' Sveg nodded towards the corner. 'We could put up a partition to give you a space that is yours and offers you a little privacy. That would be for you to look after and keep a little tidy. Your meals you could take with us, but your sleeping place would be here.'

'Also, you would be expected to help out with chores. Keep the firewood for the stove in the cottage cut and stacked in the woodshed and keep the stove going and light it in the morning. Also emptying the privy every week or so, and any other tasks that we ask you to do. Do you think you could manage all that, Gerant?'

'I guess so. It seems a fair trade.'

'Good. Oh, by the way, have you ever had a bath?'

Gerant paused for thought. 'I fell in the river once.'

'Well, that's another thing you will have to do. A regular wash every couple of days and we'll look at what we can do in terms of clothing. I can find an old shirt of mine that you can use until we find something more suitable.' A little bit of stubbornness crossed the smith's face as he continued to speak.

'We need to prove Marion wrong, Gerant. Let's work on this together. Right, let's quickly build a bed place for you. I have an old bit of screen out the back that we can fashion into something. Then I'm going to hand you over to my wife. Don't worry about that: it's what I had to agree about, and she was very insistent.'

In the same way that Sveg and Gerant looked like a good fit in working at the forge, there were able to quickly put together a little alcove that was to become Gerant's new home. Not that there was much to it or it took long. It was mostly Sveg, with Gerant fetching and carrying or holding pieces together while Sveg lashed or nailed or fashioned the pieces into something functional. The mattress was just a very basic large sack they stuffed with straw and sewed up the open end, with an old blanket over the top that had seen better days.

'I'll get you a candle and a chamber pot a little later. Or you may choose to just go to the privy, which is just up the corridor. Maybe tomorrow sometime you can go and get whatever belongings you have and bring them over. Think this will do?'

Gerant nodded. 'Much better than what I've ever had. Or at least what I can remember.'

A little later, Sveg took Gerant to the small alcove at the back of the cottage where the tub had been installed in a corner for taking baths. He then went to get Marion. Marion appeared with an apron on, her sleeves rolled up and her hair piled up in a bun. She was looking very businesslike but gave Gerant a quick smile.

'Well, my lad, let's run some hot water into the tub. This is something that Sveg put together. Some metal pipes run through the forge and the hot coals heat the water in the pipes. It saves so much effort having to heat water on the stove and then carry it from the kitchen and gradually fill up the tub.'

Marion could see that Gerant was trying to see how the tub arrangement worked. *I'll have to get Sveg to show him at some point,* she thought.

'There we go. Now strip off. Don't worry. I have seen heaps of boys' bodies and private parts looking after them in the infirmary.'

Despite Marion's assurances, Gerant took his time taking the rags off and held his hands over his nether regions. Marion's face had taken on a somewhat determined look. She poked the little pile of Gerant's discards with the end of a broom.

'Right, these can go straight into the fire. Gods know what little friends you have been carrying around with you. Well, into the tub with you.'

The no-nonsense tone didn't really give Gerant much choice. He gingerly manoeuvred himself into the water and had a huge shock. The water was pleasantly warm and not what he was expecting. The second shock was the firmness with which the woman held Gerant as she scrubbed furiously first with a large cake of soap and then assaulted him with a stiff wooden brush. He submitted with as much good grace as he could muster. The minutes continued with further pummelling, prodding and almost scraping. In between bouts of soaping and scrubbing, Marion watched her young victim's face change from wanting to get away as quickly as possible to a look of quiet resignation. The somewhat cooling water in the tub had quickly started to turn a dark grey shade similar to the colour of the local dirt. *Hmmm,* thought Marion, *it is working but we have quite a bit to go yet.*

Three changes of bathwater later, an almost unrecognisable boy was presented to Sveg wearing a chestnut-coloured cast-off shirt, cinched at the waist with a large belt.

'Hmmm. Is this the same lad I left with you, Marion? He is quite a lighter colour and must have lost weight.'

Marion joined in the gentle banter. 'Well, sir, I don't believe there are any broken bones, but I did try my hardest to get the young man clean. The redness of his skin shows how hard I scrubbed, but I am confident it will not be so noticeable in the morning. Gerant was interested in your hot water contraption, and I think that dulled the pain a little.'

'I trust that when you are next taking a bath, Gerant, it will be a bit more pleasant and relaxing activity,' noted Sveg. 'Let's hope you can learn to enjoy it! Of course, I can show you the piping to the bath: I am quite proud of the idea and how it works.'

After that, Gerant was invited to share supper with the family, and was introduced to Bree. Bree was initially shy of the new boy who she had been told by her parents would be around quite a bit from now on. But she soon saw that although the boy didn't talk much and was focused on eating the stew that her mother had made, he looked quite normal.

'You can learn your letters with me, Gerant. I already know them and can spell out some words,' boasted Bree. 'I can show you tomorrow at breakfast.'

Watching Gerant eat, Marion made a mental note to gently work on some table manners for the boy. Thinking about it, it wasn't strange at all that he hardly knew how to use the fork and spoon. These were things that Bree had taken some time to pick up, but now took for granted. *Well, at least he was clean,* she thought. *That reminds me to discuss with Sveg about what sort of clothes might be needed. And where the money for it will be coming from.* The little nest egg that Sveg had spirited away was absolutely going to called upon or Marion would never have agreed to the arrangement otherwise. But they would still need to watch the pennies. That was the reason why normally a family would still be expected to deal with feeding and clothing an apprentice. The guild made no allowance for an apprentice's keep and the surety went straight into the guild's coffers, never to reappear. Nor was a master artisan expected to pay an apprentice for living expenses. It had been difficult enough for Sveg to convince her to use a very small part of their savings to give Gerant a regular allowance of a few pennies a week.

Marion also pondered on what she had managed to get out of Gerant as she was scrubbing him. She had started gently asking about his family and one thing led to another; he almost seemed to be getting things off his chest and hadn't had anyone who he could talk to about this. It was clear that Gerant really missed his mum terribly and had almost an idyllic memory of how wonderful she had been. He hadn't shared lots of details about her, but Marion got the very strong sense that Gerant almost felt to blame that she had sickened and died. It was his fault and he should have been able to have done more, and his mother would have recovered. Marion had been hard put to resist just holding him close as she realised the import and sadness of what he had confided, in quite a dispassionate voice. There was obviously a lot going on in this boy's mind that still hadn't worked itself out. Having heard this tale of woe and what Gerant's mother still meant to him, Marion was a lot more comfortable now with him staying with them. And hopefully the rest of it would emerge in time and she could help him talk about it and focus on the good times.

After the meal, Bree and Gerant took the bowls and cutlery to the kitchen area to wash them and put them away. Bree was very quick to tell the new lodger she had been grown up enough to do this for two years now. Upon returning, the boy and the smith wandered back to the forge and the small alcove they had set up.

'This should be fine for you. It's not a lot, but it may be a little more than what you are used to. Anyway, it will be a big and important day tomorrow. I'll go to the guild and we'll see if we can get you put on formally as my apprentice. You will likely hear us when we start to move about in the morning. So just come up to the kitchen area and we can have some breakfast. See you on the morrow, Gerant.'

Gerant pondered those words and realised how strange they felt. 'Yes, see you on the morrow, Sveg.'

The smith nodded briefly, then turned and walked away. The sound of tuneless whistling gradually diminished, followed by a brief squeak and gentle thud as a door was shut and latched. Then silence.

Gerant lay down on the sack of straw, drew the blanket up his chin, and lay there, his thoughts racing from one recollection to the next of all the exciting things that had happened in the past two days. Eventually, his mind started to slip into gently pondering what the days ahead might turn into, and the boy drifted off into a comfortable and largely untroubled slumber.

Chapter 4
New Beginnings

Gerant awoke before dawn as several roosters within hearing announced the coming day. He lay on the wooden slats and the sack with his hands laced behind his head, pondering on his current circumstances. He could not remember a more comfortable night of sleep, although at various times of the night unfamiliar noises awoke him briefly. After an initial shock of trying to work out why he had woken, it was very easy to realise they were just the normal noises of the night. They were different only that his previous haunt in the corner of the remains of an unoccupied shack had other noises. He recalled the creak of one of the beams if it was a windy night and the comings and goings of various rodents in their nightly forays. Here it was a dog barking and whining at various times, a few people talking early in the evening as they walked by on the street outside, occasional doors opening and closing and snatches of conversation from nearby houses.

Some bustling noises from the direction of the cottage suggested that the others had got up and were preparing breakfast. Not in the habit of leaving his resting place tidy but guessing this would be part of what was expected, Gerant plumped up the sack of straw to get rid of the impression of his body and folded the blanket. That was the sum total of tidying: he had not lit the candle Sveg had given him. There had been no need. He knew his way around the forge enough for it not to be a problem. He had also heard that people used candles or lamps at night for things such as reading or sewing, but these were foreign to him.

Hanging back at the door to the cottage where the kitchen area was, he was first noticed by Bree.

'Gerant, we are having porridge with some apples for breakfast. The apples are really nice, but you have to make sure there are no worms in them before you bite!'

'Oh, good morning, Gerant.' Sveg had noticed him when Bree started talking and Marion gave him a quick smile of recognition. Sveg was not in his normal smithy attire and was wearing linen pants and half boots, along with a shirt and leather vest. Sveg noticed the quick scrutiny from Gerant.

'Yes, first thing will be for me to go to the guild and make a case for you to be made an apprentice under my tutelage, Gerant. After that, I can get rid of this stuff and put back on my working gear. So, after breakfast you can do what you like until I return from the guild. Maybe go and get whatever of your stuff and bring it to the forge.'

It also looked like Sveg had had a wash after Gerant's episode with Marion the previous evening and was looking clean and tidy – different from the almost 'honest' smudges and dusting that came from a day toiling at the forge.

'Oh good, I can show you my letters and how good I am at reading words,' boasted Bree.

'It might be nice to show Gerant your primer, Bree,' remarked Marion. 'I am sure he will be very interested.' Marion said this with a straight face, although the raised eyebrows were challenging him to say otherwise. Gerant thought it wise to just nod in agreement.

Bree continued. 'I can also tell you about what I am learning about The Realm. It's really interesting. Did you know that the king and queen have been looking after it for three hundred years? That's a long time, isn't it? They originally came from down south.'

Marion intervened. 'Another time, Bree. I am sure Gerant might get to hear about that stuff when he starts at the guild.'

Gerant just nodded. Again, it felt like the right thing to do.

Gerant wandered along the largely deserted streets and lanes of Ashford, naturally slipping into the old habits of skulking along the edges of thoroughfares and ducking in and out of various short-cuts and alleys. The remnants of the wooden shack where he had been camped for several weeks were strangely smaller and appeared to have shrunk. He took a quick look around to make sure no one was approaching or watching. Then he levered up the loose beam of timber that he had been placing over the small hole that led into the corner of a room that was vaguely still intact. He crouched down and wriggled in. *Good.* His small sack of keepsakes and trinkets, plus a small but rusty kitchen knife, were still there. Gerant sometimes spent a night somewhere else on occasion and his things were mostly OK for a short time. But much longer and one of the other homeless children would find the nook and take over. Competition was fierce for the few places that were relatively dry and out of the weather and not checked by the town guards. He left the pile of old rags and bits of bedding that had been like a little nest to sleep in. *Whoever took over might be grateful for them,* he thought. A last quick look to make sure nothing useful was left – not that there was much danger of that – then Gerant scooted back out through the low hole out to the lane and placed the half-rotten beam back across the entry point. He made another quick check to see no one had been watching. Then the boy set off to the smithy, only a few minutes' walk away.

The smith arrived at the guild hall and walked in through the rather ostentatious double doors with heavy brass knockers. Inside was a large open chamber with shields and other insignia depicting the guild's importance in the growing town of Ashford and its place in The Realm. A large open fireplace was along one wall with a roaring blaze. Two or three figures in guild robes, velvet flat caps and neck chains were standing in front of the fire, quietly chatting. They turned on hearing the double doors rumble shut.

'Ah, Master Martinson. We normally don't see you at our regular guild meetings. You have been here measuring where the gates will be in weeks past, but otherwise we sadly rarely see you. Have you come to tell us they are ready to install?'

The speaker was the head of the guild, Master Thomas Siffray. He was clad in the guild robes and had multiple decorative chains and insignia hanging from them, meaning whenever he moved, there was a muted shifting and clanking of metal links and medallions.

'Alas. Another week of work, tidying up and then I will bring the gates by cart and install them. No, I am here on other business. I wish to discuss the terms and gain acceptance by the guild for having a new apprentice start with me.'

'Ah, you are in luck. We have a full guild meeting in around an hour, but we could discuss this matter with you before then. I was just talking over some guild business informally with Master Viridian and Master Baldock here and they could join me in assessing your proposal. Come, Master Martinson, let us use the small guild chamber.'

Master Siffray gestured to a closed door opening off the large open room. Sveg had dealt with Master Siffray on many occasions previously. He purposely limited his appearances at the guild as it was often more interested in furthering its own reputation in the town. Some of the rules and regulations imposed on the various trades and artisans were there to only benefit the guild. Nevertheless, as Sveg followed the three guild representatives into a small room with a large rectangular table and somewhat plain wooden chairs, he reflected that the head of the guild was generally fair and reasonable in his dealings since he had been appointed five years ago. Sveg was sure there were a number of underhanded practices that involved coin changing hands to the guild's advantage and so on, but at least Master Siffray gave the appearance of running the guild as it should and the artisans, as a group, were generally content.

'So, you mentioned you have a lad that you wish to apprentice through the guild?'

'That is so. This boy's name is Gerant and I have found him to be suitable to learn smithing with me. He is very interested in the trade and appears to pick up skills very quickly.'

Master Siffray was clearly ticking off mentally the series of questions the guild needed to be satisfied with before it would agree to take on a new apprentice. 'And the boy's family have agreed to the arrangement?'

'The boy has no family. My wife and I have discussed this and Gerant will have meals with us and live in the smithy.' All three guild masters frowned and their expressions were far from positive.

'This is highly irregular, Master Martinson,' pointed out Master Baldock. 'Who will provide the surety, if there is no family?' There was a clink of coin, as a small pouch tied with a leather thong was placed by Sveg in front of him on the table.

'I will be providing the surety. It's all there.'

Master Viridian quickly reached over to grab the pouch, untied the thong and began counting. After reaching the last coin, he nodded to Master Siffray.

'Hmmm.' The head of the guild looked slightly less concerned. 'What level of learning has he?'

'It is something that needs to be worked on,' muttered Sveg. 'But Masters, you well know that many apprentices struggle with their letters and it is something I am well aware of and will be taking extra time to make sure the boy has at least some level of reading and writing.'

'He would still be expected to come to the weekly lessons with Master Klyburn that all apprentices are required to attend. No special allowance will be made if his learning is not of sufficient standard.'

'He knows that. No special treatment or extra tuition would be expected.' Sveg was starting to feel a little more hopeful about the tone of the meeting.

'Also, just because *you* are providing the surety instead of the family, the same conditions apply,' intoned Master Siffray.

Sveg knew very well that the surety was almost never seen again and was one of the sources of coin that the guild relied on to run its activities, and also to line the pockets of its senior members.

Master Siffray looked at both his fellow members and then nodded. 'If you could leave us for a few moments while I have a discussion with Master Viridian and Master Baldock, we will be able to give you the guild's decision.' Sveg nodded briefly and quietly walked out of the room.

Standing in front of the open fireplace, Sveg hoped he had convinced them sufficiently to allow Gerant to become his apprentice. Several other guild members had by now arrived into the open chamber, but were very careful to not engage with the smith and carried on their own hushed conversation in the corner of the chamber next to the double doors. After several minutes, the door to the small chamber opened and Master Siffray scanned the room and then looked at Sveg expectantly.

Upon sitting down again across the table from the three guild members, Sveg noticed with satisfaction that the pouch of coins had disappeared off the table.

'After due consideration, we are mindful of the highly unusual circumstances of the proposed apprenticeship,' began Master Viridian in an officious tone.

Sveg noticed that Master Siffray was clearly staying out of the decision and was leaning back in his chair with his eyes half closed, but still missing nothing.

'As guild Treasurer, the surety will be recorded as such and this lad, Gerald . . .'

'Gerant,' Sveg, automatically corrected.

'Gerant . . . will be expected to commence attending the guild training sessions beginning in the next week.' Viridian paused and then continued in his officious tone. 'It will take several days for the Charter scroll to be completed with all the relevant details and the usual expectations.'

Sveg was hard put to just cough and nod seriously. He fought hard to keep the grin off his face. He also realised that he should relax his hands, as he had been unconsciously gripping the frame of the seat underneath the table and was in serious danger of snapping the wood with his built-up tension.

'That is all very reasonable. Thank you, Masters. I assume that when I return to pick up the Charter, I can also be given a receipt for the surety? It would be good to have recorded that the funds were as required, in case there are any difficulties at a later time.'

All three masters nodded their heads in unison, agreeing that it was important to document all the details – exactly why the guild was needed and was trusted to deal with such weighty matters.

Having changed out of his second-best outfit and back into his normal attire, Sveg went looking for Gerant and found him sitting in his little alcove on the pallet.

'Well, you will now be officially an apprentice of the guild, Gerant. I have to return in a few days to pick up the Charter of Agreement and then you go for a morning every week to learn about how the guild operates. It is a part of being an apprentice and unfortunately it is something you will just have to put up with. But there are some useful things to learn, particularly when you eventually qualify to be a smith yourself and are wanting to train your own apprentices.'

Sveg noticed that next to the little upturned crate next to the pallet there was a small sack that had appeared and there was a small tortoise-shell comb on the crate next to the unlit candle.

'You went back and got your stuff, Gerant? That's a pretty comb.'

'It's the only thing I have of me mam's,' Gerant said softly, not looking at Sveg.

The smith realised it must be something of huge sentimental value to the young lad and thought carefully about what he could say now. 'It's always important to have keepsakes like that. It's how we remember who we are and where we came from.'

Both of them were silent for a number of moments, each thinking through important memories that they kept close to their hearts.

Sveg realised that things had gone down a dark path and that details about Gerant's past might emerge in good time. Now was not the time to dwell on it. 'Oh, I forgot to show you the tub and how I have set it up to heat water through the forge. Marion said you were very interested in it. It's something I am rather proud of.' They both walked to the side of the smithy where the water from the roof collected into the large wooden barrel circled with tight bands of iron.

'So, this iron pipe runs from the bottom of the water barrel through to the smithy, as you can see. I have made it so it runs underneath the bed of coals. It can't be in the middle of the forge, otherwise the iron would melt, but it is close enough to the heat that the water becomes quite hot. Then it runs out the other side and the pipe continues round to the tub. I just made a simple tap at the end so all you have to do is turn it on and heated water comes out. Of course, if the forge has not been on, then the water will be cold. You must also have cold water handy to mix, as sometimes you hop in and you will cook yourself if you don't test it first.'

The smith had a look of pride on his face as he explained the mechanism to the soon-to-be apprentice. 'It took me a few tries to get it to work how I had hoped it would, but I think it has saved us a lot of effort and certainly makes having a bath a lot easier and more enjoyable.

'That's why there's more to being a smith than just working metal. You need to have time to think about ideas and new ways of doing things. Anyway, I suppose we should get back to those gates for the guild. I told Master Siffray that I would have them finished within a week.'

Chapter 5
Apprenticeship

Gerant grabbed his sack from the forge, making sure he had some charcoal, a pencil and several small blank pieces of paper. Today was the second week of attending the Guild Hall where, for a morning until the early afternoon, new apprentices were instructed in the workings of the guild. They learnt how it was structured, the many rules and regulations that governed operation of the various trades: smithing, leatherwork, bookbinding, accounting, clerics, weaving – the whole spectrum.

The first week had been little more than an introductory session so that new apprentices knew where to come in future sessions and for the instructor to introduce himself. Not surprisingly, the little group of new apprentices was a motley group of various ages, sizes and attitudes. Gerant had held back and just observed. There was even a girl amongst the group of eight or so, presumably from the weaving or clothing trades. She was looking a little nervous and somewhat out of place. One of the older lads clearly thought he would become the worldly-wise and experienced lover.

'Give us a kiss, love.'

Despite her somewhat meek appearance, she had clearly dealt with these sort of approaches in past times. 'Fuck off, you idiot. Unless you want a swift kick in the cods?' That brought several wolf whistles from the others keenly watching and she was largely ignored from then on.

The instructor, when he had arrived, was of medium height but grossly overweight, so that the guild livery and tunic was struggling to contain his quivering form. His multiple chins wobbled at every step and tiny, well-inset, pig-like eyes peered out from the shiny, cushioned face. Gerant noted remnants from several previous meals that had spilled down the man's tunic in various places. A quite high-pitched, reedy voice emerged from that daunting, confronting figure.

'I am your instructor for this series of valuable lessons on your apprenticeship and the enormous privilege you have been granted in becoming part of the guild.' The tutor paused to let the apprentices appreciate the benefits they were being granted. 'My name is Master Klyburn. You should always address me as Master Klyburn. As we get to know each other a little better over the weeks, I will allow you to shorten it to just Master.'

Frequently consulting a very long scroll, Master Klyburn had proceeded to read out some initial rules and regulations regarding attendance at the weekly sessions and what equipment and bits and pieces were required for the first official session in a week's time. Gerant had developed in his relatively short lifetime the ability to zone out, wherever his imagination took him, yet being able to absorb any key points or the gist of the conversation. In this way he took in that he was to bring some reasonable scraps of paper and something to draw or write with, along with something to eat and drink at the short meal break, as the guild was absolutely not going to provide anything beyond tuition. These key details gently floated by, overlaying his main stream of thoughts. Only half listening, Gerant thought about what tasks he was going to help Sveg with this coming afternoon and what things he had been asked to have ready.

Gerant recalled all this during the short stroll to the Guild Hall this current week, having remembered with ease what he had to bring and replaying some of the more memorable aspects, not that there were many. It had quickly become apparent that Master Klyburn was only going through the motions and was there to educate the apprentices under sufferance. He had clearly not been going to stop until he had reached the end of the scroll and so droned on and on, not looking up. He did not see that several of the apprentices quickly grew bored and started making faces, mimicking Master Klyburn's actions and making rude gestures at him when they were sure he would not look up in time. One of these was a tallish, gangling youth who had, on arrival, announced to everyone that he was called Stork. He clearly expected the others to take notice of him and essentially treat him with the respect he deserved: unquestionably the leader. At least that was his own estimation of his worth. Gerant had quickly decided that this Stork was someone to avoid as much as possible. Certainly, Stork had already found among the apprentice group a small group of like-minded lads who were happy to play along for whatever benefits they could derive.

Arriving at the guild compound, the draughty room that was utilised as the apprentice instruction area was a lean-to on the left-hand side of the main building and out of sight from the main doors. Gerant picked a desk on the side of the room about midway down from the platform that Master Klyburn would use. The girl had already arrived and was seated on the opposite side of the room. She tentatively smiled a greeting, and Gerant nodded in response and attempted a quiet smile. He felt quite awkward; he didn't even know her name. A smatter of raucous laughter, pushing and shoving heralded the arrival of Stork and some of his new cronies. They gravitated to the back. Shortly thereafter, Master Klyburn appeared and stomped to the front of the room, mounted the low platform and shuffled some pieces of paper at his lectern. He quickly scanned the room to assure himself that there were at least some apprentices there, coughed, and then launched into a long monologue in the same manner of the previous week, in his reedy, high-pitched voice.

It would be fair to say that anything that Master Klyburn had to say was of minimal interest and its relevance to being an apprentice could only be vaguely discerned. Gerant continued his well-honed skill of zoning out and thinking about other more interesting aspects. He started to run through the letters that he had gone over with Bree, under his breath, just to try to get the sounds right. He was able to get through the entire set several times to the accompaniment of the steady high-pitched droning of Master Klyburn in the background. It reminded Gerant of summer days when cicadas whirred away in the trees lining the river: a constant and somehow soothing lullaby. He moved onto thinking about the filing, painting and polishing that remained to be completed on the guild gates, which Sveg had started to show him the previous afternoon. It was the first large task that Gerant was expected to look after by himself, and he was looking forward to being able to work steadily at something with Sveg only checking his progress every now and again. Already he felt the gates had a tiny bit of his hand in them and he would walk past them with a sense of pride once they had been installed.

With a momentary sense of panic, he realised that Master Klyburn had been silent for a number of seconds. However, a quick scan of the room showed that the other apprentices were looking generally bored and the tutor on his platform appeared to be reading some of his notes and shuffling through several pieces of paper. Master Klyburn must have reached a point in his notes that concluded a section. This also must have coincided with thoughts of an impending meal break.

'We will take our lunch break now and commence again on the regulations regarding monthly reporting of apprentice training and confirmation by your sponsor in due course. Please have your pages ready to note down the key points after I return from the break. You will be expected to refer to them on an ongoing basis to ensure your monthly returns are accurate and contain all the necessary details to be cross-checked by us at the guild. We will recommence in twenty minutes.'

With hardly a glance at the apprentices seated in rows before him, Master Klyburn scuttled off the platform at a remarkably rapid rate given the size and poor physical condition of the man. Clearly, the prospect of whatever luncheon the guild provided to its members was occupying Klyburn's thoughts rather more than the next stage of tuition.

Gerant did not feel the need to go to the latrine and was happy to remain at the desk and eat the small roll with ham he had brought. Perhaps he would go out for a few moments after that for a quick change of scene. The roll was at the bottom of his sack, so he got out the paper and thick pencil that were on top, and put them on the desk. He'd need them soon enough. Reaching in again for the roll, he felt a shadow cross his view and then the lanky form of the

Stork grabbed the paper and started to walk off towards one of the desks at the back.

'Knew there was something I was meant to bring. Glad you did that for me, shithead!'

It took Gerant a few shocked moments to assess the situation, then he followed the figure to the back. Up closer, Stork was a good nine inches taller, had a much longer reach that went with the lankiness and was already starting to fill out into a more adult form. His muddy-brown hair had been cropped short. A number of zits competed for space, particularly on his chin, and a few early hairs and whiskers could be seen erupting here and there on his cheeks and around his mouth.

'That piece of paper is mine. I don't have any to spare.'

'Tough shit. It's mine now.'

'You were asked to bring your own. It's not yours.'

'Whatya going to do about it?'

Stork had that supremely confident look on his face where he had been in this situation hundreds of times before. It was just a matter of stating the obvious and they always backed down. The very real sense of coming violence and getting beaten up was hanging palpably in the air.

Gerant had also been in this sort of situation before. He preferred to try to reason and negotiate his way out of trouble like this. That worked most of the time. But sometimes it didn't.

Gerant watched as Stork continued to smirk, waiting for Gerant to realise how futile his request was and just give up and learn the lesson. The expression suddenly changed to a look of surprise and worry as Stork found he wasn't able to breathe, the only noise being an almost gentle grunt as the air left his lungs following the rapid appearance of Gerant's fist into his stomach. The larger boy started to bend over, fighting to get air into his system. Gerant grasped Stork's ears and quickly yanked down. The other boy's face connected with Gerant's knee with a sickening thud. It only remained for Gerant to quickly grab the piece of paper still held loosely by the fingers of the unconscious form, walk back to his desk, grab the bread roll and the sack, and quietly slide out of the room. It was funny how the others had watched the events in shocked silence, still trying to process not only what had happened, but the speed with which it had occurred. This was another thing Gerant had learnt the hard way – if you decided that talking wasn't going to work, then don't give them any warning of what was coming.

Sveg was working at the forge the next morning when there was a cough from the street. He looked up and saw Gideon Simmons, who was another of the artisans in the town, specialising in carpentry and joinery. Simmons was a tall and willowy figure, wearing a ruby-coloured doublet, leggings and soft leather boots. Sveg knew the carpenter had a thriving business based mainly in furniture making. He didn't go much into the house-building side of things.

'Good morning to you, Master Martinson.'

'Good morning, Master Simmons. I trust I find you well?'

'Can't complain, can't complain. Although business has dropped off quite a bit with the cold weather. Is your apprentice around?'

Sveg looked behind him and pretended a frown. 'Hmm. He must have stepped out the back.'

'Well never mind. I have come to advise you I have lodged a complaint with the guild about the behaviour of your apprentice towards mine. My fellow has not been able to attend my workshop today and will be unlikely to return for at least a week. Your apprentice was responsible for significant injury to him, including some nasty bruises to the face, several loose teeth and a broken nose. There is also the matter of the stolen piece of paper, which my apprentice says was taken from him without any explanation or reason. Apparently, your apprentice forgot to bring his own and thought he would just help himself.'

The smith nodded in sympathy with his fellow artisan and appeared to consider the matter further. 'These are very serious charges, Master Simmons. You have investigated the circumstances?'

'Of course, my apprentice gave me a very detailed account.'

'Did you inquire whether my apprentice suffered any hurt from this encounter?'

'That's irrelevant, surely.'

Sveg appeared to think about what he had been told about the incident. 'I would find it odd that only your apprentice was hurt in the scuffle. Were there any witnesses to the incident?'

'Well, of course there were other apprentices that saw this. Such an unprovoked, vicious attack!'

'And it was over one piece of paper that was taken. Or are we talking several?'

'Errr, one, I believe.' Simmons' expression had changed from an almost condescending look to a worried frown. The conversation had taken an unexpected turn.

'And your apprentice described the piece of paper? It was one of yours that you had given him?'

'Of course, of course.'

'I recall last year that you bought at a very good rate a pile of paper from that bookseller in Cobham who went out of business. You showed me a piece of it. Very good quality.'

'I was very happy to acquire that lot.'

'And how big was the piece?'

'My apprentice said it was about two feet by two feet. No writing or drawing on it. A nice creamy colour.'

'Just a moment.' Sveg walked quickly to his drafting desk and selected a piece of paper from a small pile.

'I remember you showing me a sample of the paper you had bought, Master Simmons. I recall it was all about twelve inches by eight inches and bleached almost pure white, as befits the quality you bought. Here's a piece of my paper I use for my drawing and drafting. Seems a pretty good match to the description your apprentice gave you.'

Master Simmons opened and closed his mouth several times.

'Just to inform you, my apprentice told me what had happened yesterday afternoon and we had a long discussion about it. Then I went to the guild hall and talked with a number of the apprentices who were still there and who gave me a true account of the events. I suggest in future you verify the circumstances yourself, Master Simmons. Let me know when your apprentice returns for work, as I will be wanting to visit your workshop and have a private and very candid conversation with him about his habits and how he will need to drastically amend his ways. Or he will have me personally to deal with on the matter and his continuing to be licensed as an apprentice of the guild.'

Simmons had been getting progressively redder and redder in the face as he listened to his fellow artisan. Sveg had changed from quietly seeking clarification to seeming to fill the space with his well-muscled physique, his features set in a knowing, no-nonsense frown.

'I trust you enjoy the rest of your day and please come by if you need any more paper pieces at any point. You are welcome to this one.' The parting words from Martinson were polite and friendly, the tone was anything but.

'Hummph,' was all Simmons could manage as he turned abruptly and walked straight through a mud-edged puddle in the street, soaking his leggings and half boots with stinking, sticky deposits from the street.

The smith was silent for several seconds before starting to gently shake, then quietly chuckle, before he burst out into full-blown gusts of laughter, doubling over, with tears starting to trickle from eyes crinkling with merriment. He noticed that Gerant had reappeared and was a little nonplussed about whether to join in or just ignore Sveg's continued chortles.

'Well, Apprentice Gerant. That was an interesting encounter. First of all, good on you for telling me why you arrived back from the guild early yesterday. I always like to have the facts. What happened just made me angry about the other lad and I totally understood why you reacted the way you did. Hearsay is a very dangerous friend and talking to the other apprentices just confirmed what you had told me. So, when Master Simmons arrived with that demand for compensation, I thought it would be interesting to draw out what he thought he knew of the situation. It was very quickly apparent his apprentice had just made up a pack of lies to try to cover his backside.

'I much prefer to be dealing from a position of knowing the facts and trying to be calm and reasonable. You usually end up with an outcome that suits you and you can drive a harder bargain when you are sure of yourself. All the same, if you are in the wrong or can't be confident in what you are saying, you should admit it and move on. Nothing worse than someone who tries to bluster or lie or worse. I have a solid reputation in this town; people know that I will be fair and reasonable if a good argument is made.'

Sveg realised he had been rambling on and had probably said more than he had intended. 'Well, I just got a bit carried away there. Trouble is, sometimes you can't say to people exactly what you feel. I probably spoke too plainly to Master Simmons at the end, but he had it coming! OK, ready to start again? I forget what we were up to. Oh, that's right, you went to get the extra bracing.'

That evening after dinner, Sveg was relating the events with Master Simmons to Marion.

'I hope Gerant didn't think I was bitter, Marion, or that my habits are the only way to run a business. I just wanted to give him some of the lessons I have learnt the hard way.'

Marion reached over and stroked her husband's cheek tenderly.

'My dear man, what you told Gerant was just right and it's how I would expect someone of your experience to guide a young lad just at the start of their trade. He has had a far from usual beginning and needs someone to show him what's appropriate. There must be so many things that are just totally strange and bewildering.'

After a pause, she continued. 'You know, I think having Gerant as your apprentice has been really useful for you as well. You have someone to talk to about your work and it means, like today, that you can bring out things that you rarely discuss with others. You always tend to think long and hard about things, but they often stay bottled up and no one benefits from them. Gerant is giving you that opportunity, and I think that is good.'

Sveg bowed his head and submitted to his wife's tender stroking.

'You're right. You often are.'

'It's been a long day for you. Pass the lantern over and let's head off to bed.' Marion paused, with a saucy look appearing on her face as she grinned up at her husband. 'I can show you my version of smithing. I know how to keep rods stiff and strong so they don't lose their strength.'

A gasp, a giggle, a slap on cheek.

'You naughty, naughty man. Surely you can wait? You almost made me drop the lantern!'

Chapter 6
A Kiln Run

The next day dawned fair, and it started in the same routine for Gerant – get up, tidy the alcove, which took only seconds, carry wood in from the pile and get the kitchen fire lit and then breakfast with Sveg, Marion and Bree. The last part of the morning routine was also starting to feel more natural and something, thinking on it, that Gerant was liking. He particularly liked the sometimes soft, sometimes a little heated, conversation about daily events or what the family would be doing. While voices might get raised a little at times, he had yet to experience a full-blown shouting match in this household. Gerant still felt somewhat like an observer, and he wasn't yet ready to admit he felt a member of this little group. But certainly, whatever hesitancy had been quickly lost and he was involved, whether he liked it or not, in contributing to the conversation. Initially, it had taken some prompting, particularly from Marion, and Bree in her own way. Most times, he had not often said anything unless specifically asked. It had started with a series of questions.

'What do you think, Gerant?' Or, 'how would you deal with that, Gerant?'

It then graduated to one of the others looking expectantly at him to contribute something about the subject being discussed. Gerant had then been somewhat shocked to find himself saying something or expressing an opinion without thinking, just as part of the normal ebb and flow of discussion and occasional differences in viewpoint. On reflection, he couldn't remember this ever being a part of his normal life; it was rare that the street kids ever met up in groups, particularly not for debates or discussions. More likely, if it happened, it was because of fights over territory or sleeping places or things to steal that required more planning than a quick grab and run.

After breakfast, there was the next part of the daily routine. Gerant unbarred the entrance to the smithy and then got out some of the tools and brought the fire in the forge up from its nightly tamping and slumber.

'Actually, Gerant, we might leave the front shutters closed for today and not get the forge going,' mentioned Sveg when he saw that Gerant was busy getting the work area prepared.

'I have to get another batch of steel started and it is a good opportunity to show you how the kiln works. We are going to be busy doing that for a couple of days and so the forge can have a break for a bit. We're not a big enough outfit to run both at the same time, and the kiln needs constant watching to make sure we get some good pieces of steel. It needs to be fed regularly. It's a long and tiring job and we can't take a break. It needs to keep going through the night. So, we'll be pretty tired by the end.'

Sveg walked to his designing table and reached underneath the wooden-planked surface, at one of the corners. Gerant saw he had grabbed a small ring of keys, presumably hanging from a nail under the tabletop surface.

'I haven't shown you the yard with the kiln in it. A few years ago, the old man who owned the plot next door died. The wife had already died, and the children had no interest and were happy to get some money for it. So, I was able to buy the yard, which was very handy as it backs onto the forge.'

Sveg beckoned Gerant through the small door out to the back of the forge, where stacks of supplies and unused materials, spare tools, pieces of metal and sacks of charcoal were. So far, Gerant had only been out here occasionally to grab something that Sveg needed or bring in sacks of charcoal for the forge. At the wooden paling fence at the back of the storage area was a clear space in front of a small wooden gate with a chain and large padlock anchoring it shut.

After a bit of fiddling with one of the keys on the ring, Sveg opened the lock, pulled through the chain and swung open the gate.

Beyond was a small compound encircled with a fence around seven feet high with two large gates on the other side that opened onto the next street. Around the edges of the compound were lean-tos with piles of charcoal and firewood underneath them, out of the weather, along with a few wooden crates stacked here and there with the contents protected by canvas and hidden away. In the centre of the compound was a shelter with a roof and a large post at each corner, open to the air where walls would have been. In the middle of the shelter was something unfamiliar that looked like it was made of bricks. Gerant didn't quite know what it was. Sveg walked over to it and circled it, prodding it here and there with his hands.

'Well, this is the kiln. I built it a few years back with pottery bricks that Master Delaney, the master potter, put together for me. It is a design that I was taught to use when I did my apprenticeship and worked as a journeyman.'

Sveg picked up a stick lying on the ground near the forge and used it to point out the various parts of the kiln to his apprentice. 'At the top portion there we build layers of charcoal and bog iron and then light it. When it gets to the right temperature, which we have to check all the time and adjust by using the bellows, then we add more charcoal to keep the temperature constant, take off the slag, add more iron, and so on. It needs to be watched all the time to make sure you get a good quality bloom – that's where the steel forms – it could take all night and half the next day.

'There is nothing worse than spending two days preparing and running the kiln and you end up with a bloom that is useless and can't be used to forge anything. A total waste of time and effort. That's why you need to keep awake and check things every few minutes. Preparation is also the key: that's why we'll have everything ready, have some food to eat and drink, blankets, torches, shovels, and so on. And make sure everything is handy and able to be found quickly in the dark.'

Gerant could tell there were many steps to be learnt and it would take him a few tries to understand it all. But he was excited that the smith clearly trusted him enough to be his main assistant.

Even the details about the charcoal and the iron to start with was something he would never have thought much about.

'The thing is,' continued Sveg, 'when you are a small outfit like us you can't do everything yourself, so you have to rely on other suppliers that you know well and can depend on their goods. I don't have time to burn down piles of wood to make charcoal or go fossicking in the swamps to find bog iron. That's why I get it from my timber merchant and another trader who can sell me iron pieces that have been mined or collected from the forests to the north. It's important they know what you want. Martin Forsyth, the timber merchant, knows I only will buy charcoal from oak or apple, or at a pinch, cherry or hickory wood. That said, I won't get cherry from him again: it was not good enough. Pine or willow charcoal might be easy to get, but it doesn't generate enough heat in the kiln. So never bother with that sort if you are offered it, and make sure you ask what the type of wood the charcoal is made from.'

Before they started preparing the kiln for firing, they collected a few of their belongings to get them through the entire process, including grabbing some food supplies to snack on – some pieces of bread, meat, nuts – and a couple of waterskins. Sveg allocated to Gerant the task of keeping stocks of oak charcoal close at hand, by filling a small, wheeled cart with charcoal from one of the piles under a lean-to and bringing it over next to the kiln. They started a fire in the kiln with some firewood, which initially resulted in a quite intense and roaring blaze which lit the area. Soon it started to burn down, and when the kiln started to heat up, it was time to add layers of charcoal and ore. It was also time to start using the bellows attached to the kiln to build it up to a high temperature.

'The key here is to look at the bed and make sure it has that bright yellow colour. You can see it here at the base. That's what we have to watch all the time. We need to keep the temperature right – if it's not hot enough, then the bloom will not develop. But too hot and we don't get good nuggets of steel in the bloom. It's a delicate balance to maintaining the right colour, add more charcoal, more iron, work the bellows, lots to do. And you need to keep your strength up so you are able to concentrate and stay awake.'

What followed was very much a ritual. The hours went by and the light gradually faded, although it was hard not to keep focusing on the kiln and notice anything outside of that. Sveg taught Gerant to look away regularly to note other things that were happening – the normal sights and sounds of this part of town. It certainly made it easier to stay awake, otherwise Gerant could feel himself slipping into a hypnotic state with the flames and heat leading him inevitably to slumber. They talked off and on through the hours – nothing of any import – just to keep each other alert and awake. Every hour or so they stopped for a brief bite to eat and a drink, or ducked out to the privy. After a while, slag started to flow out of the bottom of the kiln, and Sveg showed Gerant how to draw it off, cool it and break it up into small pieces to be added back in with layers of charcoal and ore.

After many hours, Gerant could start to hear sounds of the coming day – cocks crowing and birds starting to call – and he could see a slight glow to the east that was clearly different from the bright and intense light in and around the kiln. There had been times when Gerant had felt himself nod off, only to almost lurch forward and then catch himself. During the night, Sveg was an imposing silhouette largely unmoving at the other end of the rough-hewn board on low stumps set up close to the kiln, occasionally getting up to add more charcoal, or nudging Gerant gently when the bellows had to be worked.

Around dawn, Sveg arose from his position seated next to the kiln and stretched, examining the kiln and the slag oozing slowly out of the bottom.

'I think we are pretty close. See how the slag has taken on that greenish tinge? And the sounds from the bloom have quietened. Things have calmed down. It's not spitting and bubbling any more. That's the change in sound you are listening for.'

Gerant perked up and could see that the slag was hardly running out and had also taken faint elements of green along with its previous metallic lustre. Apart from the gentle crackle of the charcoal bed at the top of the kiln, the lower part of the kiln in the pit still had the bright yellowish tones to show the temperature was what was needed, but it was a more constant intensity and there was less of the swirling, roiling storm of sounds that had been noticeable earlier in the night.

'Yes, I can see that.'

After a few more minutes to make sure the firing had reached its mature state, Sveg stretched once more. 'I think we can leave this now. Let's make sure everything is out of the way and can't catch fire accidentally.

'As you can now see, it's a long process that is not straightforward, and you need to stay alert. It will get easier each time you do it. I actually find it very relaxing, and I get a lot of thinking done.'

The smith checked the kiln one last time, looking for the telltale signs. 'It looks like we've earned our rest now. Go back to your pallet and just sleep. It will take a day or so for the kiln to cool down anyway. Then we can break open the bottom few tiles and see what the bloom looks like and whether we've got some nice pieces of steel and metal that we can use in the forge.'

The smith gently escorted the boy back into the workshop and made sure he was settled on the bedding in his alcove. It was but a few moments before Gerant was clearly fast asleep, breathing deeply and regularly. Sveg smiled, checked that the smithy partitions were correctly barred and then headed off up the passageway to the back of the cottage. He also was very tired and ready for bed having been awake for over a day. Before he slept, he would see if there were any leftovers kept by Marion from the night before that he could have a few bites of. There might even be some of that fruit tart left!

Gerant subconsciously registered that there were sounds of objects being moved in the forge, just outside of his alcove. They continued long enough for him to actually wake enough to wonder who it was. He jumped up and sleepily poked his head around the edge of the alcove and saw that it was Sveg. The smith noticed the boy's head had appeared around the corner, with hair very tousled and looking far from alert.

'Only me! It's late afternoon and I just wanted to do a bit of tidying up. Why don't you grab something to eat from the kitchen if you like, but go back to bed. The kiln is still way too hot to even think about looking at the bloom. It will be cool enough in the morning, so we can look then.'

'OK, I'm not hungry, so I might just rest some more.'

'That's a good choice. I am finished here, and I might also have an early night and be fresh for the morning. I'll see you on the morrow.'

The next day dawned fine and Gerant was up at his usual time just after dawn to get the kitchen fire started and clear out the privy. As well as his instruction in smithing and now the working of the kiln, Sveg had given the boy a battered primer of words and letters as he was learning to read. It had become part of the daily routine, where Gerant was expected to read out the letters and write them down, including some simple words. It had also become somewhat of a competition at mealtimes, particularly breakfast, where Bree was taking advantage of being further along in her reading and lessons. The first few times it had became clear that Bree was only asking things of Gerant because she knew the answer and also guessed he didn't. Not surprisingly, Gerant began to get annoyed at the constant questions. Both Sveg and Marion saw the expressions of suppressed anger and frustration crossing Gerant's face. So it was probably not a shock to Sveg that the matter came up in the relative privacy of the forge.

'Look, Gerant. Bree is very proud of her learning, and she is doing well. We have always encouraged her to read and work on her writing, as some families do not allow girls to learn their letters and become educated. They feel it's above their place in life. We disagree with that and feel that Bree could have many more chances to do well and lead a full life of her choice, rather than not having any opportunities for herself.'

He spoke very matter-of-factly. 'You will soon pick up reading and I suggest you play along and use it as a way to improve the way you learn. It won't be long before you catch up and then you can even learn together.'

Gerant realised this was a case of putting up with something that was not actually too difficult to swallow and to use it to his advantage. After that, he became much more relaxed when Bree started to bait him about reading at mealtimes, and actually started to enjoy the questions and actually shoot back some queries of his own. Bree got a huge shock the first time this happened.

'OK, Bree, my turn. How many words are there that sound like cat?'

'Ummm. Cat, of course. Rat. There are a few more. Oh, sat.'

It became a quiz for the adults as well. Bat, fat, vat, hat, mat.

'There are almost certainly more than that', said Marion. 'But how about you both make a list and how to write the words and we can look at your work at dinner time.'

Sveg nodded in agreement with a big smile and gave Gerant a quick wink when he could see that Bree wasn't watching.

When breakfast was over and they had set up the forge for the day, they went out into the compound to check the state of the kiln. The kiln had cooled down sufficiently for the bloom from the smelting to be collected. It was a matter of carefully hopping down into the pit the kiln was placed in and levering out the block of the bloom without destroying any of the tiles at the bottom of the kiln. It took both of them wearing leather gauntlets to manoeuvre it out of the vent holes and then hoist it out onto a set of planks at waist height that could be used as a rough table.

Looking at the lump, Gerant could see that the bloom was roughly disc shaped, but of various metallic colours and shine and pieces of metal dispersed through the block. Sveg picked up a small but heavy hammer and tapped at various places in the block.

'Depending on the amount of time, the temperature and how much charcoal and iron and slag are layered during the smelting process, you get different bits of steel that are stronger or harder and need to be used in different parts of a blade or tool, for instance. They all sound slightly different, so that's what I am checking with the hammer. Also, you can tell the different types by how easy they are to break off the main block of the bloom.

'See, this piece here is more shiny. As I tap it, it has a more ringing sound. Also, I don't have to hit it really hard to break it off. That means we collect those sort of bits off the bloom and they will be used best for blade edges. Now, this sort of piece is a duller steel colour and doesn't ring so clearly. I have to really hit it quite hard with the hammer to break the piece off. That's because it is stronger steel and we'll use that for the core of a blade or tool.'

Gerant thought through what Sveg had said and then experimented with the hammer tapping and striking on the bloom.

Most of it made sense to him, but there was something still worrying him.

'What makes the two types of steel different? There's more of the hard stuff and only little pieces of the sharper stuff here and there.'

'Hmm,' was all Sveg could think of saying. 'That's the unknown magic of what we do when we use the kiln. I have no idea and people have been trying to explain it for years and years. All I know is what I was taught by my master smith: the steel best for a blade and holding an edge is more brittle and shiny and the core steel for strength is duller and harder to break off. I am sure you could ask a mage or alchemist with more learning, but I am not sure they would tell you anything you could believe. Maybe in the future they will work out what it all means.'

Gerant pondered on this and realised that a lot of smithing was the lessons from people who had worked it out in centuries past and had passed on the skills to their apprentices without knowing why. *Oh well,* he thought, *at least I know what to look out for. That's a start.* In the course of the next few hours, he worked with Sveg to start breaking off segments of harder and softer steel from the main block of the bloom, ready for the next steps.

Chapter 7
The Book

Gerant lay on his pallet of straw in the half-dark forge, watching the sky lighten and hearing the resident roosters in the neighbourhood proclaiming a new day had arrived. He realised that it had now been several weeks that he had been an apprentice with the town's leading smith and was in a routine that he was rather comfortable to be part of. Today was a rest day, and he continued to lay there, thinking through the various aspects and the pleasure they gave him. He was actually feeling he was now doing something worthwhile and not just looking for his next meal or working out how to stay out of the way of the town guards on their regular patrols. Part of that was the satisfaction that he was actually helping out the smith more and more and not just only following simple instructions.

He ticked off with his fingers the things that might mean nothing particular to someone else but which he was very thankful for and feeling a little bit of pride. One, he had shown enough interest and potential that Sveg had decided to take him on as an apprentice. Two, the guild had been happy enough to formally enrol him as an apprentice, although Gerant was under no delusions that it was more about coin coming into the guild coffers than anything else. Three, he had managed to survive the weekly sessions with Master Klyburn. He had not really learnt anything of note and was almost only there because Sveg expected him to attend. Four, he was getting more confident in being able to recognise words and was able to read simple groups. This was a major step forward and he now enjoyed the daily lessons with Sveg and working together with Bree on their joint learnings. It had stopped being a chore and was actually something he looked forward to. It was also no longer a competition with Bree about who was smarter or better at reading; they helped each other now. And five, he had finished his first full project in the smithy. Admittedly, this was very much under the close guidance of Sveg, but all the same he was very proud of how the fireplace tools had turned out. They were finished now that a third coat of black paint had been put on carefully to seal the cast-iron pieces so they wouldn't rust. He was sure there were other things that he could use the fingers on his other hand to list, but five things were still pretty good.

Gerant recalled the steps he had gone into making the fireplace tools for the bookseller. Under Sveg's instruction, he had made a poker, a long-handled brush, a small shovel and some long-handled tongs, along with a waist-high metal stand that the various tools rested against. They were all fairly plain and functional, but following Sveg's advice they had a common spiral thread worked into the handles. That had needed quite a bit of care heating and reheating the tools after the basic shape had been made. It had required a lot of thought, care and assistance from Sveg to get the handles spiralling in the same way. Gerant had been happy how they had turned out. Even more important was that Sveg had checked them all and had pronounced they were 'not too bad'. In the short time Gerant had known the smith, he knew that Sveg would not let anything leave the smithy that he was not sufficiently happy with, so this nod of approval was the most pleasing thing that had happened.

He continued to lay back and thought about what he would do with his day of rest. Perhaps a walk with his adopted family down to the river and then to the market if Marion needed any food in the week coming, then some more book learning and reading with Bree. Most of his chores would only take a few minutes to complete and he could have a relaxing day. Part of his contentment was that he felt he had earned his day off with the tasks he had finished earlier in the week.

The following day was a normal working format and Gerant had got the forge ready after the breakfast meal and helped Sveg with a couple of small tooling tasks. Although Sveg had already mentioned this at the breakfast table, Gerant was very pleased to listen to what Sveg then had to say after the hoe had been re-edged and repaired.

'I intend to go and see Martin Forsyth about getting another cartload of oak charcoal in the next few weeks. We have a few lots of steel to make in the kiln with the work I have agreed to do. Also having you here to help as apprentice has meant I am willing to take on more work that I wouldn't have thought to do previously. That's good for business, Gerant.'

Gerant nodded and couldn't help feeling a faint flush of pleasure at what the smith had said.

'That means that I won't be able to take those fireplace tools to Aaron Galchrist, the bookseller. I feel that since you made them, Gerant, it is good for you to take them around and it is a good experience. I presume you would be able to do that?'

'Of course. I have thought about that a lot.'

Sveg watched his apprentice put on a serious look on his face, which knowing the lad quite well now, meant he had slipped into a business-like pattern of thought. He could tell without further comment that the boy was quite excited about taking the finished project round to the client, yet with a little bit of hesitation about doing something he had never tried before. Sveg had talked about this with his wife and Marion had agreed it would be a useful test to see how Gerant was progressing in being a trusted and reliable apprentice to back up Sveg.

'If you take the set to Bookseller Galchrist this morning, that would be appreciated. The price is six silver pieces, which he has paid three silver already. So, you will need to collect the outstanding three.'

It was not too much later that Gerant left the smithy clutching the fireplace toolset bundled up in a piece of sackcloth, which gently clinked as he strode out. The bookseller had a small shop in the next street from the guild compound. It took Gerant only a few minutes' walk, being mindful to keep the bundle firmly grasped so it wouldn't slip and spill the tools on the ground. It was a little strange to walk past the guild without going in and turning two corners to reach the shop belonging to the bookseller. It was clear from the building it was actually a house with the front room converted into a place to display and sell books, parchments, papers, scrolls and other reading material. Gerant paused for a moment at the front door, then pushed through; a small bell tinkled gently as his eyes adjusted to the somewhat dimly lit interior. Standing just inside the now-closed door, he had not known what to expect, but saw that the large room consisted of a series of small aisles between tables stacked with books, along with shelves also lining the aisles reaching almost to the ceiling. It had an odd, musty smell of old parchment and books, which was not unpleasant. There was also the quiet murmur of voices coming to his right. He noticed a short, balding man standing in front of a table, leafing through a leather-bound tome. At his feet was a nondescript leather satchel. Behind the table was a quite tall, thinly built man in brown, unremarkable robes, with a pair of eyeglasses perched on his nose. From Sveg's brief description to Gerant before he set out, this was the bookseller, Aaron Galchrist.

The bookseller stopped the discussion with his customer to look over the new arrival in a not unkindly fashion. 'Young man, I will be with you in some moments. I am just discussing a purchase with this gentleman. Feel free to wander about until that time.'

Gerant was somewhat unclear how to respond and so just nodded. He placed his bundle to the side of the front door and decided he should at least look like he knew his way around this sort of establishment. The fact was, he had no idea.

Walking to the closest shelves, he decided to at least get one of the books out and pretend to be looking at it. One that he chose at random had a reddish leather cover and pages inside printed with black text. It took Gerant a few moments to try to decipher the embossed letters on the spine of the book. It said, *A Treatise on*

Common Woodland Plants and Their Uses. Gerant was not sure what *treatise* meant, but he guessed the book talked about plants in the forest. When he flipped through the pages, on some of them there were printed drawings of plants he recognised from walks with Sveg, Marion and Bree. The next book was covered in black card and had printed on the hard cover, *Growing and Collecting Herbs.* After several minutes of picking up a book and mouthing out the letters and understanding its topic, Gerant realised that the books, scrolls and bound papers were grouped together by subject. While the gentle murmur continued, Gerant became more and more interested in using his developing reading skills to work out what a book was about. He was starting to enjoy himself. Moving onto a new stand of shelves, after several checks Gerant realised that these books were about crafting and trades such as tailoring and jewellery making. Tucked in between several large leather-bound books on weaving cloth and making fancier types of garments, Gerant pulled out a leather-clad, mildew-stained slim volume. There was nothing printed on the leather cover and the printing inside was rather faded, making it harder to decipher the letters. Gerant started to get quite excited; from what he could work out from some of the words and a couple of faint illustrations, this was a book about smithing and metalwork. He recognised words like forge, hammer, charcoal and others that were now part of what he did every day in the smithy. He quickly looked further into the text and only then realised that the murmuring of conversation had stopped and there was a gentle coughing that intruded into his consciousness.

'Thank you for being patient, young master. He is an important customer and regularly buys books from me. Now, how can I assist you?' The bookseller had approached Gerant, with an expression of quiet expectation on his features. Up closer, he was a little stooped, in a different way from Sveg. Gerant got the sense that he too had spent hours and hours bent over his work. His silvery-grey hair was neatly trimmed and his eyeglasses almost seemed to be part of his actual face. Warm brown eyes peered out from the glasses in a not unfriendly manner that, all the same, suggested they didn't miss much.

Gerant walked over to the bundle of sackcloth he had left near the door. 'I am actually Master Sveg Martinson's apprentice and am bringing the fireplace tools that you ordered.'

'Ah, excellent,' said the bookseller, 'I have been waiting for these. I am sure they will be used straight away. Can I have a look at them? Put them up on this table, if you don't mind.'

Gerant placed the bundle on the table indicated, unwrapped the tools from the sackcloth and showed the bookseller the tongs, the poker, the brush and the shovel and the stand they all fitted into. The bookseller hefted each in turn and then placed them leaning within the stand.

'They will go very nicely in my parlour where the fireplace is. My wife has been wanting me to get a set made for some time now. I am sure these will mean we have less clutter in the room.' The bookseller smiled softly at something he was thinking about. 'My thanks to Master Sveg; I knew they would be distinctive, yet functional.'

Gerant did not have the courage to let Master Galchrist know he had contributed most of the work and design. Gerant was now very glad that that he had rehearsed the next bit with Sveg. 'I will pass on your words to Master Sveg. He also mentioned that he would be more than happy to work on any other tasks you might have.' A pause. 'And we would welcome the three silver pieces owing on this set.'

'Ah yes, of course, of course.' The bookseller walked over to his main table and reached behind and brought out a small, elaborately carved wooden box with an ornate clasp. He took out the coins, which he passed to Gerant.

The smith had spent several sessions practising with his apprentice about the words to use when requesting payment. Gerant recalled the reasoning Sveg had given. 'What we do is of excellent quality, and we should be proud of it. I don't hold with pretending that we are of lesser worth and are the servants and need to speak keeping our eyes down and being submissive and fawning. Much better to talk to your customer as a person who is of equal standing and someone who should be recognised as such. So, look them in the eye and talk to them normally.'

'Again, my thanks,' said the bookseller. 'I couldn't help but notice you had found something that interested you.'

Gerant felt his face turning a bright red. An earlier version of himself would have denied this interest, but even the small number of months working and living at the smithy had meant Gerant decided there was no harm in at least talking about it with Master Galchrist.

'I found this. It looks like it is about smithing.' He passed the slim volume over.

'Hmmm. I had forgotten about this one. I have nothing bad to say about Master Martinson's trade, but it is a subject that many would not be interested in. I can't even remember when it came into my possession or how much I paid for it. Also, it is no longer in a good state. Let me see. If you wanted to purchase it, I could let you have it for two gold pieces.'

The bookseller peered over his eyeglasses at the boy to judge what the reaction was to the price he had named.

Gerant's face had gone white when the bookseller had mentioned the price. He tried to speak calmly and not just stutter out a reply. 'It would take me months of saving my allowance as an apprentice before I could afford to buy it. So, I will have to leave it. Thanks, anyway.'

The bookseller smiled kindly at the young lad and put the tattered book back in its place on the shelf. 'Well, as I said, it is probably not a popular subject, so it will likely be here for you when you have saved the coin you need.'

Dawdling back to the smithy, Gerant tried to remember as much as he could about what he had read in the book about his craft. How could he build up his tiny allowance for so long to be able buy it? Not that he spent his two coppers per week on anything at all. He had a small pile of coins next to his pallet that had already meant he was thinking of making himself a small leather purse to keep his allowance in. But it would take weeks and weeks to save enough to buy the book. His reading skills were not really strong enough at the moment to even work out whether it would be useful, or a waste of good coin.

He discovered he had reached the smithy, walked through into the workshop area and noted that the smith had also returned and was working at his drafting bench. All this with being so focused on his thoughts that he had got there automatically and without conscious effort. He walked up to the bench and placed the three silver coins on the smooth surface.

Sveg looked up and nodded with a quick smile, quietly hiding his relief. 'You delivered the fireplace set to Master Galchrist with no problems? I guess that must be true as you remembered to get the silver owing.'

'Yes. He passed on his thanks to you. He said he was very happy with the work. I had to wait a few minutes as he had a customer he was looking after first. I just looked at a few books while I waited.'

Sveg had already gone back to thinking about the drawing he had been working on and was only partly attending to the conversation.

'See anything of note?'

'Many of the books and printing I could only read a few words here and there. But just at the end I found an old book that was about smithing. I thought it looked interesting, but I didn't have long enough to look at it properly. And it was too much for me to use my allowance on.'

'Is that so? Hmmm.' It was then that Sveg actually took in what Gerant had said.

'Really? I am not aware of any printed work on smithing. It might be good to see what it is about. If nothing else, it could be a good way for you to continue with your reading. How much did Master Galchrist want for it?'

'Two gold pieces.' As Gerant said that, he keenly watched Sveg's face much in the same way that the bookseller had watched his own face some little time earlier.

Sveg thought through that news, musing aloud. 'Well, two gold is not a sum to sneeze at. It's not a king's ransom, but all the same there are quite a few things you can buy with that amount of coin.'

Books were not common. Many people couldn't read, and most households wouldn't own a book or other reading material. Sveg and Marion had a couple of volumes that were cherished, including the primer that Bree and now Gerant were using in their lessons.

Sveg also thought how useful it would have been to read about some of the skills in the forge when he had been learning his craft.

'Well, I will think on this a little more. I would only buy the book if it was truly about smithing and not something else. Also, you would be expected to use your allowance to eventually pay for half of it. And I would expect you to use it to improve your reading and learning even more than now. Is that a fair bargain? Do you agree?'

Gerant hardly had to think for more than a moment before he was grinning and nodding his head enthusiastically.

'Tomorrow you can go back to the bookseller, and I will give you the two gold to buy this book you found. Mind you, I expect to be able to return it to Master Galchrist and have my coins returned if I find it does not measure up. You need to make sure that is agreed before you come back with it.'

The next morning Gerant made a quick trip to the bookseller after Sveg had provided two gold pieces. The smith had initially thought to bind the apprentice to providing half of the price with some sort of written agreement, but Sveg was not interested in writing one on paper himself and did not want to waste coin on getting a scribe to put one together. He had no doubts that Gerant would honour the agreement and was secretly excited about seeing the book and what it contained.

When the door into the bookshop tinkled shut and Gerant's eyes adjusted to the somewhat dim interior, he noticed no one else that he could see apart from the bookseller, who was behind the table that he clearly used as his working area.

'Ah, young master, well met. May I presume you are here to purchase that book that interested you? I did not expect to see you so quickly.'

Gerant quickly walked over to where he had found the book on the shelves and was rather relieved that it was back in its previous place. He took it down and came up to the bookseller. 'Master Sveg has advanced me the coin to purchase it. He has not heard of a book about smithing, so was interested in it himself.' Gerant placed the two gold coins on the table.

'Much obliged, much obliged. Please pass on my thanks again to the master. The fireplace tools are very fine and they already feel like they have been there for ever.'

Gerant nodded and thanked the bookseller himself as he left the shop. He had gone only a few paces when he remembered something and ran back inside.

'I forgot to make sure that if the book is not about smithing or has some other fault, we expect to be able to return it and get our coin back.' Gerant held his breath to see what the response was. His overhearing of some conversations at the guild suggested this might lead to a disagreement. But he was relieved when the bookseller only nodded without looking up from the manuscript he was working on at the table.

'This is the case with all the books I sell. Think nothing of it. But any damage that was not there previously is your own concern.'

Arriving back at the smithy, Sveg had already started on the first work for the day, but when Gerant walked into the workshop, he took off his gauntlets, picked up a spare rag and wiped his hands. He gently took the book that Gerant had been carrying in the sack he used for his guild lessons. The smith first looked at the spine and front of the somewhat stained and well-used leather cover. As reported by Gerant, there was no printing on the cover whatsoever to indicate what lay inside. Sveg gently opened the book and peered at the title page. Then he nodded with pursed lips.

'*A Smith's Guide to Metalwork.* Hmmm, well at least the title is promising.' Sveg then spent several minutes reading out sentences here and there and looking at some of the printed illustrations.

'From what I can see, there is nothing new beyond what I have learnt in my years in the trade. But it will be useful for you, Gerant, to learn the words and techniques as an apprentice. From that point of view, it is a worthy purchase. But I have never heard of this Master Ironfist, who is supposed to have written this work. I know most of the smiths in this part of The Realm and even in The Capital. I wonder whether it is an assumed name. Of course, it could be someone from long ago who has been dead for years.'

Sveg paused as he tried to think what sort of smith could have written such a detailed account and gave up, returning to more day-to-day matters. 'Anyway, you can make it your task to learn to read from this as your particular primer, and we can spend part of each day, as before, in you reading out from a new section and making sure you know all the words. Also we can talk about what it means in terms of working in the smithy. There might be a few things I disagree about that this so-called Master Ironfist says, but we shall have to wait and see.'

Gerant had stopped on the way back to the smithy to flick through some of the pages and was even more excited about the book. Some of that showed in his face. 'Thank you, Sveg, for letting me purchase it.' A pause. 'I might need to find a candle and holder now, now that I have something to look at after dinner.'

Sveg laughed. 'Well, that can be the next job you can think about. After we have today's tasks finished, let's draw up a candle holder with a handle that you can then make for your bedtime reading.'

Gerant smiled and blushed. He took back the smithing book and quickly put it next to his pallet in his bed space on the other side of the partition.

Two evenings later, the candle holder had been completed. Up until that point in the late afternoon and twilight, Gerant's routine had been the same and comfortingly normal. He would have helped Sveg pack up the forge, dampen down the coals ready for the next day and pulled closed the outer partitions to the workshop area. Then a quick wash to remove the grime accumulated during the day – full baths were taken twice a week nowadays – and the family chores such as bringing in more firewood for the kitchen fire, checking the privy and some quiet time before dinner. With the failing light he would quickly complete any tasks that had been set by Master Klyburn at the guild. Or, for a bit of fun, practising his dagger throwing out in the kiln courtyard where an old post had been set up in the middle. This meant it was away from prying eyes, although some neighbours had wondered about a periodic *thunk*, sometimes followed by quiet cursing, that they could hear occasionally.

Gerant was unaware that occasionally the smith stood in the shadows of the workshop watching the progress and nodding his head with satisfaction at the steady improvement. This was also being seen in the apprentice's ability to strike exactly where he had intended on the heated bar of metal on the anvil. Sveg pondered on this growing skill and thought it was almost time to fashion a couple of daggers for Gerant that he could wear when he went out. They would only be needed if a situation turned nasty or there was an immediate need for protection of life and limb.

After the family dinner with Marion, Sveg and Bree, Gerant had helped pack up dishes and leftover food with Bree and then had excused himself. The previous routine since he had been staying in the alcove was to lie on his pallet for some time in the dark, thinking of the day's events, or what was to come on the morrow, or anything else he pondered on before sleep took him. This evening, he took a candle into the workshop, stuck the wick carefully against one of the still slowly burning coals and waited while it lit. He then took it back to his sleeping place and pushed it onto the spike of his newly fashioned candle holder. He placed it carefully on the small chest that was now next to the pallet and that held his schooling materials and his very few personal belongings. The alcove was a rather small space and now was totally visible in the soft candle glow.

Gerant smiled and thought of the candle holder and what had happened up to the point before this. Of course, the family had a number of candle holders scattered around the cottage, but Gerant decided to see what else might be worth incorporating into his design. So he had walked around to the chandler's shop in another part of the town and seen several different candle holders available. The chandler had been disappointed when Gerant had indicated he was only there to look, and not to buy. He had liked one design, which was slightly different from the ones in the cottage. Coming back to the workshop, he had worked with Sveg to draw up what it would look like when made up and the key parts to it. The smith had suggested that they make it up in brass, which Gerant had not worked with before. Sveg showed him that it should not be heated too strongly, more in the dark orange to bright red range, and to use only light taps. The shape of the candle holder had come together progressively. Not that there was anything particularly complicated about it, but Gerant felt a weight of pressure on him in a way he had not felt before. Sure, he had designed and made Master Galchrist's fireplace set to a large extent, but that had been under Sveg's unobtrusive oversight. In this case, the piece of work was for himself, and Sveg had been willing to let Gerant take the lead in terms of the design and what steps needed to be followed. After an hour or so of steady work, the brass candle holder was complete, apart from filing the joins to smooth them and a final polish. Gerant suddenly realised how drained he felt and smiled in relief as he saw Sveg watching him closely with care on his face.

'You see how much thinking there is in even a simple project like this. That's why you need to take your regular breaks and not wear yourself into the ground. If a customer asks me how long a job will take, I work that out in my head and then double the time. Not because it will always be more difficult, but because you need to pace yourself so you can work well day in and day out.'

The memories of making the candle holder still brought a grin to his thoughts. Now it was possible every evening to spend some time before sleep to continue learning his letters, words, reading and writing. He reached for the smithing book and was pleased that the printing was able to be seen clearly enough in the candlelight. Gerant picked a page and mouthed the words. He was also able to look at the printed drawings and diagrams scattered infrequently throughout the slim tome and recognise some of the processes illustrated based on what he already knew working at the forge. He looked up and realised the candle had burned down quite a bit – he had been looking at the book for some time. He remembered what Sveg had said the previous day and the need to pace himself. So, he decided to stop this evening and pick up again the next night. But he was curious where the book finished. He turned to the final leaf before the cover and saw that there were a lot of words he could read, but some were unknown to him. As he was about to close the volume, he noticed a small slit between the last page and the battered and scuffed leather cover. Looking more closely in the candlelight, he saw something within the slit. Pulling carefully revealed a slender fold of parchment pieces that came out with a bit of pressure and wiggling. There was some faintish writing in ordered lines on the parchment. The writing was hard to discern and after several moments Gerant could only see one word he could recognise: it said "blade". But even with that, he was not all that confident. He sighed and realised that he would need Sveg's help. Gerant wondered what the writing said and why it appeared to have been hidden with purpose inside the lining of the book.

As he lay on his pallet after blowing out the candle and lying back, his mind could not stop thinking about his discovery. *What did it mean? Who had put it there? Was it important?* All these questions went round and round in his mind. Gerant forced himself to think about the work he needed to help Sveg with in the morning, and gradually his thoughts started to calm down. After a few more moments, he slowly drifted off to sleep.

Chapter 8
Magicks of Bladecraft

In the morning before they started work for the day, Gerant mentioned to Sveg what he had found. He showed the smith the slit in the inside cover and pulled out the folded parchment pieces with the faint writing on them. Sveg attempted to read the writing in the somewhat dim light of the workshop and read a few words aloud.

'Welcome, thou student of the blade. Here be some magicks of bladecraft which are hereby passed to you in great secrecy.'

'The writing is very faint and in an odd manner that is not easy to read,' pondered Sveg. 'It looks very interesting, but perhaps it will be easier to look at it out in the full daylight during our mid-morning break. We could sit out in the courtyard.'

Gerant nodded, but couldn't help feel somewhat disappointed that he would have to wait a little longer. They finished putting together some metal brackets that were needed for the guard post at the town bridge and took their break. The pair carried a wooden bench from the smithy to sit on in the courtyard. Sitting next to Gerant, Sveg carefully held the scraps of parchment so he could view the writing in the strong morning sunlight.

'Well, this is much better, although the ink has faded quite a bit and the writing is in an old-fashioned style. Let's see . . .' Slowly, and with regular halts where it was difficult for the smith to discern the words, Sveg read aloud from the parchment pieces.

'Welcome, thou student of the blade. Here be some magicks of bladecraft which are hereby passed to you in great secrecy. They are known to very few and are of great worth. Several have killed for details of them in generations past. Knowing of them is a great boon but also a great curse if they are not kept close. I give you four lores that will make you a master weaponmaker and be the envy of all in the kingdom. Do not betray this trust.'

'Nothing particularly important to smithing here', said Sveg after reading this passage. 'Apart from the details are to be kept secret and are to be told to but a few. Also it talks about a kingdom. Maybe it is from a foreign place or this was written in times well before The Realm was called that.'

Gerant was wide-eyed with anticipation and just nodded. What Sveg had read so far sounded like a bedtime story that would have magic and spells and monsters and legendary warriors wielding fantastic weapons. 'What's next, Sveg?'

'Ahhh, this might be more interesting . . .'

'In making swords and other bladecraft, the master of skill knows of two sorts of steel: hard steel and soft steel. These can be selected after controlling the amount of charcoal and iron in the kiln and being expert in how they look within the bloom. Someone who has become a grand master after years of training will be able to select those pieces that are of hard steel, soft steel and a medium steel.'

'Hmmm, I am familiar with hard and soft steel and how to sort it from the bloom. I have already started to show you that. The only difference is I have learnt to call this hard steel as edge steel and the other one is named as core steel. This medium steel I am thinking is in between the two and it should be possible to sort the bloom pieces into three lots instead of two. I wonder why that is important?' Sveg kept reading aloud.

'Anyone of ordinary skill in the arts will be able to forge a weapon made wholly of hard steel, sufficient as a club or a mace or a sword of lesser quality. A drawing of the blade of such a crude weapon could be shown thus:'

Sveg showed the boy the drawing of the blade. 'Nothing new there. That's what we do for ordinary tools and pieces. You already could do that.'

Gerant nodded in agreement.

'A master swordsmith who understands the forging of a blade with hard and soft steel will be able to make a finer weapon. This will have an outer edge of hard steel that can take a superior edge, but the inner core of soft steel has a greater strength and resilience and will resist breaking. The master smith is able to forge the blade so that it can be shown like this:"

'There are occasions where I use this sort of technique, if I am wanting to make a particularly robust plough blade. If the town guards need any daggers or swords, I would use this approach of hard and soft steel to make a better sort of blade. If you like, we could make up a pair of throwing daggers for you in this way. Would you like that?'

Gerant couldn't keep the excitement out of his voice. 'That would be terrific,' gushed Gerant. 'But would that affect the balance and they wouldn't throw well?'

'A good point and something to consider. If anything, the balance may actually be improved. We shall have to see. Also, you can help balance the dagger by shaping the handle and what sort of wood you use. How dense the wood for the handle will affect things and whether it is heavy towards the point or the hilt.'

The smith kept reading. His interest in the ancient manuscript pages had also been piqued.

'A true grand master smith known throughout the kingdom will be able to forge a weapon that befits a champion warrior and who deserves the best blade. They will forge an inner core of soft steel, a tip and edges of hard steel and layers of medium steel around the core to provide the benefits of both hard and soft steels. Such a blade takes many weeks to make and only one blade in ten will have the correct strength, sharpness and balance to be worthy of a sword champion and truly meet the standards. The secret of this six-layer forging is known to only two or three masters of the craft and should only be passed on to a trusted and worthy successor. The six-layer blade made by such a master looks like:'

Sveg showed his apprentice the third drawing, pointing out each of the layers and what sort of steel they must be forged from.

'Well, I understand now about the three qualities of steel you would need. I must confess I have never heard of this six-layer mastery. It would only be needed for a very valuable weapon, such as a sword used by a lord or the king, or the king's champion. From a smithing point of view, I believe I could master it, but for the likes of what we do around here in Ashford, there is little use for this. Even the captain of the town guard wouldn't merit a blade like this.'

Sveg looked at the faint writing and got to the end of the first sheet of parchment. 'Well, that seems to be all that this mysterious teacher has to impart about making these sorts of blades. It is very useful information that would be good to pass on to any apprentice, but I must confess this six-layer forging is beyond me. Hmm.'

And Sveg started to read out the next section, on the second folded sheet of parchment.

'The second lore I leave to you is the use of talium in your forging. The metal known as talium is a powerful addition to any blade, giving it both enormous strength and a lightness like swansdown. Add one portion of talium to nine portions of best quality iron in the kiln to give a steel of unrivalled merit. Talium is only found in one mine in the foothills of the Greenthorn Mountains to the west, a short ride from Osmount. In searching within the tunnels, seek the veins of ore that glow with a greenish hue in lantern light. Many search, but few can find it. Talium has a shining, greenish cast and flakes off with uncommon ease. It is of unrivalled value and is worth many times its weight of gold. Beware of its attraction. Evil people will kill all those who find it, so they can take it for their own.'

The smith spoke softly, as he recalled aspects he had not thought about for many years.

'I have heard of this talium, but never seen it or worked with it. I knew it was only found in the one mine past Osmount. I had heard that there was no talium left and it was even more valued than before.'

'Does it say anything more about what it does?' asked Gerant.

'No, nothing of note. It would be interesting to try it if we ever got hold of some, but I can hardly think that will ever happen. Again, it would only be used in valuable weapons that would be used in The Capital for kings, lords and other important people.'

Sveg turned to the third piece of parchment.

'Few know the secret of how to harden the edge of a blade even more than from regular forging and using hard steel for the outside of the blade. As a third lore, I give to you the secret recipe that should not be shared with others, unless they are to inherit your mastery. The recipe uses ingredients that are often hard to find and are known to impart their properties of hardness. You will need a piece of the tusk from the spotted tusktooth, ground into small pieces. This creature lives in the waters of the far north. It will not give up its life easily. You will also need ash made from burning the wood of the hedge apple. This tree of moderate size is found in open forest in the eastern lands, often on the edge of farmland and has a large green fruit that should not be eaten. Any forester or woodcutter should be able to find a tree. While they are not common, they are also not rare. The final ingredient is clay taken from a stream bank that has a golden tinge like the newly risen sun. Mix up six parts of clay, two parts of ash from the hedge apple and two parts of the ground tusk tooth. The mixture is applied to the blade carefully so the paste is thicker on the spine and very sparse on the cutting edge. Be careful to then heat the blade in the forge very slowly and carefully, if possible in a darkened workshop. When the temperature of the blade changes from dull red to bright red, the blade should be quenched quickly in a bath of water. You will find that the hardness from the hedge apple and tusk tooth have been imparted to the blade, with the brightness from the sun-hued clay. It is then but a matter of polishing and sharpening to give a weapon that has a bright, keen edge that will take much use before it becomes even a little less sharp.'

'This sounds very far-fetched! When I was a child, I was told stories of these tusktooths, which are found in the icy waters to the north of the town I come from. There is a village called North Haven on the coast that I believe they are hunted from. Even if you had a piece of the tusk, then you need charcoal from this hedge apple, which I have never seen in any of my travels. And then a special kind of clay! Who knows where you get that? This is very much for a master sword smith to use, even if it was true. They may know of this lore in The Capital, but I have never heard of the like.'

Gerant nodded in agreement, although he wasn't sure why he was nodding. It sounded like a wonderful recipe that he would be keen to try. He heard the tone of reservation in Sveg's voice, but couldn't help think about what sort of blade it would make and how much better it would become. He realised the smith had started reading from the last two sheets of parchment, and from his reciting of the words, was having difficulty in reading the words without commenting immediately.

'The fourth and final secret art I give to you is one that uses a magic lore I learnt from a powerful archmage. I do not understand the means by which it works, and he was not willing to teach me this aspect or perhaps even he did not know. But I have seen that the spells gives weapons a mystical and powerful effect. I impart to you four Words of Power that can be used to control the use of a blade. Each uses a different gem, a different paste and a different spell to impart its property. The Words of Power are Fast, Slow, Strong and Weak.

'To instil a blade with the power word Fast, you must have an emerald ring or pendant and make a paste of ground-up anise seeds. When the paste is applied to the pommel, the following spell is said while holding the sword and wearing the gem:

> To weave and carve the very air,
> No eyes can follow this deathly dance.
> Yon blade is now beyond compare,
> It sings like in a lethal trance.'

'To use the power word Slow, you must have a gem of cinnabar and make a paste of hops. The paste is applied to the pommel and this spell is recited:

> Thy looks are still the very same,
> Yet feeling leaves no glow.
> It has no hope to beat or tame,
> Being thrice as dull and slow.'

'To use the power word Strong, have a ruby ring or pendant and make a paste of purslane. The purslane paste is applied to the pommel and a spell for Strong is said:

> Be like the bear, of magical strength:
> Best all who threaten thy will,
> Never to tire, an endless length
> Majestic calling shall fulfil.'

'To use the power word Weak, a ring of amber is needed and a paste made from the Carduus thistle. After applying the paste to the pommel, a spell is recited:

> Make this blade grow truly pale,
> Lacking strength, might or speed.

A thing that will be known to fail
Hear my spell, obey, take heed.'

'The power word Weak can only be used on a sword once, as it will shatter the blade the first time the weapon is used in anger and the word is spoken.

'After the sword has been imparted with a Word of Power, the ring or pendant must be near to the weapon for the spell to work. Each Word of Power can only be used once each day. For the spell to take effect, the Word must be spoken clearly at the time of choosing and the weapon will become like the Word of Power, for better or ill. The spell will last for a short time and then cannot be summoned again until the next day. This power is a great gift to someone who is given the enchanted blade, the ring or pendant and the secret Word of Power. That is why the Words of Power are the opposite of each other, and mayhap will bring some sort of balance to those who choose to impart these spells and their use.'

Sveg paused as he turned to the final piece of parchment.

'I teach you these four gifts, that will enable you to become a master in crafting swords and other blades that will have renown throughout the kingdom and beyond. Many will seek to learn your teachings and use these lores. But choose wisely who you then teach these gifts to. Many will use honeyed words and compliments to be taught these crafts. Few are worthy and deserving of this trust. Choose wisely, my friend, or it will be at your peril.'

Sveg reassembled the pieces of parchment together, carefully holding them as he pondered. He stared out into the yard for several moments, then turned to Gerant sitting beside him.

'I wonder who this smith was. The last couple of lores appear to be more in the arts of magic and wizardry than smithing. The first two lores made some sense to me as a master of smithing, but the third one about the tusk tooth and then these spells to change how a weapon behaves is fantasy!' He looked into the distance, gently shuffling through the pieces of parchment as he kept thinking. Then he carefully folded the pieces of parchment and slid them back into the inside the leather cover of the old book.

'Well, this was an interesting way to spend our break, but let's go back to these brackets. Here, Gerant, you can keep these old writings on the parchment to amuse you and use the printed book to continue in your reading and writing skills. I still believe it will be useful for that.'

'Is it still possible to make the throwing daggers with the two layers?'

Sveg sighed, as he could see the excitement in Gerant's face had not diminished.

'Of course, my young friend. I did say we would do that, so let's start on that in the next few days. Mind, I still want you to work hard on your reading and writing using the book as your primer.'

Chapter 9
An Excursion

As Sveg had promised, two mornings later they began working on a couple of daggers that could also be used for throwing. Sveg got out some rough bars of steel that he had stored away at the back of the workshop.

'This should be sufficient for the blades of two small daggers. See how the steel looks slightly different to each other?'

Gerant could see one bar was slightly shinier and a little lighter than the other.

'So we have the two sorts of steel, which I know as edge steel and core steel. First of all we need to forge the bars, heating them and hammering and bending them. That way we can get rid of any impurities from the kiln and the blades will be stronger and less likely to snap. After that we can weld the two together, so that the bar of core steel in inside strips of edge steel, so that they fuse together. Then we can hammer them into the shape of the dagger blades.'

Although they had worked on other smithing jobs in between, it had taken several days to reach the step where Sveg was satisfied with the two dagger blades. He held them both up to the light and sighted along them, then got Gerant to do the same.

'If you were only using these for throwing, you would keep the edge blunt and only have the point sharp. But I think they should be more useful if they have a sharp edge and can be used as a dagger or knife as well. That's why we made them with a diamond profile, so we can put an edge on both sides, as well as the point. That is another reason to have the core steel in the middle and weld the edge steel around the outside.'

This made sense to Gerant, now that Sveg had explained it. 'But if you put an edge on both sides and the point is sharp, how can you grab and throw or hold it to cut something?'

Sveg smiled, pleased that his apprentice was thinking about the next steps needed to finish the weapons.

'True. We will rivet on a small wooden handle. I have some seasoned cherry wood somewhere that should suit. We'll just make it very simple and only long enough for your hand to grip. Making it fancy will only mean it doesn't fly well when you throw it. Also having a plain wooden handle and just the blade makes it less likely for someone to notice it and covet it. You will be the only one that knows its purpose and how useful it is.'

Another few hours' work was spent fitting the plain wooden handles and making sure both daggers were as similar as possible and balanced in the hand. Gerant polished the finished handles with beeswax and put edges on the blades as Sveg had taught him. Hefting each dagger in his right hand, he could not tell any difference in their weight or how they felt.

They went out to the courtyard and Sveg watched with arms folded as Gerant walked away from the post until he got to the mark on the ground that showed he was ten feet away. He looked at Sveg, who nodded. *Thunk . . . thunk.*

Sveg walked to the post. Two daggers were buried into the wood at his head height within two inches of each other.

'Not bad, not bad. Did they feel good in the hand before you threw them?'

'Yes, they felt the same,' responded Gerant.

'Well, let's finish this work off. We can fashion a couple of sheaths out of some leather scraps I have left over from another job. I think you should have one strapped to your calf and the other in the small of your back on a belt around your waist. Then they are not obvious to anyone under your clothing, but you can quickly get to them if you need them. As well as keeping up your throwing practice, remember every now and again to make sure that you can reach them quickly if you need to. It's often best to slowly reach for them. If you do it in a hurry, then the other people will realise you are reaching for a weapon and might strike first.'

Gerant nodded in understanding, but with large eyes as he tried not to think about a situation where he needed to get out the daggers and use them for real. All the same, he would dedicate several times during the day to work on his throwing, so if it came to a situation in the future, gods forbid, it would be just instinct to throw, and throw accurately, should he need to.

One morning, Marion mentioned to Gerant something that clearly had been discussed with Sveg for a little time.

'Gerant, we are going soon to take a trip north to show Bree where her father came from and for her to meet some of the family at Rivernook.'

'Yes,' added Sveg, 'It is a good time to shut the forge for a little while before business starts to increase with the longer summer hours. I have not been back for some years, and it will be a welcome opportunity for my parents to meet their granddaughter, who they have never seen.

'Of course, the forge will be closed for a few weeks. I have already told the guild of my plans. I guess it would be possible for you to stay in the smithy, but what will you do? I know you have only just heard of this, but do you have any plans yourself?'

Gerant absorbed this surprising news. He sensed that although Marion and Sveg were saying he could remain in his alcove in the workshop, they might be more comfortable if this was not the case. It would be no issue for him to move back to one of his old haunts for the week or so they were away. That said, it would feel a little strange and he would need to think more on how that would go. He certainly had no desire to come across some of his previous acquaintances now or live in the sort of conditions that he had taken for granted even a year ago. Gerant admitted to himself that he would not want to go back to that style of living – not knowing where his next meal would be coming from, or trying to stay one step ahead of the town guards.

Thinking further, he realised he could perhaps take on something that he had only contemplated as he mused on some of the writings from the mysterious scribe about the smithing lore. But he was not yet ready to tell Sveg exactly what he was thinking and what he wanted to explore.

'Actually, I was wondering about spending some time going to other places to see what they have to offer. I have never been outside the town boundaries. Perhaps I will take a few days here and there to see what lies outside of Ashford. Maybe I might walk to Cobham and spend a day or so in the town. Or take the road west and see how far I get in a week or so.'

Marion was relieved to hear the Gerant didn't appear to be too crestfallen that they would be leaving him to his own devices for a little time.

'I think that sounds like an excellent plan, Gerant. Perhaps I will make a batch of loaves that could be used as food on the road. We will take some to Rivernook and you can take your share as well.'

Gerant walked into the guild complex for his weekly tuition, then round to the instruction room and sat down at his usual desk. He smiled and said hello to Rachel. Rachel had been the girl from the first week who had seemed shy and then put one of the older lads in their place. They had become friends in the class and looked forward to seeing each other each week. Rachel had moved to a desk close to Gerant and they often spent break times chatting or working together on tasks that Master Klyburn set.

They both turned as they heard loud voices from the group of apprentice lads approaching the door to the rear of the room, along with the sounds of back slapping and welcoming. Both of them watched as three or four youths all swaggered in, along with the just-returned figure of Stork. Gerant looked with interest at his face and saw that he had the same roughly cropped hair and a new batch of zits. The bridge of his nose started down straight from between his eyebrows and then wandered a little left before reaching its end. The break had healed enough for him to return but would always announce that some sort of accident had occurred in the past. Stork had the remnants of a smile on his face following the shouts of welcome and back-slapping from the others. As he looked around the room, he saw Gerant watching him intently. The smile very quickly disappeared, and Stork looked for the nearest desk and sat down quickly; he seemed to be examining the desktop carefully. Rachel had been watching this and grinned at Gerant. They were both thinking that the remaining classes at the guild would still be boring, but at least there was no need for Gerant to be always watching his back.

Master Klyburn continued to drone on about the correct details for a formalised contract. Sveg had already told Gerant that most jobs were by word of mouth and honoured on completion, but occasionally there were situations where it was a very large piece of work, it was for The Realm or one of the official departments. Or where there were some concerns about aspects of the work, perhaps to ensure a decent job or so that payment could be delivered.

'Four. The terms of the payment should be agreed upon. Common conditions are full payment before work commences, half at the commencement and half at completion. Or one tenth as a deposit and the remainder at completion or at specified stages towards completion. This should be agreed with the client and before the notary drafts up the agreement.'

Master Klyburn continued without looking up, so did not see that his audience was only barely paying attention, or looking at other areas of the room, drawing on scraps of paper or even with their heads on their folded arms on the desktops. Gerant continued looking at the tutor on the podium in front of him, vaguely comprehending what was being said, but actually pondering on Marion's news from earlier. He recalled there was a large map of The Realm fixed to one of the walls in the reception chamber of the guild, which might help in working out his own plans. He decided at the short lunch break to eat his bread roll with cheese quickly and then look at the chart. That way he could work out some details about his idea that was slowly solidifying in his mind.

Gazing up at the depiction of The Realm on the wall of the chamber, Gerant got a sense of how big it was. He could only remember ever being in Ashford and could see where the town was compared with the other places that Sveg and Marion had mentioned on occasion. He mouthed the names as he spelt the letters out. Cobham was pretty close and then a bit farther again was The Capital, on the coast. He could see Rivernook to the north, and why it would take them a number of days to get to there. And then on the road west from Ashford was Osmount, around which his idea had taken shape. He looked at the chart and tried to etch in his mind some of the key details. The main feature was where the road crossed the River Greenthorn, which looked to be about halfway between the two towns. There were various other things drawn that showed trees and hills that the road went near, but Gerant couldn't decide if it would be like that in real life or just drawn on the map for decoration. He at least now had a bit of an idea of what he might find. He knew Cobham was a good three or four hours' walk from Ashford. If the chart had been drawn well, then Osmount was a solid two or three days away, so he would have to camp out there and back. There was no way he had the coin to hire a horse to ride there, even if he knew how to ride! Gerant suddenly realised he had been standing there thinking for several minutes. He rushed back to the tutor's room, hoping that Master Klyburn had taken a little longer over his lunch.

A few mornings later, Gerant stood outside the workshop with Sveg, Marion and Bree. He had walked with Sveg to pick up a horse and cart that was to be used by the family for the trip north to Rivernook. It appeared there was some long-standing agreement with Coran Smalltop, whose business was carting produce to and from The Capital. As Sveg mentioned briefly on the way to the carter's yard, he repaired any of the ironwork on the carts, including hoops on the wheels, in return for having the use of a horse and cart when required. Gerant did not know anything about horses and was a little nervous, but this was a horse that Sveg had used on other occasions, and he was content that it was quiet and well trained.

'Maybe on another occasion when I need to borrow the cart, I'll teach you how to drive. There are just a few things to remember, but mostly it's about understanding the horse and knowing where you want the cart to go. But we should get back and load up, as I want to get at least as far as Cobham before we stop for the night. Even better, there is a small hamlet a few miles farther north that would suit us.'

Gerant nodded but kept his hands firmly wrapped around the edges of the seat, as the cart seemed to be prone to random swayings and sudden small shifts in movement.

Upon their return to the smithy, Gerant helped put into the cart the various sacks, boxes and trunks that the family were taking north, all covered over by a large tarpaulin. Part of his training at the guild had been to learn several types of knots and how to lash down coverings, so Gerant was confident of the way he worked with Sveg to make the load secure. Sveg walked round the cart, testing all the lashings and knots and gave Gerant a nod of approval.

Gerant had put together his bedroll and pack ready just after dawn and had already checked and re-checked it several times. So, he was also ready to head off. There was almost a ceremonial threading of the large chain through the sliding partitions of the smithy and the healthy click as the large and forbidding padlock was closed on the ends of the chain. Then the somewhat awkward pause while the small group realised now was the actual time of the parting, albeit for only a few weeks.

'Well, my young fellow, I trust you have an adequate time and keep out of mischief. I will look forward to hearing of your adventures when we return. You know where the spare key to the padlock is, if you get back early and we are still to return.'

Sveg's very firm hand gripped his in farewell, along with almost a shy smile.

'Oh, you, come here.' To Gerant's utter surprise, he was suddenly enfolded in a huge hug from Marion, quickly joined by Bree. Gerant didn't know what to do, so just hugged back. After a few seconds, Marion giggled a little, as she tried to surreptitiously wipe a few stray tears off her cheeks. Sveg was just standing with his hands on his hips, along with a huge grin on his face.

'Well, up you go, young miss,' he grunted as he lifted Bree onto the seat of the cart. He gently assisted Marion up next to her, then climbed up onto the right of the bench himself. He nodded to Gerant, who had quickly got out of the way of the cart and clucked gently to the horse while loosening the reins. The cart moved off down the street and turned to the right at the end, towards the main road heading to Cobham. The last sight Gerant had was a furiously waving Bree sitting in between the figures of her mother and father.

Gerant picked up his pack with the bedroll strapped to the top and shucked his arms through the straps, adjusting them high as Sveg had shown him, to minimise the true weight of the pack, particularly towards the end of a day of tramping. He grabbed the stout wooden staff leaning next to the entrance to the workshop. He had selected this yesterday from a wooded grove at the northern edge of town on the riverbank: another tip from Sveg. He also headed off to the end of the street, but turned left, heading in the direction towards the River Greenthorn and the continuation of the road from Cobham, towards the interior of The Realm.

Some hours later, Gerant was starting to feel the muscles in his thighs and calves, telling him he needed to rest. Work in the forge was often quite strenuous, but he could not recall when he had walked this far. Normally it was down to the guild and back once a week, or various short errands within the town that Sveg asked him to do. He began to look for a likely camping place, remembering again the smith's advice about what to look for.

As twilight deepened into full night, Gerant ate a little more of the rabbit that he had roasted on a spit over the small camp-fire. He had come around a corner of the road not really paying attention – he could not recall what he had been thinking about – when he saw a sudden movement to the side in his peripheral vision. Stopping without sound, he saw to his left several rabbits had frozen in fear maybe ten feet off the path. He got the sense that as soon as he moved farther, they would duck straight into the bushes or down a hole. He slowly reached to the back of his waist and in one fluid movement threw the dagger at the closest form. The other rabbits quickly scuttled away, but there was one that did not move apart from a few quick shudders, as the dagger handle had appeared sticking out of its furry body just as it turned. A quick twist of its neck and Gerant was already thinking that he would have some fresh meat to have with the bread Marion had made for him to take on his travels. It looked like all that practice throwing with the daggers had paid off – not only did he feel more confident in being able to protect himself, it would be a good way to get fresh meat should the opportunity arise.

Gerant packed away the half of the rabbit he was going to save for tomorrow's dinner, and undid his bedroll, laying it out a few feet away from the fire. He was well satisfied with his first day of walking towards Osmount and should reach the crossing over the River Greenthorn around the middle of the next day. Then it was about another day to the town. He looked around the little clearing he was camped in, listening to the wind gently rustling in the branches and the birds settling down to their night of rest. He recalled Sveg's thoughts on choosing a good campsite.

'Most people you meet on the road are fine and no problem to other travellers. But there are a few that you should avoid, and you certainly don't want to have them come across you when you have camped. I have learnt that from bitter experience.

'So, when you are ready to stop for the day, move off the road a little distance. Somewhere close to a stream or running water, perhaps, down the bank from the road. There is also nothing wrong with going up the hill from the road a little, and over the brow. Just not too far from the road, but out of sight. Keep your fire small as you don't need to tell everyone where you are. A good woodsman will smell the smoke and work it out from there, but they are not the people you are concerned about. Better to be prudent and stay away from those who are wanting to rob you, or worse.'

Gerant had remembered that advice and taken a faint animal trail up the ridge. After a hundred yards or so, he had reached the brow and just over the top was a secluded opening in the trees covered in leaf litter. It had been a few moments to find some loose rocks to make a quick ring for a fireplace, collect some twigs and small logs, then start a small, well-contained blaze within the ring, using his flint and steel. Once it was going steadily, he quickly went back to the road and was heartened that he couldn't see any firelight. Hopefully, no one would know he was there. Then it had been back to skin and prepare the rabbit and make a little spit to roast it.

Lying on his bedroll next to the still faintly warm coals of his little fire somewhat later, he thought more of his trip and what he would find. He had not been willing to tell Sveg that he was still very excited about the ancient parchment pages hidden in the cover of the smithing book and was going to see if he could find some talium. It was too risky to bring the book with him as it might get rained on, and he was not even sure he would be in places where he would be able to take it out to read. So he had memorised the passage on the parchment about finding talium in the mine somewhere near Osmount. He was not even sure what he would do when he got to the town. He had four silver pieces and a few coppers from the coin he had scraped together from his allowance over the past months. Even that might disappear having to find a room at Osmount and buying some supplies. Maybe he should stay just out of town and camp out to save coin. So far, he had had a reasonable day with no disasters. The rabbit had been an unexpected bonus.

Chapter 10
The Confrontation

After waking with the birds and the slow lightening of the forest clearing, Gerant left the rocks around the fireplace as they were. It was possible he would camp here again on the way back, as it was a secluded spot where he had been undisturbed and was clearly only travelled through by the creatures of the forest. After a quick snack of bread and a drink at a running streamlet that crossed the road near his resting place, Gerant shouldered his pack and headed off west again on the road towards Osmount. He had developed a steady pace that ate up the miles regularly, yet it was not so rushed that he didn't have time to absorb the country he was walking through and watch for anything unexpected around the next curve in the road. He was thankful that he had got used to walking with the staff, which gave a pleasing regularity to his stride. The road was hardly a highway, but it was relatively well-maintained with only the occasional pothole filled with the remains of the last downpour. He could also see clear wheel tracks in the surface of the road but had yet to meet or pass any carts. So far, all he had seen were two men on horseback coming from the Osmount direction, who had given a brief nod to the young man leaning on a sturdy staff having just stepped off the road to allow the horsemen through. They were clearly in no mood to spend the time of day with a youth of nondescript appearance a long way from the nearest town or village, which also suited Gerant.

As the sun approached its highest point, Gerant stood looking down the road ahead, where it moved in gentle curves to the river, and what appeared from this distance, between some trees, to be a small stone bridge. After studying the large map in the guild chamber several times, Gerant knew this was the river that passed through Ashford, but farther up in the hills towards the Greenthorn Mountains, where it must arise. From here, he knew that the road crossed to the southern side of the River Greenthorn and then took a turn more directly towards Osmount, which was still a little over a day's walk.

After seeing nothing of note to concern him, Gerant began walking down the right-hand edge of the road towards the stone bridge. After briefly clambering down to the river itself to fill his water bottle, he walked on up the gently rising slope and entered a lightly wooded grove on either side of the road, with the branches of the trees either side almost forming a living, leafy archway above the road surface. It was while still thinking about his next place to camp that Gerant heard a loud click coming from a fork in the tree to the right of the path. He noticed a lanky, but scruffy man balanced in the fork of the two large tree limbs about eight feet above the ground, holding a crossbow loosely pointed at him. The man had dark ginger hair and a beard, wearing a motley array of bits of leather clothing. And he was grinning wildly. Gerant looked around quickly and then noticed a taller man with a closely trimmed black beard and hair leaning against a large trunk on the left of the road, who had appeared from behind it, about fifteen or twenty feet away. He had a drawn sword around three feet long that he was idly examining and was dressed in a blackish doublet and boots that reached his thighs, along with a whitish frilly shirt that perhaps was lacking a good wash. What might be thought to be foppish on another man was clearly meant to portray standing and power in this individual. Gerant heard behind him some scuffling and two more figures emerged from behind trees. A short balding individual with shifty eyes and buck teeth was armed with a cutlass with clear nicks in the blade edge. Also emerging was a very large man who would have been at least six foot four inches tall and very broad, holding a club that he thumped slowly and steadily into his left open palm. He was also grinning, and gently chuckling with no particular purpose. His smile showed that he didn't appear to have any teeth left and his look was somewhat vacant.

'Well, my young fellow,' drawled the clear leader, as he continued to examine his sword. 'Fancy meeting you here in the middle of nowhere. Where are you headed?'

Gerant thought quickly about whether to answer or not. 'To Osmount.'

'Well, you have not too far to go. It's an easy walk from here. You should get there tomorrow. That's why you should leave your pack and your coin purse with us.' Gerant eased off his pack and placed it carefully on the ground next to him.

'Very good, my lad. We don't want anyone to get hurt, do we?'

The scruffy man in the tree fork grinned even wider and there was a snicker of laughter from the shortish man with the cutlass. Gerant had not moved, apart from placing his pack down. He felt like the time he had been confronted by the Stork at the guild. He knew exactly what he was going to do, but he had to wait for them to move first.

'Come on, my good fellow. Step away from your sack.' The leader looked even more bored and was looking closely at his blade, as though it had a small flat spot that honing had missed.

Gerant did not move for a number of seconds, waiting for their next move.

'Enough. Clive, you know what to do.'

Clearly the boss of this gang was tiring of the situation. Clive, the man in the tree, clicked his tongue a few times in pretended disappointment and started to raise the crossbow to point directly at Gerant. A second later, the crossbow thumped into the ground at the foot of the tree and the bolt discharged harmlessly into the bushes. Another second later, the body of Clive collapsed in a tangled heap on top of the crossbow. A small throwing knife had mysteriously appeared just above Clive's right eye, buried to the hilt. Already, a trickle of blood coursed down over his unmoving face. There was a swift intake of breath from the two men behind Gerant. The leader had a look of disbelief on his face as he stood up rapidly, the shocked look rapidly being replaced by pure anger and malice.

'Well, my young friend. A pretty trick, but what now? The dagger is in Clive, and you are over there, and I am just about to fillet you like I would a deer. No one does that to the Black Fox or any of my gang and lives to tell the tale.'

The Black Fox continued to stalk closer and closer to Gerant, starting to weave his sword in a furious little pattern that made the blade make little hissing sounds as he got closer and closer. As the man approached, Gerant slowly bent down, and his right hand slid to the back of his calf. He straightened again. The Black Fox was now about ten feet away and was about to say something, but all he could manage was a loud gurgle. He dropped the sword and with wide eyes reached for the handle of the second dagger which was now buried in his throat. A look of wonderment and then distance crossed his eyes, as he slowly toppled forward to the ground, the pulse of blood rapidly spurting and turning the top of his ruffled shirt a very bright reddish tinge.

'Shit, shit.'

Gerant glanced behind him and could hear that the other two accomplices had quickly come to the decision – they wanted no further part of this failed attempt. The sounds of rapid snapping of branches and heavy footfalls receded into the forest lining the road, to be eventually replaced by silence. Almost in a daze, he held his right hand out in front of him and saw how much it was shaking. His thoughts became almost matter of fact, just to distract himself somehow from the horror and abruptness of what had just happened. He quickly moved to the two bodies. This was a very clear lesson why you were wise to carry two daggers in convenient but hidden places. One was sufficient for most situations, but thank the gods he had the second ready. And also thank the gods that the Black Fox had assumed he only had one.

He started searching the two bodies, in much the same way he had learnt on the streets before he had met Sveg. It had been Crawface and Snappy – larger, older boys bordering on young men – who tended to lead a confrontation if it got to that. Usually it was just scuffles or fistfights, but there had been several occasions where blood had been drawn or even deaths. He recalled one occasion where there had been an older gent who had confronted the gang, one thing led to another and Snappy had lost it and stabbed him, then couldn't stop. There had been a collective gasp when they all realised what had happened, then they had just quickly searched the crumpled body, grabbed some coin and cleared out. He didn't recall that with any pleasure and that was probably the main reason why he had slowly dropped out of gang activities.

Gerant put those thoughts to one side as he searched, and came across a few scraps of food, a dagger each and then the coin purses. Clive had two silver pieces and a few coppers only, but the Black Fox's purse had a ring with some sort of gemstone set in it, five gold and seven silver pieces in it. Gerant transferred the coin to his own purse and left the ring. He quickly scanned the ground for anything he had missed and decided that the others may soon be back, possibly with other gang members seeking revenge. As quickly as he could he dragged the bodies off the beaten path, then rapidly cut some branches off nearby bushes to drape over the two men. It wasn't pretty and someone might follow the drag marks and drops of blood and find them, but at least it was less obvious. A traveller walking or riding focused on their own thoughts might just miss the signs and keep going. After a quick check that no one was coming, he scuffed up some of the marks on the trail with his boot. Picking up his pack, he adjusted it quickly, then grabbed his walking staff, which had fallen just off the road surface. He started to dog-trot down the road away from the river. He thought it would be sensible to put a few miles distance in place straight away, just to be sure he would have no further trouble.

As the afternoon drew to a close, Gerant found himself at least six miles farther down the road. After trotting for a mile or so, he had stopped briefly. About to get up, he realised he was still shaking quite a bit, particularly as he thought over what had happened and how instinct had just taken over. Now he had time to realise how lucky he had been, as it could have gone horribly wrong. He grabbed a quick gulp of water and a mouthful of rabbit. Even that little bit of sustenance helped after a few minutes, and his hands became steady again. He adjusted his pack and staff and headed off.

It had taken him some time to learn that the white-painted large boulders at regular intervals to the right of the roadway were actually mile markers. By reading the symbol on each and mouthing his numbers, Gerant was able to confirm the marker he had come across later had a large O carved above a figure eight. That probably meant he had about eight miles to walk until he hit the town of Osmount.

It was time to look for a camp site. He had not seen a soul on the road, even though he had approached each curve or crest in the road with a little hesitation of what he might see coming. He had been ready to quickly step off into the bushes to avoid a meeting or confrontation. And he had regularly looked behind him to check for any pursuit. Where he was, the road had curved down to a shallow dip in which a chuckling stream met the roadway. The crossing through the water had been uneventful, and it had only reached up to his calves. Upon reaching the other bank, he had walked away from the road through willows lining the bank until he reached a curve in the stream out of sight from the ford. There was a large willow leaning at an angle over the water, behind which was a little alcove nestled in the exposed tree roots and finger-like lower trunk. It was there that he built a little camp-fire. The remains of the rabbit tasted even better than the night before, perhaps because Gerant felt he had rightly earned the meal. He was hungrier than what he was willing to admit.

Just then, he froze and realised he could hear voices drifting up from the road. He rapidly snuck along the bank, being as silent as he could, carefully parting a bush so he could observe the road unseen. He immediately recognised the two figures from earlier, the short, balding fellow and the giant, chuckling man. They were standing just at the crossing, having a discussion.

'Look, matey, we should have caught up to him by know. I was really looking forward to pulling him apart piece by piece.'

The shorter man then spoke. 'That may be so, Tiny. Maybe he got hold of a horse or turned off somewhere. Let's go on for a bit to make sure. We probably should then head back to base and work out what we are going to do. We might have to talk to some other people about joining them. The Fox could be an arsehole sometimes but he wasn't too bad, all the same. We'll go on for another mile and then call it quits. You OK with that?'

'Whatever you think, Albert. I'm here for the muscle, not to do the thinking.'

Gerant hadn't really considered that the other gang members would have come after him, so he was very glad he had turned off the road to find a quiet, secluded camping spot. He quickly finished the meal and washed his dishes in the brook chuckling just to his left, then rolled out his bedroll next to the remains of the fire. He found it hard to get to sleep. His mind kept going back to the fight earlier in the day. It had affected him deeply and it was going to play on his mind at odd times. He decided it was a good thing that he didn't take it for granted; a person's life was special and valuable, and even thugs deserved the benefit of the doubt, if possible. He continued to lie with his hands behind his head, thinking over the day's adventure and what it meant. Without realising it, the sky had well and truly darkened with the odd star starting to emerge. He listened to the emerging sounds of the evening and then slipped into slumber.

He struggled against the tight bindings and watched fearfully his captors.

'Well, my young lad . . . Gerant, isn't it? Things aren't going to go all that well for you. See, Tiny here enjoys dishing out pain and he'll just start with your finger joints and break each one, and we'll see how you feel after that. He's rather good at making things hurt but not so bad that you don't appreciate his special attentions.'

The giant figure of Tiny giggled for several seconds and started to move forward.

'Your turn will be soon, Tiny,' warned the Black Fox, leaning up comfortably against the trunk of the tree. 'But first there are a few things I need to find out from Gerant. Like why he was headed to Osmount and what he was going to do. Most people don't come this way unless there is something important to be had. He needs to tell me about that.'

He then spoke directly to his captive. 'I wouldn't hold back, you know. Tiny will get it out of you, regardless, so you may as well save yourself some pain. I've only got your own best interests, at heart, after all.' The Black Fox paused for a few moments and then his face took on a more grim countenance.

Gerant suddenly woke, heart pounding, thrashing about before he realised he could actually move. It took a moment to comprehend he was at his little camping spot just off the road, that nobody was accosting him, and that things were quiet, apart from the normal nighttime sounds. He lay awake on this bedroll, slowly assuring himself this had been a bad dream, not surprising given the horrific and unexpected events earlier. *This has affected me more than I thought,* he mused. *Gods, I hope it's not going to be like this every night.* After a few minutes of reassuring himself, he turned over and tried to get back to sleep.

Chapter 11
Osmount

Being in the countryside for two days and away from towns and villages, Gerant was surprised that he could actually smell and hear that he was getting near to Osmount. The road had been climbing steadily up a valley and then reached a steeper ridge where it snaked back and forth a little as it climbed the slope. Before Gerant crested the ridge, the faint waft of smoke came down the gentle breeze and he could hear an occasional strike of something on metal, faint thuds or dogs barking. He realised these were just the normal random sounds of people living together in a town or village. The sky had a few high clouds and just above the trees lining the top of the ridge was a layer of grey, smoke from the many fires in the town that had dispersed. The road carved through the trees along the ridgetop and Gerant could now see a town, smaller than Ashford, nestled in the hills about half a mile farther on. It almost seemed be cradled in a large bowl-like valley, cupped within the steeper hills and behind it ridges marching up to the snow-capped mountains.

Gerant wandered down the road that headed to the town gates. As soon as he had crested the ridge and the road meandered gently towards the township, the amount of foot and horse traffic had suddenly gone from nothing to a dozen or so. He got the impression that the inhabitants had business within the large valley that the town was laid out in, but seldom needed to travel farther. No one paid any particular attention to the youth with a pack and bedroll walking quietly towards the gates and carefully stepping out of the way of people bustling towards him on their way to some further task or meeting, or those on horseback picking their way along the thoroughfare in no particular hurry. After wandering through the stone archway with a couple town guards idly watching some children chasing each other, Gerant noticed a two-storey building across the other side of the small square from the guardhouse. He looked up at the sign with a green painted figure, which hung above a doorway. He mouthed out the letters and confirmed the name of the tavern was what the picture showed. Looking around the square, he saw many other buildings, with some appearing to be houses, some like shops, but he found nothing similar. Gerant sighed and walked up to the tavern entrance and through the double doors into a large dim room. As his eyes adjusted to the lower light, he could see a long bar top along one side of the room and a number of round tables and chairs set up in the open area. There was an older woman with grey hair in a bun and wearing a white apron, standing behind the bar with her back turned, putting glasses and tankards away on shelves on the wall. He stood just inside the doorway taking all the details in.

'Young sir, you are a little eager if you are wanting a drink. We will not start serving until this afternoon.' The woman had turned and noticed the figure just inside the door.

'Umm, I was actually wanting to get lodging for tonight. Do you have rooms?'

'Well, that's different.' The woman smiled in greeting. 'I am Mother Gimlet, the proprietor of The Green Dragon. I could let you have a room for five silver for the night. Included is dinner and breakfast. Nothing fancy, but honest food. That suit you?'

Gerant thought quickly and then nodded. Five silver sounded a lot of money, but the first impression of Mother Gimlet was that she appeared honest and not trying to take any obvious advantage.

'Harry! Harry!' The owner turned her head and shouted towards an arch leading out of the taproom next to the end of the bar. In a normal voice she asked, 'Just arrived?'

Gerant nodded. 'From Ashford.'

'You walked?'

Another nod. Gerant could see her sizing him up and noting the pack with the bedroll.

'It's not a bad road or trip. Although we have been hearing whispers that the Black Fox has been working the area.'

He decided not to say anything.

'Harry! Harry!'

'Coming, coming', wafted through the archway. A few seconds later a portly youth with blond hair and the beginnings of a beard arrived. He was wearing an apron, which had a few splotches of dirt on it, and was panting slightly.

'Was just putting this week's barrels in the cellar, Mother.' He looked at the proprietor with a questioning look.

'This is . . .'

'Gerant.'

'. . . Gerant. Put him in Number Five for tonight.' She smiled at the young guest. 'Harry will take you up to your room, show you where the privy is, bathroom, meals room and so on. Anything you need, see Harry or myself.'

Mother Gimlet was a little curious about a lad from another town travelling by himself. 'You just need the one night? What brings you to Osmount?'

'I have to see a few people and I want to look around a bit. Maybe look for some work. I might need another night or two later on, but I won't know until I talk to these people.'

The proprietor smiled and nodded. *How many times have I heard this story?* She continued to muse. *If he's looking for work, how come he has enough coin to stay here? Well, as long as he pays and doesn't cause any trouble, I don't care. But he needs to work on getting his story together a little better.*

Harry waited just at the inside archway while Gerant picked up his pack and walked over. About to follow Harry out of the taproom, the voice of Mother Gimlet spoke out.

'A moment, Gerant.'

Gerant turned and the proprietor still had a smile on her face, but she had her hand out. 'We normally accept payment in advance.

Then we don't get into any arguments about whether customers have paid or not.'

Gerant turned bright red. He reached into his coin purse and took out five silver pieces, placing them on Mother Gimlet's palm. 'Sorry, Mother.'

Mother Gimlet chuckled and turned back to putting the glasses away ready for opening the bar later. *That boy was definitely green! Well, it would be good for him to learn how things worked.* She finished with the glasses and started wiping the counter down.

Gerant followed Harry through the various rooms that a guest might need. The other lad was clearly following a rehearsed script and showed Gerant the large privy just outside the taproom on an inner courtyard, the kitchen and meals room opening off the kitchen, then up a narrow staircase to the second floor where the guest rooms were. They walked along a narrow corridor with doors opening on either side. Harry stopped outside a door that had a *5* painted above the lintel and pulled the door ajar. He waited while Gerant sidled past him into the room. Gerant put down his pack next to the basic bed with a china jug on a stand next to it. There was also a lone wooden chair in front of a small window that looked out over the courtyard, but no other furniture. Still, it was clean.

'No key?' asked Gerant.

'Not for five silver. You have to pay more for one of the rooms with a lock.'

'Oh.'

'That it?' Harry was clearly wanting to go back to his barrels in the cellar.

'Yup.'

Gerant watched Harry head off down the corridor almost before he had responded. He shut the door and sat on the bed, swinging his feet. *Well, it's not like I have much that would be worth taking.* He had his coin purse on him, plus his two throwing daggers in their sheaths. The only thing in his pack was a water bottle, a leather vest, what was left of the bread Marion had packed and his bedroll on top. After putting the pack and bedroll as far under the bed as he could, he walked out, shut the door and wandered back down to the taproom.

Mother Gimlet was wiping chairs and tables in the main part of the tavern. She heard the soft footfalls and turned.

'Was the room suitable . . . Gerant?'

Mother Gimlet had that learnt gift of being able to remember patron names, as her business required.

'It's fine.' Gerant paused. 'I wanted to ask you about a couple of things, as I don't know the town.'

'Ask away, young man.'

'If I wanted to have a look at the talium mine, what do I need to do? Where is it?'

A piece of the puzzle about this lad and why he was in Osmount clicked into place. 'Well, there's a story. You can't just head up to the mine and hope no one notices. There are very clear regulations that have to be gone through and the town guards regularly visit the mine to check for permits. No, Gerant, you need to go and see Master Fergal Hardcross and obtain a permit to go to the mine. His house is the biggest one across the square. I hope you have plenty of coin.'

'Oh, I just want to have a chat in the first instance.'

'Of course, of course.' The proprietor smiled. *I bet this lad will leave Osmount within the day, not having any coin left.*

'I also need to get a few general supplies, like candles, a lantern and a pick. Is there a shop where I can get them?'

'Hmm. I would go to Anton's store, which is only a few minutes away. Turn right out of The Green Dragon, then left and about halfway along is Anton's. It is the one with the bags of flour and the shovel on the sign. He will give you an honest price.'

Mother Gimlet looked over at Gerant and kept the smile up, even though her thoughts took a sadder turn. *Here's another young fool hoping to make his fortune. Well, he's in for a harsh lesson and it might do him good. Surely his parents would have warned him about these sort of hare-brained schemes to get rich? Well, it's not my job to be his mother! All the same, he seems to be a nice boy.*

'Thank you, Mother.'

The proprietor nodded and moved back to wiping some chairs. Without turning, she heard the double doors to the street waft open and then gently clatter shut as the lad left.

As Gerant reached the street outside The Green Dragon, he realised for the second time what he had said, which was so out of character for him. *I called her Mother*, he thought, uneasily. *But, somehow it just feels right.* He shrugged his shoulders in wonderment and walked with purpose towards an imposing building lining the square.

The doorkeeper looked up as a slender youth quickly walked through the main door and approached his desk. He quickly assessed the new arrival as someone wanting to sell something to Master Hardcross and while his face was composed in a welcoming smile, he was ready to express sincerely felt regrets that the master was, unfortunately, not available.

Gerant saw a man that reminded him of the tutor at the guild, Master Klyburn. Weeks of reading Klyburn's face had given Gerant the ability to understand that the smile of greeting was false, and the true feeling was more of impatience and boredom.

'I have been told that I need obtain a permit from Master Fergal Hardcross to go to the talium mine. Is he available?'

Gerant was secretly pleased with the manner in which he had framed his request. The hard work that Sveg had put in might help him out in this situation.

'Talium, you say. One moment.'

The doorkeeper had been very clearly instructed that enquirers about the talium mine were not to be kept waiting and were certainly not to be shown the door. His boss had been very insistent about that. After a few minutes, he came back out of an interior door and beckoned to Gerant.

'Master Hardcross will see you now. Follow me.'

Gerant tailed him into a large room with a healthy fire within a stone fireplace. There were a number of books on shelves, along with vases and other ornaments that were clearly very valuable. A middle-sized man with greying hair and velvet robes rose as Gerant walked in, then sat down again behind his desk as he realised that a somewhat callow youth had appeared.

'Well, young man, you mentioned talium?'

'I have read an old parchment that mentions that the mine near Osmount is the only place to find talium. But there are regulations about going to the mine.'

'Of course. Talium is a rare metal and even moreso these days. To approach the mine and even to go in will cost you a silver to have the necessary authority. I can provide that to you.'

Master Hardcross had changed from being very quick to dismiss this young fellow to realising here was another stupid adventurer who could be quickly fleeced of all his coin. 'Of course, the path to the mine is jealously guarded and not easy to find. You will need an official map to show you how to get there. That would be another silver.'

He paused briefly. 'And then you would require a strong lantern as there is no light in the mine and it is very dark. Of course, that will cost you a gold coin. Also a prospecting pick carefully designed by successful talium miners to check that you have talium ore of sufficient quality. That would be five gold. And rations that have been found to be best suited for keeping up one's strength far underground and away from a store. Another silver per day, of course. So that would be a minimum of six gold and three silver. And then there would be the hire of a pack pony, sacks and water bags, bedding, firewood, all manner of necessary supplies.'

'Just the permit and the map, if you please.'

Hardcross was somewhat perplexed that his usual patter had not resulted in the extra coin being outlayed immediately, as happened when most of the gullible enquirers were confronted by these choices.

'Well, I suppose that can be arranged.' He pulled two pieces of paper from a drawer in the desk, scrawling one with a quick signature at the bottom of some previously written text. 'I am also required by officials to record who the permit has been issued to. Your name?'

Gerant thought quickly. In the previous similar situation with Mother Gimlet, it had felt perfectly natural to tell her his real name and where he was from. The man in front of him had given him quite a different feeling, using everything to his advantage and so far had been arrogant and disdainful.

'William.'

'And you are from?'

'The Capital.'

'William of The Capital. Well, we will be sure to track you down even in so big a city if we need to. Not that I foresee any need at this point.'

These details were quickly written in an imposing ledger kept at the side of the desk. After handing the two pieces of paper to the lad and quickly pocketing the two silver coins, he revealed his final condition.

'You know that by His Lordship's direction and as laid out in the relevant Realm bylaw, with any talium acquired from the mine, there is a ten per cent tax. Either payment in gold or in talium ore. That is to be passed over to me as the duly authorised representative of his lordship, on your return.'

As he was announcing this, Hardcross hardly watched the boy. No one had got any useful amount of talium from the mine for ten years or more. It was one of the stupid regulations from The Capital that Hardcross had to abide by to keep his position. It was best to keep his lordship happy and his accountants not suspecting that this had never been followed.

'If that is everything, I am a very busy man. There is a lot happening in Osmount, and I am expected to administer it all and collect duties for his lordship. Good day to you.'

He did not look up and was already busy with some loose papers sprawled in front on him. As if he had been carefully listening on the other side, the door to the room opened and the doorkeeper beckoned impatiently to Gerant. After a rapid escort through the outer lobby-like room, Gerant was almost pushed back out as the large wooden door to the street closed firmly after him. He found a quiet corner in the square and took out the two pieces of paper. The one covered in neatly written black ink took a few minutes for Gerant to decipher. He spelt out enough words to get the gist that this was the permit allowing him to go to the talium mine and enter. It was mostly about the penalties for not having the permit ready to be inspected by town guards at any time and that the permit could not be given to someone else or sold. Things like that. The other piece featured a crudely drawn map, showing that the path or road to the mine left from the western side of town and appeared to be only a mile or two away. There were a few places where other paths intersected along the way to the mine and there was a stream crossing with a bridge marked. Gerant did wonder why such a simple map had cost him a whole silver. The whole experience with Whitecross had not been pleasant and he was glad it was over. Well, there was still plenty of time left in the day, and he had one other place in the town to go to.

As he walked past The Green Dragon, heading farther down the street, there were several men waiting impatiently just outside. He espied Harry as he bustled out of the double doors, swinging them open and around so he could hook them ajar. The men laughed and pushed each other good-naturedly as they walked into the tavern. Clearly, The Green Dragon had just opened for its main business for the day. After a quick scan of the square, Harry walked back inside, having seen nothing to note, apart from the usual hustle and bustle in the town.

After turning left when he reached an intersection, Gerant looked out for a sign with bags and a shovel. He saw this about fifty yards farther on the left side of the street. Approaching, he could see a long wooden counter with shutters above it that could be partitioned open if the weather allowed it or kept closed during rain or storms, or at night. At the moment they were all open in keeping with a mild winter's day that held no hint of rain. The second storey, which seemed to be a dwelling, meant that the interior of the store could not be seen very well from where Gerant had stopped, about ten yards away on the other side of the street. It appeared to be full of various bits of equipment and items that were stocked, and the owner, presumably the man on the inside of the counter, disappeared briefly several times and returned with various items. After completing his purchases, a customer gave some coin to the man and picked up his items, passing close to the boy across the street. He tried to see what the man had bought, but they had been put in a large sack and were not visible.

Gerant looked up and down the street, checked that there was no one who had come up to the counter, and walked over. As he approached, he could now see that the interior of the shop was a little like the bookshop in Ashford, in that it was cluttered with lots of items with small clear spaces to walk up and down. The shop owner must have a very good memory of what he had, as there didn't appear to be any rhyme or reason for where things were placed.

Gerant had not heard the owner, Anton, approach him on the other side of the counter.

'Something?'

Anton was an older man not much taller than Gerant with a tuft of black hair and a moustache.

'I have come from Mother Gimlet. She suggested you would have what I need.'

Anton smiled and nodded. 'Mother Gimlet and I have a long-standing relationship. She sends me those who need supplies and I send her those who have a thirst or need wholesome food or a bed for the night. I have most things, but I don't have everything. But I can usually get it within the week.'

'All I need are some candles and a lantern. And a small pick and five hessian sacks of medium size.'

'One moment.' Anton went quickly into the shop and disappeared around various piles of hoes, sacks of grain, barrels and other stacked items. He reappeared promptly and laid on the counter five large candles, a basic lantern of non-descript iron with a hinged shutter and a two-bladed pick with a short wooden handle. Next to it he put the hessian pieces sewn together with rough twine into sacks.

Gerant looked quickly at the lantern and then examined the pick. From his training he could see it was forged as one piece of iron. The iron looked like it was of reasonable quality, so it should be quite sturdy. The wooden handle was well-shaped, sanded down well and fitted into the metal part tightly. It was something he would be quite content to have made himself.

'I might need a few more things next time. But that will be all for now.'

Gerant watched Anton make a quick addition in his head as he glanced at each of the items.

'That will be two gold and five silver.'

Walking back to The Green Dragon with his purchases together in one of the hessian sacks, Gerant was grateful that he had asked Mother Gimlet where to buy the supplies. Despite a little shock over the final amount he had been asked to pay, he felt he had been charged a fair price for the goods and would be happy to go back to Anton should he need more gear and after he had at least seen the mine. He was also relieved that despite the coin he had laid out today, he still had more than half of the funds he had acquired left. Arriving at the double doors of the tavern, he walked inside and was amazed at the change in the taproom, which was around half-full with mostly men and a couple of women, laughing, talking, drinking and clearly enjoying themselves. He navigated through the archway to the other part of the tavern and climbed the stairs to his room.

After pushing the sack of gear under the bed with his other stuff, Gerant went out again to look around the town. He was keen to at least find the road leading to the mine which, according to the crude map, left from the western edge of town. After a couple of false starts, he found what must be the road he was seeking. It left the town through a smaller gateway on the side of the town facing the main mountain range, crossing a ditch. He walked along it for a few hundred yards. The road quickly changed from a width suitable for two carts to pass one another, to a pot-holed surface that narrowed after the first turn. He stopped once the path had become little more than a cleared grassy path just wide enough for a narrow cart, as shown by the faint wheel marks just scraping past the tree trunks which encroached on the grassy surface.

There was nothing else that took his fancy when he returned through the west gate and explored a little more of the town. He eventually found what looked to be the town smithy down a side street near to the main gate and square. This was an open space with only the forge under cover, although that was boarded up and he could not see in. Either this was only used in warmer weather, or the business was not doing well. Gerant thought it a little strange that a town as big as Osmount didn't have a smith busily working away in the later afternoon light. He would try to remember to ask Sveg about it when he got back. Apart from houses and cottages and a few other shops, the only other place Gerant saw was another tavern near the northern gate. Like The Green Dragon, this establishment also had a slowly swinging wooden board above the doorway. Based on the design, it must be named the Hammer and Sickle. Gerant could not work out why taverns had to have particular types of names. That said, he had not seen very many. But Green Dragon, Hammer and Sickle, Wheatsheaf – they all had a certain rhythm and sound to them. He poked his head in the door and quickly made his mind up to keep walking. What he saw was a smaller, darker room with a few patrons silently drinking from tankards. The smell was also quite different, being a strange mixture of smoke, stale sweat, tobacco and some things he had no idea what they were. He got the sense that this tavern catered for a different set of townfolk, who probably didn't mix much with the customers from The Green Dragon.

As darkness approached, Gerant came down from his room and quietly moved around to the meals room. He could hear that the main taproom was getting a little louder with conversation and the occasional shouts and laughter contributing to a steady pulse of sound. The meals room had a few large tables and chairs in the middle of the room and a small counter and hatch to the kitchen. There were some people sitting at the tables already, talking quietly to themselves, with one or two people sitting by themselves and eating.

A thin, wrinkled, somewhat elderly woman wearing a cloth cap and an apron stood at the kitchen hatch. She saw Gerant approach.

'Which room?'

'Five.'

The woman looked to her right, picked up a large piece of chalk and crossed a number off a board.

'Tonight is mutton stew. One bowl and a tankard of ale. If you want more food or drink, then that will be extra. When you have finished, bring you leavings back here. Stay in the meals room to eat.'

The woman, who Gerant presumed was the cook, walked over to a large tureen and ladled out a bowl of the stew and poured out some liquid into a tankard from a large ceramic jug. Gerant realised she was like that Harry fellow from earlier in the day, following a well-rehearsed script that told him what he needed to know, and no more. She brought the bowl and tankard over to the hatch, along with a carved wooden spoon for the stew. She watched while Gerant collected them with a brief thanks and moved off. Faced with the prospects of not knowing anyone at the tables, Gerant chose to hunker down against the wall facing the internal courtyard and watch the other guests. The first mouthful of the stew showed it was quite tasty, with real bits of mutton and various pieces of vegetables in a savoury broth. He continued eating, watching peoples' faces and expressions. He noticed that there were no children. It looked like there were two couples, quietly talking to each other. Both couples were dressed in good quality clothes without being particularly fine.

There were three men who had sat at the tables a little away from any others. Gerant guessed that they might be in business and traders of some sort, perhaps visiting Osmount as part of a regular trip. The final pair were quite different when he looked over them. Both of the men were dressed in clothing that was clearly not typical of these parts; they were wearing blue, flowing robes and leather boots. They also had turbans wound around their heads and trimmed beards. Perhaps the most noticeable feature was their brownish skin colour, which Gerant had never seen before. They talked quietly in a language that Gerant could hear was different but could not understand any words. Yet he had the sense that they also might be traders or skilled workmen, particularly since they were here in the tavern. One of the men must have felt eyes on him, as he stopped talking and started to turn to look at whoever was staring at him. Sitting on the floor with his legs out, Gerant hurriedly looked down at his bowl and ate a few spoonfuls, only looking up when he heard the unknown conversation between the two men start up again. Gerant wondered who they were and where they were from. *Perhaps from the south where the weather was hotter. This is something I can ask Sveg about.* He tried to make sure he could remember the types of clothing they were wearing and what they looked like.

He reached for the tankard and took a swallow without thinking. It was only then that he realised this was the first ale he had ever tried. At the cottage, they normally only had cool water or occasionally some cow's milk or freshly squeezed fruit juice if it was available at a good price from the market where Marion shopped. Gerant thought the taste was a little odd, not unpleasant but slightly sour. He would be willing to have it again, but it wasn't something he would clamour for next time. The stew was going down well. After about ten minutes, he had finished the contents of the bowl and the tankard. There had been a few small bones with the meat, as you would expect. He quickly got up holding the bowl and tankard. Suddenly, the room lurched a little and he grabbed for the nearby wall to steady himself. After a few seconds, he felt that the room was not going to move again and he carefully walked to the hatch, put the items down, nodded to the chef and carefully walked up to his room. He reflected that maybe he should take a little bit more time over his next tankard of ale and not rush through to finish it as quickly. After a few minutes lying on the bed, Gerant got up again, took the chair by the window and levered it against the knob on the inside of the door. He climbed back into bed. His arrangement wouldn't stop a determined intruder but at least the crash of the chair falling to the floor should wake him easily. With that realisation in his head and plans of the coming day and walking to the talium mine, Gerant drifted off to sleep.

Chapter 12
The Mine

It was a little chilly and overcast when he looked out at the early morning light streaming in from the small window in the guest room. Gerant decided he wanted to make an early start, so he went down to the meals room not long after sunup. There was only one other person eating a hurried meal. He saw that a small bowl of apples was at the kitchen's hatch, along with some small bread rolls and a few wedges of cheese. Gerant grabbed one of each sort and walked back up to his room. It took only a few moments to fill his water bottle at a pump in the square and head to the western gate he had found the previous afternoon. The pack and bedroll were on his back as previously, but he also carried the sack of gear he had bought from Anton's across one shoulder. He soon reached the point at which he had turned back the day before. The way to the mine continued to get narrower and narrower and soon gave up the pretence of being a road for carts. It began to follow a fast-running stream emerging out of a valley where the hills and mountains started to hunker closer on either side. The trees also changed from evergreens to some sort of pine, and the only sound was a quiet whisper of the breeze through the branches. After about half an hour, he crossed two tracks that appeared suddenly from the forest. Without looking at the map, he remembered these had been drawn in. After the second of the two, he knew he was getting close. The valley with the rushing stream got narrower and the mountain slopes drew closer in. Suddenly, the head of the valley stopped at a very steep face of rock, with a rickety little bridge where the path crossed the water. On the other side, flanked by leaning trees, was a dark gaping hole at the bottom of the rock face.

'This must be the mine,' muttered Gerant to himself. He noticed a leaning post to one side with two short pieces nailed across each other in an X-shape. He could almost feel the warning the post was indicating, even though he could not see any letters written on it. Looking around, he noticed a ring of stones and ash from a long-forgotten fire, along with a few beams of timber and scraps of canvas. Perhaps this was where the town guards set up and stayed whenever they came out to inspect the mine.

He had a quick drink of water and filled the bottle up again at the stream. The flow of water appeared to emerge from a cleft in the rockface not far to the left of the mine entrance, but the bushes and trees in front of the rock wall made it too dangerous to go and look. He used flint and steel to light a candle and placed it carefully in the lantern. The light appeared to be steady and would be fine for several hours. Putting his pack back on carefully and with the sack back over his shoulder, Gerant picked up the lantern, had a last look around the small open area and walked carefully into the darkness of the mine.

After walking in about ten feet from the entrance, he stopped and listened. By the light of the lantern, the tunnel seemed to be about ten feet high and bored more or less straight into the mountain side. The walls were rough-cut with jagged edges sticking out here and there, but the floor was relatively smooth, with a layer of dirt or dust about half an inch or so thick. The intense darkness reached everywhere beyond the relatively small light thrown out. Also, there was little sound, apart from a *drip, drip* of water somewhere ahead. He moved forward another fifty feet or so and stopped. Looking back, he could clearly see the circle of daylight. He also noticed every twenty or so feet there were unlit torch brackets placed about six feet or so up from the tunnel floor. *If this continues*, he thought, *it will be a useful reference point.* The air had a musty feel to it but so far was OK.

After passing another five torch brackets, Gerant could almost feel a faint breath of air coming from the left, confirmed when he shone his lantern to show that he had reached a side tunnel. Looking down it, he could see it continued to head off in a straight line until it curved away beyond the lantern light's reach. Looking at the floor, there were still many footprints that continued down the main tunnel, with only a couple of prints going into the branch. Gerant decided that he would continue down the main heading, but was already concerned if he came across many more branches. It would be difficult to decide which direction to take and, more importantly, hard to remember what was the correct way back.

Thankfully, there did not appear to be too many side tunnels and it was fairly easy to work out what was the main tunnel farther into the mine. He was also able to keep track with the torch brackets. The tunnel did start to get slightly smaller, but generally stayed the same height, although it did climb up and down a little and had small bends at various points. He had long since walked beyond where he could see back to the outside exit. And the blackness was now complete, apart from the little light the lantern threw out.

After another period of time, Gerant reached a junction in the tunnel system, with the one he was following stopping at a blank wall, a tunnel heading off to the left and another to the right. He was unsure which direction to go down, and picked right. The torch brackets continued down that path, which was a good sign. It then curved to the left and then back to the right. A little farther on, it curved again to the left, looking like there was a sharp corner coming up. Strangely, Gerant also thought he could see a faint glimmer of light slowly growing in the darkness as he moved forward. He pressed on, step by step, stopping every few paces to stop and listen. And yes, there did appear to be a light up ahead. He wondered what that meant. Perhaps he had come to another entrance to the mine. It had a different look to daylight – more like a candle or a lantern. He approached the corner slowly and although he couldn't see very clearly beyond the corner, the space looked like it might be opening up to some sort of cavern. Turning the corner, he took in the open space ahead, with some tools and equipment lying on the ground. Just as he peered around with his lantern held high, there was a sudden and frightening eruption of barking that burst out. Coming straight towards him was a large, brindle-coloured dog with a studded metal collar, snarling and barking. It was hard to decide who had been more surprised, Gerant or the dog. The dog stopped about six feet away and did not approach any closer. But it continued to snarl and bark.

Up ahead a lantern suddenly shifted and a quavering voice yelled out. 'Hold, Fang. Don't let him get away.'

The dog continued to bark and caper but did not move forward. Gerant had not moved, but he continued to grip one of the daggers in its sheath on the belt around his waist.

He watched as a silhouette of a figure approached holding a lantern aloft. As it approached, the dog subsided to a steady and deep grumbling growl. It also crouched down on the floor of the cavern, clearly ready to spring and go for the throat if the intruder moved.

The figure with the lantern approached and stopped next to the dog. Gerant could see that person was a wiry old man with a shock of white hair and flowing beard, dressed in dusty robes and with a floppy hat of indeterminate colour on his head.

'What do you want? Go away, you are not welcome here. This part is mine and there is nothing for you.'

Gerant digested what this strange old man had said. 'I didn't know you were here. I was just having a look.'

'Well, push off. Or Fang will make you push off. Leave me to my work. You can go anywhere else, but this tunnel's mine. Not that you'll have any luck. I'm very close to finding the last vein and I don't need busybodies like you disturbing me. So push off, I say.'

The dog began to growl louder, and it showed its large teeth in a slobbering grimace. Gerant kept the lantern in one hand and held the other palm out in a gesture of appeasement. 'All right, old man. No harm intended. I'm just going.' He started to back away slowly. The dog followed his movements, growling steadily. He reached the corner, backed out of sight of the old man and his guard dog, then walked back to the branching of the tunnel, and sat down to think.

This was like the encounter with the Black Fox, Gerant thought. He could see his hand was shaking in the dim lantern light. And it brought back some confronting memories of when he was with the gang and they had had some scary moments with large dogs protecting houses or cottages they were trying to look into. He now had no idea what to do. Clearly there was no point in going back to the old miner and trying to reason with him. The only thing that would happen would be to get attacked by his dog. So that was a lost cause. The only thing was to keep going down the other tunnel. But if what the old miner had said was right, there was no talium down that other way.

After eating the apple he had taken from the tavern at breakfast, Gerant headed down the other shaft. This tunnel had no torch brackets, which was not a good sign. He walked on for a few more hundred feet, and after rounding a slight curve in the tunnel, the lantern light showed only a solid wall ahead. The tunnel just stopped. Gerant shone the lantern all over the surface but it was solid. Whoever had tunnelled this far had just given up. He even got out the pick and tapped it all over the places he could reach and there was a dull thud every time of solid rock. Feeling very flat, Gerant realised that his dreams of finding a hidden store of talium were probably over. He turned around and began to walk slowly back to where the tunnel had split.

He was thinking about whether there was any point in not just going back to Ashford when he realised he had stopped for some reason. He looked around and the wall to his left appeared to be slightly different. As he held the lantern aloft, Gerant saw there was a split in the rock about five feet high and about eighteen inches wide. Shining the lantern through, he thought he could see it stayed that width for a few feet or so and then opened up again. Gerant's heart started to beat a little faster in hope. Then he thought this would be just another false start leading nowhere. But he decided to shrug off his pack and bedroll and put down the sack. He would squeeze through with only the lantern and go in for just a little bit until he got to the end, which would be surely just a few feet farther on. There were no problems getting through once he had turned sideways and sidled in. The surface of the split was quite rough but not too bad. As the lantern light had indicated, it opened up a little more, although the height of the rocky roof closed in so that Gerant had to crouch. After another ten feet, the opening began to head downwards quite steeply until it again flattened out. And then after another twenty feet, the lantern light picked out that the opening stopped when it dropped suddenly again, this time into a pool of water. *So that is that,* Gerant thought. It was the end of this little tunnel and there was no talium.

Gerant had been half-expecting something like this. And yet he couldn't help wondering whether the tunnel did keep going past the water. He was probably just being very stupid in this, but for some niggling reason he thought he would give it one last try. There were many reasons why this wouldn't work. He was a long way from help, he was about to jump into probably really cold water and he couldn't swim. There were probably many other considerations why this was a dumb idea. But he felt he had to try.

He stripped off his clothing down to his leggings, took off his knives and scabbards and his coin purse and left them in a small pile next to the lantern. The candle was still going well and had about another hour of light left. The shock of the cold water as he eased himself into the pool almost convinced him straight away to jump back out, but he steeled himself to continue. He felt as far along as he could with his head just out of the water and the opening did appear to continue on. With a quick shudder and thought of his foolishness, he took a large breath and tried to pull himself along the side wall. He kept his eyes shut and tried not to bump his head too much on the roof as he scrabbled along. He was not sure how far he had been able to drag himself – certainly no more than five or six feet. He started to panic about needing to keep holding his breath, and the water was freezing. He was about to turn around and head back when he realised he could not feel any rock above him. His head broke the surface of the water and he opened his eyes and took in great gasps of breath. He couldn't see anything. Feeling around, he was able to find the edge of the water and pull himself out. He started shivering with cold, but noticed that the air was not too bad and didn't smell. Crawling in the dark a few feet, he could sense he was in a small space and it was only a short way until he hit rock in every direction that he turned. So this was not any better, particularly since he had no light to see. But some little voice of instinct in his head said to him that it might be worth trying to get the lantern down here somehow so he could have a proper look. That probably wasn't possible. The first thing, though, was to get back through the water and into his clothes before he shivered to death. He felt for the water and dropped back in. After a few quick inhales and exhales, he again held his breath. This time it was a little quicker because as he pulled himself along, he opened his eyes and could see the very faint light approaching through the water.

Gerant broke the surface and pulled himself up next to the lantern. He dressed quickly, already starting to feel a little warmer as he put on his shirt, vest and half boots. Then the two knives and their scabbards and the money purse. Picking up the lantern he clambered and shuffled back up the small tunnel, reaching the narrow opening which he sidled through. His pack and other gear were exactly as he had left them. He carefully found his way back to where the tunnel split and followed the main path with the torch brackets back to the surface. Seeing the gradually growing circle of daylight approaching as he paced up towards the entrance was one of the most relieving things he had ever experienced. To celebrate his return to the outside, he quickly checked the old fireplace was still the same, set up a small fire from a few hastily collected pieces of wood and then spent the next hour or so warming himself up close to the crackling flames.

As he felt like he was now thawed out and feeling that the effects of the cold dipping had now passed, Gerant spent some time thinking about the problem he had encountered in the mine. The main thing was to get some light through to the little cavern he had felt having passed the flooded tunnel section. Only then would he be able to tell whether his instinct was correct or just wishful thinking. But how could he do that? The only way he could think of was to take a lantern, candles, and his flint and steel kit along with a little quick-starting tinder or rags. But it would get wet being pushed through the water section and then would be useless to try to light a candle and use the lantern. He might be able to put them in some sort of container that didn't let the water in. But that was not possible with what he had. He decided he would have to go back into Osmount and talk with the general store trader, Anton. That was all he could do. He couldn't see the point in taking all his gear all the way into Osmount and back, so he looked around for somewhere in the bushes to stash it. After poking around between where the trees started again and the steep rising of the rocky slope, he came across an overhanging bush. He parted the leafy stalks and peered in. Some sort of animal had been using the space under the leafy roof as a shelter, based on the scratchings he saw in the earth and the odd dried-up scat.

This should be quite suitable, he thought. He wandered back to the fireplace and grabbed the gear he didn't need and carefully knelt down and pushed it in under the cleared space within the drooping bush. Backing out, the stalks re-arranged themselves somewhat and he tugged a few here and there to give further coverage. Looking back from six feet away, it would have been impossible to guess that under this bushy outcrop was his pack, bedroll and other bits and pieces. He made a quick walk back to the fire and kicked dirt on it to make sure it would be out. Then he grabbed the hessian sack he had left out with the water bottle and some food and walked off in the direction of Osmount. The sun still had a few hours left in the sky, but Gerant thought it would go down a little earlier up here, because of the tall mountains that stood in the way to the west.

Arriving back in the town, Gerant went directly to the shop he had visited the day before. There was no one waiting to be served, but as soon as he approached the counter, the storekeeper stood up and came across. Gerant saw that he had a chair placed just in front of a barrel with shovels, axes and other tools, where he could watch the street and see who came along.

'Something?'

He saw that the warm brown eyes were nonetheless watching him very keenly as the shopkeeper unconsciously stroked his moustache. Gerant realised that Anton might be thinking he had come to return the gear he had bought yesterday or had some fault with it.

'The stuff you gave me yesterday was more than sufficient. But I forgot a few things. My flint and steel kit is getting a little worn, so could I get another one? I would also like some wadding or similar to light it with. And another lantern like the one you sold me yesterday and some more candles.'

The storekeeper nodded. 'I have one more lantern. Any more and you will have to come back in a week.'

The youth in front of him nodded and waited, as if making up his mind.

'And?'

'I need to have something that can keep stuff dry when it is under water. Like a sack or a box. Do you have anything like that?'

The man scratched his tufty black hair and smoothed his moustache as he thought. He asked some questions about how big it had to be and how much protection from the water was needed. 'Probably the best I could give you is some waxed canvas that you can fold around the things as a little sack. If you tie the opening with some waxed twine, it should keep the things inside dry. But not forever. It will be only a temporary fix.'

Gerant tried to envisage what Anton had described to him and thought it would work well. He nodded.

'That will be eight silver and five coppers. Including the kit, the lantern and the extra candles. Wait a few minutes while I prepare this.'

Anton disappeared into the bowels of his store and Gerant could hear items being shifted and material being cut. After a short period, the storekeeper appeared again and placed on the counter a small tin, another lantern of the same design as the one Gerant already had, some more candles, a folded piece of waxy material and two feet or so of waxed twine. Gerant counted out the coin and gave it to the storekeeper, placed his new items in the sack, thanked the storekeeper and walked off. He turned after a bit and saw that the storekeeper had not moved and was watching him with his hands on the counter of the store. The boy turned again and started the hike back to the campsite outside the mine. He should be able to get there before night set in.

With the fire gently crackling and a meal of some bread and the cheese from The Green Dragon, Gerant reviewed the day's events and was well satisfied. Tomorrow might be another story, but he would just have to see what happened then. He had already tested making up the waxed canvas into a little sack with the new lantern, candles, pick, flint and steel, then tightly wrapping the neck with the waxed cord and holding it carefully under the water of the rushing stream for a minute or so. When he pulled it out and took it back to the camp-fire and unwound the cord, the items inside had stayed dry. Gerant pursed his lips and nodded to himself. *Maybe this will work*, he thought. He laid out his bedroll next to the fire and after a few moments, fell asleep.

In the morning, it took only a few moments for Gerant to eat a scrap of bread and a small piece of beef, wash his hands and face in the brook, and put the gear he didn't need under the drooping bush behind the open clearing. He put the rest of his stuff in one of the hessian sacks, lit one of the lanterns and looked around to make sure there was nothing left to show he had camped there. It was a much quicker trip to the pool of water than previously, as he now knew the way and had much less to encumber him as he squeezed through the crack in the tunnel wall he had stumbled across. It took but a few moments to prepare the sack of waxed canvas with the things he would need on the other side. Then he stripped off again, leaving his clothes and other stuff in a small pile not far from the pool. He pondered whether to blow out the existing lantern, but decided he wouldn't, as he would probably have returned with no success in a short while.

He grabbed the canvas sack and eased himself into the water. The water felt no warmer than yesterday. He held his breath and kicked out. Although the weight of the sack held him back a little, he soon broke the surface at the other end and heaved himself out. It was a little difficult trying to undo the cord wrapped around the neck of the sack in the complete darkness and put each of the items within feeling reach. After some time, he was able to manage and then was grateful he had used the flint and steel all the time in recent days and was well practiced. There were a few sparks and he carefully blew on a piece of the wadding that Anton had provided. A tiny glow of red appeared as he blew on the wadding, until it was sufficient to light the candle. He carefully placed it in the lantern, made sure it was steadily alight and only then raised the lantern and looked around. Water dripped off his hair onto his shoulders without being noticed, as he stood there for many seconds with his mouth agape with wonder.

The lantern light showed a rough-hewn little chamber of rock no more than fifteen feet from the surface of the water to a wall of rock and about ten feet across. The rock ceiling was five or maybe six feet high. What was arresting was that on one of the side walls were two seams of something that glowed faintly with a greenish-black tinge in the yellowish cast of the lantern light. Compared to the dull surface of the rock, this material had a shiny look about it, with small protuberances that were jagged and sheer-cut, where they stuck out from the surface of the base rock. The two seams of what must be talium wandered across the wall about three or four feet above the floor towards where the cavern stopped. It was almost inviting someone to come along and snap it out of the surrounding rock. Gerant went back to his canvas sack and hefted the pick. He brought the lantern over to where the upper seam of talium was about four or five inches wide and there were a series of little blocks protruding out of the mother rock. He picked one seam and struck tentatively with the pick. A small amount of the greeny-black pieces of talium dropped down to the cavern floor where the pick tip had struck. Gerant hit the place again with more force this time. He could feel through the pick head that the talium itself was neither hard nor soft, but the rock underneath was quite hard. Squatting down with the lantern, Gerant picked up a few large flakes of talium. It had that same greenish-black tinge in the lantern light, had some sheen to it and seemed to be a little transparent. It reminded him of pieces of toffee, but much darker. Marion had made some toffee once for him and Bree as a treat. In the same way the toffee had come out as a sheet, the shards of talium had that same look when they had been broken off.

He kept working for ten minutes or so and soon hit a rhythm a little like Sveg had taught him in the smith: one-two-three-four-five-six-seven, and rest. There was now a little pile of talium shards on the ground below the veins. He could see that he had broken off a handspan of talium from one seam, but there would be at least a month's solid work to get at what he could see in this cavern. In his rest breaks between periods of hammering with the pick, he thought about how much he should take. Perhaps he could see how much he would get after three or four days. It would also depend on how long the candles would last and how heavy the talium was to take back out through the pool of water. There were a thousand things to think through. He placed the lantern closer and scooped up with his hands the fragments and put them in the hessian sack he had brought. It didn't amount to much: about half a handful. There was quite a bit still on the ground as smaller pieces that would be difficult to scoop up. Maybe he could find a bit of cloth to lay on the floor of the cavern underneath the seams while he worked. That way most of what he broke off should land on the cloth and he could collect it that way. Also, he didn't have too much food left. It looked like he would have to go back into Osmount again. He was not sure that he wanted to go back to Anton's again for the cloth. The merchant had been watching him intently as he left the last time, and he might get more suspicious if he appeared again. Gerant would have to look for other places for any further supplies and he was sure he had gone past a bakery on his first afternoon when he had wandered through the town. That would do for now. It was a tiny start, but it might be better to pace himself and not rush things too much. The physical work had also meant he was warm enough now, which was some blessing after the cold dunking. That might help things and make it easier to work well. Gerant looked through the gear he had brought through the pool and decided to leave the flint and steel kit, the pick and the second lantern. No one would be coming to take it and he made sure he left them within reach of where he would come out of the pool of water on the way back in. He carefully put the little bit of talium he had broken off in the hessian bag in the larger waxed canvas and tied off the neck. He placed the lantern down next to the pick and tin box, opened the door and blew out the candle. As he grabbed the sack and eased himself into the water, there was a faint, eerie but steady greenish-black glow coming from the wall of the cavern. Somehow in a way he did not understand, the talium had taken on some of the candlelight. He shook his head in amazement, held his breath and headed back under water to the other side of the pool.

Back at the campsite outside the mine entrance, things were as he had left them. He had been very relieved that coming back through the cavern pool and surfacing, he could see that the original lantern was still alight, although the candle had burned down quite a bit. When he was doing this in the future, it would be best to save his candles on either side and light them in the dark. He was glad he had already thought about that ahead of time and bought the second lantern and the extra steel and flint box. Gerant ummed and ahhed a little about whether it was safe to leave the small sack of talium under the spreading bush with his other gear. Then he realised it was as good a hiding place as any. He made a quick scoot around to collect some firewood for later and left it behind a nearby tree, then he walked back on the path towards Osmount.

Chapter 13
Talium

Gerant was feeling pleased with himself as he ambled back from the town later that afternoon. After wandering some of the main streets, he had found a small stall where a woman was selling woven stuff and sewing equipment. He had no idea what to get, but ended up getting some cloth that had a pattern of red and white checks on it. He had pretended to the woman that he was buying it for his mother as a birthday present and needed a piece about three arm lengths long in a square piece. She was happy to oblige and was most concerned for Gerant to let her know if his mother liked it. Not far from this stall he found the bakery. He bought some small loaves of bread and a couple of small beef pies. That should last him for a week if he took care to ration his meals. On the street leading to the western gate, he looked behind him and noticed that the same man who had been walking about twenty feet behind him was still there. Alarm bells started to go off in Gerant's head. He stopped and pretended to look into his sack and rearrange a few things. The man walked past, got to just before the gate and then turned down an alleyway to the left that ran along inside the town wall. As Gerant stood up and walked forward, he could see the man reach a doorway to a house and go in, disappearing from view. A relieved young man continued to walk back up the grassed track to the mine, occasionally stopping and looking behind him to make sure he was travelling alone.

Thereafter followed a routine that Gerant developed over the next four days. He would get up sometime after dawn, have a leisurely breakfast, drink from the rushing stream and collect firewood. Then he would pack away his gear under the weeping bush, light one of the lanterns and walk into the mine to the outer side of the pool blocking off the small side tunnel. He would strip off his clothes apart from his leggings, blow out the candle and swim through with whatever gear he needed in the waxed canvas pouch. On the other side, he would grope for the other lantern, the steel and flint kit and then light a candle. The pick and that lantern stayed on that side of the pool. He worked it out by trialling things.

Working at mining the talium from the wall for the time that two candles lasted was a good day's work and he was very hungry by the time he made it back to the camp. The chequered cloth had been a huge boon and meant that the talium that he broke off the seam with the pick fell onto it and could be collected at the end of the time he allowed himself. At the end of the first day of this strange new work routine, Gerant hefted one of the hessian sacks now containing talium. It weighed a goodly amount without being overly heavy and was over half-full with flakes of the ore. The key had been to work for a number of hours at chipping it out and then stop. With the small handful he had collected on the first day, he now had something approaching a small bucket full.

It was on the morning of the fourth day, as Gerant was carefully arranging under the weeping bush his growing pile of gear, bedroll and two-and-a-bit sacks of talium ore, that he could hear voices faintly approaching. He stopped his movement and sat quietly under the leafy fronds. He couldn't see out, but the voices got louder and he could hear footsteps echoing a little as they crossed the bridge. It sounded like there were two men. One spoke with the same measured tone and deepness, similar to Sveg's voice. The other voice was a little higher-pitched and sounded somewhat younger. The voices reached the fireplace and halted. Then Gerant could hear them moving around, kicking the ground, walking back to the bridge and then returning.

The deeper voice spoke first. 'Looks like someone has been using this very recently. Well, we didn't see anyone on the way here, so maybe they are in the mine. Or just spent a night here. We'll have to report this.'

The younger voice replied. 'It's probably just that crazy, old Harold that came out to get a breath of fresh air for a change. It must be terribly lonely working in there all these years and nothing much to show for it. I would come out now and again just to see the sunlight.'

The deeper voice spoke again. 'You might be right. But we still need to report it to the captain. We should go back and then tomorrow bring a few others to do a proper search and go into the mine a bit and look for fresh footprints.'

'I tell you it will be Harold, for sure. You're just making work for us.'

'That's what we get paid to do. If you don't want to be in the guard, say so. There are plenty who would willing to take your place.'

The younger voice spoke up again. 'Sure, sure, grandfather. We can go back and report and then come back with some of the lads tomorrow.' There was no dissent. 'Let's go then.'

The footfalls headed back to the bridge and the voices became softer and softer as the two town guards returned to Osmount. Gerant waited for some time and all he heard was the breeze in the tree branches and the occasional bird. He popped out of the bush, dusted himself off and made a decision that today's work would be his last. What he didn't need was to run into these guards and have the talium he had mined confiscated from him using some obscure regulation that Hardcross had not told him about.

The day, such as it was in the darkness and dim candlelight in the mine, was the same as the previous ones. Gerant worked steadily at the rockface with the seams of talium ore. Towards the end of the second candle, he stopped to collect the fragments from the chequered cloth. It made up more than half of a sack. By his reckoning he now had around three hessian sacks full of talium to take back with him. He decided to stop now. Holding the lantern aloft, he could see he had worked along the two seams for a distance of five or so feet. The greenish glow from the talium in the candlelight still followed the seams for the remaining feet until the veins disappeared into the mother rock. There was still a good few weeks' worth of material there if he ever needed to come back. He had no firm idea about the amount he had collected and how long it would last. The old parchment had been silent on that account. But it was clear that what he had chipped off was worth a lot of gold, if the stories were right. It was clearly a waste to leave some of the gear, but Gerant was worried about the amount he would have to lug back to Ashford. Even the sacks of talium would need some careful thought about how to get it there. Or he would just have to accept it would be a slow road back. So he left the pick, the lantern, the candles he hadn't used and the flint and steel tin on the floor of the cavern. The cloth would also have to stay here. Then he put the sack of talium in the waxed canvas for the last time, carefully wound the neck tight with the twine, blew out the lantern, and eased himself into the water. As on previous occasions, the remaining talium in the wall of the cavern above him softly glowed with its greenish presence.

Things had gone smoothly on the way out of the mine, until he reached the junction where the tunnels split. He was just about to turn and follow the torch brackets back up the main tunnel to the mine exit when he realised he could hear a soft mournful, baying coming from the tunnel to the right. It sounded like that guard dog. Against his better judgement, Gerant decided to investigate. After walking down as silently as he could down the tunnel, he turned the final corner where he had suddenly encountered the dog and where the space opened up into a larger cavern. This time there was no lantern light ahead and all he could hear was some scrabbling sounds and the same soft, mournful howling. The lantern light showed quite a different scene. The tools and equipment were still scattered around the cavern floor, but Gerant could see the large, brindle dog standing in front of a large pile of pieces of rock and rubble that fanned out from a vertical wall of stone on the far side of the cavern. The dog saw the youth with the lantern approaching, but this time it did not rush to attack him and continued to scrabble at the edge of the rubble and softly howl.

Gerant could piece together what had happened. It looked like the old miner, who he presumed was called Harold, had been working away at his usual place. For whatever reason, a rock fall had been triggered and he had not been fast enough to jump out of the way. That made sense with the dog pawing at the pile of rocks spilling out from the face. It suggested that poor old Harold was buried underneath. He thought there was at least a few tonnes of rock that had fallen down. The gods only knew how long ago this had occurred.

'Well, Fang, or whatever your name is, your master might have met his doom.'

The dog looked up quickly when he heard Gerant's voice. Gerant was not willing to leave the dog to its fate, and then had an idea. He reached into his sack and pulled out a portion of one of the beef pies he had been saving.

'Here.' And he laid the pie piece on the ground in front of him. Fang took one look and bounded over, wolfing down the piece in two big gulps, licking the ground for any missing crumbs. If a dog could feel relief, it seemed to be showing that on its face and if it could talk, Gerant imagined it would say something like, 'Well, about time! I was starving.'

What was noticeable after being fed was that Fang became friendly and accepting to the boy. Gerant looked around with the lantern at the bits and pieces lying around and noticed a rickety bedframe and hessian sacking stretched across it, a few boxes, and mostly mining tools and equipment. He grabbed a coil of rope and cut off about ten feet. He also noticed a hand-made wooden cart with an open top, two wheels and a wooden handle to pull it. He thought that might just do the trick for what he was thinking. Certainly, it was clear that Harold would not have any further use for it.

Gerant decided to see what happened and called out to the dog. 'Let's go, Fang.' He approached the dog warily and slipped the length of rope through the studded collar and tied it on. Fang sat there with patience and did not react.

Phew. He put the last sack of talium in the handcart, picked up the lantern and the end of the rope, grabbed the handle and started to walk off. 'Come on, time to leave.' To Gerant's immense relief, there was a brief tug on the rope and then the large dog followed him out of the cavern and up the tunnel towards the surface.

Outside the mine entrance, he briefly tied Fang to the leaning post with the crossed boards. Fang laid down, closed his eyes and was content to patiently wait. Gerant wheeled the handcart towards the drooping bush and quickly ferried out his pack, bedroll and the two full sacks of talium. A quick repacking of things and he placed the talium in the handcart and hefted the handle. It was not too bad and might work. There was no way he could have managed things without this contraption. Fang watched with lowered eyes the bustling of his new friend. Gerant left a couple of small things in his hideaway under the bush to save weight, put on the pack with the bedroll, untied Fang and started off towards the bridge. Having to pull the handcart with the sacks of talium in it was a little cumbersome and slow, making Gerant feel somewhat vulnerable, but this was balanced by the large dog walking beside him for protection. He listened ahead for sounds of anyone approaching and continued down the grassy track with the faint impression of foot traffic and the wheel marks. He started to look out on either side for somewhere suitable to stop, planning and thinking as he wheeled the cart, mulling over the next stage.

'This might work,' he muttered to himself. Off on the right of the track, he could see down the bank with a glimpse of a fallen log showing here and there. He tied Fang to a sapling on the edge of the path and quickly snaked down the bank. As he had hoped, the log had fallen across twenty feet or so of ground, with little mounds and holes in the uneven ground that it lay across. Clambering over the trunk, Gerant dropped down the other side and soon found a hollow of about two feet that he quickly enlarged with his hands. He clambered back over the log and ran up to the track. Over several trips back and forth he transferred his pack, bedroll and the sacks of talium to the other side of the log and into the hollow. The handcart was a problem. He gave up trying to figure out how to push it into the hollow and just positioned it at the opening. He spent ten minutes or so cutting ferns and branches of bushes and positioned them over the upturned cart and the opening of the hollow. He stepped back and looked at this work. It looked OK, but it was also not the best. In his mind it was hardly as hidden as the drooping bush he had used near the cave entrance. It would have to do; he would only need it to work for a day or two. By then he should be back and the cut stems and ferns shouldn't have wilted too much. After carefully brushing the ground a little smoother where he had slid down the bank, he untied Fang and continued towards the town with only one sack containing some food, the water bottle and his vest. Importantly, he had apportioned into one of his spare hessian sacks a small amount of the talium ore that he placed in the larger sack with the other stuff.

Arriving at The Green Dragon, Gerant wondered what he would do with Fang and then walked around the back of the tavern courtyard and tied the dog to a post near a timber fence. As before, Fang lay down without prompting and seemed to accept that his new master would be back fairly soon. Walking through the taproom, there were already several patrons sitting at the tables, chatting and drinking. He noticed that Mother Gimlet was wearing a fresh apron and was chatting away to a couple of men sitting on stools at the bar. She noticed the youth come into the room and make his way towards her.

'Excuse me, gentlemen. Ah, young ... Gerant. You are back. Everything has gone well?'

'Yes, Mother. Would I be able to have a room again for the night?' He laid five silver on the bar counter.

Mother Gimlet nodded in approval. 'Of course. You can probably have the same room. Harry! Harry!'

'Actually, you know where it is and what the arrangements are.'

'I also have a dog now. He is tied up around the back. Is it OK to keep him here?'

Nothing could surprise Mother Gimlet. 'That should be fine, as long as he stays outside. You can tie him up at the stables.'

'Would it be possible to get him a little meat or something to feed him?'

Mother Gimlet was inclined just to let Gerant have some scraps for the dog, but business was business. 'Give me a couple of coppers and that should cover it. Just go to the kitchen door and tell chef I said it was OK to give you something for the dog.'

'Thank you, Mother.'

Gerant went back up the stairs to the rooms and saw that room five was exactly as he had first seen it. He pushed his sack under the bed again and walked out to go and find the cook and take whatever she gave him back to Fang. After that, he had a couple of tasks to complete in the town.

Gerant hurried to the bakery he had found the previous week and got there in the late afternoon sun just as they were closing up. The choice was limited as they had sold much of the day's baking. But he was still able to buy a small loaf and then two beef pies and one of chicken that he would share on the road back to Ashford with Fang. Putting away his purchases, he quickly felt to make sure he had the other small sack in the bottom. It was still there, of course, but he had to make sure. Then it was off back to the main square through the streets busy with townspeople on their afternoon business.

The doorkeeper at the Hardcross residence put away his materials, went into the study and put a couple more logs on the fire merrily burning in the large fireplace. He shut the door to the study just as the front door opened and Gerant walked in. The doorkeeper recognised the youth that had come during the previous week.

'Master Hardcross is not available to see you. He is attending an important meeting with the Mayor and will not be back until tomorrow. If you come then, he might be able to spare a few moments to see you. But he is very busy.'

The doorkeeper noticed the boy had an infuriating knowing smile on his face. 'That is not a problem. I only wanted to leave Master Hardcross something that he asked to be given.'

With that a brownish sack with some twine tied across the neck was produced that was laid on the doorkeeper's desk with a soft clinking noise.

The man was taken aback.

'Will the master know what this is?'

'I believe he will. If he has any questions, I can be found at The Green Dragon. Good day to you.' Gerant had been practising in his mind the words he would use and was quite pleased with how they had come out.

The doorkeeper watched the youth nod to him, turn and walk to the door and slip out before he could think of an appropriate response.

After a quick dinner of shepherd's pie in the meals room of the tavern, Gerant went up to the room and got ready for bed. He suddenly felt rather tired and was looking forward to an undisturbed sleep in a proper bed.

Gerant awoke suddenly in a sweat and quickly sat up. It took a moment for him to realise he was safe in the room in The Green Dragon, with no idea how long he had been asleep. He had been having a very vivid dream where he was working next to old Harold in the talium mine. In between swinging their picks at the talium, Harold had been telling him a story of when he was a boy and stealing apples from the churchyard and the thrashing he got from his father when he found out. Suddenly, there was a low rumble and the cavern in which they were working started to shake and bits of rock and stone broke off the face and fell around them. Then the whole rockface started to slowly lean and crumble towards them.

'Get out, get out!' yelled Harold, and that was when Gerant had woken.

Clearly it had been a nightmare. But some instinct, like when he was in the dark of the mine after passing through the pool of water, urged him to listen. He sat there on the bed for a few minutes, debating whether he was being silly and go back to sleep, or take heed. In the end, he thought he would be leaving Osmount tomorrow anyway, so nothing much would be lost. He quickly grabbed his stuff from under the bed, quietly closed the door and crept down the stairway. There were still sounds coming from the taproom. There was no babble of voices, only a few scrapes and gentle thumps of stuff being moved around. Maybe the tavern had closed. He walked down to the stable area. Fang heard him coming and started whining and wagging his tail, at the end of the rope. The boy just checked he hadn't left anything here with Fang. He noted the bucket of water he had left for the dog to drink from, next to a couple of old blankets that he had found in the stables for the dog to lie on. The germ of an idea came forward.

'I'll be back in a few moments,' said Gerant to the dog, as he grabbed the blankets and went back upstairs briefly. He returned, untied Fang and they both quietly kept to the shadows as they stole out of the tavern courtyard and headed off to the western gate.

Gerant took his time, so he would see any patrolling guards well before they saw him.

Harry finished rearranging the chairs around the tables in the taproom and thought about bed. It had been a normal night with many of the usual regulars coming. He had helped the last few out the doors and then gone through the nightly routine of cleaning up and getting the bar ready for tomorrow. He still had to bring up a new barrel of ale, but that could wait until the morning. He heard the main door open and close and some footsteps approaching.

'We're closed for the night.'

He put the chair down and was about to turn to see who had come in when he was clamped in a bear hug by two steely arms. The man held him tight, breathing on the back of his neck in regular little gasps as he held the struggling youth. Another man appeared in Harry's vision as he tried to fight against the rugged grip. The second man was tall and tending to fat, dressed in dark clothes and had several knife scars on his cheeks. He reached out with large hands and started to steadily squeeze Harry's throat. He brought his face up to Harry's, squeezing harder. His breath stank.

'The boy called William from The Capital. Which room is he in?' He loosened his grip slightly to allow a response.

'Don't know no William. Ow, ow! Must be the lad in five.'

The man in front shoved Harry in the chest just as the man behind him released his bear hug. The youth fell backwards on the floor, knocking over a chair. He looked with frightened eyes at the two men in black standing over him.

'We were never here. If we find out you ratted on us, we'll seek you out and we'll cut you.'

Harry scuttled backward around the side of the bar and out of sight.

Two dark shapes stood carefully on either side of the door to room five and listened. They were almost invisible in the darkened corridor apart from the slight sheen reflecting off their drawn daggers.

'One, two, three,' one of them mouthed.

They wrenched the door open, strode to the bed and plunged their knives into the sleeping form curled up on the bed. Something didn't feel right. One of the men ripped back the cover and cursed when he saw that all they had ripped open were a couple of old blankets squashed around a pillow that was now bleeding feathers.

'He must have got warning, somehow. We might have a quiet chat to that idiot downstairs tomorrow about this.'

'Yup. Hardcross is not going to be happy. He said this was going to be easy.'

'Well, nothing more we can do tonight. We'll tell him in the morning. Let's go.'

Two figures clattered down the stairs, passed through the taproom and out into the night. After a few minutes, a hesitant Harry came out from behind the bar counter, latched the two doors and turned the lock, then groped his way towards the kitchen.

Chapter 14
A New Companion

The moonlight, only occasionally obscured by brief scuds of cloud, helped Gerant and Fang make it back to the cache of talium and gear without trouble. Gerant tied the dog's rope to a small tree a few feet away and then pulled out his bedroll. The ferns and cut stalks from the bushes went under the rolled-out padding, making the unyielding ground slightly more forgiving. He lay back with his arms behind his head and tried to get a few hours' sleep before the forest birds would start calling to announce the new day. Fang stood up from where he had hunkered down watching the movements and plopped down next to him, with a soft grunt. A hand reached down and stroked the large, spade-shaped head for a few moments.

Morning showed the slimmish figure of a youth pulling a handcart along the road from Osmount towards Ashford and The Capital, with what seemed to be sacks and other provisions under a canvas cover. A bedroll poked out at the rear. Keeping pace on a short rope lead was a very well-built brindle mastiff with almost over-sized paws and a heavily muscled neck. The dog's solid head and shoulders were almost on a level with the youth's hips. The length of rope tied into the animal's studded collar was, at best, a token. It was fortunate that the animal appeared to be well trained and docile, given it was such a large, threatening-looking beast.

The pair had soon got back to within sight of the western gate and then cut across on a well-travelled side path that had linked up to the main road coming into Osmount from the east. The cart now had all Gerant's gear in it, along with the sacks of talium. It required steady effort to pull it down the well-kept roadway. He stopped every half-mile or so for a bit of a break. Even with the recent use of the pick and the daily use of tools in the forge, he could feel the beginnings of some blisters starting on the palms of his hands where the wooden handle had been rubbing. Although the pace was quite a bit less than when he had been walking in the other direction, Gerant was content that he would make it back to the smithy within four full days or thereabouts. Having the dog pacing next to him gave him a lot of relief. Certainly, the encounters with fellow travellers so far on the road had been interesting to experience. There had been several riders who had come up from behind or approached from the other direction and had not stopped, although quickly moving to the other side of the road and looping past. Because he was still able to keep up a steady pace, so far no one had overtaken the pair on foot from the direction they had come from.

Coming towards Osmount, there had been a steady trickle of people approaching the pair. There had been a few men with vegetables or packages, several couples and even a family of four perhaps coming in for market day. Gerant watched them coming up and could see their expressions as they got closer and what they revealed. In most cases, they all could see a figure pulling a cart and what looked like some sort of animal next to the figure. As they got closer, Gerant could see on their faces the gradual realisation that the creature next to the lad was a very big dog, who was watching them approach with close attention. The approaching travellers invariably started to edge to the other side of the road as the pair from Osmount got closer. Some would even stop and move off the road. All of them watched carefully as Gerant and Fang walked past until they had definitely moved on. It was obvious they were worried that the huge dog would suddenly jump after them and attack them. The first couple of times, Gerant had spoken quietly to Fang and hitched in the lead a little shorter. Apart from the head of the mastiff swinging round to keep a steady eye on the people approaching and the occasional soft rumble from his throat, Fang would continue to pace next to the cart, occasionally looking back. Gerant was not sure what would have happened if someone stopped for a chat or questioned him, but for the first few miles nothing like that had eventuated.

At the little camp-fire that evening, Gerant and Fang shared a basic meal of a little of the bread loaf and a part of one of the pies. Despite the clear protection of having the large dog to discourage those considering mischief, Gerant thought it prudent to continue to camp off the road a bit, out of sight. The cart had made it a little harder, but he had found a spot where it could be wheeled through the open ground under a grouping of tall trees and over a small bank. Although only thirty yards or so from the edge of the road, the small pile of burning wood could not be viewed when Gerant went back to the road and checked. He could smell the smoke from the fire, but Fang would give him warning long before anyone approached.

The next day, Gerant stood with Fang watching ahead for any sign of movement. After several hours of travel, they had passed the odd traveller walking in the other direction. And there had also been one middle-aged man hunched on the seat of a cart filled with chopped wood and pulled by an elderly grey horse. They had now reached the grove where Gerant had been ambushed by the Black Fox and his band. Looking ahead, he could not see anything untoward. Certainly, there didn't appear to be any bodies lying in the positions that he remembered. He left the handcart and carefully wandered up the fifty feet or so with Fang on the rope lead to the tree with the large fork a little over head height. A few minutes of quick searching around showed nothing. The crossbow was gone, and there was no sword. There were a few scuff and drag marks in the ground. Fang was very intently sniffing the ground where there were still two slightly darker patches in the dirt near the neighbouring trees. It took a little bit of effort to pull the dog away, but Gerant succeeded after a few strong tugs. They walked back to the cart and continued over the stone bridge at the bottom of the gradual slope.

It was in the afternoon two days later that the travellers finally arrived outside the smithy. Gerant dropped the rope and let down the handle of the cart and stretched wearily. He was relieved to see that although the shutters to the forge were firmly closed, the large padlock and chain were not to be seen. He quickly tied the rope to the cart, told Fang to stay put and went around the back and over the paling fence so he could lift up the cross bar. He pulled the cart into the workshop and re-barred the shutters. Fang was taken out to the courtyard where the kiln was and tied up to a post. Gerant quickly went back in and filled up a small bucket of water and placed it next to the dog.

'Welcome to your new home, Fang,' said Gerant as he patted the dog. 'At least, I hope it will be.'

Gerant grabbed his gear and the bedroll and walked into his alcove. Nothing had changed, although it looked very small. It took him but a few moments to pack everything neatly away and then he set off up the passageway from the forge towards the cottage.

'Hello . . . hello . . . hello . . .' he called gently as he approached the kitchen area.

The door quickly burst open and out rushed a blonde figure with plaits who tackled Gerant in a huge hug. He returned the hug fiercely. Bree was full of excitement with things to tell Gerant.

'We got back yesterday. It was a long trip. I got to meet my grandpa and grandma and some cousins. The food was kinda funny but tasted OK. We saw a fox one day that ran across the road. Mother is inside changing the beds and Father has gone down to the market to get some vegetables and some meat for dinner. He should be back soon.'

That was a lot of information to take in, but Gerant just smiled and chatted with Bree. He realised how much he had missed the family that had taken him in.

That night over dinner, Gerant learnt more about the trip north, which appeared to have been without incident and had been a welcome change of pace with different things to do. Bree had enjoyed the trip in the cart, although Gerant could see that Sveg and Marion were glad the journey had not taken any longer. Then it was Gerant's turn. He took his time and tried to remember as much of his own trek west as he could. Sveg had been surprised and perplexed when Gerant started off saying he had been to Osmount. This generated a flurry of questioning from the smith and Marion.

'What possessed you to go all the way to Osmount?'

'Just to see a bit of the countryside.'

'That was a long way to travel to do that. Why didn't you look around Ashford or walk to Cobham and back?'

Gerant looked at Sveg. 'Do you remember the old parchment describing the talium mine near Osmount?'

'Hmmm. Let's start at the beginning and give us the whole tale.'

Marion nodded in agreement. Sveg had a look that said, 'This will be interesting and I not make any snap judgements until I hear it all.' Bree just looked excited and agog with anticipation in equal measure.

So Gerant started with him seeing the cart leave the smithy and walking off towards the river road. When his tale got to the point where he had crossed the bridge and he had spied the man in the tree fork and the dark-clad man leaning against another tree, Sveg and Marion passed a quick look between each other.

'Right, young lady. Time for you to take the dishes and tidy up and then off to bed,' said Marion.

'But, Mother, the story is just getting interesting. I want to hear what the nice man said to Gerant.'

'Shoosh, shoosh. Gerant can tell us about it tomorrow. You've had a big day and time to think about a good night's rest. Don't forget you've got schooling in the morning.'

With that, Marion helped her daughter pick up some dishes and they both disappeared farther into the cottage. Sveg and Gerant talked about the family's trip north for a little longer until Marion reappeared and snuggled up next to her husband. Gerant picked up where he had left off. He talked quietly for another hour or so.

Marion could see that the young man in front of her was going through a range of emotions as he relived his journey. The event with the gang was truly frightening and even Sveg had looked shocked. She paused.

'Two men were killed. So did you tell the town guards when you got to Osmount? This is serious stuff that happened.'

Gerant looked crestfallen and he realised Marion was shocked and disappointed in him. 'No, it happened so fast, and I was just defending myself. I didn't start it. They did. And the guards wouldn't have believed me. Also, it happened miles away from the town and when I went through on the way home the bodies and stuff had gone and it was all peaceful.'

Sveg broke into the conversation. 'Marion is right that you should have reported this to the authorities in Osmount and let them deal with any issues. That said, I have been in my share of fights and brawls when I was younger. I know you just tend to react instinctively and it sounds like you could easily have come out of this situation the worse for wear…or not even come back.' He paused as he continued thinking through what Gerant had spoken about.

'Well, I'm truly pleased I taught you the knife throwing, but I never thought you would need it so soon, or that your life would be in so much peril. Or that it ended up with such a dire outcome. I know you didn't go looking for this encounter. It shows just how careful you need to be and ever watchful. Most people are good folk but there are always the odd bad egg or two, no matter where you are.'

After another hour or so of Gerant relating his visit to Osmount, staying at The Green Dragon and journeying to the mine, Sveg could see the lad starting to flag.

'That's probably enough for this evening. It sounds like you have certainly experienced some new things, some even I haven't experienced. We can take it up again tomorrow at dinner time. I know Bree will want to hear about the meeting in the forest, but perhaps you could skip over that bit. Are there any more things like that coming up?'

'Weeell, a few things that were a little scary, but nothing as bad as that.'

The relief on Marion's face was clearly apparent. Sveg also had a look of concern on his face that lessened somewhat knowing tomorrow's tale might be less harrowing.

'Gerant, I was not planning to work tomorrow and just wanted to get the forge ready for the next day. There are a few little fixing chores that Marion has need for, so you can help me with them. Then we can get back into it. I called into the guild this afternoon. Once I had filled in a form covering your absence because your supervisor had been away, they were a bit more relaxed. And they kept for me the smithing jobs that have built up in my absence. We will be quite busy for some days with those. Nothing complicated, but a good pile of work.'

'I would be happy to help,' said Gerant, smiling at Marion. She smiled back.

It was only as he was lying on his pallet back in the workshop that Gerant remembered the dog. 'Damn, I forgot to tell them and ask whether he can stay here,' he muttered to himself.

He jumped up and rooted around in the sack next to him and found the leftovers of a pie he had been saving as a reserve ration in case his journey had taken longer. He felt his way out to the courtyard. Fang heard him coming and whined with pleasure, his tail thumping on the ground.

'Here, Fang. Sorry.' The dog wolfed down the pie and washed it down with some gulps of water from the bucket next to him.

'Good boy. I'll be back in the morning and you can meet Sveg and the others.' Fang seemed to understand and lay down again, his tail wagging gently. 'Good night, boy.'

At breakfast the next morning, Gerant remembered about Fang. 'Ummm, I can continue my tale at dinner . . .'

'Yes please,' agreed Bree.

'There are a few things to show you as well. You see, one of the things I came back with was a dog.'

Bree's mouth was formed into a huge O with surprise. Marion and Sveg were a little more experienced in dealing with unexpected news, but their eyebrows were quietly raised.

'I can tell you later how it happened. But he has been very well behaved and hopefully he won't be any trouble. He can stay in the courtyard and guard the forge. Do you want to go and have a look at Fang?'

Bree was nodding enthusiastically. Marion was looking at her husband and the look on her face clearly communicated, 'This is your problem, husband.'

'Really? Well, let's go and have a look at this hound.' Sveg was not looking pleased.

They trooped out of the kitchen and headed to the courtyard. As they walked in, the huge dog stood silently and recognised his new friend. But the other people he didn't recognise and he started to stare threateningly at them.

Bree had stopped, as had Sveg and Marion.

Marion spoke after a few seconds.

'He's, umm, very big,' she uttered slowly as she held her daughter by the shoulder. Bree partly hid behind her mother's skirts, peeking out and watching the dog with a very hesitant, worried glance.

'He's OK, Sveg.' Gerant walked up to Fang and patted his head.

Sveg also walked up and allowed the dog to sniff his hand. Fang continued to squat and began wagging his tail. He clearly recognised the leader of this new group that his friend had brought along.

Gerant gave an unspoken look towards Sveg. The smith interpreted it correctly and after a few seconds of thought, gave a brief nod.

'Bree, would you like to come up and pat the dog? His name is Fang.'

The girl looked up at her mother to see what she would say. Marion looked at her husband with a questioning expression and Sveg squinted slightly as he nodded slowly.

Despite any misgivings she might have had, Marion paused and then uttered, 'Gerant, come and help Bree to say hello to the dog.'

Gerant walked forward and took Bree by the hand and led her to the squatting large hound. As if understanding what was happening, the dog did not move. A small hand patted the huge head gently.

'Would you like to scratch his belly?'

A hesitant nod. Gerant hoped this would go well. 'Roll over, Fang.' And he gently rolled the dog onto its belly.

'Like this.' And he scratched Fang's belly, resulting in an uncontrolled spasm of leg movements. Bree tried next and had the same effect. She smiled shyly at her mother and father. Gerant sighed internally with relief.

After several minutes, it had almost got to the point when Marion and Sveg had to stop Bree playing with her new friend.

'That's really fine, Bree. I need to chat with Gerant for a minute. Perhaps you could do your reading practise with your mother? You were doing so well when you read to me last night.'

Sveg and Gerant sat in the smithy talking, although the smith was being rather blunt. Sveg's anger had subsided a little, although he was still somewhat annoyed at being in a position where he felt he had lost a little control and had less room to move regarding the decision he would have to make.

'Let's talk about the dog. For you to expect us to take it on, there are some clear things that need to happen. And no slipping up.' He paused. 'Or the dog goes.'

Sveg marshalled his thoughts. 'First, it is your responsibility to look after him and make sure he is well-cared for. Second, the dog stays in the courtyard. Third, you need to make sure he goes for a walk regularly. I don't want a brute like that wrecking the yard or the kiln because it doesn't have anything to do. And four, food is entirely your responsibility and you will need to work that out and pay for anything you have to buy.'

Gerant quickly thought about each point that Sveg had laid down in his no-nonsense manner and slowly nodded.

Sveg relented a little. 'You might want to go to Zacchary the butcher to see if you can get some meat scraps regularly. If he wants more than four coppers per week, then it comes out of your allowance.'

'There's something else I need to show you.'

'Yes?' The smith folded his arms and raised his eyebrows in enquiry. His look clearly displayed that nothing more would surprise him.

Gerant went into his alcove and brought out one of the sacks and quickly unravelled the twine holding the throat of the sack closed. 'This is what I went travelling to Osmount for. This is talium.'

Sveg couldn't help himself and delved quickly into the sack, pulling out a fistful of the contents. He opened his hand carefully, then began gently pushing the talium flakes around on his palm with his index finger. 'So that's what it looks like. It's very strange. Not what I was expecting.'

A few thoughts occurred to Sveg. *Gods, this is a small fortune here! Wow, it will be really interesting to play around with this stuff and see if it is a good as what that old parchment promises . . . but hang on, if word gets out about this, things could get pretty dicey. Imagine the shady characters that would turn up. I'm not so happy about this . . . if any harm came to Bree . . . or Marion . . . Hmmm, I don't want to put Gerant off, but need to think fast about how to deal with this.*

He confined himself to a curt, 'Just this sack?'

Gerant couldn't help himself and blurted out, 'No, there's another two just like this.'

Sveg nodded slowly, trying to digest what his apprentice had just told him. 'If what the parchment says is true and from what little I have heard, what you have collected is a small fortune. Does anyone know what you got?'

Gerant shook his head.

'Well, we need to hide this away. If the wrong people knew about this stash of talium, we would all be in trouble. Now, where would be a good spot? Hmmm, how about we put them at the bottom of one of the woodpiles and stack firewood back around it. It will just look like it always does. And that dog can make sure no one thinks to just look around out here for the fun of it.'

Sveg thought more and changed tack a little. 'We will look forward to the rest of your tale tonight. I am now very curious about this stuff. We can read over the parchment again and maybe try it in the kiln and smith it. First things first, though. We shift the wood and get it hidden away. Maybe it would be smart to put a small amount in a separate little sack that we can get at easier. Also, we need to do those jobs that Marion has for us. Best not to forget them, or there will be hell to pay.'

Gerant paused for a few moments, looking very seriously at Sveg. 'Thank you. I am sorry about this talium and sorry about the dog. I just wanted to go and see if what was written in the old parchment was true and then things just happened.'

Sveg had a distant look on his face. 'You are not the only one this sort of thing has happened to. Mind you, your adventure trumps any tale I had when I was your age or a little older. But I remember when I saw something that looked interesting and wanted to see more. Then one thing led to another. You see, there was an interesting-looking girl in the next village. Things just happened, and now I have this lovely wife and a beautiful daughter!'

They looked at each other and then together burst out laughing.

Several days later, Gerant went to his alcove and got the smithing book and the folds of parchment in the slit of the cover. With the talium that Gerant had brought back, it had become more than curious whether the cryptic instructions were true or just fanciful musings. They pored over the section in the parchment leaves again.

'Add one portion of talium to nine portions of best quality iron in the kiln to give a steel of unrivalled merit,' intoned Sveg. 'Well, the portions are fairly clear, but we have no further word on what the bloom will look like. We also don't have any idea about how the kiln will behave or whether it will be just like it usually is. I guess we will just have to try and see what happens.'

Gerant got the kiln ready as Sveg had shown him. He had now helped out a few times, and he was hopeful he would do better in staying awake. Also being able to watch the kiln fire to monitor when more charcoal needed to be added and when more iron was put in and the slag broken up and added back in. It would be even more interesting because they would be adding the talium as part of the firing. Goodness knows what would happen after adding in the ore that he had collected on his trip.

The smith and his apprentice shared the night sitting next to the kiln after the initial heating with firewood to get the coals going. Fang had been somewhat edgy for the first hour or so, not used to having Sveg and Gerant staying in the courtyard, but had settled down when the two had spent the first part time quietly sitting and talking. Things had got quickly into the same routine. The point of difference had been when they had added the talium to the iron in the required amounts mentioned in the parchment, at the point when they layered the ore with the charcoal. They discussed whether the temperature they kept the kiln at needed to change, but nothing in the lore said anything about it. So they kept it going with the same bright yellow glow as normally used. As far as they could tell, the bloom looked and sounded exactly as expected. They spent the long hours through the night talking about Gerant's trip, allowing Sveg to ask more questions and hear more details than before. It helped to pass the time, occasionally getting up to put more materials in the kiln, keeping the temperature up, a bite to eat, some water, and so on.

Around dawn, Sveg and Gerant looked at the kiln and saw that the slag coming off had its greenish tinge and the bloom had quietened down and was only gently bubbling. Sveg had another look at the slag.

'See! I believe that the slag is a different green from usual. It looks a little darker . . .'

Gerant also looked on. He pondered about what Sveg had remarked and thought back to the first time he had seen the vein of talium ore after the pool of water flooding the tunnel. 'It almost looks the same sort of glowing greeny-black as the talium in the cave wall. Maybe that means it has melted and is now part of the steel.'

'You might be right. But I think we should let the kiln cool and then we can take out the bloom tomorrow or so. Let's grab a bite to eat and then we can head off to bed. This watching the kiln doesn't get any easier! I am just glad we were able to talk through the hours and keep each other awake.'

Gerant smiled tiredly and helped Sveg tidy up and move everything away from the kiln.

'Goodnight, Fang.' Gerant ruffled the large dog's ears. He checked the rope lead was securely tied and that the dog could not reach the kiln, in case something unexpected happened as it was cooling down and it somehow fell apart. Sveg had already gone back to the cottage and Gerant could not believe how welcome his bedding felt after the long night. He quickly fell asleep, hoping that the bloom had the talium in it and the steel was now somehow stronger but lighter like the old parchment said should happen.

The following afternoon, after both had slept in a little and had a refreshing rest, Sveg and Gerant worked to take the pieces of steel from the bloom and sort it into core and edge steel. They discussed the greenish hue that the steel hinted at and whether this meant the talium had changed the way the steel would behave. Sorting through the pieces chipped off from the main block, there appeared to be enough to forge a new blade, perhaps enough for a sword of normal length. And after discussing the next steps, that was as far as they got.

Thinking later on of what had happened next, Gerant realised he had been annoyed that the message from the guild had arrived. He now recognised it was a very worthwhile project and indicated Sveg's standing in the district as a master smith. Reading a little slowly and with some hesitation after Sveg had passed the scrap of paper to him, Gerant saw that the smith was respectfully requested to visit the guild, at his earliest opportunity, to discuss the drawing up of a new contract for a major piece of work in Cobham.

'I like those bits the best,' muttered Sveg proudly when Gerant passed the paper back. 'Respectfully request. And at your earliest opportunity. Quite different from the way the guild normally writes!' Apparently, the town committee of Cobham had heard about and then seen the gates built by Sveg for the guild in Ashford. They wanted a similar set of metal gates to be built leading into the town on the road from The Capital. Even Gerant could tell that this would take several months of work and would need lots of discussion and working with the authorities in Cobham before they were happy to commence work. It would also lead to some significant coin coming to the smithy and only enhance Sveg's reputation as one of The Realm's best craftsmen working in metal.

'This must be very welcome news,' suggested Gerant.

Sveg humphed. 'Well, I suppose so.'

Gerant could tell, however, that the smith was very pleased with the letter. He was not surprised by what Sveg said next.

'I'll have to go to the guild and see what's involved. Sorry to say, but we might have to leave this talium thing for a little while, and maybe come back to it when we have more free time.'

Gerant nodded, although he knew the decision had already been made for them.

Sveg was also thinking through what this new work meant. 'Of course, I'm content with my lot here. You know what to expect living and working in a place like this.'

'Sure, I could have built up a thriving business in The Capital. On the other hand, there are so many more unscrupulous and shady operators in that place who are just full of words and false promises.

Most of the gentry class are good for custom and patronage, but there are always a few who make a habit of using their position to take what they want knowing that the law will look the other way. Once bitten, twice shy.' Sveg paused as he recalled some of his bad experiences. 'Enough of all this, just remember to keep your eyes open, Gerant. Not everyone is as honest and trustworthy as we like to think we are. At least with this one, we will have our guild helping out. They also don't want to be taken advantage of and particularly not be cheated by their rival town!'

Chapter 15
Growing Up

One-two-three-four-five-six-seven. The figure in the smithy was working with the economical, well-rehearsed rhythm he had been taught. A handspan or so under six feet, still slim in figure, but with well-defined cords of muscles in the arms from working metals every day. It was the same dark and tousled hair, almost shoulder-length, but quite clean and tied at the back with a leather thong. Of note was a somewhat scraggly brown moustache and wispy makings of a beard. The brown eyes sat amid an unremarkable face that clearly could stare off into the distance when the mind was imagining thoughts, yet become very intense when needed. Such as when the young man checked the drawing of the sword he was fashioning, to ensure the hilt was coming together as planned.

Gerant had grown in the two years or so, shooting up quite a bit, with his face becoming a little more angular as it took on an adult form. He would not reach Sveg's height, but was reassured that there was now no question that he would be mistaken for a youth or growing boy. He would also likely retain his slim form and never be as muscled as the older smith. He smiled as he recalled several occasions when other apprentices had foolishly taken him on in arm-wrestling games, only later realising their mistake when those deceptively defined cords of fibres had shown their true strength.

Things had gone fairly smoothly with his apprenticeship and the interactions with the other apprentices. Stork and some of the other troublemakers respected his growing height and strength and kept well away, which suited him. He counted Rachel as a friend and they often worked on group tasks together. That said, he didn't know much of her personal circumstances and only saw her during the regular sessions at the guild.

And there had been no confronting follow ups to his finding the vein of talium at the mine outside Osmount. Gerant had spent a number of sleepless nights early on expecting the door of the smithy to be battered down and a horde of masked ruffians grab the talium and beat him up for the fun of it. Even worse had been the nightmares where they grabbed Bree or Marion and started to hurt them. He had discussed all this with Sveg many times and whether 'William from The Capital' would be tracked back to here or if the associates of Master Hardcross had journeyed to look for him in the big city. In the end, they decided it was enough to keep their eyes out for strangers hanging around the street, interested in the forge. They were confident the talium was well hidden and they certainly didn't chat about it to strangers. Besides, Ashford was a fair distance from The Capital and news of happenings that occurred in that thriving bustle only filtered down to them occasionally. So, after a few months of concern and wariness, but with nothing happening, they had both relaxed a bit and got on with their work and the growing trade that was coming Sveg's way.

More and more, Sveg was content to leave a significant portion of the smithing work coming in to the workshop in Gerant's hands. That meant there were some more complex tasks that Sveg could now take on, either using his years of experience or truly working as a close team to complete projects he would never have accepted when working alone. The gates at Cobham had been weeks of work for the two of them, but it had become a source of pride in how they had turned out. There were now many commissions coming in for Sveg, whose reputation as a true artisan in metalwork had grown in the last couple of years. He could now pick and choose, as coin was not a problem – he could charge what he wanted and even refuse some commissions – and he mostly took jobs that interested him or had an element that called on his skill as a master of his trade.

The piece that Gerant was working on at the moment was something that was engrossing him for a number of reasons. As part of finishing his apprenticeship, he was required by the guild to produce a piece that showed he was worthy to receive the qualification, to be regarded as a journeyman and no longer an apprentice. He had thought a long time about what to make for this defining project and discussed it many times with Sveg. Gerant wanted to make something that had a purpose and would be used, and was less interested in a decorative piece. All the same, Sveg had cautioned him that it had to be an item that was sufficiently complicated and difficult to make and that demonstrated his skill as a smith. Without having to say it, Sveg was also ensuring that the project would reflect well on him. No apprentice of his would ever leave his workshop who was not a highly skilled maker of metal pieces. After much discussion, they had settled on a plainly decorated but extremely well-crafted sword. It would have all the elements of being well-designed and superbly made, also allowing Gerant to make it out of talium steel. Part of the growing success and renown that Sveg had developed in the past year or so had meant there had been little chance to work more with talium. They had been able to fashion a small dagger of talium steel, which showed enormous promise, but had yet to make anything larger. The project to be used as Gerant's test piece for his apprenticeship was also going to answer that question.

During a break from finishing off the sword, Gerant thought of the steps he and Sveg had gone through to get to this point. Once they had decided that a basic but expertly made sword would be a worthy project, they took a morning off and went to the town armoury. First, Sveg had found Captain Amos Moorhead, the head of the town guard in Ashford. He had been on patrol with a couple of guards near the main gate leading out to The Capital and had been more than happy to have a distraction to show them the armoury and its stored equipment. Surprisingly to Gerant, Captain Moorhead was not an imposing figure and must have reached his station perhaps by other skills apart from an overbearing physique and strength. Although now slightly portly and clearly showing his love of a good meal, the guard captain's build suggested he had once been a handy fighter, where speed and agility were his major weapons rather than brute strength. It appeared to Gerant that he and Sveg were almost long-lost brothers. The two had quickly dropped any pretence of official speech and spent the short walk to the armoury talking about past times, people they both knew or those they hadn't heard from for some time. Amos was more than happy to leave Sveg and Gerant to wander through the dimly lit storage area, just asking that they latch the outside door after they had finished.

Sveg and Gerant wandered through the area, looking at various swords, cutlasses and sabres that were placed in racks ready to be issued if need arose. Often Sveg would pick up a weapon and briefly make a comment before replacing it.

'Poorly made. Won't last long once used in earnest.'

'Not too bad. The blade is OK, but they could have put more effort into forging a decent hilt.'

'Just a toy. It wouldn't stop anything.'

'Hmmm. Reasonable blade matched to a fancy hilt. They have used lost wax to fashion that part of it. I would say it's a bit decorative for my tastes, but well-made all the same.'

Gerant pondered the sabre for a few moments and asked Sveg about lost wax.

'Well, I have read a few parchments about it and was shown the basic steps. But I have never really tried to do it very much. Not much call in the line of jobs I normally work on. It is sometimes known as "seer pursue" by some. I think that is an ancient language. Anyway, that is something that a few craftsmen in The Capital are expert in, but I would never lay claim to.'

Gerant didn't respond but would ponder on this news later. They looked at many of the weapons and the apprentice made some sketches on some scraps of paper with a stick of charcoal. These were the ideas that Gerant had worked into his drawing of the sword blade and hilt he was hoping to forge. It was a straightforward and simple design that combined the elements needed to be a functional weapon, with curving lines in the hilt and handle that pleased the eye. Or that was the intention. Of particular satisfaction had been the working of the kiln and making a bar each of the two sorts of talium steel to forge into a blade. Gerant had forged them himself and then melded the two types into a blade that had the core steel edged with the harder steel. They had also discussed the merits of putting in a fuller along either side of the blade to save a bit of weight and add a pleasing profile. Gerant had popped back to the town armoury to get an idea of how fullers were used on other weapons, developing a template to guide their forging.

What was particularly interesting to both of them was the faint greenish tinge of the metal showed that the talium was now part of the blade. Once the fairly plainly designed guard (Sveg had told him these were more correctly known as a quillon), hilt and pommel had been fitted over the tang of the blade, it would be ready for final adjusting, polishing and sharpening. Gerant had spent quite a bit of time trying to get a good balance in the sword. Adding the talium had made it a little lighter in weight than expected, so he had to carefully consider that in crafting the other metal pieces to attach to the blade itself. After lengthy discussion with Sveg, Gerant had kept the design simple without compromising on the strength of the pieces by making them flimsy. That was why they had decided to use a simple braided leather grip rather than wire wrapping, and a plain pommel without a heavy solid metal end. He could balance the sword easily when his two fingers were about two inches from the hilt. Gerant had gone and found Captain Moorhead a few weeks after their initial visit. The captain was very willing to give Gerant a quick lesson in some tips to check how correctly made a sword was and showed the apprentice how to balance the blade on two fingers and see where it sat.

'A correctly made sword should balance steadily about three or four fingers width from the hilt. Too much farther down the blade or closer to the hilt will mean it is extra work to swing. A good sword should be an extension of your arm and your hand. You shouldn't even notice you are holding it.'

The balance was pretty good. Gerant felt a sense of relief and was so glad he wouldn't have to change the pommel or quillons or, gods be thanked, work on the blade to change its length or thickness to get it right.

He took one last look at the weapon and sheathed it gently into a leather scabbard that he had crafted. He was satisfied that he had made a very balanced and well-crafted weapon that would be worthy of a skilled swordsman and be used for many years. He recalled the sheen of the blade with its faint green-grey lustre. At the last minute he had decided to add some gold highlights to the hilt and pommel, using a little gold leaf rubbed onto some of the surfaces. Sveg had initially bridled at the cost, but had subsequently approved when Gerant showed him the way that the gold highlights complimented the greyish sheen of the blade itself.

'Just enough. It is not too flashy but with just an understated elegance that I like. Your instinct was good.'

Gerant flushed with pleasure.

'Don't forget to think about your response once the guild panel have asked you something. Don't rush to say the first thing that occurs to you. It is much better to ask yourself why they are asking the question and what the best response would be. It is a balance of giving them enough information to satisfy them, yet not so much that they think you are above yourself and trying to score a point. They won't like that.'

Sveg stopped and then made some more points. 'Master Fullham will have been asked to come in to provide expertise in smithing when they talk with you. He is a steady, well-known fellow and should be able to judge that your work is of a sufficient standard. He probably won't know anything about talium, so tell him fairly plainly about it. If I am any judge, he will pretend he knows about it and will agree with what you tell him, as long as you don't try to give any details that are too far-fetched. The rest of the guild will look to him to ask any questions about your smithing expertise. I will also let them know I am very happy with your progress once they call me in.'

The day of the apprenticeship assessments dawned fine and cool, with Sveg and Gerant walking the ten minutes or so to the guild compound. Despite Sveg's reassurances, Gerant was feeling distracted and gave only short replies to Sveg's almost random questions and comments. They arrived into the large open chamber, the main room of the guild building. There were a number of masters and apprentices grouped in pairs around the room, clearly waiting for their time. Some twenty minutes later, Master Klyburn emerged from a door, looked around and weaved his way to Sveg.

The rather high-pitched voice emerged out of the large, robed figure, multiple chins gently wobbling.

'Ah, Master Martinson. We are ready for your apprentice. We will then call you in at the end. Come, young man.'

Gerant followed the tutor through the door, clutching a loosely wrapped bundle in both hands. He almost shone, having been scrubbed until he was pink by Marion earlier that morning. His hair and moustache had been carefully trimmed, along with his tunic, pants and half boots that had all been thoroughly washed and cleaned.

The small chamber had a large bench set up across the room with the solemnly dressed figures evenly spaced out behind it. There was a chair on the other side of the table and a plain stool that appeared to have been taken from the tutorial room. Gerant didn't need to guess where he was meant to sit, with the chair reserved for the artisan when they were asked in at a later point. Once perched on the stool, Gerant saw that the guild members were reading pieces of paper and not noticing the new apprentice, apart from an older man at one end. The man was quite bald apart from the band of grey hair around the sides and back, with a large, well-trimmed grey moustache. His grey eyes had a neutral look. The linen shirt and leather waistcoat looked a little at odds with the well-defined muscled arms emerging from the shirt, as one would expect from someone working in a smithy on a daily basis. Although Gerant had not met the members of the guild, the brief description by Sveg meant that he knew he was facing Master Baldock, Master Viridian and the head of the guild, Master Siffray. Of course, he knew Master Klyburn, who was seated at the other end, with a pile of papers in front of him. What followed was really just a series of easily answered questions about how the guild operated and what was expected from a member who recognised its functions. Gerant gave short answers to these enquiries, largely parroting parts of the lengthy lectures given by Master Klyburn. Then followed the more interesting part.

'What is the piece that you are submitting so we can judge your expertise?' intoned Master Siffray.

Gerant pushed forward the wrapped bundle and uncovered the sword in its scabbard.

'Master Fullham, if you would be so kind?'

The balding smith smiled and reached for the weapon and spent several minutes examining it. 'Describe to me how you have made this.' The visiting smith's voice was quite deep and melodic. In other circumstances it would have been a pleasure to listen to in a tavern, or other more informal setting.

Gerant remembered Sveg's advice and stuck to a list of the key points, not really elaborating beyond a very brief description of the kiln process, forging the blade, adding the fuller to both profiles and then attaching the tang of the blade to the quillon, hilt and pommel.

'And tell me particularly about the blade. It appears to have a colour to it that has a greenish tone – more than what I would expect.'

Gerant gave a very short explanation about adding talium to the iron during the kiln process, which resulted in a lighter but stronger blade with the almost eerie green cast. The master smith's face initially had a very curious look where he might have been hoping to gain more details, but quickly changed to a knowing set of features where he nodded briefly. It seemed as if Gerant's words were exactly what he would have expected, given his clear knowledge of talium and how it could be used.

'I have no further questions,' finished Trent Fullham.

'Very well. Apprentice Gerant, you may be excused. Please ask Master Martinson to come in. You may leave your piece.'

The instructions by Master Siffray were clearly part of the process, regardless of how well or otherwise the apprentice had performed. Gerant was quite relieved to leave the chamber and nodded to Sveg as he emerged into the larger chamber.

'Went OK?' muttered Sveg as he walked past, heading for the smaller chamber.

Gerant nodded and decided to go for a breath of fresh air in the guild compound.

After a few minutes of trying to calm his nerves, Gerant walked back into the main chamber. Luckily, he had just come back when the small door opened again, Master Klyburn looked around and beckoned him in. He walked into the smaller chamber and sat back down on the stool, next to Sveg, who had an uncharacteristically serious look on his features.

Master Thomas Siffray pretended to consult a piece of paper, before coughing gently.

'Well, Apprentice Gerant...' Master Siffray consulted the paper very quickly and muttered, 'No other name. How odd!'

'Well, Apprentice Gerant, the guild has considered your answers, noted the comments of Master Fullham and also has been provided with a number of assurances from your supervisor, Master Martinson, as to your skill and suitability. After careful discussion, we find that you have fulfilled the requirements of the guild and can now be considered to have completed your apprenticeship. From now, on you will be regarded as a journeyman. If you return in two days' time, you can pick up the warrant that states you have been adjudged worthy by the Ashford guild. Have you anything you wish to say?'

Gerant was caught unawares. Sveg had not talked with him about this part of the examination. He gathered he was meant to thank the guild but decided to embellish a little. What came out was rather more formal than what he would normally say. He certainly could not have said anything of this sort even a year ago.

'I would like to thank the guild for allowing me to take on this apprenticeship, which has made me a much better person for the opportunity. I thank also Master Fullham for travelling and lending his expertise today and particularly Sveg Martinson for taking a chance and believing in me. I could not have had a better teacher.'

'Hmmm, hmmm. Of course, we are keen to foster talent in our town and wish you the best,' intoned Master Siffray. The other guild members nodded seriously in agreement, apart from Master Klyburn who had a shocked expression on his face. Clearly, he had made a greater impression on this young man than he had realised!

'The sword is very well made. It is a credit to you.' This was from Trent Fullham.

Sveg did not say anything, but his beaming face did not require any words to indicate how he felt.

Two tankards of ale clinked together before Sveg and Gerant took a long couple of swallows. The light in the Wheatsheaf tavern was a little dim and a few of the regulars were talking quietly at the various benches. Sveg took another long pull.

'Where did you get that guff at the end about thanking the guild and thanking Trent and thanking me? I reckon that it might have come out of your rear end. I certainly didn't put you up for it.'

Sveg was clearly in a very good mood after they had left the guild and then decided have a quick stop at the tavern before going home. The older smith had come to realise he had been a lot more nervous about the process than what he had expected and was prepared to admit. When he had been called in to the guild room, he had appeared very calm and gave very measured answers, leaving no doubt that Gerant had become a very competent smith and there was no reason to suggest otherwise. In fact, he had enjoyed the short discussion he had with Trent about the sword and its quality. They had also covered the many other projects that Gerant had worked on with him or crafted himself. The guild members watched the byplay between the two smiths with satisfaction. Some of the more detailed aspects they could not follow, but the sense of the conversation gave no doubts about this particular apprentice. This was one of the easier ones they had to deal with today. The merits of some other apprentices would need a lot more discussion before they could be considered worthy.

'I guess what came out is what you taught me.' Gerant then realised what he had just said. 'Sorry, I didn't mean you taught me to bullshit. Rather, about how to talk calmly and steadily about what you are trying to get across.'

Sveg chuckled and then they clinked tankards again. 'There is a real skill in speaking bullshit that sounds reasonable. That Master Klyburn is someone I could actually take lessons off.'

They finished their drinks after a few more minutes of recounting the meeting at the guild and what they had both been feeling.

'There's one thing we should discuss, however. Do you have any plans? You are welcome to take your time deciding and you can stay at the smithy until you do.'

Gerant had been dreading this conversation somewhat. 'As you know, I am still very interested in the old parchment and doing some more with making weapons and using talium.'

'Go on,' said Sveg, clearly not surprised but interested to hear where this would go.

'You made a comment some time ago about lost wax casting. I would like to learn that, as I can see it could be a really useful art to use in crafting swords and such, mainly the quillons and pommels. I would still want to learn more about using talium in the blades, but the other parts are where I would focus on using this sort of casting. Do you know of any masters that you could recommend that could teach me this?'

Sveg paused while he thought through the names that came to mind, instantly dismissing most of them. 'Lost wax casting is usually only used for the more precious metals like silver or gold, although it is pretty straightforward for things like bronze or copper. Many of the craftsmen that use lost wax that I know are more in the jewellery line and I wouldn't recommend them for the sort of work you would like to do. There is one artisan in The Capital that is known to me and uses this sort of casting for other things besides trinkets. At least occasionally, if I recollect. His name is Trantor Shagreen, apparently preferring to be known as Maestro Shagreen. That tells you something, I would say. He is not someone I know well or have seen much of his work. I do know he has a very good reputation with the nobility, as they are the only ones that can afford his type of pieces. Next time I go to The Capital, I can look him up and see if he would be willing to take you on as a journeyman. Hmmm.'

Gerant could tell that the smith was less than enthusiastic about where the conversation had ended up, but Sveg was willing to do what he could to help.

'I appreciate what you may be able to organise,' Gerant said. 'I am sure I will learn nothing new about bladework or the types of smithing you do, but I really want to try out lost wax casting and what it can be used for.'

Sveg nodded and realised that the nestling was ready to spread his wings and it would happen regardless of what he wished. It would be much better for both of them to make sure the landing was as easy as he could make it.

'Well, Marion will tan our hides if we keep going here. I also said I would grab some fresh butter from Mrs Comfrey's dairy on the way back. Let's go, Journeyman Gerant!'

Captain Moorhead was patrolling with several of his guardsmen the next day when he noticed Sveg and his offsider approaching. The young man was carrying a wrapped bundle. 'To what do I owe this visit on such a fine day, Master Martinson?' remarked the captain, with a twinkle in his eye.

'It's your lucky day, Amos. Well, Gerant, go on.'

'Captain Moorhead, thanks for your help in allowing us to look at some of the weapons in your armoury and talking to me about what makes a balanced weapon. I have finished my training and I hoped you might like to try a sword I made and perhaps find a use for it.'

'Well, this is an unexpected turn of events. Is this it?'

To cover his nervousness, Gerant quickly unfolded the cloth covering and presented the sheathed sword. The guard captain drew it from its scabbard, spending some long moments looking at the workmanship and then tried a few swings and thrusts.

'It's nicely balanced. It feels quite light in the hand, and I like the way it almost anticipates your next move. What's the nature of the steel? It has an unusual glimmer to it.'

Gerant explained to the captain about the talium and how the sword weighed less but was actually much stronger than it felt.

'Hmmm. There is an easy way to check this. Ox, let's see how it goes against you.' The captain gestured to one of his guards, who now that Gerant looked at him, realised that the man was at least a head taller than Sveg and massively built. Captain Moorhead continued on in explanation.

'We call Guardsman Davies the Ox, for obvious reasons. He is quicker than what he looks, and we have yet to find his match in swordplay. He just blocks you and then batters you down with massive blows. He's impossible to best.'

The Ox sheepishly drew his sword and got ready to confront his captain. He would have to be careful not to damage his captain too much – certainly not draw blood – but at least he could prove again how dangerous he was in sword fighting.

Sveg and Gerant did not know what to expect, but the other guards started grinning in anticipation and the expectation that the Ox would again best the captain after a short flurry of blows. It certainly followed that pattern, although the captain appeared to be moving a little faster than usual and was able to parry many of the Ox's strikes or briefly fend them off before jumping aside. The two combatants continued in this manner for a number of seconds. The guards became quite absorbed when the captain blocked a heavy strike from the Ox and then retaliated briefly with his own blow. This did no damage to the Ox but the shock registered on the massive man's face.

'Huh!' was all Captain Moorhead muttered.

Even the two visitors could see the growing frustration and anger emerging on the Ox's features. This had continued far longer than normal, and he had not really been able to land any telling blows. His frown grew grimmer, and he started to growl softly in between huge grunts as he carved a path of fearsome blows towards the captain. Yet every blow was thwarted with a wicked parry, or a quick jab or blows from the captain that he had to defend. He was moving the captain back slowly, but not really gaining any clear advantage. The Ox undertook a rapid and massive series of blows that his superior would not be able to avoid. The captain was progressively pummelled under this rain of blows and was not able to retreat, as they came faster and faster with massive force. All he could do was to give slightly and bend his knees to try to absorb the blows and fend them off with his new weapon. The Ox snarled and went in for the killing blow, all thoughts of relenting on the captain clearly forgotten. The other guards were yelling encouragement as they cheered the Ox on. A last huge blow was launched at the captain that he only just caught with his blade. The Ox's sword slid down the other blade towards the hilt of the captain's sword with massive intent. Then, there was a sudden *kting*.

The Ox looked at the abrupt jagged blade stump which was all that was left of his weapon and realised that the captain's sword was held against his throat. After a few moments when both of them continued panting heavily, Captain Moorhead withdrew the edge from the Ox's throat.

'I believe you will have to concede that one to me, Guardsman Davies. But because of the worthy tussle and what has happened to your blade, you can have my old one. That's the least I can do.'

Sveg began to chuckle as the captain unsheathed his old sword and presented it to the Ox. The other guards also began chuckling and slapping the Ox on the back with appreciation. The Ox just looked confused. He had been bested in a swordfight for the first time since he had been a hulking lad, but they were congratulating him on it.

Amos Moorhead had a very serious look on his face as he continued to examine the talium sword. 'Not even the faintest nick. Gods, this felt so light and nothing can usually survive blows like the Ox uses. Tell me about this blade. I have never seen anything like it!'

Gerant talked about adding talium to the iron during the kiln process. He decided not to mention the old parchment, as it would sound a little far-fetched and part of some sort of black magic.

The captain nodded along as he heard the story and looked at Gerant with a new-found appreciation. 'What you have made is a special thing and I would be more than delighted to retain it. This will be the stuff of many stories of my prowess with the sword. Of course, it has nothing to do with such an amazing blade.' He winked. 'If this is anything to judge you by, you have a long and prosperous future in front of you, young man.'

The guard captain peered at Sveg. 'This lad has come a long way. You taught him everything useful, of course?'

'Hrrrmph. Of course, Amos. But that is the subject of a longer conversation over a tankard of ale. You are buying, I take it?'

The banter between the guard captain and the smith had clearly resumed as part of their long-standing acquaintance. 'Perhaps at sundown, Master Martinson. But first I need to get these lads back to the business of protecting the town. And also try to repair the Ox's pride, of course.'

The guard captain gestured to his troop with a smile, and they began to move off towards the southern gate.

The two smiths worked seamlessly on a new project to build iron supports for one of the bridges over the River Greenthorn. Several carters had been complaining to the guild that heavily laden carts of produce and timber were causing some alarming groans in the timber bridge, and they were concerned it would give way. The guild had ignored them for several years but now a delegation of some of the more influential merchants had joined forces with the carters and they could no longer be put off. Sveg and Gerant quietly moved around each other, anticipating each other's move, and compensating for it with practice built up seemingly over many years, even though it was much less than that. They also were very practiced in keeping up a running conversation during the short breaks between using the anvil, checking pieces of metal in the forge and the usual routines needed in the workshop.

'So, how are you going to afford living The Capital as a journeyman? It doesn't pay all that well and expenses in the big city are so much larger.'

One-two-three-four-five-six-seven. 'I was thinking of using some of the talium ore and selling it for coin. Is that far-fetched?'

Sveg pondered on this during the next cycle. 'No, but you would have to be careful. You might need my help on this. I have a few contacts I could approach who might give a fair price. It would get people talking if a country lad turned up with some talium to sell. It would not go so well.'

One-two-three-four-five-six-seven. 'You're right, of course. I hadn't thought enough about it. I will be hard-pressed to find some lodging and have the coin to pay for it.' Gerant grabbed the drawings so they could see where this particular metal flange fitted into the crosspiece they were working on.

They both looked over the design and then they were ready to start working again. Before they did, Sveg continued the conversation.

'Why don't I make a quick trip to The Capital? I can look at selling some talium for you and also look up Maestro Shagreen and see whether he would be willing to take you on. I also have a few bits and pieces myself to look into.'

'That would be terrific, Sveg. I would have no idea about doing any of that sort of stuff.' Gerant thought about asking what the extra things were going to be on the trip, but he decided Sveg would tell him in due course if he wished to.

Chapter 16
The Capital

Sveg checked the pack horse one last time and made sure he had everything. He clasped arms with Gerant and gave Marion and Bree huge hugs.

'Safe trip, husband.' Marion was matter of fact but still had love and concern showing.

Sveg swung up and made sure things were balanced. Then he smiled, waved briefly to his farewell audience, gently flapped the reins and clucked to the horse to get it to walk off. Marion and Bree held each other tightly as Sveg disappeared up the street. Bree had certainly shot up in the last year and was becoming a capable young woman. Not surprisingly with the parents she had, she was someone with a mind of her own. Gerant had felt more and more like an older brother and was quite comfortable with giving and receiving some of the spontaneous shows of affection he was subjected to. The three of them walked into the smithy, Gerant remaining there and the other two continuing on to the cottage.

As Sveg plodded off, he recalled how earlier he and Gerant had uncovered one of the sacks of talium ore from its hiding place in the woodpile and portioned out enough for a pouch sufficient to hold a few oranges. That was one of the items they carefully had packed onto the horse, down the bottom of one of the leather panniers, well out of sight.

He had outlined for Gerant a little of what he was intending. 'This will take me a few days, probably closer to a week, by the time I get everything finished. It will be important to take my time and not rush things. Luckily it should be no issue with staying at Redman's Inn for the days I need.'

Two mornings later, Sveg stopped the horse and pulled to the side of the road, looking over the view ahead. Every time he crested this ridge, he always spent a few moments to take in this first view of The Capital. It never ceased to impress him. The smoke from cooking and kitchens hung in a slight cloud over the valley ahead. Rising above this on the extensive promontory above the mouth of the River Greenthorn was the multitude of buildings making up the main city of The Realm. The sunlight brightened each building and gave them an extra glow, casting each of them with a yellowish tinge in the early morning clear light. Sveg was glad he didn't live here – it would be a challenging place to make ends meet – but all the same he looked forward to his visits and particularly enjoyed this initial view. The road wound up to the start of the expanding cityscape and then disappeared into the clutter of houses, shops, rooftops, spires and other buildings too far away to work out their purpose, with the castle brooding over all at the top of the promontory. All the parts made up a thriving city still several miles away and silhouetted against the sky.

Arriving at one of the imposing gatehouses sitting astride the road from the west, Sveg dismounted from his horse and nodded to the guards standing passively at either side of the archway. He could follow the main thoroughfare through the city to the River Quarter and Redman's Inn, but he had long ago found a short-cut through some of the twisty laneways that were quite narrow but easy enough if leading the horse. Some little time later, he saw the comfortable-looking brick and timber facing of the inn, with the large sign of a silhouetted figure outlined in red. Tying up the horse at the hitching post, Sveg wandered in and was immediately noticed by a short but overweight man with muttonchop sideburns extending down from his snowy mop of hair, ruddy cheeks and who was wearing a nondescript tunic affair over a mainly white apron.

'Well, look who's here! Sveg from Ashford, clearly wanting to complete his usual shady business deals before escaping again into the countryside.'

'Always the same patter, Dorian.' Sveg grinned. 'Yes, I am from Ashford, but my business is totally above the board. It should take me maybe three or four nights. And I need stabling for Corporal.'

'Well, your usual room just happens to be free and has just been cleaned, so we'll call it the usual rate. I need to look after our regular customers,' said the innkeeper, chuckling.

'Thanks. I'll take Corporal round the back and bed him down. Then I've got a few chores to do and need to head out for the afternoon. I'll see you about supper time, I guess.'

A short stroll up the hill took Sveg to the Argent Quarter. He always found the noise of The Capital a little overbearing for a few hours, compared with the sleepy sounds of his hometown. That was another reason why he preferred living where he did. He turned onto a cross-street to the main thoroughfare that headed up to the castle. About halfway along was a two-storey house that had been converted into a series of apartments and small businesses. Climbing up the narrow wooden stairs, he reached a desk in the corridor with a slim, bespectacled man busily scribbling in a large ledger. The man looked up as Sveg approached.

'I would like to see Hamish if he is in.'

'He is expecting you?'

'No, but he knows me from long past. Tell him Sveg is here to see him about a delicate matter.'

The man focused again at the visitor and a look of recognition passed over his face. 'My apologies, Master Martinson. I get so immersed in the accounts I often don't recognise a known visitor. I am sure that Master Wheelwright will see you right away. Just a moment.'

The bookkeeper smiled apologetically and hurried through a door just past his desk. A hurried but muffled conversation ensued. Shortly thereafter, a second man emerged and came forward with his hand outstretched in greeting.

'This is a lovely surprise! It must be at least a year since you last came by. Come in, come in.'

Hamish Wheelwright was a tallish individual with prominent wrinkles around his grey eyes and carefully trimmed brownish hair tending to grey. He was wearing a purple velvet tunic, linen pants and soft shoes. As Sveg followed him into his office, he gestured to a comfortable armchair on the other side of his large table, covered in a multitude of ledgers and loose papers. Each part of the table had a separate pile with a large stone on top. Clearly the metal trader was a very systematic man who liked to be well organised in his affairs. He leant back with his fingers splayed across his mouth, waiting for Sveg to indicate why he had come. Many years in business had taught him to be patient and not rush things.

'We have known each other for a long time. You have always given me fair price for any metals I have been wanting to buy.'

Hamish nodded, leaving his fingers steepled. So far, he had not heard anything new.

'Normally I have bought iron or copper or other things. But I know you also trade in many metals and also buy ore and metals, including silver and gold.'

'True.' Again, he had heard nothing new.

'It turns out I have a little bit of ore I would like to sell for the right price.'

Another nod. In other words, continue.

'By unusual circumstances, it turns out I have some very pure talium ore that I would like to sell. Interested?'

Although his fingers stayed steepled around his mouth, the metal trader's eyes became even more focused, drilling into Sveg's. Nothing was said for a number of seconds.

'As you know, I trade in all metals: copper, brass, nickel, iron, lead, silver, gold, many others. There is always a market and it is just a matter of knowing the market price and adding a small amount to cover my costs. But talium.'

Hamish paused again for many heartbeats, ordering his thoughts. 'I used to trade in talium. As you would know, it is very, very rare and many people are interested in it. That is part of the problem. When I was much younger and much less experienced, I tried to set up a deal involving talium. I won't go into the details. Let me just say that people are prepared to do almost anything to get talium, often way beyond the market price. I ended up being badly beaten up after I delivered the talium and it took me many months to recover.'

The trader sighed at the memories. 'Never again. My apologies. I would be happy to buy any metal from you – gold or silver – and give you fair market price, but I draw the line at talium. It is not worth my safety. I am too old these days. And too wise, perhaps.'

Sveg now felt terrible for having brought this subject up. He had always found Hamish to be a very calm and thoughtful person, and to watch the play of emotions that had crossed his face at the memories of what he had experienced was quite confronting. He was glad he didn't know any of the details. 'My friend, I have asked you something that I had no idea would be so troubling for you. Forget I spoke.'

'No, no, I am long past these memories. But I am also afraid I cannot help you in this instance.'

'I do understand. Nevertheless, I do have an amount of very pure talium ore to exchange into gold coin. Is there someone else you could recommend who I could approach?'

A pause. 'There are very few who would have the connections and be able to deal with this. The only one I could suggest is Sterling Capuchin. But you would know that I put his name forward with some reservation.'

Sveg almost choked and then burst out laughing. 'The so-called Count? Gods, is that the only alternative?'

Hamish spoke in a measured voice and very calmly. 'Despite his somewhat unusual ways of working and his keenness to talk about his prowess, he does appear to have the necessary connections to take this sort of trade on. Not many can. He knows everyone in The Capital and everyone knows him.'

After his initial outburst, Sveg thought through what the trader was suggesting and realised there was little choice. He recalled the brief number of times he had dealt with the count. Everyone knew that Sterling Capuchin's family links with the nobility were tenuous at best, and it was merely an affectation to try to increase his prestige and bargaining position. Clearly, the more times he had said it to people, the more people had believed him, particularly those more gullible, who were entranced with the flashy, impeccably dressed individual and his now famous mannerisms and way of speaking. Despite the flowery and complimentary words, there was a steely resolve to beat down anyone to a low price and cheat them out of a fair deal. Sveg had been told once by someone in the trading game to know the market price of what you were trying to exchange. If you didn't, then when someone like the count got around to naming their price, work out five times that value and start bargaining from there. When you had dropped down to around three times the starting price, that was often fairly close to what the market was paying. Much lower than that and you would be making a poor deal. Sveg had also heard a number of stories that despite the respectable appearances, Capuchin was quite happy to arrange little incidents to his advantage. Of course, nothing could be traced back to Count Sterling Capuchin, who would be as shocked as anyone at what had happened.

'Well, I will just have to go in with my eyes wide open and watch things very carefully.' Sveg's features were grim, clearly showing he would not put up with any nonsense.

'My apologies again. I have been in this business for many, many years and part of the reason I am still trading is I keep away from talium. I believe the count is able to do this only because he plays to win and so far has been very lucky. Or else he has powerful protection. Or his competitors are not willing to cross him unless they are really feeling brave.'

The two men caught up on their news for some time, then shook hands and Sveg left the Wheelwright premises. At least he didn't have far to go. It was only farther up the Argent Quarter and close to The Park – where the castle was – and where the very prosperous citizens had their mansions.

Following the main thoroughfare towards the palace and The Park, the houses went from functional to being larger, finer and more decorative. The number of carts, horses and people had also dropped away. This was not the thoroughfare to the Port or Market Quarters and taken up with everyday folk going about their business or moving produce, hard-earned goods or handcrafted items. This was more for merchants and other traders bringing food and other needed goods up to those wealthy enough to pay for the delivery and not bother getting it themselves. The road itself was paved in stone rather than lower down where it was well-worn packed earth with clear wheel ruts. In this aura of wealth and prosperity, the very large and well-made mansion flanked the avenue on the right-hand side, almost abutting the ornamental gatehouse leading to the top of the promontory and where the royalty lived. The stone ramparts and wall of the old citadel from centuries ago had been well maintained but now functioned as a visual barrier to remind the people of the centre of power for The Realm. Sterling Capuchin had clearly been trying to have his residence as close to this privileged area of influence and authority as he possibly could. Sveg walked through the twin entrance doors with expensive glass panes. Inside was a large salon with several seated individuals along one wall and a man in an embroidered purple coat with gold trim standing behind an ornate counter. All in the room looked up when the smith walked in, with those in the chairs quickly going back to their various musings. Having experienced this several times in the past, Sveg knew that those sitting were hoping to get an audience with the count and having to wait until they passed into the next room to wait again, under the watchful eye of a slightly more senior flunkey. He walked up to the man behind the counter.

'My name is Master Sveg Martinson. I am here to discuss a trade with the count that I am sure he will be interested in.'

'You have an appointment?'

'No, I have only just arrived in The Capital.'

'And the nature of your business?'

'That is for the ears of the count. A matter of great import and a rare opportunity. He knows me and also knows I would not waste his time. I came immediately as soon as I realised that the count was the only person in The Realm capable of handling it.' This was said with a straight face. Sveg knew from past experience that to get to see the count, a certain amount of flattery was needed.

'Ahem. Well, I will take your name, and someone will attend to you in due course. The count is a very busy man and unfortunately cannot see everyone. Please take a seat here.'

Sveg found a chair and resigned himself to a long wait. After what seemed several hours, but may have been half an hour, Sveg had progressed through several waiting rooms and had actually made it up to the second floor. He recognised he was getting close and had finally whispered, 'Talium', to a more senior and experienced but similarly uniformed man in an upstairs room. Significantly, there were only three chairs in this room and no one else currently waiting.

'Talium, talium,' muttered the man softly as he repeated the word Sveg had whispered to him. He suddenly recalled what the word meant, and his eyes widened. 'Of course, Master Martinson. I am sure the count will be very interested. Wait but a moment and I will see if he is available to see you straight away.'

Without looking at Sveg for a response, he quickly ducked through a door at the end of the room and was gone for only a minute or so.

The person that emerged through the same door was the actual count himself. Sterling Capuchin was a moderately tall person who had been slender in former days, but many years of luxurious living were starting to show in his build and now rounded facial features. He was wearing a superbly fashioned cream-coloured silken doublet, copper-coloured tights and soft leather boots that encased his lower legs up to the knee. Sveg could see a number of silver and gold rings with precious stones on his fingers and he wore several slender golden chains about his neck and wrists. His flowing, golden locks were beneath a small velvet cap and reached shoulder-length. Clearly, he spent several hours each morning being dressed and manicured before he began any weighty discussions and business deals. As he approached Sveg, the count smiled in welcome. Sveg had experienced this peacock-like visage on previous occasions, which tended to suggest to visitors that this fop must be simple minded and that negotiations could only end up in their favour. He noticed that despite the carefully composed and welcoming features, the almost-black eyes of the count did not change their careful looks and remained very observant.

'Ah, my apologies, my old friend. I have been run off my feet today and they only just told me you had arrived. Otherwise I would have been out straight away. Also, when Manners told me you had come to discuss talium, I had to hear more. Do tell, old friend. I am all ears.'

Sveg let the various half-truths and embellishments go past without comment. 'I won't waste words, Sterling, as I know your time is valuable.'

The count nodded that this was, of course, the situation, but his eyes didn't waver from Sveg's face.

'I don't need to give you the details, but into my possession has come a quantity of very high-grade talium ore. Clearly this is a very precious and unusual item to sell. Only a handful in The Realm could put it into the right hands, as only very few know its worth and what it can be used for. You were someone who I thought could find a buyer.'

Although the expression on the count maintained its benevolent, welcoming look, Sveg thought he could now see a quick flash of greed, which was quickly masked.

'Well, finding a buyer for talium is always difficult. It has perhaps some value, but it is often very hard to arrange things so it ends up in the right hands. Quite a hard challenge. I would have to think about it a bit more.'

Sveg could feel the bargaining already starting to occur.

'How much talium are you offering? You have it here?' The count looked at Sveg politely with eyebrows arched.

'All together, a small sack of maybe a half a pound or a little more in weight. Say, the equivalent of four oranges. I didn't bring it all with me in case you were not interested, but in here I have a sample.'

Sveg knew exactly how much talium he had brought. He and Gerant had very carefully discussed how much to bring and then weighed out that amount using a borrowed set of scales. In the sack was enough talium to be the equivalent weight of one hundred gold coin. Clearly there was far less coin than this in the cottage, or in Sveg's carefully hidden hoard. With some careful sums they had weighed the talium against the small pile of coin and done the transfer in smaller batches.

Sveg passed a small leather pouch with a drawstring to the count and waited while the taller man opened the pouch and poked a finger into the contents, peering in carefully. After a few moments, he passed the pouch back.

'Well, I may be able to organise something. But it will take me a little time to test some contacts. Would you be able to come back here in say, three hours, and we can continue the discussion? I have someone who I think would be interested. When you come back, we might be able to agree on a price and arrange delivery. You are staying at Redman's Inn, as usual?'

Sveg covered his shock at the count knowing exactly where he was staying. 'I can return around then. I have a few other errands to complete that will fill in the time. Of course, we may not be able to agree on a price. I have to look after my interests as well . . .'

'My dear man, of course we will be able to agree on a price. When has it never been so? I have a reputation of fairness to live up to. Come, Manners will show you out. I'll cancel my other meetings and go and see a couple of acquaintances about this. Good morning to you, Sveg.'

As Sveg wandered almost aimlessly in the Market Quarter sometime later, he reviewed the conversation and started to think about what arguments he would make when talking about price. As with all these sorts of arrangements, it was a matter of putting together truths, half-truths and the occasional lie to build a convincing argument. Hopefully the person you were negotiating either agreed with what you said or at least knew it was just part of the process of bartering and a price somewhere in between could be agreed on. Sveg had already settled on what he was willing to be bargained down to. It had been very helpful just at the end when Hamish Wheelwright had told him what a reasonable exchange rate for talium might be. It was then a matter of seeing whether the count had different ideas on how little he could outlay to get the talium. Also, whether he believed there might be other buyers that Sveg could consider. The truth was, Sveg dreaded having to find others to approach, which would take a lot more time and effort to seek out. He reached the clothing stall he had been ambling towards and started inspecting the wares on offer. The older woman with grey hair in a bun rose from her stool as she recognised a potential customer and came forward.

After dropping off his purchases at Redman's Inn on the way back, Sveg climbed back up into the Argent Quarter to the count's mansion. This time there was no waiting or formalities. As soon as the first liveried man saw the smith walk in, he hurried forward and escorted Sveg straight upstairs. The several traders and other visitors waiting on their chairs frowned in frustration and disappointment that someone clearly more important was able to be taken straight through.

Sveg was taken to a large salon with a number of paintings and clearly expensive furniture scattered in strategic parts of the room. Several large rugs covered the polished floorboards. Count Sterling Capuchin was leaning against the mantelpiece reading from a piece of paper to one side of the fire set in the hearth. He looked up when the smith walked in, with the flunky quietly closing the double doors behind the smith.

The count walked over to a desk set against the wall, dropped the paper and gestured to Sveg to join him by the window where two comfortable armchairs were set up on either side of a small round table. After a minute or so of bland comments about the weather, the state of The Realm, increasing taxes and so forth, the count got to the point. 'I have been able to speak to several contacts and they might be interested. The market for talium was very strong two years ago, but just at the moment they are less enthusiastic. But because you are known to me, I would be able to offer you the equivalent weight in gold coin for the talium you have brought.'

The count sat back a little with his professional smile in place, but his dark eyes watched Sveg eagerly to see his response.

So the bargaining has begun, thought Sveg. 'That is an interesting offer. I am not sure who your contacts are, but my own contacts have indicated they can never get enough talium and it is always in very short supply. These very well-respected buyers would be willing to offer me five times the weight of gold coin. But because you have such an important standing in The Realm and this is such a good amount of talium, I should give you the right of the first offer.'

Sveg also leant back and watched for the response. The count nodded briefly, seemingly acknowledging that this counter-offer was as expected and that some of Sveg's words may not be true, but that was to be expected in this dialogue.

'Well, I suppose I could see if they were willing to move a little on the price. As you say, I have good standing with them. If I could get them to accept double the weight in coin, would we have a deal? This may not be possible, and I would have to call in some big favours, of course.'

Here we go, thought Sveg. *Lucky I have already thought about my next offer.* He took a slow deep breath and launched into his counter-offer. 'I respect your contacts and their standing, but I believe they have forgotten how much effort goes into getting this amount of high-grade talium. We have the high price of a permit to prospect, the dangers of the mining and how little talium ore is left in the mine at Osmount. Then they need to consider that most of what is coming out of Osmount is floor sweepings and flint pieces made to look like talium. You have seen the quality of what I am offering. You will not find better. In these circumstances, the people I represent might be able to accept three times the weight of gold coin, but not a copper less.'

The smile on the count had not changed – these dealings and being able to come out on top were what he most enjoyed – but his eyes had hardened even more.

'Well, I have the feeling that we are splitting hairs. My offer of twice the weight in coin was more than reasonable. Perhaps I could convince them to pay another silver in weight. Or if you wanted to wait while I check another contact who might be interested, we might come to a slightly higher price.'

The longer this bartering to and fro went on, the more Sveg felt that he would lose out. The count was far too practiced at this; this was what he did every day and the stories of how he had made enormous profits by bartering down unfortunates and then selling the next day for a fortune regularly circulated around The Capital. Sveg decided to call the bluff and go for everything.

'I appreciate the efforts you have made on my behalf, Count. It is unfortunate your buyers are not as understanding as you. I'll follow up with my other contacts, who have already been wanting to purchase. I thank you for your time and am much obliged. I will be happy to see myself out. Good day.'

Sveg had carefully composed his features to indicate regret and looked anywhere but at the count's face as he stood up and started to walk towards the double doors leading out of the salon.

'Wait but a moment. Come and sit back down. Let's not be hasty.'

Sveg's hand rested on the door handle, and he smiled secretly at the door, before turning with his features carefully composed. He walked back to the armchair and sat down, watching the count's face. The professional smile was still in place, but Sveg thought he could see a degree of quiet fury. Or maybe he was imagining things.

'My client was very insistent that he would pay more only if I guaranteed the quality of the talium and that it had not been obtained by illegal means. If the rest of the talium matches the sample you showed me, I am willing to confirm the first point. Because I know you and your standing, I am also willing to stand by the second point. These are very unusual circumstances, but I am authorised to offer you . . .' The count paused. '. . . offer you three times the weight of gold coin for your talium. Is that acceptable?'

Sveg did not speak but offered his hand in acceptance. The professional smile on his adversary slipped a little.

'Shall we say you return in the morning with the full amount of the talium and we can arrange the exchange for coin? Of course, this deal is a matter of great secrecy, as my client is very well known and would not want the details to be known to the public.'

'Of course. I will not say a word. Ever. And I should be able to bring the talium here by about mid-morning. A pleasure doing business with you, as always.'

Sveg shook hands with the count again, noting how the grip was very loose and felt like a cold, clammy fish.

Walking down the main stairs of the mansion, Sveg could not help thinking that the unusual circumstances were that for once Count Sterling Capuchin had been forced to pay actual market price for something. The need for secrecy was probably nothing to do with the mysterious buyer and more about the news reaching anyone influential that things had not gone as planned, as far as the count was concerned. He could not resist skipping a little down the stairs before he resumed his normal tread at the bottom and left through the heavy double doors at the front of the mansion.

Chapter 17
Closing the Deal

Arriving back at Redman's, Sveg entered the side door leading to the upper floor and quickly glanced into the bar area as he walked past on the way to the stairs. He had got a few paces when there was a loud, 'Sveg'. He retraced his steps just as the inn owner popped his head around the corner of the doorway.

'I thought you should know that there was a stranger asking after you. I said you were out and they were satisfied with that. I asked if there was any message or a name and they didn't answer and just walked off.'

'Hmmm. Thanks.'

Sveg started up the stairs to his room. Odd. Very few people would know he was in The Capital. Who was this person and what was their business with him? He opened the door to his room, still thinking who it might be. As he glanced about not really paying attention, he suddenly tried to remember exactly where the packages from the market had ended up when he had come back earlier. He was sure one of them had ended up near the pillow on the bed when he had tossed them. Now both of them were together towards the foot. He looked around carefully, trying to picture how things had been placed. He walked over to the large pack he had brought from Ashford. Working through the contents, he saw that they had been carefully arranged, but slightly different to the order he knew he had packed at the cottage. Going back to his market purchases, he could see that the cord tying them had been carefully undone and then retied.

Sveg clattered downstairs and headed around to the stables at the side of the inn. He found Corporal and gave him a quick pat on the neck and a small lump of sugar. He walked into the stall the horse was in. Looking up into the dimly lit roof area, he reached up and carefully felt in a narrow gap between the top of the wooden planks and the roof beams. He was relieved to feel the leather sack which gave slightly when he prodded it. Making sure it remained undisturbed, he gave the horse another pat and headed back inside.

In the bar area, Sveg found the innkeeper talking with one of his staff.

'A moment, Dorian, if you don't mind.'

'We can come back to this order in a few minutes. I won't be long.'

They found a quiet corner to talk. Sveg outlined to the inn owner what he thought had happened. The usually cheerful-faced older man's countenance got progressively grimmer once he realised the consequences of what Sveg told him. The smith had already worked out what he wanted to do.

'If I can keep the room for another day, I might actually go to the Crafty Fox and stay there until I go back to Ashford. Keep pretending I am staying here, of course. Also, have you got a long ladder that I could use?'

Dorian thought for a moment and then nodded.

'Here's what I would like to do.'

A little-used door at the rear of Redman's Inn giving access to the back laneway opened with a slight squeak. A cloaked and hooded figure just under six feet in height stopped and peered in both directions carefully. Satisfied, Sveg slipped quietly down the alley used to deliver barrels of ale to the inn and headed deeper into the River Quarter towards the Crafty Fox, another inn he had stayed at on occasion.

In the morning, Sveg Martinson appeared at the mansion of Count Sterling Capuchin. He was wearing a loose-fitting cloak that hid his clothing underneath. He also appeared to have put on a little weight in recent times, although this had to be a guess as the cloak hid everything rather effectively. Similar to his previous visit, the smith was shown directly in when he reached the first liveried man, but was taken to a small chamber on the ground floor towards the back of the mansion. Another liveried man was already standing next to a table on which a large set of scales and some plain sacks had been placed. There was also an enormous individual with long moustaches and dark brown hair tied loosely at the back. He stood against the wall with his heavily muscled arms crossed, scowling without saying anything.

'He will be here very soon,' twittered the smaller man nervously.

The Count almost immediately arrived, all pretence of delight and pleasure missing from his features. 'You have the talium?'

Sveg opened his cloak and undid the twine holding the sack tied to his waist, placing it on the table. The count spent several minutes sorting through the talium, making sure it was the same quality as what he had seen in the small pouch the day before.

'Let's get this done quickly. I have several important meetings to get to. Cooksley will weigh the talium and calculate the exchange for gold coin. Bear is here just because there is a lot of coin in the bargain and to make sure that no funny business happens.'

At the mention of his name, Bear scowled even more but still said nothing. Cooksley then placed the sack of talium on one arm of the scales and piled gold coins on the other arm, softly counting. The count pretended disinterest and examined his nails and checked his rings. Sveg had no need to pretend and watched every action of Cooksley with rapt attention.

'Ninety-five, ninety-six ...' The dish containing the growing pile of coins started to waver a little as the arms of the balance started to have equal weight on either arm.

'Ninety-eight, ninety-nine ...' The needle on the dial of the scales was almost vertical.

'One hundred gold coin is the correct amount. Three-fold is thus three hundred gold.'

'Yes, yes, just get on with it,' muttered the count loudly.

Cooksley seemed to be secretly enjoying the process but quickly ahemed, twittering nervously, and counted out another two hundred coin. He placed the entire amount in a leather sack before quickly tying it closed with a leather cord.

'As witnessed by myself, you, Cooksley and Bear, the trade is complete. As requested by my client, there will be no written record of this.' The count had a grim smile on his face. 'I must be off. Good day.'

He left the room without a further word. Sveg carefully tied the sack to his belt and re-arranged the cloak over it. Although it looked like he had suddenly become trimmer in his figure, he noticed how much heavier his hidden stash of coin was. He nodded to Cooksley and noticed that Bear had not moved or changed expression, but the brown eyes followed him out the door of the small chamber.

The cloaked figure walked down the main thoroughfare of the Argent Quarter and into the River Quarter, occasionally stopping to look at shop windows or move out of the way of riders or the occasional cart. It had only been a few minutes of subtle checking behind him before Sveg thought he had identified the two figures following him about fifty or so paces back. He was careful not to fully turn around, which would have indicated he knew he was being trailed.

After ten minutes or so, Sveg reached Redman's Inn. He paused at the door to the bar room as if in thought, and noted that the figure in the grey cloak ducked quickly into a doorway a little down the street and disappeared from view. He had not seen the fellow in the blue outfit for several minutes but was sure he was within call somewhere close. He walked into the bar area and tapped a finger on his nose as he walked past on the way to the stairs and the guest rooms. Dorian was behind the bar. The owner grinned and also tapped his nose with one finger.

The window of one of the inn guest rooms was suddenly hitched up so that it was open. A hooded and cloaked figure carefully climbed out and onto a ladder that had been left leaning onto the wall below the window. After climbing down, the figure checked that their climb down had not been observed and carefully placed the ladder lengthwise against the base of the inn wall. The figure checked again and then carefully turned into the back alley and headed off farther into the River Quarter.

Sveg climbed down wearily off Corporal and threaded the reins through one of the slats next to the smithy doorway and tied them loosely. He realised how tired he was and how much he was glad to be home. He ferried the bits and pieces lashed onto the saddle and put them in the forge. Gerant wasn't working, although the coals looked like they had been recently fired and there were some pieces of curved iron laid next to the anvil. Sveg realised it was just after midday and probably Gerant was having a short break for lunch. He grabbed a couple of the packages and headed up the walkway to the cottage.

'Hello, hello, I'm back.'

There was a squeal of delight and Bree ran full pelt into Sveg from out of the meals area, causing a whoomph of surprise as his daughter barrelled into him. The response from the other two were more measured. Marion smiled as she walked up for a deep hug.

'Welcome, husband of mine. A successful trip?'

Gerant hung back, smiling with pleasure that Sveg had returned, as expected.

'Is there any food from lunch left? I came straight from Cobham and haven't eaten yet.'

As the four of them sat around the kitchen table, Sveg related his news, or at least some of the bits. He had already decided that he would tell his wife and Gerant the full story at a later point. There was no need to frighten Bree and so he would stick to recounting the pleasant bits.

'So I managed to get a fair price and had no issue with exchanging the talium for coin.' With a flourish, Sveg reached down and deposited a leather sack onto the table with a heavy clink.

No one was willing to ask, until Bree blurted out, 'How much is in there?'

'Only three hundred gold.' Sveg laughed uproariously at the shocked expressions on their faces. Then his face took on a serious tone.

'I have never seen so much coin in one place, and I am sure you all haven't either. We need to put it somewhere safe very soon and with the rest of the talium and our own coin, we are running out of places to secrete things away. So my suggestion, Gerant, is that we both take it to Banker Croker in the morning and leave it with him. He charges a small fee to look after it and it also means you will have to come back to visit every now and again to get extra coin when you run out in The Capital. Another nice thing with that sort of arrangement is we will get to see you on those occasions, I would hope.'

Gerant realised he hadn't thought far enough ahead about this and was grateful that the smith had clearly spent the ride back from The Capital working out these details.

'I was trying to work out where to keep the rest of the talium when I start in The Capital. I hadn't even thought about the coin. Your suggestion is very good. I'm very glad you thought of it.'

Bree had been eyeing off the other packages that Sveg had carried in. 'So what did you bring me from The Capital, Father?'

'Bree!' Marion's instant reaction of horror at the forwardness of her daughter was replaced by relief when she saw the cheeky grin on the young lady's face, matched by the knowing features on her husband's face as he had quickly realised the manner in which the question had been made.

'Well, my brazen little wench, I did go to the market and bought a few things.' Sveg reached into one of the packages and pulled out a couple of small items that he presented to his wife and daughter. Inside were beautiful bracelets where thongs of leather had been woven into a complicated design after being threaded with several sorts of coloured beads. He received several big hugs for these.

'And to make an appropriate impression on the people in The Capital, a new journeyman needs to have at least one outfit when meeting important people and patrons. Hopefully it will fit well, although I am sure you could ask Marion if she would make any necessary adjustments.' With that, Sveg presented Gerant with a larger package. Gerant coloured red with embarrassment, particularly with the realisation that they were all watching him expectedly. He quickly undid the wrapping and held up a doublet in dark brown that appeared to be made from a velvet-like material.

'This is too much,' he said, looking at Sveg and Marion in turn.

Marion looked at him with fondness. 'No. You are family now. This is the least we could have done.'

The embarrassment continued when he was forced to parade around the kitchen in his new doublet, which fitted him rather well and wouldn't need much adjusting.

That night after dinner, Sveg, Marion and Gerant sat around the kitchen table, with Sveg talking more about his trip and some of the more unfortunate parts. Bree had headed off to her room, as she had some schoolwork to finish for tomorrow. They had laughed at Sveg's account of the negotiation over the price to be paid for the talium, and shook their heads with relief when he talked about being followed and his climbing down the ladder in case the ruffians had tried to accost him in the room at Redman's Inn.

'You took a huge risk, Sveg,' marvelled Marion. 'Weren't you frightened?'

'I won't even pretend that I wasn't. But often I didn't have time to think about what could happen if things went poorly. It was only on the ride back that I truly pondered on how fortunate I had been.'

Gerant realised that now was as good a time as any to bring up what he had decided. During the afternoon, he had quietly sifted through the sack of coins, letting them slide gently through his fingers over and over as he realised what this meant for his future life in The Capital. He could now spend a little more time, if he needed to, finding some suitable lodging and he hoped this Maestro Shagreen would agree to take him on as a journeyman. He knew he could always stay working with Sveg. But he wanted to show Sveg and Marion how much they meant to him. So, he carefully counted out some of the coin and put it in a small pouch.

'Sveg and Marion . . .'

They both looked up, knowing that Gerant was going to say something important.

'I wanted to give you this as a small thing to say how much I want to thank you for letting me come and live here. It is only ten gold, but I hope you will accept it.'

He placed the small pouch on the table. Sveg appeared suddenly to be very angry. 'We refuse. That was not the reason we have done this. It is not about wanting to take money from you for your board and lodging. It was something else. You will need all the coin you can amass to survive in The Capital.'

Gerant smiled at them both with the same sort of cheeky grin that Bree had displayed earlier. 'But this is strictly a business deal. This is rent for keeping most of the talium here in its safe place. The other condition is that when I come back to visit, there is no charge. Also maybe a bit of an upgrade on where I stay. Perhaps in the cottage? Doesn't need to be fancy, but I think I've outgrown the alcove a little. And I also expect no charge for Fang and he gets a choice steak for his dinner every night. Agreed?'

There was a shocked silence. A range of emotions crossed Sveg's face. Anger was replaced by confusion, then astonishment, then a huge grin and a roar of delight erupted. 'You cheeky young pup!' he yelled as he reached over to furiously ruffle Gerant's hair.

Marion burst into tears and rushed around the table to envelop Gerant in a huge hug. It was now clear that they all felt that Gerant belonged in this family and, even more, how important it was to all of them.

Chapter 18
Relocation

Gerant was slowly getting used to the slightly uneasy feeling of the rhythmic and rather gentle swaying as he sat on Corporal's back as they slowly walked along the road to Cobham. Fang padded along next to the horse. The past few weeks had involved Gerant going down to Coran Smalltop's yard, leading out Corporal, saddling him and then riding out with the trader so he would get comfortable riding.

'No, Gerant, just relax. You are too tense. They can feel it if you are afraid. Just enjoy it and be part of the horse. Corporal is far too well trained to do something stupid and bolt off.'

It had taken Gerant several sessions before the trader was happy that Gerant could saddle a horse by himself and be still atop at the end of the journey.

Over a tankard of ale Coran discussed things with Sveg. 'The lad will never be a natural horseman. He's still way too stiff and needs a really quiet mount like Corporal.'

Smalltop had refused anything but a token payment of a single silver for what the three of them had discussed. Gerant would take Corporal to The Capital and would leave him at Redman's Inn once he had finished. Coran was in The Capital at least every week ferrying goods and it was no issue to pick the horse up. If Gerant had need of a horse to come back to Ashford, he need only leave word with Dorian Redman and the news would get back to the trader. Corporal or another quiet mount would be left at the inn stables within a few days.

The leave-taking had been hard but full of fond memories. Sveg was like an old mother duck, constantly reminding Gerant of new things to remember, or items to get, or places to check out in The Capital.

In the end, Marion had spoken sharply to the smith. 'For the God's sake, Sveg, that's enough advice. This is the fourth time you have mentioned that leather merchant in the Florian Quarter. I am sure he has remembered.'

Most touching had been Bree. She had only appeared at the last moment. Gerant had been starting to think she wouldn't appear. But she had walked out of the dimness of the forge just as Gerant checked for the last time he had everything and Fang was slumped down calmly awaiting whatever was going to happen. It happened very quickly. Bree walked up to the young man and gave him a freshly picked daisy. She gave him a very quick hug, stood taller on her tippy-toes and whispered in his ear.

'Good luck and come back soon ... brother.' Then the young lady quickly disappeared back into the forge and towards the back of the cottage. Sveg and Marion shared a private look of contentment when they realised what had happened.

Gerant laughed again as he recalled Marion's reaction to the many words of advice and instructions Sveg had given him before leaving. All the same, he had never been to The Capital and was grateful that with all the preparation he pretty well knew where he was and what to expect on the road.

'About an hour from the city, you will come to a little village called Nutley. Just a dozen cottages and a tavern. But you know you are getting close, so follow the road up the slope and once you are at the ridgetop you can see The Capital. I always stop for a look there.'

As Sveg had forewarned, Nutley was a small grouping of dwellings on the side of the road, along with a small building with a door and one window – perhaps a tavern or a shop – with woodsmoke leaking out of the chimney. The couple working in the vegetable gardens did not look up as Gerant, the horse and dog ambled past. The road saw a lot of cart traffic and groups going from and towards The Capital. But they did look up when a troop of soldiers clattering past on mounts, before going back to the planting and weeding.

The road followed the gentle rising of the land towards the ridge, which had a line of oak trees that marked the top of the slope. At the summit, a small clearing and the remains of campfires showed where travellers often stopped before braving the challenges of the large city sprawled across the end of the promontory at the other end of the valley. Gerant slipped off Corporal and held the reins while he looked ahead. He realised that the inside of his thighs were starting to ache. He would be glad to stop riding, although resigned himself to an hour or so more. The road ahead curved to the left towards the river and disappeared into a grove of trees, reappearing at the bottom of the slope. It looped gently along the valley floor, always about a hundred yards or so away from the water. The houses commenced about two miles or so farther down, initially lining the main road but increasingly spilling out into the fields. According to Sveg, this was now known as the New Town Quarter. A little to the right, the buildings looked larger and closer together. That must be the Market Quarter. Farther still, Gerant could see the blue of what must be the sea. He guessed that from books he had looked at and from Sveg's description this would be where the Port Quarter would be, where ships left and arrived with goods from all over The Realm. Following what must be the path of the river back from the sea, it looked like there might be a couple of large bridges crossing the water. But he could not be totally sure as it was a long way away and the lingering wood smoke from many fires made details not as clear as they might be. The city was like a carpet laying on the side of the promontory. More and more towards the top, the buildings were fewer, but they were much larger, probably indicating wealth. It was impossible to guess whether they were houses or large public buildings like the guild hall. One stood out, and Gerant thought it might be some sort of church based on the drawings in a book he had looked at. Even at this distance, the old city wall could be seen like a browny-grey thick ring encircling the oldest part of The Capital. There were less but larger again buildings sitting farther up behind the wall and there appeared to be quite a few trees and some open spaces. Sveg had said this was The Park – where the ruling family lived in park-like gardens and that if he had the chance he should just walk around there, provided the guards let him enter. Going into the palace buildings was not allowed unless you had specific business with the ruling family or the central administration, and had an appointment.

After a few more minutes looking over The Capital and realising just how new everything was going to feel, Gerant tied Fang's long lead to the pommel of the saddle and levered up onto Corporal again. 'Come on, Fang. Try to behave yourself, as there's going to be a lot of people to go past.' He clicked the horse into motion, and they started off around the curve and down off the ridge towards the now much larger and slower-flowing River Greenthorn.

There were so many sights and sounds to take in. Gerant had followed the road down and reached the beginnings of the city. Even here, there was lots going on, with people going in and out of buildings and builders working on the skeletons of new dwellings on either side of the road. The Capital looked like it was rapidly expanding. Gerant could count ten or twelve half-finished houses within sight and other groups of men clearing areas where wooden stakes had been driven into the ground indicating where new buildings would be started. He reached the main bridge over the River Greenthorn. It was a sturdy construction of stone with several spans, arching over the hundred feet or so of slowly flowing current. At that point he hopped off the horse and started walking, leaving Fang's lead tied to the saddle. It was going to be easier leading the horse; he stopped frequently to almost ogle a new sight, or marvel at the hustle and bustle of the city, the number of people, children running in and out of the crowds, carts and drays, riders and the occasional horse-drawn carriage.

After some time, he recognised one of the landmarks Sveg had mentioned. 'After the bridge, you will eventually come to The Cross. Continuing on, you will enter the Argent Quarter and eventually get to the Old Wall. Left is to the Florian Quarter and right is to the River Quarter. So turn right and about two hundred yards farther on is Redman's Inn. The sign at the inn makes it obvious.'

He was glad he was leading Corporal as it was easier to edge his way to the right and turn down that large street. One of the things that he had already noticed was that everyone knew exactly where they were going and did not slow down as they ducked in between overladen carts or riders walking rapidly towards them. The many men, women and children on foot changed direction seemingly at random as they went about their business. Appearing up ahead was a two-storey timber building with a swinging sign on hooks showing the outline of a man picked out in red. Gerant tied up Corporal, told Fang to lie down and not move. He considered taking the little baggage he had inside but realised Fang was a far greater deterrent if someone was unwise enough to approach Corporal. So, he just went inside to find a person matching the description of Dorian Redman.

Such a person was found at the bottom of a set of stairs after Gerant had recognised and then followed the squat figure out of the bar talking rapidly to another man, both of them in dark clothing and linen aprons. 'Excuse me, Master Redman.'

Dorian turned to see who had mentioned his name and saw a youngish man somewhat taller than him (not that that was hard to achieve) and of slim build, with dark hair tied in a thong at the back and with dark brown eyes. The man's expression was solemn without being threatening, not smiling but also not sad or angry. There was a certain alertness to the features that Dorian couldn't define further. He was clean-shaven, although it looked like he hadn't touched a razor for a day or so. 'IIow can I help you, young man?'

'My name is Gerant. I believe you know Sveg Martinson. Sveg said to see you and hopefully be able to stay here until I find somewhere in the longer run.'

'Ah yes. Gerant. Sveg did mention you might be along at some point. We will put you in the room Sveg normally uses. Our rates are seven silver a night, including meals and things like stabling a horse and such. Have you got Corporal? This is almost a second home to him.'

The innkeeper chuckled quietly at his own joke and Gerant couldn't help smiling along with him. He already felt that this man was a friend and that he could ask him for advice about living in this big city.

'Yes, there is Corporal . . . and my dog who is no trouble. I can leave him here as well?' Gerant hoped he would get a positive answer.

Dorian didn't miss a beat. He had over the years witnessed many strange requests and this one was not even particularly difficult. 'Oh, just bring him round the back and tie him up. He'll be fine.'

Dorian thought again. 'Sveg also mentioned that you would be looking for somewhere to stay. You could stay here, of course, but I am running a business, and you would likely run out of coin fairly soon. I have asked around and there might be something quite suitable not so far from here. Mrs Lamming lost her husband a few years back and her previous lodger took up a post in Pearl City. So she has been looking for someone suitable. It's a small but tidy cottage, the rate is very reasonable, and she is looking for someone who can help her out with shopping and any heavy things and to look after her garden. She will provide meals and such, that will be included in the lodging price.'

The innkeeper noticed that despite his slim build, Gerant's arms looked like they were very used to hard work. Thinking further, it was not surprising given his trade.

Gerant made a mental note to again thank Sveg for planning and thinking ahead. He didn't have a clue where to start and had been dreading having to look around strange streets and try to ask strangers about places to live. 'My thanks, . . .'

'Oh, call me Dorian. We don't need to bother with this mister this, master that here.'

'I am very grateful, Dorian. This sounds exactly like what I will need. Where does this Mrs Lamming live?'

The innkeeper took Gerant out to the stable area and showed him where to bring Corporal and where he could keep Fang for now. He also explained very quickly some directions.

'Just walk out to the street and keep on going. Take the next street to the right and head towards the river. You are looking for a short street on the left with a brown stone house on the corner with timber trim painted blue. About four doors down that street on the right there is a small white timber cottage with a wooden paling fence. That is where Mrs Lamming lives. The plot is somewhere in the New Town Quarter and she could show you if you both agree about becoming the new lodger.'

After getting Corporal settled, he tied Fang to the post on the edge of the stable door. 'Back soon, boy.' Fang had become quite used to this sort of thing. He knew his master would return at meal times and for a quick game. This new spot had some interesting new smells and sounds. He snuffled and stretched out, shut his eyes and started to snore. The nose sniffed occasionally, checking an interesting smell wafting on the gentle breeze.

Gerant opened the little wooden gate carefully and stepped through. The few plants in the tiny garden between the fence and the front wall of the cottage were neatly maintained. The whole front of the cottage was only about ten feet wide, nestling in between the two neighbouring houses. It looked like it was single storey and who knew how far back it went. It felt like it was going to be quite small. Likely it was not even as big as the quite compact cottage at the back of the smithy at Ashford. He knocked on the painted white door. After a few seconds there were sounds of quiet shuffling approaching.

'Who is it?' The door stayed shut.

'My name is Gerant. I have just come from Redman's Inn. I believe you are looking for a new lodger.'

There was silence for a few moments and then the door opened slowly to reveal a small, slightly hunched figure of an older woman with carefully brushed white hair drawn into a bun. Her face was a mass of wrinkles and she looked at the young man on her doorstep with eyes squinting, as though her eyesight was not as good as it used to be. She appeared sufficiently satisfied with what she saw.

'Come in, young man. My apologies, but it pays to be careful. The neighbourhood is not as safe as it used to be.'

Gerant shut the door, while she watched him doing it, and then followed the older lady down a short corridor, past a room that looked like a parlour or sitting room, a shut door and then a kitchen area with a table and chairs, wooden cupboard, stove and a bench against a window. There was a small room opening off the kitchen, presumably which the lodger would use, next to another closed door that probably went to the outside. Gerant sat down at the table where Mrs Lamming indicated.

The conversation over the next twenty minutes or so was a series of questions about Gerant's intentions, where he came from, what he was going to do and many other aspects. He got the impression it was partly to satisfy her need about someone who might end up being her next lodger, but mainly about Mrs Lamming having someone to talk to. So, he was quite happy to give the old lady some details of his past, the reason he had come to The Capital and so forth. When he got to the part about telling her about Fang, his size made her start to mutter a little.

'So big. This place is tiny. He's this big?' Being seated, she held her hand level with her neck. Gerant wondered how he could convince her and then had a really great idea.

'He is really well behaved and spends most of the day sleeping. He is a great guard dog and would not let anyone come in or make any threatening actions towards you. You would feel really safe with Fang around.'

The old woman pondered on this as she talked to herself. 'Fang sounds like a very dangerous name. But I like the idea of having someone around during the day. I would certainly feel safer opening the door when someone knocks. We used to have a dog years ago. That was only a little thing, though.' She continued on without a break, this time to Gerant. 'Maybe you could bring the dog around at some point and we can see.'

And so on to a hundred other things. Suddenly, the conversation took an unexpected turn. Then he realised that Mrs Lamming had already made her mind up.

'As you can see, the room is not very big, but it should suffice. I will cook all the meals for you and you help clear up. And I would like you to come with me to the market every few days as carrying food all the way back is getting harder and harder. Also you would need to keep the plot weeded and growing vegetables and such. It saves so much coin that way and the food is always nicer made with fresh stuff straight from the garden.'

'Umm, where is the plot, Mrs Lamming?'

'I can show you tomorrow. We could go to the market, and it is ten minutes' or so walk farther on. There is a small shed with some tools in it. Make sure I don't forget the key before we go.'

Gerant digested this news and what it meant. It all sounded perfect. She liked to talk but that was all. He would get used to that. Anyway, he would be away for most of the day working and she had said she would provide meals, wash clothes and things like that. It was too good to be true.

'And the lodging costs?' Gerant waited with his breath held, steeling himself for the bad news.

'Since my husband passed, there has been no one to do the heavy work and keep the plot going. I would really like an honest, hard-working young man like you to help out. I realise it may be too much to ask, but would a gold piece a month be too much?'

The old lady watched Gerant keenly and waited in silence for a response. Gerant couldn't believe his ears. He had been expecting to pay at least that much every week.

He paused. 'I think that would be something I could afford.' Gerant felt a little bad that it sounded like the amount was almost too much, but realised he had already said it and couldn't unsay the words.

'Oh, young man, my heart skipped a beat just now. I thought you were going to refuse.' Mrs Lamming beamed in delight. 'Here, let me put some water on to boil for a hot drink. Now, do you want to bring your stuff tomorrow and then we can go to the market?'

A comfortable hour was spent talking with Mrs Lamming. Gerant had then been shown the room that would become his, opening off the kitchen. Mrs Lamming had a concerned look on her face, as if her prospective lodger was going find the space too pokey. Gerant interpreted the look correctly.

'This is actually quite roomy, Mrs Lamming. It's much bigger than I am used to.'

Afterwards, he walked back to the inn. He was feeling rather pleased with how things had gone so far. Checking the path of the sun, he saw it was mid-afternoon and still some hours before sunset. He decided to work out where Master Shagreen lived and see if his luck would continue.

Arriving at Redman's, Gerant found Dorian behind the bar, keeping an eye on a couple of early customers seated and enjoying their first ale. His reaction indicated genuine pleasure that the young man had found suitable lodging and would move out in the morning. He rapidly listed directions to the Florian Quarter and getting to Maestro Shagreen's residence. He smiled quickly at Gerant before turning and welcoming a new customer who had just walked in, clearly looking for a drink.

Gerant wandered up to The Cross, walking slowly and taking in the frantic noise and hubbub of the city. He looked briefly to the right and stopped against a convenient wall to take in the wide street leading up to the old wall some way off, clearly visible in the afternoon light. After a few minutes, he continued on across the busy crossroads and into the Florian Quarter. Very soon he reached the house described by the innkeeper and sat down on the edge of a water trough to look it over. The two-storey house was well-built in stone and had a number of windows looking onto the street. The main entrance was inset into a stone-faced arch, with three steps leading up to the panelled door painted in grey, with white trim. Gerant could not recall any house in Ashford that was nearly as fancy. From what Sveg had told him of the owner, it was a fair reflection of his status. The owner was someone who was extremely well regarded in their craft, having built up their reputation by providing valuable and well-designed pieces to the ruling class and others who could afford to pay for the best. The building, its cleanliness and how well-looked after it was told of success and good fortune. Gerant could not see if Master Shagreen and his artisans did any of the crafting work at the house. Maybe there were work areas out the back, out of view, or there was a separate workshop somewhere nearby. He would have to find out. After a few more minutes looking things over, he walked up to the door within the stone archway and knocked. After some moments, the door opened and he was looking at a figure standing expectantly. The young woman had black curly, shoulder-length hair, a naturally friendly face, blue eyes and an upturned snub nose above rosy lips held in a gentle smile. While she could hardly be called tall or even of moderate height, the green dress accentuated her feminine hips and well-developed bustline. Her eyebrows were raised in gentle enquiry.

'I was hoping Maestro Trantor Shagreen was home. I would like to discuss with him about an opening he may have for a journeyman smith.'

The young lady had clearly been expecting someone else, perhaps a visitor calling for another purpose. 'Oh, that's odd. He didn't mention anything like that. The family is away today but will be back tomorrow. Perhaps it would be best if you could come back then.'

The news was given in a polite way, but Gerant could feel that this conversation was about to end.

'I will come tomorrow then. Is there a particular time that would be best?'

'No, but I will let him know you called.' There was a pause, laden with unsaid questions. 'I didn't catch your name.'

'Gerant. I believe Master Sveg Martinson has mentioned me to the maestro.'

'I am sure you are right, but I wasn't told.'

Silence followed. Gerant couldn't stop looking at her and then finally thought of something to say. 'I didn't catch your name either.'

As the young lady started to close the heavy front door, her smile widened. 'Molly.' The door shut firmly and Gerant was left wondering what had just happened.

Chapter 19
Settling In

Gerant led Corporal past the quaint wooden cottage with the paling fence and around the corner to the narrow back lane. Fang padded alongside obediently. The night at Redman's Inn had been uneventful. He had supped on the beef pie and vegetables along with a tankard of ale, sitting in a corner of the bar room, just watching. The noise around the bar swirled as bits and pieces of conversation reached his ears from all sides, along with random clinks, thumps and snatches of laughter and shouting. He had made a quick check of Corporal in the stable and taken some offcuts of meat for Fang and then headed off to bed. He was now quite practiced at saddling up Corporal and tying on the various sacks, pouches and panniers that he had brought with him. He quickly reached the back of Mrs Lamming's cottage and the small open area between the neighbouring dwellings and the alley. There was a small stone sink abutting the back door, presumably for washing clothes, along with a small set of shelves with a few pots, some hand tools and wooden boxes. He unloaded Corporal and stacked his gear near the back door. Then he looped Fang's lead and Corporal's reins around a post on the edge of the alley. Rather than give Mrs Lamming a fright with someone suddenly banging on her back door, he told Fang to lie down and walked back down the lane and around to the street. He knocked.

'It's Gerant, Mrs Lamming.'

The shuffling noises approached the door and this time the door opened straight away. The old woman stood there beaming at him. 'How lovely to see you, Gerant. I was just starting to wonder what the strange noises were outside the back door, but I assume that was you?'

Gerant followed her down to the kitchen. 'I dumped my gear there and have to take the horse back to the inn. Also, I put Fang out there so you could take your time to know him.' *And for him to get to know you*, Gerant thought, not saying that aloud.

He opened the back door. The horse turned its head around at the noise and the large brindled mastiff sat up quickly and started wagging when it recognised the figure in the doorway.

'My, he is big. He won't hurt me, will he?'

'No, don't worry, he is well trained. And he is tied up over there and won't move unless I tell him to. Maybe let's leave the door ajar so he can get used to the sounds and see you moving about. And it would be helpful if you are able to talk to him a little, so he gets used to your voice.'

The old lady took it all in, in her hesitant way.

'I just have to take the horse back to the inn and then we can go to the market.'

Mrs Lamming gripped the doorpost and watched the huge dog very carefully. She nodded slowly. 'He won't get loose, will he?' she trembled.

'No, he's well behaved. Lie down, Fang. Stay. Stay. Good lad.'

Gerant unlooped the reins off the post and paused. 'I will be back as soon as I can, Mrs Lamming. It should be only for a short time.'

Mrs Lamming nodded again, her eyes not leaving the dog lying down in her small rear yard. Fang lay there, not moving, with his massive paws on either side of his spade-shaped head. Gerant slowly started to walk off with Corporal, watching the large dog carefully. With a final, 'Stay, Fang', he headed off to Redman's Inn as fast as he could.

Gerant hastily pulled up the end of the girth strap until he could unhook the strap and quickly pull the saddle off Corporal. He gave a quick wipe down of the horse with some straw, making sure the bridle and reins were hooked up on the wall and the horse had some chaff and water. After a last quick check, Gerant almost ran the short distance back to the cottage. This could be the shortest lodging ever if things had gone badly while he was away. He rounded the corner into the alley and forced himself to slow to a walk. He carefully came up to where he could see into the yard. Phew, Fang was still there, tied up, with his paws next to his head. Coming farther in, Gerant got a shock, then started smiling. He saw an odd sight. Mrs Lamming had brought a kitchen chair and was seated in the doorway, knitting rapidly while she chatted away to Fang. She looked up as she saw a shadowy figure appear from the alley. Squinting a little, she recognised her new lodger. She smiled broadly.

'I have been telling Fang all about what we will look for at the market. I am hoping there are some fresh beans and maybe a nice leg of lamb that will last several days. He is a very good listener.'

Fang's furry brows seemed to react as he recognised his name and the tail started to swipe back and forth gently. Gerant let out his breath in a gentle sigh of relief.

A short time later, the older woman and young man started off for the Market Quarter on the other side of the River Greenthorn. Gerant was holding a canvas pouch while Mrs Lamming turned the key, locking the front door to the cottage. He suddenly remembered about the garden plot they were also going to visit.

'I knew I would forget the shed key. Just one moment while I get it.' She unlocked the door again, disappeared inside and came out again brandishing a small key on a pink ribbon.

They headed off. This was all new to Gerant and he was happy to walk at the gentle pace set by Mrs Lamming, taking in the sights, as she chattered away next to him. He would gently interrupt the flow of words with the odd question about what he was seeing.

'This is a different bridge to the one I came over yesterday?' Then, 'Is that the port there? Are those ships?' And once they had arrived at their destination, 'Does this market serve the whole city?' This latter question was as he followed around the old lady, who knew exactly where she was going and which stalls to visit. As well as its fair share of cottages, houses, shops and other buildings, there was a very large square surrounded on the four sides with buildings up to two or three stories in height. The market was a swirling mass of chattering, shouting people, dodging in and out of aisles between stalls and oncoming handcarts piled high with produce. Most of the stalls were set up in the open, but here and there were others grouped underneath roofed areas with no walls, so as to provide as much space under cover as possible. Gerant had on occasion been to the market in Ashford with Sveg or Marion, but The Capital market was many times larger and busier. If it had been a little quieter, he would have spent more time looking at some of the stalls. There was some food and produce he did not even recognise. Perhaps it came from other parts of The Realm and wasn't grown locally.

Mrs Lamming quickly made some purchases for meals in the coming days and handed a leg of lamb, some beans, apples and a small paper bag of sugar to Gerant to stow into the canvas pouch. At the butcher stall, for a few coppers Gerant had bought some meat scraps and a couple of bones for Fang.

'How do you know what you want and which stalls to buy it from?' Gerant asked.

'I have been coming here for years. Since Mr Lamming passed and my boarder left, I have only been coming once a week. I am very glad you are here, as I can start buying things on a more frequent basis and making some things I haven't for a little while.'

The garden plot was about ten minutes' walk farther on, on the edge between the Market Quarter and New Town. Gerant noticed that the houses were a little smaller than in the older parts of the city and were crowded together more. Here and there, there was a small open area that hadn't been built on. He surmised from the carefully fenced and tended ground that this was used by the residents to grow a few extra things to eat, particularly fruit and vegetables. Quite close to the river, Mrs Lamming led him to a small open area bounded by the wall of a house at the back and on either side. It was probably no more than twenty feet wide and twenty feet deep, with a small shed-like structure in the corner.

'My husband had a bit of coin at one time to buy this small plot. He had big plans to build a cottage on it, but we never got around to it before he passed. He did used to come down here and enjoyed digging the soil and growing a few things.'

It looked like the weeds were starting to take over a little, but the old lady very proudly showed Gerant some beds with potatoes in it, a small area with carrots and some other vegetables that she told him were cabbage. He could see there was maybe a day's work to get things back to some sort of neatness and then maybe an hour once a week to weed, check on growing plants and start on new things.

'It is very little work, really. And we can buy seeds at the market, and I will show you what needs to be done. It's just the work is too heavy for me to do by myself.'

Gerant was more than happy to agree to this small chore, given how little he was going to pay for lodging. Together, they walked over to the shed, which was only five feet high on all sides, with a corrugated iron roof and a small door closed with a chain and padlock. It took him a bit of fiddling to get the door open with the key on the pink ribbon, and he tried to remember next time to bring a little bit of oil to work into the lock mechanism. He opened the small door and crouched to look in. There were a couple of small wooden boxes with packets of bits and pieces. Mrs Lamming told him they were seeds and other things. Leaning up against the back wall was a long-handled spade, a hoe and a few other tools that he recognised from working on similar items at the smithy in Ashford. He took each one out and inspected the metalwork in the daylight. They were nothing fancy, but not too badly put together. He might take a couple and reinforce them and make the shafts fit more snugly, if he managed to get a place with Maestro Shagreen. He had a quick thought and looked at the floor of the shed. It was fashioned with wooden slats sitting on a couple of larger blocks of wood placed on the ground. He reached down and tugged them a little. They were set reasonably solidly. He thought about this a little more. It would be pretty easy to saw through the ends near the back so some of them could be levered up. It would be an easy matter to dig a hole underneath and place a leather sack in there, replace the floorboards, put the tools back and close the small door with its chain and the padlock clasped shut. No one would suspect anything other than some gardening tools and such were being kept in the tiny shed. It would be a perfect place to keep the talium he needed for his smithing and bladework. The stash hidden in the woodpile at the Ashford smithy would be the main stock, but he could safely keep some here in The Capital. It was well away from where he hoped to be working, or even Mrs Lamming's cottage. Even more so, only a few people knew about her small garden and where it was.

Walking back to the cottage with the purchases from the market and a small bunch of baby carrots from the plot, Gerant easily stayed in step with Mrs Lamming and that meant he could think more on his plans while walking. In the next day or so he would take the sack of talium currently being guarded by Fang once he had modified the wooden floor of the little shed. Then it would be perfectly natural to go and do a little weeding and planting every now and again, taking a canvas pouch or similar with him to bring back whatever was ready to harvest from the plot. And underneath the cabbages or potatoes or whatever would be the amount of talium he needed for a kiln run. As Sveg had shown him several times, if things looked normal and it was what people were expecting, then there would be no trouble or awkward questions about what he was carrying. Gerant became quiet nervous thinking further about these next steps. Here he was making all these grand plans for using talium and making wonderful daggers, swords and other weapons. But he had yet to introduce himself to Maestro Shagreen, who might refuse to take him on. As he continued walking next to the old lady, he resolved to return to the residence in the Florian Quarter and see if Maestro Shagreen would see him. Of course, first he had to get Mrs Lamming back safely to the cottage, before he hurried off to confront what was building up inside himself as a real turning point. He liked to think he would be welcomed with open arms, but it was certainly conceivable that he would be given little chance to explain his value and be shown the door very rapidly. That nice young lady had been a bright spot yesterday, but he was now more than a little worried that his meeting with the maestro might not go well. Or even worse, he thought, he wouldn't even get that far.

A short while later, Gerant headed off on his next task. He had carried the shopping in and checked Fang had some water and given him one of the bones to gnaw on. The large mastiff was quite content, particularly with the bone. Mrs Lamming also was quite comfortable now with the second of her two lodgers and was happy to have Fang off the lead. The dog plopped down a few feet from the open back door, happily destroying the beef bone, while his new older friend chattered away to him about the trip to the market and what stalls had stocked what food and the prices. Gerant smiled contentedly as he headed off. How quickly some things changed.

He wondered if he would have more luck today as he knocked again on the white door filling the arch-shaped entrance at the Shagreen residence. A brief pause and the door opened, revealing the same young woman. Today her hair was tied up with a green ribbon that matched her dress. Her face had a serious expression as she opened the door, changing to a cheeky grin as she saw who was standing there.

'Ah, Mister Gerant No-other-name! Maestro Shagreen knew of you and should be able to see you. One moment while I check.'

Gerant was left standing for some moments not knowing whether he was meant to follow. He thought it prudent to wait on the doorstep. A soft cough and a beckoning young woman at the beginning of a hallway opening off the open entrance hall suggested otherwise. The front room he walked across was tastefully furnished and had an engraving on one wall of a large town that he recognised as an older version of The Capital. There was also a generously proportioned wooden staircase that spiralled down from the second floor to spill out to the left of the front door and across from the hallway where Molly waited. Gerant followed her down the hallway, where various closed doors opened off to the left and to the right. Molly reached a door on the right, knocking quietly. After opening it, she gestured the visitor through. Gerant found himself in a large room lined with bookcases and several windows that allowed the strong morning light to flood the room. After he had entered, Molly quietly closed the door behind him. Seated at a large desk was a man of maybe thirty years or so, dressed in a navy-coloured doublet and trousers. He had carefully combed slightly curled ginger hair cropped short and a goatee beard that was a little darker, with more brown shades in it. He finished drawing a line on a piece of paper and put it into a drawer in the desk, before shutting it. Gerant saw briefly before it was put away that it appeared to be a design for a sword hilt.

The man watched him without speaking. He stood up, and Gerant saw that the man was quite tall – maybe three inches over six feet – and with a strong build. There didn't appear to be any fat on his frame. In contrast to his height and build, he noticed the man's hands were delicately shaped and on the thin side. *Artisan's hands*, Gerant thought. On his right hand was a ring with a large gem – possibly an emerald. The man opened another drawer in the desk and took out another piece of paper and read it briefly again. The maestro spoke, in a moderate baritone, neither softly nor loudly. He was clearly used to people listening to what he had to say and dispensed with any formalities.

'This says that you were apprenticed to Master Martinson and that he is very happy with your skills and training. You have your warrant?'

Gerant handed it over. Shagreen barely glanced at it and handed it back. 'Tell me what you can do.'

Thereafter followed a long interrogation about what Gerant had learnt. He could tell that the maestro had a good basic understanding of working with a forge and metalwork. After some time, the older man stopped and gestured to a nearby chair while he sat down again at the desk.

'My particular skill and reputation is making superb pieces for those who have sufficient coin to pay. That means many of my clients are from the gentry. I specialise particularly in metalwork using lost wax casting. I am now wanting to branch out a little and make highly desirable weapons using a combination of lost wax for the more elegant parts combined with superbly forged blades. There is a strong and growing market for well-made blades with the upper classes. That is why I am willing to take you on.'

Gerant was hard put not to start smiling and kept his features serious.

'You will be on three months' trial. Should your work be satisfactory, I will keep you on for longer. One gold piece.'

'Thank you.' Gerant thought that was very generous. He wasn't expecting a gold a week.

'I pay you one gold piece a month.' The maestro had been watching Gerant's face and realised what the younger man had assumed.

'But as a journeyman I thought I would get at least five silver a week for my work. That's what the guild always said.'

Shagreen dropped any pretence of friendliness and told it exactly how it was from his view. 'I am taking you on only because my current smith is proficient in lost wax casting but has little experience in forging blades or using a kiln. You benefit from working for the best metal artisan in The Realm. You will learn things that you could not get from anywhere else. That's why you get a gold a month. Many fellows would pay for the privilege of working with me.'

The maestro smiled grimly and continued. 'I have a reputation to uphold and so you will work exactly as I tell you to, using my designs. I also have important clients coming here and you will be elsewhere out of sight. You only come here when needed and work away at the workshop, which is not far away. Molly will show you later. And you are to show the proper respect to my wife and my children. That's all. Anything else and you can organise it through Molly.'

The audience was apparently over. The maestro ignored Gerant, took out the design and started working on it again. Gerant stumbled up to the door, walked through and did his very best to close it quietly, even though his strong urge was to slam it so hard it fell off its hinges.

Molly looked at the ashen face of the young journeyman and guessed how the conversation had gone. 'He can be a bit abrupt and often talks very plainly.'

Gerant nodded in frustration. He was going to have to think about what he wanted to do. He didn't want to walk out, but this was a turn of events he hadn't ever considered. 'He mentioned that you could show me the workshop and answer a few questions. And that I was only to approach him through you.'

Molly grinned again at this news. 'Between you and me, I only put up with it because he pays me well to run things for him and be nice to his brats.'

'But I will get very little! Far less than what I should as a qualified tradesman!'

She nodded in understanding. 'He didn't get to where he is without making sure he looks after himself. It's a dog-eat-dog world here in The Capital, after all.'

By then, they had reached the main entrance with the impressive spiral staircase curving down from above. 'Come, let's go to the workshop and you can meet Ray and see if it suits. We can chat on the way, and I will try to answer some things for you.'

Along the way to the workshop and farther into the Florian Quarter, Molly talked about the situation with the maestro. Apparently, he had burst onto the scene from down south and immediately made an impression on the well-to-do and gentry, who now lined up for his work. He had started in a small workshop in the River Quarter, but quickly moved up, until a few years ago he had bought the current large house. Molly was not a true judge of his work, but much of it was beautiful and the maestro was a talented artist and able to convert a drawn design to the finished product that was, if anything, even more stunning in real life. As his acclaim and success had grown, he had quickly stopped making pieces and doing the metalwork himself and currently had Raymond working for him. He focused on designing and meeting wealthy clients, receiving their astounded gasps of admiration and the significant pile of gold coin that his pieces attracted. All this was delivered by Molly with a straight face and a look of 'that is just how it is'.

They had reached a small gateway, opening off one of the long streets crossing the slope of the promontory heading west away from the sea. The gate closed off a short corridor between two buildings facing onto the street and appeared to open out into an open space after about thirty feet or so.

'The workshop is in here. So it's only a few minutes' walk.' Molly gestured Gerant to follow. Past the narrow access alley between the buildings was a small, paved area in front of a low stone building with a single door and a couple of windows facing onto the paved area. The door opened into a large open area with walls on three sides and the fourth side open to the air with large round posts sunk in a line and holding up the roof. The area had a look of organised clutter, with various barrels, boxes and tools stacked between work benches and around the poles supporting the roof. There was also a plain door on the far wall leading into some more room space, currently closed. The forge was built in the rear corner between the last two posts, covered under the roof but with no walls surrounding it so it would get all the airflow. Gerant could see how this would be quite useful and allow you to work in the outdoors and indoors at the same time, largely independent of the day's weather. Beyond the forge, there was a small outer area under a lean-to arrangement where what looked like a small kiln was positioned under a sloping tiled roof supported by four large posts.

'Gerant, this is Raymond. Raymond, Gerant. Gerant will be the new journeyman smith.'

Gerant's eyes had gone straight to the forge and the kiln, and he had totally not taken in that there was a man seated in the other corner of the workshop at a large table.

Raymond put down the piece he had been working on, looked at the new arrival briefly. 'Most people call me Ray.'

The voice was nondescript, soft and hesitant and pitched just enough to be heard. Although still sitting on the work stool, Gerant thought Ray was about his height and build. He had curly brown hair in a messy mop, a large nose and slightly bulging eyes. He regularly gave a little slurp and licked his lips and prominent teeth, not in a frightening or disconcerting manner, just something that he did unconsciously.

Molly continued. 'Ray stays here and has a small room out the back. He comes to the house for his meals, so I suppose when you are working you could also come for a quick lunch. He knows all the suppliers and where things are. Just work out what supplies you need for the workshop. Let me know and I will arrange payment.'

Ray nodded in agreement. 'I can show you where things are. One good thing is that we have all the right gear and if you need materials to make a piece, that is no problem. You just need to order it a little ahead of time, if you can.'

Gerant looked around and could see that Ray had everything well-organised and hanging up on hooks or neatly arranged close to where it would be needed. Some of the tools and gear he didn't recognise, so he assumed these might be used for lost wax casting. It looked like Ray was working on something interesting at the moment using fine wire and small pliers. That would be great to ask about later, even just to watch.

'Tomorrow, I might bring my gear up here and settle in. Where do I go?'

Molly responded, nodding, as it was a perfectly reasonable question. 'Ray will set up another worktable just against the wall there and you can use that space closer to the forge. I imagine you will be using it all the time. Ray doesn't use it all that often.'

Ray nodded. 'I use the kiln to fire the clay moulds and if I have a lot of metal to melt, but only use the forge if I am using a small crucible.'

Gerant nodded as if he understood all that. He wasn't really sure exactly what Ray was referring to. He had only a very basic understanding of lost wax casting and assumed he would find out all this very soon and become familiar with it.

'OK, see you tomorrow. Thanks.'

Ray seemed a little confused at being thanked and quickly turned back to the bench and started working again. Gerant got the impression he was quite happy to work on his own and certainly wouldn't be a regular down at the local tavern interested in talking with any stranger that turned up with a tale to tell.

On the way back, he quizzed Molly further. She was quite happy to answer his many questions. 'So Ray lives there behind the workshop?'

Molly sighed, seeing where this was heading. 'Yes, it's a little complicated. Ray is incredibly good at what he does but you wouldn't know it if you tried to talk to him. He also doesn't have any family locally and lives for his work. So it was easiest for the maestro to set him up with a small room at the workshop. He eats at the kitchen at the house and gets a very small living allowance. He is content enough and that satisfies him, apparently.'

The young lady continued as they strolled farther on. 'I think it would be fine if you come for your lunch when Ray comes. The maestro won't even know you have come. But there's no room for both of you to live at the workshop and anyway you have you own place, don't you?'

'If you call a room as a lodger in an old lady's cottage . . .'

'Ray is a lovely fellow, but I wouldn't want to share a place with him, so you are lucky to have something separate.'

'So, what happens with supplies for the workshop?'

'Ray will be able to tell you the suppliers we use. I can't remember them all or what specific supplies they cater to. I have enough trouble remembering the ones we use for running the household. Just order what you need, tell me and I will arrange the payment. The maestro checks the orders every now and again but, as Ray said, making the best requires the best and so it has never been an issue.'

Another thing to ask Ray about in the morning, thought Gerant. 'And I just wait until I'm told what to work on?'

Molly grinned this time.

'He likes to pretend he just gives orders and never gets his hands dirty, but he can't help himself. If it goes well, you will be bombarded with tasks to do and projects to work on. I overheard him talking to his wife the other day about this. He is quite passionate about this new direction in weapons he hopes to design and then craft. Not that he will let you know that, but you will see it in his actions and the many ideas you are expected to work on.'

With all his questions and pondering on the responses, Gerant suddenly realised they had arrived back at the large house.

Molly continued. 'You will need to get used to coming around the back. The front door is really only for clients and important visitors.'

They walked around the side of the building to a small wrought-iron gate with a large latch set in a narrow open passage between the Shagreen residence and the next house. Past the gate was the rear of the house, which had a wooden single-storey construction leading into the fancier two-storey stone building.

'This is the kitchen and other rooms the staff use. Just come this way with Ray for your midday meal. Also, if you are looking for me, I am often in this part of the house. Just come in and start calling for me. I won't be far away.'

She gave Gerant a quick smile. 'I probably should get back to see if I have missed anything. Sometimes he gets quite annoyed if I am not instantly there or the children are misbehaving or need their lessons. I suppose I will see you at lunch tomorrow.'

She gave Gerant another small grin and a quick squeeze of his hand before disappearing into the kitchen area. Gerant again was left not knowing what to think and slowly walked off, gently shutting the iron gate and wandering off towards the River Quarter. He had a lot to ponder on and only vaguely registered people coming the other way and automatically moving out of the way of riders or carts of produce.

Gerant spent a quiet afternoon settling in at the cottage and putting away some of his clothes and a few prized items like the book of smithing with the old parchment carefully folded away in the back cover. Until he had a chance to borrow a few tools from the workshop to do the alterations at the garden plot, he decided to push the sack of talium into the far corner under his bed, along with the book. To discourage anyone, he arranged some clothes and small boxes in front. It should be safe for a night or two and Mrs Lamming could always call Fang if some stranger arrived interested in the new lodger. But that was almost certain not to happen. All the same, he would sleep easier once the talium was no longer in the cottage and safely in its new hiding place. He had also noticed that the front door of the cottage was a little stiff to open. It would be really simple to plane the timber of the door to get it working properly. A good excuse to grab the tools he'd need.

He helped Mrs Lamming clear up after their simple dinner. Gerant thought the beef sausages and boiled vegetables were very tasty and went down well with some water from the pump at the end of the street. The old lady had been apologetic about the meal.

'Just lately, I have only had to worry about myself and only cook every two or three days. Also I don't eat much.'

'Truly, Mrs Lamming, it was a dish fit for a king!'

She took a moment to work out Gerant had been complimenting her at the same time as trying to make a little joke. She smiled in appreciation at the attempt.

'And you may call me Dierdre if you would like. We don't need to stay with formalities in the house, but outside and particularly at the market or if I come across friends of mine, I would prefer you still call me by my proper name.'

'Of course, of course . . . Dierdre. I will make sure that I will use Mrs Lamming when we are out. That is no problem at all.'

Gerant noticed that it had darkened a lot since they were clearing up after dinner and their little conversation. 'Tomorrow is my first day working at my new position. So I might feed Fang, then do a little reading in my room and then retire for the night.'

The older woman nodded.

'I might just do a little more knitting in the sitting room and then head off for bed myself. Goodnight, Gerant.'

'Goodnight.'

He headed out the rear door with some meat scraps and the leftover water in the jug.

Chapter 20
A New Post

He woke rather early after thinking he had spent most of the night mulling over the things to do in the next few days, but also realising he must has slept reasonably well and for some hours. Mrs Lamming wasn't up yet and he quickly fed Fang and slipped out the rear door and to the lane with a couple of sacks of gear and stuff. He was wearing his usual work attire of short-sleeved tunic, leather vest, cloth pants and half boots. His hair he had tied with the thong so it was out of the way. And he had had a quick shave. He quite liked a moustache but just at the moment it was a little sparse for his liking. After proving the point towards the end of his apprenticeship, he had gone back to shaving every couple of days. But he would see if it ended up growing more steadily in a few months or so. Also, once he got into a bit more of a routine at the workshop and had sounded things out.

Arriving at the workshop in the Florian Quarter, Gerant walked through the doorway and said good morning to Ray. Ray was already at work at his bench. Around ten feet away was another bench that had been placed closer to the forge overnight. Gerant plonked his gear down in front of it and started to get some tools and equipment out. He turned around to Ray, who was watching him unpack, unconsciously licking his lips and teeth and making a gently slurping noise every now and again.

'I have thought of a whole lot of things that you could answer for me, Ray. Matters such as who to order materials from, and the like.'

Ray nodded his head. 'We can do that when you get back. At breakfast Molly said for me to pass on that the maestro needed to see you about a new piece. I have seen the design but he has other instructions for you.'

'Oh. OK. I guess I had better go straight there.'

Gerant reached the Shagreen residence some minutes later and remembered to go around the back through the side gate. He reached the kitchen area and popped his head in the door. It was a well-appointed room with flagstones and a large fireplace along one wall and lots of cooking equipment on hooks or on open shelves around a massive table. There were a number of chairs around the table, so it appeared to be used for both preparing food and where the house staff ate their meals. A solidly built woman with short black hair and ruddy cheeks was wearing a large white apron. She was in the process of pummelling a lump of dough on part of the flour-strewn table.

'I am looking for Molly. She sent a message.'

The woman looked up, stopped kneading for a moment and smiled. 'You must be Gerant. I'm Faith, the cook. Molly is somewhere in the house but won't be far away. Through there.' She nodded at a doorway at the far end of the kitchen that must head into the main part of the building.

'Thanks.' Gerant walked through the door, which led to a short hall, with various doors opening off it. Walking past one, he noticed a familiar figure and knocked on the lintel. Molly looked up and smiled in greeting.

'Great. You got my message. He has been wanting to show you the design for a new piece. This will be your first project you will be involved in, so he wants to make sure you understand it and what is required.' She paused briefly. 'Remember what I said yesterday. Best to take it all in and agree. He doesn't realise the way he says things can lead to offence or not respecting others' skills.' She looked sideways at Gerant as they walked farther into the house.

'Sure.' Gerant didn't know what else to say.

After a few moments, he recognised the same door as yesterday. As Molly knocked and then ushered Gerant in, he tried to remember the directions they had taken so he would know for next time. The maestro was again seated at his desk, but this time was studying a small book. Seeing Gerant, he nodded in greeting and gestured for his new artisan to pull up a chair next to him. After sifting through a drawer, he pulled out some paper and passed it over to Gerant. Studying it, Gerant could see a well-drawn design for a dagger featuring elaborate but still functional quillons, hilt and pommel. The detail was mainly in those parts and the blade was only briefly sketched in. Maestro Shagreen started to talk.

'This is an important commission for Viscount Urbright. If this work goes well, I can see this leading to many other nobles wishing to have my designs. So there can be no mistakes.'

He paused. Gerant nodded. So far, there was nothing particularly surprising.

'Ray has already seen my design and will fashion the hilt and other parts using lost wax. The garnets and tourmalines have already been ordered from Purslip, the jeweller we use. The blade will be left to you in terms of fashioning, edges and length. Martinson said you are sufficiently skilled to do that. I know a good blade when I see one, so I expect nothing but the best.'

Gerant paused and then slowly nodded. This was more along what Molly had warned him. He resented the implications, but chose not to comment.

'That's all. Bring it to me when you and Ray have completed it. It will also require a suitably decorated scabbard which Ray knows about. You have a week to finish this.'

A week? Gerant screamed to himself. If this was to be his best, it would have to be from talium steel and he would have to set up a kiln run – that took three days minimum – and then there was sorting the core steel from the edge steel, fashioning that into separate bars and then forming them together into the one blade. And working at a new forge and kiln he wasn't used to using. He would need more time than that. Without thinking about Molly's words, he spoke out in an icy tone.

'Maestro, you expect the best and I will give you the best. But to achieve this in a week is not possible.' He rapidly sorted through what he would need. 'I have to source the best iron from a supplier, make sure I have oak or apple wood for the kiln run, add my own special ore, then form the metal into bars. Then days of work to forge the blade and to fit it to whatever Ray makes.' He totted up the time for each task in his head. 'I need three weeks, preferably four. Anything less than this and you will get a second-rate piece that neither of us would be willing to admit to.'

As he finished, Gerant realised what he had said. *Oh no,* he thought, *you have done it now. I should have kept my mouth shut. Lucky I didn't set out my gear earlier.* He waited not daring to breath, watching the maestro's face.

Trantor Shagreen was a master artisan and often had clients who he forced to wait for a commission long after they thought it should have been completed. The young man initially appeared to have taken in his instructions and looked like he would be as pliable and obedient as Ray. Ray just did what he was told, didn't ask any questions and turned out immaculate work that the maestro passed off as his own. Things had been going exactly like that.

And then the journeyman's face had started to go pale as he took in what Trantor was saying and particularly the deadline of a week. Shagreen could see his eyes not focusing as he seemed to be forming words silently, trying to think through details in his head. Then he had started talking, in a tone that Trantor had not heard for a long time. The young man looked steadily at him and his tone was measured and calm, but there was an icy chill to his words as well. Listening to what he was actually saying, a sudden thought rose in Trantor's mind that maybe this fellow actually knew his stuff and what had been proposed was not workable and going to fail. He thought back to when he was this sort of age and just starting to show his talents. He felt a small sense of kindred spirit, which he quickly stopped thinking about. What nonsense! There was no way that this fellow had any of the talent and potential he had shown! But the sneaky thought would not go away.

Gerant had watched the maestro, whose eyes had started to widen in shock when he realised what Gerant was saying and the curt, almost rude manner in which it had been delivered. He looked like he was going to interrupt. But then the maestro listened through to the end. His eyes lost a little focus and seemed to be remembering some memories from the past. Eventually he nodded, perhaps with a small amount of respect showing in his eyes and a somewhat grim smile.

'I will give you three weeks, not a day more. And it will be perfection, or as near to that as you can make it. Otherwise, you can pack your things.'

He reached for the drawing. 'Take this to refer to. Ray won't need it but if it will assist you to discuss the best manner to meld the blade to the hilt and such, do so.'

Gerant nodded, grabbed the piece of paper without a further word and walked out, closing the door gently behind him. He lent against the wall for a few moments to try to compose his thoughts and then wandered back to try to find Molly.

He found her in the same room as before, where she ran the household from. Gerant guessed she had a room for sleeping somewhere else in the house. He related the conversation with the maestro. Molly followed his recounting nodding here and there and then became wide-eyed and mute when he related the last bits.

'You took an enormous risk. He would normally fly off in a temper and start yelling. I have even seen him pick people up and then throw them down in a heap on the ground. What were you thinking of?'

'I don't know. He has little idea of what you have to do to make a blade that is the quality he expects. I have to start from scratch. There is no other way. But I was just thinking that in my head and then realised I was actually saying it to him. Then I couldn't unsay it. So I just had to wait for the explosion and him saying I was out and don't come back.'

'Well, perhaps he could see the talent you are meant to have. But next time, please try to hold your tongue a little. The outcome may not go so well. From the sounds of it, he will be expecting something amazing.'

'Hmmm. You are right. The standard expected might have gone up even further. Well, I will just have to take my time, work steadily and do it right the first time. Sveg taught me to work step by step, take breaks to make sure it is progressing as you expect and check against your drawings or what is in your mind.'

Molly had a sympathetic expression on her face as she tried to understand what Gerant was saying. 'We should chat again, Gerant, so I can understand more about what you do. Ray just works away and it is hard to get him to talk about it. Right now, I need to check up whether Master Purslip has sourced the gems we need for this dagger. He was confident he could get them, but that was a week ago.'

Gerant realised that the young lady was very practiced at ending a conversation without the listener feeling like they were being cut off, or that their company was not valued. 'Well, I also need to head off. I need to set up the forge to my liking and also I have a lot of questions to ask Ray about the workshop and supplies.'

'Agreed. I'll see you for the meal at lunch. Just come with Ray.'

Gerant walked back to the kitchen. Faith had formed the pastry into a pie dish and was chopping up some meat and vegetables. She gestured with the knife and the journeyman waved in reply as he crossed to the outer door and the rear courtyard.

Gerant slowly unpacked his gear and tried to find places for the various bits and pieces that made sense and could be grabbed easily as needed. He tried to put the few tools he had brought in the spot around the forge as they had been in the workshop in Ashford. There were also tools that Ray used and that were common to any smith or artisan using a forge or kiln. In between these tasks, he asked Ray, whose voice was a little muffled as he continued to work on his own project while answering Gerant's questions.

'Who do you use to supply metals and ores like iron and such? Or do you have several?'

A short pause.

'No, we just go to Hamish Wheelwright for all our needs. We possibly pay a little more than from others, but the quality is always really good and reliable. And he has been able to supply most of what we are after.'

'Sveg, the master I worked with in Ashford, has mentioned him and said good things. I will have to go and introduce myself. There are some things I'll need for this new project.'

He spent a few more minutes of arranging things. 'What about gems and jewellery? The maestro mentioned someone called Purslip.'

'Yup. Adam Purslip. He is a good jeweller and can get most things after a week or so. Anything really rare like diamonds or sapphires, that would be more difficult. And any really fiddly jewellery work, we get him to do it directly. But most things I can manage.'

Gerant fiddled with some of the coal chisels while he thought more. 'I need to use particular types of firewood for the kiln and sometimes for the forge. What do you use?'

Ray stopped working for a minute while he pondered the question. 'Mostly apple or cherry, which Levy is able to get most of the time. What are you after?'

'That might be good enough, but I would prefer oak if this Levy fellow can get it.'

'He will be able to give you an answer quickly. It depends on his suppliers. Firewood has to come from out of The Capital and where they are cutting trees within carting distance.'

Gerant made a mental note to visit this wood trader the next day to arrange getting his preferred type. 'Are there other traders or merchants you use?'

He could see Ray thinking as he continued filing away at the metal piece he was working on. 'No, I can't think of anyone else. They are the main ones. We did try Count Capuchin a couple of times. It didn't work out. He was too expensive for the quality of what he provided. It should have been better given his reputation. I wasn't there, but I heard from Molly that there was a big argument with the maestro and they were accusing things of each other and it almost came to blows. So we stay clear of that fellow. We're not the only one.'

Gerant thought about the tale that Sveg had related about talium and was not surprised at what Ray had said. He decided to visit this Hamish Wheelwright after lunch. He would make up his own mind but also trusted Sveg's judgement. 'OK, thanks. I'll let you get back to your work.'

Ray glanced outside and estimated the time of the day. 'Well, actually it is almost time for lunch.'

He stood up and folded up his coverall and looked expectantly at his new colleague. Gerant smiled to himself as he followed Ray out of the workshop. Ray was clearly a creature of habit and his meals at the Shagreen residence were part of this routine. To his companion's surprise, Ray ventured a comment without being asked.

'Chicken pie is almost my favourite dish. Faith promised me she was going to make one for today's lunch.'

Ray and Gerant walked into the kitchen and already there were three or four people seated at the large table, including Faith. Ray headed straight to the sideboard and grabbed a plate with a generous portion of pie on it, handing an empty plate to Gerant. He sat down next to Faith and started eating immediately. Gerant followed suit and sat down a little away from the others and tasted the pie. It was very good. Molly arrived from the door leading to the main part of the house and noticed Gerant.

'Everyone, this is Gerant.'

They all stopped and made welcoming noises, continuing to eat. As well as Molly, Faith and Ray, there was another man, somewhat older and two more women, one quite young and another in middle age. They all chattered to each other in between enjoying the chicken pie, not ignoring Gerant but not asking him lots of questions. He had not been looking forward to being asked a thousand things about where he came from, who his parents were, what he most like to eat, and so forth and so on. Instead, he took his time finishing his meal, listening to the scraps of conversation happening about him. He realised that Molly was standing next to him.

'Don't worry about this. I'll introduce them all in the coming days. It's just they only get fifteen minutes or so to have their meal break, so they eat fast and talk fast. Also don't worry once you finish. Faith will clean up before she starts preparing dinner.'

That explained quite a bit. 'Thanks. I want to go to meet Master Hamish Wheelwright to talk about some things I will need. Is that alright?'

'Yes. Just let me know what you have ordered so that I can arrange payment.'

Molly gave Gerant directions where the metal trader was to be found. After a few more minutes as he listened again to the chatter and finished the last of the pie, Gerant slipped out. He saw that Molly was having a lively conversation with the other man that he had yet to meet. *I wonder who that fellow is*, thought Gerant, as he moved off.

At The Cross, he turned left towards the old wall. This was an area he had not entered previously. He knew it was called the Argent Quarter, where the well-to-do lived. If he kept going on this main street he would reach the old city wall, beyond which only the gentry and titled people resided, at the top of the promontory that The Capital was built on. Already he could see what looked to be a wall of stone, maybe two or three stories high, peeking out between buildings up the road a little. Molly's direction sent him down a side street and he arrived at a house with wooden half-doors painted a glossy black. There was a steady stream of people going in and out of the doors. Walking in during a brief lull in foot traffic, Gerant's eyes took a moment to adjust from the bright outdoor light. There was a large lobby with various doors opening off it and a corridor marching down to the rear of the building, with further doors along it. People appeared and disappeared out of the doors moving about their own business and ignoring the young man with dark hair and working clothes trying to get his bearings. He saw the narrow stairs to the right and followed them up. The corridor at the head of the stairs was a little wider. Here and there, doors opened off it as it tracked to the rear of the house. A man at a desk strategically placed where the corridor started was bent over a large book and looked up quickly when a shadow crossed the large open page covered with columns of numbers and text. The man pursed his lips.

'To see?'

'Master Hamish Wheelwright about supplies of metal and ores.'

'Hmm. He has a meeting in one hour farther up the quarter. If it is quick, he might be able see you briefly. I just need to finish this invoice for Quilty's. Then I will ask.'

The man paused, with eyebrows raised in query. Gerant suddenly realised what he was waiting for. 'Umm, my name is Gerant. I was recently apprenticed to Master Sveg Martinson.'

'Ahh.' The man's face brightened. 'Master Martinson was here just the other month. Such a fine fellow.'

The accountant, or whoever he was, wrote quickly on a piece of paper and disappeared with it into a door on the left about ten yards down the corridor. After a few moments he reappeared into the corridor, walked back a little to a door on the right and knocked, then disappeared again. About a minute elapsed before the man appeared for the third time, this time leaning his head out into the corridor and beckoning.

After passing the accountant at the door, Gerant found himself in a comfortably furnished room with large windows showing views towards the River Greenthorn where it emptied into the sea. A man with greying brown hair and comfortable clothes stood and introduced himself as Hamish Wheelwright, before gesturing to Gerant to sit in a chair close to a large desk. Wheelwright also sat and gently smiled.

'Sveg mentioned when he last visited that you might come. For purchasing of metals or ore . . . or even just to talk and other things I might be able to advise on.' He stopped, looking over more closely the young man in front of him. 'Are you starting to settle in?' the older man asked carefully.

'Well, yes and no.' Gerant had already warmed to this man and decided to be more frank about how things stood than what he had originally intended to be. 'I have found lodging with an old woman in the River Quarter, which will probably work out alright. I have to look after a garden plot she has, but the lodging is all that I need, and the cost is very reasonable.'

Hamish nodded, without comment. After a few moments, Gerant continued.

'I have started with Maestro Trantor Shagreen, which is why I have come to you. We have been commissioned to craft a dagger of the finest quality and I need to start from scratch.'

'Maestro Shagreen has been a client of mine for the time he has been based in The Capital. He is certainly known for his fine work.' There was a reasonable pause. 'He is also known as someone difficult to work with – a perfectionist would be one way to express it.'

The look in Gerant's eyes was that he heartily agreed, but he kept silent and tried to keep his expression neutral. 'I hope to be able to make this work. Only time will tell.'

The older man sighed quietly. 'A very careful answer, my friend.' He paused again. 'So how can I be of assistance?'

Thereafter followed a quite technical discussion about Gerant getting sufficient iron-containing material for using in the kiln. Hamish Wheelwright leant back in his chair and shut his eyes briefly, steepling his fingers across his mouth as he thought. After a few moments, he sat back up and quietly gave Gerant a choice. 'I could provide you with enough bog iron for a couple of kiln runs. It comes from the southern marshes and my supplier has just delivered a new lot. The quality is as you would expect, so you might need to sort through it somewhat before you do a run.'

Gerant nodded that this sounded agreeable to what he required.

'There is also something else. Wait here for a moment while I get a sample.' The older man disappeared out the door and was back in a couple of minutes carrying a small canvas pouch. He opened it and passed over the pouch. Gerant looked inside and could see some sort of ore that looked to be strongly reddish-brown in colour, some of it like dirt with other larger pieces the size of a pea up to the size of a flattened apricot.

'I have only just started to obtain this. It comes by ship from a kingdom far to the south, from a mine, I believe. The amount of iron in this ore is more than the bog iron, and it is a matter of crushing it to a powder and adding it to the kiln. I have seen some bars made with this material and they are very fine in quality.'

Gerant continued poking the material in the pouch, as he thought of the possibilities it provided. This could be really exciting to try in the kiln.

Hamish Wheelwright watched the growing excitement showing on the young man's face and spoke again gently.

'Of course, I have not been able to obtain large supplies yet and it comes by ship from a long way away. So, the price is five times higher than the bog iron.'

Gerant thought about this for a few moments. Then he recalled what both Molly and Ray had told him about using the best materials for the maestro's work. After a bit more discussion, the new journeyman and the trader agreed on a combination of bog iron and some of the new ore supply from the other kingdom. They agreed on the price and that the materials could be picked up the next day. Gerant suddenly blushed when he realised he had brought only some coppers and a silver for emergency. Hamish Wheelwright could clearly read his thoughts.

'Payment now is not needed. I have a very good system going with the maestro through his housekeeper, Molly. Frederick provides an account every month and she arranges payment.'

After handshakes and a promise that he would come around at some point for a hot drink and a chat, Gerant took his leave of the metal trader. He was quite excited about the new iron ore and wanted to ask Ray whether he had ever used a similar stock. He hurried back to the workshop to continue getting the forge ready. He wanted to take a close look at the kiln and see how different it might be to the one in Sveg's workshop. He also made a mental note to order some oak firewood for a kiln run. And to look at the maestro's design again and start discussing it with Ray. And he would also have to smuggle enough talium to the workshop for a kiln run. Was there somewhere close to the kiln that he could hide it? Oh, also to take a few tools to the cottage to rehang the front door and to modify the wooden floor of the shed at the plot. He realised there were so many things now to think about. Gerant smiled to himself as he thought about how busy he had suddenly become. He punched the gate gently in excitement as he got back to the workshop and saw Ray at his usual place hunched over his workbench.

'Ah, Gerant, here you are,' remarked Mrs Lamming as she heard him come in behind her through the rear door. He had grabbed a few tools he would need and a small oil-can from the workshop when he had finished up for the day. He had also scrounged a few odd lengths of timber plank from out the back near the kiln. He was sure no one was going to miss them.

'Hello, Dierdre.' It would still take him some time to get used to calling the old lady by her first name when they were alone. 'I am just going to fix the front door and then take Fang out for a walk and go down to the garden plot.'

'Oh, good. That door has been bothering me for some time. It's getting harder and harder to open. I should have had someone to look at it ages ago, but I keep on forgetting.'

Mrs Lamming continued chopping up some vegetables for dinner as Gerant, with a series of expert, economical actions, hammered out the pins on the door hinges, leant the door sideways against the lintel, planed and filed the bottom and side where it was sticking, rehung the door and gave the hinges and door handle a quick oiling. It was a matter of five minutes' work. He made a final check by swinging the timber door backwards and forwards. The opening action was very smooth, and the latch fitted straight into the striker plate.

With that task finished, he quickly ferreted the sack of talium out from under his bed, grabbed an extra small sack and a loose piece of canvas, the tools and bits of planking he had left near the back door.

'Come on, Fang. Time for a walk.' Fang stood up and padded quietly next to him as they headed out through the alley towards the near bridge over the river.

During the walk, no one was particularly interested in the slim, dark-haired figure with a large sack looped over one shoulder, a small satchel that clanked occasionally with metallic sounds and an armful of wooden planks of various lengths. A good reason not to approach the figure was the large, brindled mastiff with the studded collar that marched in tandem with the young man. The animal looked around at all the sights and sounds but was silent as it stalked along. The people passing by all thought it must be well trained, thankfully, as a lead of around eight to ten feet, attached to the collar, trailed in the dirt, clearly not needed. But all the same, it was better to be safe than sorry. So the various city folk noted the little procession and kept going about their own business.

At the garden plot, Gerant quickly looked around and saw that nothing had changed. Fang plopped down next to the shed and watched the proceedings vaguely, his sides gently panting.

'First, a bit of oil to loosen up the workings in the padlock.' Gerant talked to himself as he worked. He realised that maybe he was talking to Fang, like Mrs Lamming seemed to enjoy doing.

'That's better,' he muttered as the key turned with a smooth click.

'Right, let's move this gear out of the way for now.' It took only a few moments to quickly pile the small boxes, spade, hoe and other tools on the ground next to Fang.

He grabbed the spade and dug around the ends of the floor planks so he could lever them up. 'About halfway, I reckon.'

He sawed each plank, stacked the pieces outside and then attacked the ground at the far end, quickly digging a square-shaped hole about two feet along each side and two feet deep. Then it was a matter of sawing the bits of timber he had brought to fit the bottom and sides.

'OK, let's line this little hiding place.' He used the short-handled maul to knock the planks down so that the pieces on the base were level. After that, the side pieces fitted together in the corners snugly.

'Right, now to take out some talium for the workshop.' Gerant had looked this afternoon at where he could make a hiding place and found some loose cobblestones near the privy at the back of the workshop. They could be levered up and a small hole dug underneath.

He looked around to see if he could see anyone watching and then quickly filled the small canvas sack with talium, carefully winding some cord around the neck. He placed it next to the lying dog and took the large leather sack into the tiny shed.

'Good. It fits well, once I plump it down to fill out to the corners. Now the canvas piece goes on top.' There was a short pause as he muttered to himself. 'Then the base boards and smooth a little dirt over to set them and make it seem like they have not been disturbed.' There was another longer pause while the boxes of seeds, other bits and pieces and the tools were arranged roughly in the same places.

Gerant dusted his hands and nodded with approval at his handiwork. 'I am just going to grab some carrots, Fang. Then we can go back.'

In the late afternoon sun, it was a few more minutes' work to grab several bunches of carrots from the bed in the plot. He dusted them off and gave one to Fang, who crunched it quickly and with apparent enjoyment. Gerant had another quick look inside the shed, locked the door and grabbed the satchel of tools and the small canvas sack on the ground next to Fang.

'Let's go, boy. I wonder what Mrs Lamming has made?' The pair wandered off.

'You know, Fang, I really should learn how to cook some simple meals. I am sure she would be happy to teach me.'

Chapter 21
His Own Master

After several days of preparation, Gerant was almost ready for his first kiln run. He had heard from Ray the steps the other artisan followed. While he respected Ray's expertise and experience working with lost wax and design work, it was clear that the other artisan used the kiln only for enabling a steady and sustained high temperature for heating his crucibles or firing the clay moulds and nothing beyond that.

Ray listened with consternation of Gerant's account of the sustained period over which the kiln had to be watched and fed almost as if it was alive.

'Rather you than me. I don't get paid enough!'

Gerant thought it wasn't worth mentioning that he was actually paid less than normal so he could benefit from the maestro's tutelage. Rather, he focused on making sure the whole run would go as smoothly as possible and lead to a successful outcome. In a final step, Gerant pleaded a bit of stomach-ache and not feeling up to lunch with the household staff. Ray was quite shocked at his workmate missing a free meal. As Ray left, Gerant knew he had a bit over half an hour of uninterrupted time and spent it carefully prising up a few pavers next to the privy, digging a quick hole to put the sack of talium into, then replacing everything including throwing higgledy-piggledy the remnants of a few broken wooden crates over the area to disguise the recently turned earth.

He had looked over the kiln very carefully. While it looked a little different from the one that Sveg used, it was built in similar fashion and he was confident it would behave the same way, more or less. The sacks of charcoal from oak logs had arrived at the workshop and Gerant had helped the carter stack them neatly close to the kiln ready to use as needed. The set of bellows had also been taken from the forge and were also conveniently lying close to the kiln. On one trip to the market with Mrs Lamming, Gerant had seen a small stall run by a man bent over with arthritis, selling pieces of wooden furniture and dressed timber. For a silver piece, he bought some pieces of dressed timber. The old man had told him it was chestnut and there was sufficient to put together a simple little bench to sit on next to the kiln. He planned to cut, chisel and plane it together while he waited for the kiln to go up to temperature and he started feeding in the ore and charcoal. Hopefully it would only take him an hour or so, after which he would have his project to sit on while he checked the kiln every now and again. He had also brought his bedroll and blanket – not to sleep on while the kiln was running – but after. Past experience had shown him how tired you got staying awake the whole afternoon and night and he had dreaded having to stumble home to Mrs Lamming's cottage and his own bed in that sort of state. While he was also pretty trusting of Ray, nonetheless he had come early one of the days when he knew the other artisan would be still away at breakfast, quickly dug up the small sack of talium and hid it temporarily in the pile of charcoal sacks near the kiln. The bog iron he had smashed and sorted and some of the new iron ore from down south was also ready to be layered.

After a quick walk with Ray to have their midday meal at the Shagreen residence, Gerant was ready. The kiln was lit without issue and soon got to the point where he could start adding the oak charcoal to build up the temperature in the kiln to the intense yellowy colour, showing it was ready for the ore. While he was waiting, Gerant started working on his bench with saw, hammer, chisel and plane. In between he checked the kiln, grabbing the bellows as needed and using a steel poker to even out the bed of coals before adding more charcoal. At one point he went to the privy, drank some water and ate a little jerky to keep himself going. Ray periodically came out from the workshop to observe the start of the firing run, shaking his head in disbelief and disappearing back inside without a word.

Around the time when the kiln's temperature had risen so that the bed of coals was an intense, throbbing yellow, the bench was finished. Gerant would have to do a final sanding and maybe coat it with a light layer of linseed oil to protect the timber, but he was quite happy with it, particularly as the pieces had fitted together well and there was only a little give when he wiggled on it as he sat. Then it was time to start layering the interior of the kiln with layers of charcoal, then the layer of bog iron mixed equally with iron ore. On this metal layer Gerant carefully sprinkled the precious talium from the small sack – one part talium to nine parts iron – as the old parchment decreed. Gerant and Sveg had found this mixture certainly produced the superb steel but had not tried other portions of talium to the iron. It was so valuable and they didn't have cartloads of it to try different amounts. Then it was a matter of waiting and waiting, keeping an eye on the kiln, checking the slag and adding more layers.

Gerant continued to sit throughout the hours, checking progress, adding more charcoal, breaking up the slag and adding it back, along with quick breaks for a drink of water or to go to the privy. Much of the time he sat on his newly made bench and let his mind wander. He vaguely heard and saw Ray head off for his evening meal and return some time later. The daylight gradually faded. The light of a lantern came on in the rear of the workshop where Ray had his room and then went out about an hour later. Gerant tried to stay awake by inventing games such as trying to throw pebbles as close as he could to a particular sack of charcoal while sitting on the bench. Or running up to the gate opening onto the street and back to the kiln a few times to get his heart going and become less sleepy. It was also interesting to listen to the sounds of the night and try to work out what they were and where they were coming from. On a couple of occasions, Gerant would suddenly catch himself from falling forward off the bench, as he realised that he was about to fall asleep. Then it was time for a sprint to the gate, or a round of pebble tossing, checking the kiln, judging the colour of the bed of coals, listening to the soft bubble and hiss and the other little signs that Sveg had shown him.

Towards dawn, Gerant progressively watched the sky as it slowly gained colour and previously dark shadows gradually emerged into the familiar houses and buildings around the workshop. It was also the time when the signs and sounds from the kiln meant it was getting closer to the critical point when the iron and talium were melting together into the required blend. This part of the run was always the most interesting and the easiest to stay alert. Several hours passed without him realising and when he next took stock, daylight had well and truly come and it was firmly morning. Of note was that the slag slowly oozing from the bottom of the kiln had taken on that greenish tinge, even more noticeable with the talium now in the kiln and melded within the steel. Ray emerged from the workshop yawning and stretching a little. He came over and looked at the kiln for a few moments, taking it in.

'You were here all night?'

Gerant just nodded, giving the bed of coals a little stir with the poker.

'Crazy. Coming for breakfast?'

'No, I need to keep an eye on things. This is the most important part.'

'Suit yourself,' muttered Ray, as he walked off towards the gate and turned left out of sight.

Within another half hour, the noises from the kiln had died down to a gentle burble and the slag had stopped flowing. Gerant knew that the talium had formed into the steel and he could let the kiln die down and rest. Gods, he was tired! He quickly moved any stray coals or bits of wood away from the kiln and went to the privy. He splashed his face with some cold water and had a quick drink. Then it was a matter of a few moments to lay out his bedroll along the boundary fence close to the kiln, under a tree growing in the yard. He lay down and pulled the blanket around himself. Within a few minutes, the reclined form was breathing deeply, but otherwise not moving.

A feminine figure with black curly hair and wearing a brown dress with white trim came through the workshop past the forge. Molly looked at the kiln with bits and pieces scattered around it and a simple bench about three feet in front of it. She looked around and then noticed to her left a sleeping form on a bedroll on the ground, lying up against the back fence of the workshop property. She smiled gently, went back into the workshop, and came back with a small wooden box. She quietly laid the box next to the sleeping figure and placed on it the plate of food she had brought. She gently adjusted the blanket so it covered the young man a little better, then silently walked off. The figure on the ground muttered a little without waking, rolled onto their other side and kept on sleeping.

Gerant continued to finish weeding the row of beans at the plot. He looked up and Fang had returned, his sides gently panting. A deep, gruff voice emerged from the mastiff's lips as he seemed to grin. 'I saw that collie off after I roughed him up a little. That's the last time he'll try to pee on our cabbages.'

This must be a dream, thought Gerant. *And I thought I was at the workshop.* He slowly opened his eyes and sat up, the blanket slipping off his shoulders. It looked like it was in the afternoon sometime, based on where the sun was. He noticed a small crate next to his bedroll, with a bread roll, some cut meat and cheese on a plate. It didn't last long – he had only had a few pieces of jerky all night – and it was very welcome. Taking the last pieces with him, he walked over to the kiln and checked it. It was still way too hot to access the bloom. It would need the next night to have properly cooled down. So there was nothing he could do for now. As he quickly rolled up the bedding and tightened the two belts, Gerant could hear work sounds coming from the workshop.

'Who left the food for me? That was thoughtful.'

Ray had a mouthful of small tacks he was using to mark out the design he was working on. 'Mwrorry.'

'Oh . . . Look, I'm going to head home and get a proper sleep. I'll break into the kiln tomorrow and start sorting through the steel.'

Ray nodded and looked up briefly before continuing to tap the tacks into the block of wax.

After a restful long sleep at the cottage and a wonderful breakfast cooked by Mrs Lamming, Gerant turned up at the workshop to see how the kiln run had gone. When he broke into the bloom, he could see the mottled greeny-grey tones throughout, showing that the talium had melded into the steel and he would be able to carefully break up the chunks into core and edge steel based on the colour, shininess and feel. He set up a bench between the kiln and the forge, so he could work in the open air and take advantage of the strong light to put chunks of bloom into two growing little piles of the two grades of steel fragments. The morning was gone before he had fully broken up the bloom and had a medium canvas sack of each type. He estimated once he had condensed the steel fragments into crude bars, he would have more than enough for a dagger. What he didn't need he could store for future projects. It should be sufficient, he thought, for several smaller weapons or probably enough for a sabre or sword.

It took a fair amount of the afternoon to prepare the forge to be operating for the next day, to have the long-dead coals raked and ready for lighting. It also took time to lay out the hammers, mauls, pincers and other tools he needed within arm's reach of the anvil, plus a score of other aspects prepared for the first serious session with the forge. At last he was done and he gave the forge area one last check before saying farewell to Ray and heading off to the cottage.

The days following were a blur of activity, where Gerant re-enacted all the training he had undertaken with Sveg. At the core were the efficient movements and unhurried actions to achieve the next step in the process and the regular rhythm of activity, followed by a break to assess progress and judge what was needed next. As such, the dagger blade emerged slowly but steadily from the forge and anvil, with Gerant stopping frequently to check and refer to the maestro's drawing. He had looked at the design and decided on a blade of about ten inches in length that would emerge out of the elegant but finely crafted hilt and pommel arrangement, gently tapering to the point. It was still around an inch in width – a compromise of not being too chunky and heavy-looking – yet also not too slight so it would not be able to deliver a hefty, fatal blow if needed. He was going to use the design in the old parchment of having the core steel enfolded by the edge steel to give a strong and balanced structure. All in all, it took him three days of steady work at the forge and on the anvil until he had crafted the double-edged blade between two and three handspans long and a shorter tapering tang over which the quillons and grip would sit. Ray had already fashioned these, so it was easy to use them as guides as he worked the bars of talium steel, melded the core steel with edge steel surrounding it and then repeatedly heated and hammered the emerging blade into its final form. Knowing the overall length of the dagger being fashioned had allowed Ray to also start working on a scabbard using burgundy-coloured leather, with some details similar to the design in the quillons, grip and pommel.

Gerant spent the last morning carefully checking over the blade before he started the final polishing and sharpening. It all looked exactly as he had seen in his mind and the simple drawing he had made the previous week was also a good representation of the finished product. He was quite tired in his mind even though it was not long after breakfast, as he had been concentrating carefully for days now and needed to take a break and do something different for a change. But first he needed to focus on completing the final steps. After the polishing and sharpening, along with some very small adjustments, Gerant and Ray inserted the tang through the quillons and the hollowed grip, checked it was a very snug fit and then anchored the blade with several small steel pins. After that, he gave the weapon a careful final rub and polish along with a last sharpening of the edges.

The two artisans stood back to admire the finished dagger lying on some white cloth on the workbench, with the leather scabbard lying next to it.

'A really fine job, Ray,' breathed Gerant, not yet ready to think of what they had achieved.

'Yes, he should be pretty happy with this,' agreed Ray.

The silvery-grey surface of the dagger blade had a distinctive darker greenish tinge to its colouring, noticeably different from the usual steel weapons. The surface mirrored the light and dark parts of the workshop, broken up by the fuller impressed into each side that gave the blade a very pleasing profile. The quillons curved gently and intertwined to still fulfil their protective function, but the design was pleasing to the eye and had no sharp joins or corners. Here and there braided wire wove in and out of the quillon openings and small garnets and tourmalines were set within the metal to complement the design. The pommel also featured a scattering of gemstones, and the grip was fashioned from a piece of stingray leather stained to the same burgundy hue and interlaced with the braided wire.

Gerant sheathed the dagger and carefully wrapped it in the cloth.

'Do you want to take it to the maestro?'

Ray spent very little time considering. 'Not particularly. It's probably best for you to do it. Besides, it's time to go to the house for our meal.'

The two artisans walked the short way to the Shagreen residence, one carrying a small bundle of pale cloth. Gerant still couldn't understand Ray. He was clearly a master craftsman in his own right, but not interested in any fame or recognition. What seemed to be most important to him was that he had a bed to sleep in and regular meals. Gerant gently shook his head as he followed Ray into the kitchen area.

The red-headed man leant back in his chair, with his long legs stretched out in front of him and his hands interlaced behind his head. Trantor thought more about whether he should make an appointment to visit the earl to finalise the design for the iron screen doors and permission to commence crafting them. The initial drawings had been well received and he was very confident that it was only a formality. You still needed to follow protocol, he mused, or else there would be hell to pay. Hopefully it would not be too long before they were clamouring for his work and he could dispense with this tiptoing around.

There was a gentle knocking at the door.

'Come.' He sat up quickly and watched as the new journeyman walked in quietly and placed a small cloth bundle on the desk. Gerant's face remained expressionless.

Trantor's pulse started to beat a little quicker. Perhaps this was the dagger. It would be around three weeks since that the little shit had called him out about how long it would take to fashion. With a few quick tugs, he unwrapped the contents. He saw a very elegant dagger in a decorated but functional leather sheath. *Gods, this already looks good.* He picked up the scabbard – he had only given brief instructions to Ray but this was his usual fine work. He also complimented himself on his beautiful design of the dagger grip and quillons emerging from the scabbard. Well, everything was as expected so far. His hand enclosed the grip of the dagger as he slid the scabbard off. And he couldn't help but stop and marvel at the blade. He spent several minutes twisting the dagger this way and that and admiring the polished surface of the dagger. It was highly unusual. It had a quite attractive vaguely greenish sheen to the surface that he had never seen in a weapon before. He balanced the dagger on his finger like he had seen expert swordsmen do and it sat motionless, not tipping one way or another. It was a sturdy little weapon, but somehow it felt notably lighter than what he would have expected. He tested the edges with his thumb. *Gods, it's sharp!*

The maestro had spent several minutes now closely examining the dagger from every angle, balancing it on his fingers and checking the sharpness of the edge. He glanced only briefly at the scabbard and the dagger handle. His face did not give any thoughts away.

'These channels that are worked into the blade? They are?'

'Fullers. They make the whole dagger slightly lighter without affecting the strength or flexibility of the blade. And they add a pleasing profile. They are often used on better quality weapons.'

'Tell me about this greenish cast to the steel. I am not familiar with this.'

Watching his new smith, the Maestro saw a flash of pleasure cross his face before it was quickly masked.

Gerant continued calmly. 'The blade has a covering of edge steel surrounding a centre of core steel. I made the steel using the techniques Master Martinson taught me, which took a week. In addition, I used an old but uncommon method to add another type of metal to the blade, which accounts for the greenish colour. It gives it additional strength and lightness.'

The maestro pondered on the explanation, then nodded, satisfied.

Trantor was truly impressed with the quality of the dagger blade, but he was careful not to show it in his expression or words.

This lad had made something notable, and he had actually not seen anything to match it. He allowed himself a moment of genuine relief. And the possibilities! He had been thinking of charging Urbright one hundred and fifty gold for the dagger, but thought he would insist on two hundred. Urbright was a bit of a fool, but you couldn't doubt his knowledge of weaponry and what a superb dagger would look and feel like. If the maestro was any judge, Urbright would be delighted. And an extra fifty gold would be paid without question. Trantor was sure he would show his friends the new dagger and interest in getting weapons made by Maestro Shagreen would quickly grow. And grow and grow. Now, what was the best way to make sure this new fellow got just enough acknowledgement of the quality so he would continue, but not think it was all down to him? *Hmmm*, he thought.

'The blade is not too bad as a first try and I will keep you on as long as your work continues to improve. I will let Molly know when I have the next piece designed ready for you to start working on. There will be more blade work in the weeks to come, but there is another project starting soon that you and Ray can also work on. That will be all for now.'

'Thank you, Maestro. I will get going. I have a few things to tidy up at the workshop.'

Gerant waited until he had closed the door and headed back to the kitchen area before he allowed himself to grin in delight and relief. He also went to find Molly to tell her the good news. Molly was talking to Faith at the kitchen table. The remains of the meal had been cleared away and Faith was starting to prepare dinner as she talked to Molly. Both women looked up as Gerant walked in with a grin on his face.

'It was a little hard to judge, but I think he was happy with the dagger. So I can stay.'

'Oh, Gerant, that's wonderful news!' Molly beamed and Faith smiled and muttered, 'Well done!'

'I need to go and tell Ray. He probably won't say much but he did a terrific job.'

Gerant smiled in farewell, but turned back as he remembered something. 'And I want to thank you for leaving that plate of food for me after I had finished the kiln run.'

Molly blushed, and quickly muttered, 'It was Faith's idea.'

Gerant paused briefly at the doorway to the courtyard. He saw Faith silently mouth some words after she checked Molly couldn't see her. As he walked through the iron gate on the way to the street, he realised she had been mouthing, 'No, it wasn't me.' He pondered what that meant as he walked back to the workshop.

Chapter 22
A Different Project

Through various means, Gerant understood that the dagger had been presented to Viscount Urbright and the coin collected without a murmur. Ray had participated in conversations about it at the kitchen table and Molly had overheard directly from the maestro. The maestro was apparently very happy to relay to Molly the viscount's reaction. If this was to be believed, he had immediately gone to the fencing salon to practice with it and was already praising its merits to whomever would listen. Shagreen was highly confident that there would be a host of new commissions for similar pieces of work or even more substantial weapons. As well as thinking of ordering a matching sword, the viscount had shown his cousin, the Earl Sherrington, who had been intrigued, according to the viscount, and was also thinking of contacting the maestro to discuss future commissions for weapons. This was in addition to the cast-iron screen doors that he had already approved. As Molly explained, this could cement the maestro as one of the main suppliers of weaponry to the ruling class. The earl was extremely influential in those circles and was very close to the actual royal family, being head of one of the minor branches.

Gerant had barely time to complete the first phase of a tidy up and make a few minor repairs and adjustments to tools and the forge before he was summoned to see the maestro. Things had not changed appreciably in the manner in which Gerant was told about the next piece of work. As he sat next to the maestro's desk absorbing the details, he could see this project was quite different. It brought to mind immediately some of the work on gates that he had assisted Sveg with during his apprenticeship, those at the entrance to the guild compound and then the set positioned at the bridge at Cobham. This work was to be a commission for Earl Sherrington, which would commence once the final set of drawings had been seen and approved. With the status of the earl in The Realm, Gerant needed no reminders how important this work was going to be. Nevertheless, the maestro spent several minutes emphasising the honour of being entrusted with these screens and the necessity to make them perfect. Shagreen explained the concept for the design and the working drawing based on the space to be filled by the wrought-iron work. It was a depiction of grape vines, where the screens would be filled with intertwining and twisting metallic vine tendrils with leaves, spiralling shoots and clusters of grapes. To provide structure around the outside of the arched screens that also doubled as open doorways, the maestro had drawn in the trunks of the vines. Gerant was truly impressed and could see how the wrought iron would be made to look like a living, growing mass of plants made from blackened metal. His part in making this complicated mass of iron work was to interlink the many lost wax castings of leaves, bunches of grapes and textured vines with sections of cast iron to represent the larger twigs, branches and trunks. Ray would be doing all the lost wax work, which would take several weeks to complete. He took the large piece of paper with the drawing, rolled it into a tube and tied it with the ribbon. He was then entrusted with two carvings in wax that the maestro had made, to be given to Ray as templates for the casting. Apart from drawings, this was the first example of crafting that he had seen from the maestro. He had only a few moments to view them before they were carefully packed away in a small wooden box lined with wood shavings. But what he did see was a masterful depiction of vine leaves and a small bunch of grapes with many small details carved into the wax that almost made them come to life. It showed a mastery of this form of crafting that the maestro clearly had. It certainly tied in with what Molly had told him, that the maestro had a background using lost wax and carving, which was certainly apt given his long, slender fingers a little at odds with his tall, well-built and athletic figure.

'You have everything you need to start work on this? Between the drawings and the wax carvings, Ray should be able to do the castings. Tell him to bring a sample of them for me to check once the first sets have been made.'

Gerant paused after he had received the instructions and thought about the parts of the work he would be particularly responsible for. 'Maestro, you have indicated the dimensions of the overall space where the screens will be installed. To make sure I forge the frame so it fits snugly with no gaps and so the arch structure follows the angle truly, I feel I need to look where it will be installed. I would also need to check how best to attach the screens to the supporting walls and the best type of brackets to use.'

The look on the Maestro's face suggested that he had been focused on filling the space with a pleasing design and spent less time on any structural considerations. 'That might be possible, if it means you can be more confident in what you are putting together. See Molly and she can find out a whether a special permit can be granted to go to Earl Sherrington's chateau to view where the screens will be installed. I have been there several times at the invitation of the earl, but this is something quite different. It is rather an unusual request.'

Gerant thought it was a perfectly reasonable request, but he had no experience with dealing with the aristocracy. He would have to check with Molly before he took the wax carvings and drawing back to the workshop. 'Thank you, Maestro. We'll get working on this right away.'

Gerant was already deep in thought about the first steps as he closed the door carefully and headed off towards the back of the house. Molly was sitting in her small room looking at several pieces of paper when he knocked on the doorframe. She looked up and smiled.

'He gave me the wax carvings to take back to the workshop and give to Ray.'

She nodded.

'But I would also like to look at where the doorway is going to be installed. I can see from the drawing that it will look amazing when finished, but the details I need are not there. The maestro said you might be able to organise some sort of pass letter to get me in. But he said it could be quite difficult to arrange.'

Molly grinned and clicked her tongue, as she slowly shook her head. 'He is very fond of exaggerating. It will be really easy. I just need to talk with the earl's chief steward. Where is the doorway?'

Gerant realised he didn't know. 'I have no idea, Molly. Just somewhere at the earl's residence.'

'Hmm. I am sure Steward Waterford will know. I can probably go this afternoon and get your letter. It's a good excuse to get out of here for an hour or so. Sometimes he just expects me to be here at his beck and call.'

Gerant couldn't help grinning in sympathy with Molly. It wasn't hard to guess that she was referring to the maestro, who clearly insisted on being the centre of attention.

'That would be great. I want to start watching Ray as he starts the lost wax process, but it would be good to go and look, maybe tomorrow or the day after.'

Molly agreed she would let Gerant know as soon as she had the signed permission. He headed off to the workshop, carefully holding the small wooden box with the wax carvings to give to Ray. He balanced the rolled-up drawing on top.

They pored over the drawing and now Gerant had a really good look at the wax carvings. He was even more impressed. The vine leaves were lifelike in the way they bent a little, with veins in the surface and a little roughened texture. The only thing missing was that they were the yellow, waxy colour instead of various shades of green and brown. The wax carving of a small bunch of grapes was only about half an inch thick, but the way the grapes were carved made them look like they were plump and rounded. He shook his head in admiration as he appreciated the way perspective had been taken into account by the maestro.

'This is the biggest project we've had for a while,' pondered Ray. 'It looks complicated, but the main bit is just chipping away at making the moulds and putting it all together bit by bit. Once we have the first stages done, then it's a matter of following the same routine each day to build up sets of castings. Then you can forge them together as we go and then the gates are done!'

'Sure, Ray, sounds easy.'

Ray nodded, not picking up that Gerant was being more than a little sarcastic. 'I really want you to show me each step of the lost wax process. I have heard talk about it and seen the odd finished product, but only have a basic understanding of how you do it.'

'Right,' said Ray. 'The first steps are about making the main moulds that we do the whole casting process off. Like these ones.' He got down a wooden box with a whole lot of clay moulds packed away in straw.

'These are some that I've kept from previous jobs.' Gerant had a quick look through them. There were various hollow shapes there that he could see. In each case there appeared to be matching pairs of moulds, where one of the moulds was one half of the shape to be made and the other was the mirror side. Ray took the two wax carvings done by the maestro and placed them carefully on his workbench, Gerant sitting next to him so he could see every step.

'First thing is to have a little clay handy so you can make one side of the mould. I knew these were coming, so I went round to Hanson's and got some fresh stock.'

Gerant now knew that Evelyn Hanson was an experienced pottery maker who had a workshop a few streets away in the Florian Quarter. He had met her on an earlier trip with Ray. As well as making pottery and other wares for sale, she was happy to sell locally sourced clay that could be used for casting.

Ray carefully brushed the two wax carvings with some oil. He then took small pieces of clay and pressed them gently into one side of the wax carving. Using a variety of small wooden tools, he built up the clay on one side of the carving, working it gently into some of the design. 'The main thing is to take your time. You need to do it carefully as you can't afford to break the wax carving.'

Ray was frowning with concentration and Gerant also couldn't help but frown with concentration in sympathy. He could see this was a really important step. As he took in what Ray had told him, he realised that the other artisan had talked normally when he was concentrating on his work or explaining technical aspects. There was none of the licking of lips or quiet slurping. In more casual or social situations, Ray got a little nervous and was more on edge. While Gerant pondered on this, another question occurred to him.

'How do you get the clay to follow the little details in the wax?'

'You need to have the clay at just the right consistency. Not too stiff and not too runny. Just a matter of experience.'

Eventually, the clay had covered one side of the wax carving. Ray built up the thickness so it was about an inch thick. He also added clay to the sides so there was about an inch around the outside of the wax. Then he gently pressed it on the surface of the workbench so it was totally flat on the back side. He squared off the edges with a knife and also carefully added a few more scraps of clay and carved some off so that the inside surface was also flat. Gerant could see that the wax carving looked a little like something floating on a bowl of clay-coloured water, with the bottom half of the shape hidden because it was underneath the surface.

'The last step is to put in a little channel so you can add the wax when you have the moulds together. I use a little twig like this just to press the clay before it sets.'

Gerant nodded that he understood that part, but something else puzzled him. 'What is the oil for?'

Ray's answer hinted that it was obvious what its purpose was. 'You want the clay halves to come apart easily. The oil helps grease things a little so they don't snap and break.'

'Of course. I wasn't thinking.'

Ray smiled and started working on the second wax mould of the vine leaf, using the same careful process adding clay to surround one half of the wax carving. 'Right, that's it. We just leave them out in the sun to cure and harden up. I leave them for two days. You could quicken things by putting them near the forge or somewhere hot, but they don't cure evenly, in my experience. Or they could even crack if they dry too fast. Better to be patient.'

Gerant secretly agreed. He was still very interested in the next steps, but resigned himself to wait until Ray was ready. Besides, he would hopefully be able to go and look at where the screen doors for Earl Sherrington were going to be installed. Plus, there were quite a few little forge tasks to do in preparation.

When Gerant arrived the next morning, Ray told him that Molly had a message for him. Hoping it would be what he thought it might be, he grabbed the rolled-up drawing of the doors, a pencil, a measuring tape, hammer and a couple of tacks. The various bits and pieces he put into a wooden tray and headed off to the maestro's residence.

Molly was in the corridor leading to the kitchen talking with one of the other staff. 'Just a minute,' she said as she walked off to her working room.

She returned and handed Gerant a small, folded piece of paper with writing on the outside in blue ink and with a wax seal that had been opened. Gerant opened the folds and slowly read what it contained within, then reading aloud. Molly waited impatiently for him to finish.

'The bearer, Master Gerant from Maestro Trantor Shagreen's studio, is hereby authorised to visit Earl Sherrington's chateau for the purpose of installing the new cast-iron screens at the rear staircase. Should further visits to inspect the work area be needed, he is to present himself with this authority on each occasion.

By order, Chief Steward Waterford.'

The order was signed with a scrawl in a different coloured ink. Gerant looked at the seal – impressed into the red wax was a stag on its hind legs with spears on either side. Molly was watching.

'That is the seal of Earl Sherrington's family. It is to show that this is a genuine authority for you to visit more than once. You'll need to take it every time.'

Gerant nodded. This was all beyond his experience. There was one little detail he was a little embarrassed to ask. 'Umm, where do I go?'

Molly burst out laughing. Gerant couldn't see what was so funny.

'Well, country boy, you go up to The Cross and keep walking up the hill through the Argent Quarter. When you get to the gatehouse in the old wall, you will need to show this order to the guards. Then go to the earl's chateau and present yourself at the front door. I imagine Steward Waterford will come down to meet you and then take you to wherever these doors are to go. Think you can remember the way back?' Molly grinned mischievously.

'Ha, ha, ha,' muttered Gerant as he walked off.

'Oh, and you should go home and put on your best. You want to make a good impression.'

Gerant walked in from the back lane and fondled Fang's ears for a moment, before walking in the back door.

'It's me, Dierdre. I just need to change.'

Mrs Lamming emerged from the front room with some knitting, surprised that her lodger had appeared in the middle of the day. Gerant gave her a quick explanation of where he was going, showing her the piece of paper. Mrs Lamming was clearly very impressed.

'Oooh, la. It looks very official and important. The Earl Sherrington? He is very well regarded in The Capital, so folk say. You need to tell me all the details when you get back.'

Gerant looked in mild surprise at the older woman and slowly nodded. It was interesting how you only found out about someone's interests after some time. But he was happy to tell Mrs Lamming all about it, as it was going to be a new experience for him, as well. He quickly changed into the dark brown doublet that Sveg had brought back from The Capital and his better set of half boots. He gave a quick tidy up of his hair and he was as ready as he would ever be.

After reaching The Cross and turning to the right, Gerant walked upslope towards the top of the ridge from which the original city had grown. He passed the street down which the metal trader, Hamish Wheelwright, had his premises, but continued on. This was all new to him and he discretely gawped, sometimes stopping to take things in, particularly the larger and larger buildings, some clearly houses, that lined the street he followed. Around a gentle curve in the avenue, the stone archway where the street stopped slowly emerged. Gerant could see a stone wall, maybe two stories high, linking the archway, bits of which he could see in between the various buildings built in front. *This must be the gatehouse*, he surmised. He paused for a moment, about a hundred feet away, and noticed that almost all the people rushing here and there had moved off into side streets. Any horses or carts had also peeled off. Now that he had watched for a bit, there were very few people or riders actually approaching the gatehouse. Gerant also noted a pair of guards who were stationed on either side of the gatehouse, leaning on long spears. There was another pair of guards standing a little farther back, and he also saw the occasional glint of some sort of weapon in the narrow slits within the gatehouse itself, suggesting that other guards were within call, if required. He checked that he had the authority with him and wandered up to the archway, looking around him eagerly.

The guards watched the young man carrying what looked like a wooden tray with some things in it. Balanced on top of the tray was a rolled-up piece of paper. When it became clear the man was approaching the gatehouse and the arched entry, they looked at each other and one of them nodded. Gerant noticed one of the guards step towards him, holding up a hand while he continued to grip the long spear with the other.

'What's your business?'

Gerant didn't say anything but passed over the pass. The guard harumphed and leant the spear shaft against his shoulder while he opened the folded paper and scanned the contents. Gerant could see that the guard held the paper with the writing upside down, so he quickly worked out this was just for show.

After perusing the paper for a few moments, the guard turned his head towards the archway and yelled, 'Sergeant!' There was a clatter of footsteps coming down a stairwell and an older man with greying hair and a moustache arrived, buckling on his breastplate.

The older man took a good long look at Gerant. The guard handed the paper to the sergeant without a word. The sergeant read the contents, after first turning the paper the right way up.

'Been here before, lad?'

Gerant shook his head. 'First time.'

'Right, whenever you come, either show this pass to one of these fine gentlemen, or we will start to recognise you and let you through. Head on up towards the palace and the road reaches a roundabout with a fountain in the middle. Take the left branch and about one hundred yards farther on there is Earl Sherrington's chateau. Ask for Chief Steward Waterford at the main door.'

'Thank you.' Gerant was glad the sergeant had given him some directions, as he had forgotten to ask Molly.

Walking farther up the now gentle slope, he realised how quiet it had become. Very little of the hustle and bustle of the city below reached this level. It was like walking through a very neat forest park, with the occasional building peeking out between the trees. There was nothing like the feel down below where the buildings crowded on top of and next to each other. And there were very few people. He could see the odd person walking on carefully groomed paths and a man with a hoe, presumably a gardener, working away in a garden bed off to the right. He reached the fountain with the road circling its perimeter and saw farther up that it continued on to a sprawling three- and four-storey stone building sitting atop the ridge. *That must be the palace*, he thought. *I guess there will be lots of guards there and you would need a special pass.*

At the fountain, he turned left, walking slowly up the edge of the road. A somewhat smaller but still impressive two-storey stone building with red roof tiles gradually emerged from the park-like surrounds. *This must be the chateau of Earl Sherrington*, he surmised. Feeling somewhat overwhelmed, Gerant walked up the five marble steps to the large arched doors. He wondered if he should knock and then saw a small brass bell with a braided rope. He gave it some discrete tugs and the four ringing sounds announced to whoever that Journeyman Gerant of Maestro Shagreen's studio had come to look at the location where the cast-iron screen doors would be installed.

One of the large doors gently creaked open and a man appeared, wearing green hose, green long-sleeved undertunic and a pale-yellow tabard showing a rearing stag and spears embroidered on the front. 'Yes?'

Gerant handed the folded paper to him. 'If the chief steward is available, I am here to measure the archway where the new iron screens are to be placed.'

The man read the pass. 'You are Gerant?' The younger man nodded. 'Come in and wait here while I find him.'

He gestured to Gerant to follow him and pointed at a small, padded sofa in the large, marble-tiled foyer, before walking off. Gerant was hard-pressed not to gawp open-mouthed at the sparsely furnished but opulent space. Sitting on the edge of the sofa, he could see various paintings on the wall, around half showing individuals, presumably important family members. A grand staircase curved up from the right-hand side of the room to a second floor and the open space was emphasised with having the ceiling the full height of two floors. He had never seen anything so fine as this, shuddering to think what the actual palace was like given it was likely to be fancier still. Gazing about him, he suddenly realised an older man with grey shoulder-length hair and a similar tabard but with gold braid as additional decoration had quietly approached. The chief steward handed back the paper and had an enquiring look on his face.

'I am here to check again the measurements for the cast-iron screen. We are about to start crafting it and I also need to check the walls and how best to anchor them.' He presumed this was what the chief steward was expecting to hear.

'It would be best to check all this, given the cost of this commission. It would be rather unfortunate if they didn't fit perfectly.' The chief steward spoke in a rich baritone, not disguising that he was speaking to a tradesman, no matter how skilled he was. Further, that he represented the earl, one of the foremost men in The Realm. 'Follow me.'

They walked through a number of corridors, staying on the ground floor and emerging from a small side door at the back of the chateau, clearly part of the staff quarters. There was a short walk across some mowed lawn, and they arrived at a back entrance of the chateau, where a wide path approached from between the trees and gardens.

'This is where the screens are to be placed, right at the bottom of these stairs up to the second floor.'

Gerant put down the rolled-up drawing and the wooden tray and eyed up the double doorway. There was a stone archway about nine or ten feet high in which two wooden doors had been built, which were currently hooked open. The area above the doors had been filled in with wood panels to close off the space. 'I have to measure from the top of the stone arch. Could I trouble you for a small stool or box I could stand on?'

The chief steward seemed a little perplexed at the request, but after a few moments he nodded. 'I will get one of the staff to bring something suitable. When you are finished, leave it with them.' And he walked up the stairs without waiting for a response.

Within a few minutes, a young man in the earl's colours arrived with a small wooden stool. 'Will this do? I am to assist you with your work and then take you around the outside when you are finished.'

Gerant was glad that he had someone to help and unrolled the paper with the design. Then it was a matter of getting his new partner to hold a measuring tape to the ground where the two doors met while he checked off the distance to the archway. He was glad he had come. Most of the measurements were generally correct but some were out by at least an inch. He spent quite a bit of time checking and double-checking the angles of the archway and inking in on the paper the distances. Gerant also spent quite a bit of time inspecting the archway itself, as he would need to anchor the screens to the stonework. By listening to the sound as he knocked on suitable parts, he decided that three hinges for each half screen would be sufficient to anchor the structure solidly. The drawing done by the maestro had not even indicated what the arrangement was to be to attach them to the stonework. This was another reason why it had been important to come and confirm things.

While he was making some final checks and confirming his new measurements, he heard footsteps and voices coming along the path towards the stairway. Approaching were three figures in riding gear, carrying gloves and short crops: two women and a man. The shorter and slimmish blond-haired lady and the tall young man wore similar loose white shirts, black leather pants and riding boots to the knee. The other woman was about Gerant's height, had a ruffled white shirt, brown leather pants and boots. These last two had black curly hair and deep brown eyes, copper-coloured skin and were clearly related. Their conversation halted as they approached the stairs, carefully walking through to avoid the large drawing and scattered tools, then journeyed up the stairs and disappeared at the top into the chateau.

A male voice drifted down from above. 'That fellow must be something to do with the new screens your father has ordered. Must mean they are starting soon.'

Chapter 23
Grapes and Vines

The two clay half-moulds of the bunch of grapes were placed together so they matched, and twine was carefully but firmly wrapped around so the halves couldn't wiggle.

'Now we can pour in the wax, and it should turn out exactly the same as the original piece the maestro gave us. At least, that is the plan. We can also use these moulds to make as many copies as we need to complete the screen.'

Gerant nodded to Ray that he understood. Ray had already got the small brazier of coals heating the container of wax. He had explained it was often not worth firing up the forge just to heat some wax, so he used a brazier for that. If Gerant was working with the forge, then Ray would place the wax container just on the side. When they were working with molten metal to go into the final lost wax moulds, they would need the heat of the forge to keep the crucibles of liquid metal at a sufficiently high temperature.

The other pair of moulds in the shape of the vine leaf was also soon ready.

'Right, it's just a matter of being very patient and slowly pouring in the wax through the channel we made using the piece of twig. Like this. Also make sure you are wearing gloves, as they will start to heat up and you don't want to suddenly drop them.' Ray frowned in concentration as he carefully let a stream of liquid wax disappear into the channels. When the inside space within the moulds was full, he quickly checked that there was no wax leaking out between the two halves. Then he carefully packed the two sets of moulds in a straw-filled box so they sat up and the wax wasn't going to pour out again.

'We leave them overnight for the wax to cure and they will be ready to open tomorrow.'

Gerant could see that when all the steps had been done once, Ray would be able to string them all together so he was doing them all in the one day, always having things to do and be keeping busy.

'Ray, this is really smart. I am impressed.'

Ray smiled in satisfaction, giving a little slurp at the compliment. 'Well, I have been doing this for a bit, so I know what I'm doing. Also the maestro will start to ask questions if we don't have it finished as soon as we can.'

As Ray continued working on his lost wax steps, Gerant looked over the measurements he had taken the previous day and the design for the screens that the maestro had drawn. He still was impressed with the idea of making the doors look like a depiction of a grape vine in black cast iron, but a feeling had been niggling at him that it could be improved. Sure, the artistry was amazing and as much as possible the design should depict a rambling grape vine with branches, stems, leaves and small bunches of grapes here and there. The problem was that the entire screens would weigh several hundredweight and they may not be able to support themselves and function as a strong door barring passage up the stairs. That was the problem he had been mulling over while he was making his measurements at the chateau. He grabbed a small piece of blank paper and after several attempts on other scraps, he drew what he was thinking. He was careful to use the tips that Sveg had drilled into him, using strong lines and simple diagrams to show the key points. He sat back and checked his new drawing again, then rolled up the larger original chart with his new drawings.

'I'm just going to get approval for something from the maestro.'

Ray nodded his head without looking up as he maintained his concentration on his castings.

Trantor looked again at his design for a dagger and sword set for Viscount Joffrey. It followed the main features of the dagger made for Urbright, but used citrine and yellow garnets for decoration. That was very appropriate since this commission had come directly from Urbright boasting about his new dagger and how fine it was. Now, he needed just a few minor changes to the lines and it would be ready to show Joffrey and talk about the quality of the weapons he would receive. It would also be a good chance to gauge the final price he could charge and how much the viscount would be prepared to pay so he had one of the first examples of a Shagreen weapon. Shagreen weapon, he mouthed silently. That certainly had a fine ring to it! He then realised there had been a knocking at the door for several seconds.

'Come.'

A very hesitant Gerant popped his head around the corner.

'I couldn't find Molly.'

'Look, I am about to go and discuss a dagger and sword combination with Viscount Joffrey. Will this be quick?'

As an answer, his journeyman walked in bringing some drawings and sat down in the spare chair next to the desk.

'Maestro, your measurements for the new screen matched well.' Gerant hesitated. 'In looking at the design and where the doors will hang, I feel they might need to be reinforced a little, without taking away from the strong design and the intertwined features of the grape vine.' He rapidly laid out the drawings and talked through his idea.

Trantor looked at his original design and then the clear sketch that Gerant had made to show the proposed alterations. *Hmmm, I can see the issue now it has been explained.* He had been focused on bringing out the features of a naturally growing grapevine and not taken any note of how the work must still function as a gateway that could be closed when necessary. *The little shit is right,* he mused. He also saw that the key elements of his design had not been changed, but by running some iron struts up the design, suitably disguised as pieces of vine branch, the doors would become much stronger and rigid. He wished he had thought of this. *At least someone had taught this lad how to draw a design clearly.* He could see this was a useful enhancement that would lead to a better piece of work. That said, it would be easy enough for him to pass it off as his own idea once it had been finished!

'Look, your suggestion has some merit and I get the base of the idea. Just make sure you put in these pieces so they look like vine branches and have the texture that suggests it. Ray can help you with that. I have to go now. I also expect to see the first lot of cast-iron work very soon. When will that be?'

The maestro gave these rapid-fire instructions as he packed up the drawing he had been working on and put them into a fine leather satchel.

'Oh, Ray has already commenced and I would hope we would have something to show you early next week.'

'Good,' was the only and abrupt response given as the maestro left the room.

Gerant packed up his drawings and mused that this had probably been a useful step forward, although every time he was left feeling he was being a huge inconvenience.

The following weeks were a blur of activity and routine, which Gerant really enjoyed as it gave him a sense of purpose. He would get up of a morning, sometimes go down to the garden plot and do a little weeding and collecting some fresh vegetables with Fang constantly at his side. Then it was off to the workshop, where Ray would often have already started work. Together they would carefully pull apart the clay moulds to reveal a new waxy bunch of grapes or vine leaf, which had to be trimmed and from which a new lost wax mould would be made. These next set of moulds would be heated to let the wax run out ready for the molten metal. Then the earlier set of moulds had molten iron poured in very carefully and set aside to cool. The now cooled set of moulds from the previous day were broken open to reveal the bunch of grapes or vine leaves made now in iron, that had to be trimmed and filed to get rid of any small imperfections from the casting. With Ray's help, Gerant would heat them a little in the forge and then fuse them onto the growing screens, which were laid out on pairs of trestles near to the forge. He had also worked with Ray to make a stamp made of harder steel with indentations and ridges worked into the surface.

When this stamp was hammered into a piece of iron strip glowing cherry red from the forge, it left a pattern on the now-cooling iron that resembled the surface of a vine branch. In this way, he was able to reinforce the screen so it would still function as a working door, yet make it seem like it was part of the rambling grape vine design.

All these steps were repeated each day, plus getting in more materials, firewood, charcoal and the other small jobs to keep the workshop and forge running. Often there was time in the afternoon after he and Ray had progressed their work for Gerant to do other little projects or think about extra work. The maestro had made it clear to them that for now the screens for Earl Sherrington were of the first importance, but mentioned that several orders for daggers and swords had started to come in. These were the items that he mulled over in the afternoon, including getting ready for a new kiln run to make some more talium steel. He also brought along the book about smithing and the old parchment leaves hidden in the inside cover and read that again when he had time. Ray had initially shown some curiosity in what Gerant was reading.

'Oh, it's just an old book about smithing. I like to read it to see how they did it in the old days.'

With that explanation, Ray quickly lost interest and went back to his own work. Gerant carefully got out the parchment sheets and reread some of the parts. He decided he would stick to using the two-layer method for making his talium blades. The six-layer secret sounded like it would take years of practice and experimenting before he could master that technique. It was something not to forget about, merely that it was not the next teaching from the old parchment he would like to try. What did pique his interest particularly was the description of hardening the blade to make it even keener and retain its sharpness for much longer. He quietly read out the section to himself.

'Few know the secret of how to harden the edge of a blade even more than from regular forging and using hard steel for the outside of the blade. I give to you the secret recipe that should not be shared with others, unless they are to inherit your mastery. The recipe uses ingredients that are often hard to find and are known to impart their properties of hardness. You will need a piece of the tusk from the spotted tusktooth, ground into small pieces. This creature lives in the waters of the far north. It will not give up its life easily.'

Gerant recalled what Sveg had said about this creature and the place called North Haven in the far north of The Realm. He decided to ask around. Ray had not heard of North Haven. At the lunch table, the maestro's staff all shook their heads when Gerant raised the question.

It was Molly who actually then spoke.

'Actually, I think my mam told me this place is far to the north somewhere and it is often really cold. But I don't know anything more than that.'

'Thanks. I'll keep asking.'

'Why the interest in this place, Gerant?' Molly couldn't help but be curious.

'I am just interested in different parts of The Realm. I might go there one day.'

'Well, you can use the time when everything is shut for the midsummer festival and go there!' suggested Faith.

Gerant had forgotten about this holiday lasting a week, that was celebrated all over The Realm. It had meant at Ashford there was no apprentice instruction at the guild. Sveg had not formally closed the forge but only worked half days. In the afternoons, they all went down to the river for picnics or visited some of the friends in the town the family were close to. Gerant had tagged along and enjoyed everything, although these sorts of things were a bit strange to him, particularly just deciding on the spur of the moment to visit acquaintances and enjoying their company.

There was a lively discussion around the table about what plans they all had for the festival and break. Gerant only half-listened as the banter went back and forth. Who else could he ask? He mentally listed his acquaintances. *There is no way I am going to ask the maestro. Dierdre will probably not know. Maybe Dorian Redman will, because his inn had travellers from all over The Realm. Hamish Wheelwright . . . Hamish Wheelwright! He could well know of this place because he trades materials from all over The Realm and beyond. That iron ore came from another kingdom to the south.*

The sounds of packing up intruded on his thoughts, signalling to him that lunch was over. He distractedly wandered off with Ray back to the workshop, planning another visit to the metal trader.

'Gerant, always a pleasure. I trust the iron ore from down south is suitable for what you require?' The metal trader smiled gently, all the same watching Gerant carefully after inviting him in and offering a chair.

'The quality is really good. The bog iron is what you would expect and would be sufficient for most projects, but for forging weapon blades, I am thinking about just using the ore. I know it costs more, but the results far outweigh the extra coin needed.'

'I should also tell you I am starting to hear from several people I associate with that Maestro Shagreen has turned out some superior arms that have got people talking about the superb quality and there have already been several orders placed. Is that you?'

Gerant nodded, knowing that he could not only trust Hamish, but that the trader had quickly realised who was actually crafting the pieces. He decided to be open about why he had come. There were few in The Capital he did feel he could trust and Hamish Wheelwright was one of them.

'I actually came because I want to keep building my expertise in making weapons. Sveg and I found an old work on smithing and it talks about a method to enhance the sharpness of the blade. You need to make a paste from three ingredients. One of them is the powder from a tusktooth horn, whatever that is. I am trying to find that out and Sveg told me they hunt for these animals in the far north at a place called North Haven.'

The metal trader nodded slowly and then spent several minutes thinking. 'That sort of thing is not in my line and I can't think who would supply it. As a last resort, you could try Count Capuchin, but I wouldn't counsel that.' The metal trader continued thinking. 'I have been to North Haven many years ago. It is about five day's travel north of here. I have a map of The Realm somewhere.'

After some minutes searching in the room, Hamish gave a soft, 'Ah', and pulled out a large piece of thick paper. Bringing it over to the desk, they pored over it. Gerant could see that the road north left The Capital and then joined with another road coming from

Cobham. He followed the path north through to Rivernook, which he recognised as the place where Sveg and Marion had grown up. Farther again was North Haven, which appeared to be where the road ended. He could see that North Haven was on the edge of the sea. He asked Hamish about tusktooths.

'Well, I have heard of them but nothing more, apart from them being large sea creatures. My memory of North Haven is that it is where a lot of fishing and such is done, although I am sure smaller places also hunt the tusktooth and large fish in the sea. My suggestion would be to go to an inn there and see if you can find some sort of fisherman or experienced hunter that could take you out looking for them. Or even easier, sell to you what you need. My sense, for what it is worth, is these tusks are very hard to come by and that makes them worth many gold.'

Listening to what the older man was saying reminded Gerant of his search for talium and the difficulties in obtaining it. Perhaps he should have expected this. These ancient techniques were not only known to but a few, but also used expensive and hard-to-obtain materials. This ground tusktooth sounded the same. At least he had a better idea of where he had to go to try and find some.

'Would I be able to make a copy of this map, Hamish? This North Haven is far to the north and knowing the path would be important.'

'I agree. It is not a place where you can afford to get lost, as the weather can be very punishing. I'll find you a quill and ink and some spare paper and you can transfer whatever details you think you need. I have some notes to write, so just work here until you are finished.'

So Gerant sat at a small side table and inked in his own map. He worked particularly on the details north of The Capital and only sketched in the outlines of the other parts of The Realm, towns and rivers. After half an hour of companionable silence working near to the metal trader, he had finished to his satisfaction. Hamish had been quietly writing at his desk and consulting a number of ledgers, but looked up when the young man stood and stretched.

'Do I owe you anything for this?', Gerant enquired.

'No, just a full account when you return from your journey. I am always interested in tales of places farther away. And any interesting metals or ores you happen to hear about. I am not aware of any mines up that way of import, but they may have opened up something new that I would like to know about. Regardless, safe travels when you go.'

Ray brushed the last bunch of grapes with the black paint and they both stood back to admire the two screen doors. This was the second coat and they had one more to put on the next day.

'Damn, this looks good,' muttered Ray. Gerant agreed.

There had been a minor issue towards the end when Gerant had not been happy with one of the internal supporting struts. It had ended up too straight and wasn't looking like a vine branch. So he cut it out of the almost finished right screen and fashioned it again, this time bending it a little more here and there and emphasising the branch texture using the stamp they had made. This time it looked much better and they both remarked on the improvement.

As they packed up, the gate at the street front squeaked slightly and they both looked up. It was quite rare to have visitors to the workshop. In strode the maestro, followed a little shyly by Molly. Gerant gave her a little half-wave and noticed she was wearing a cornflower blue dress with a matching ribbon and soft leather shoes in a similar shade. She smiled back.

'So these are the finished screens?' The maestro was about to reach out to touch one of the screen doors lying on top of the trestles.

'Don't touch!' The maestro froze.

'Sorry, Maestro, we only just finished putting the second coat of paint on and they will still be wet.' Gerant hoped his outburst would be forgiven.

The maestro only nodded and confined his inspection to peering closely at various parts of the design and then stepping back for a longer look. 'And you are satisfied with the strength of the doors? And I see you will hang each screen using three hinges?'

Gerant nodded and summarised what he had done to make the screens ready for hanging. Ray held back and watched the exchange. His contribution to the work was not under any scrutiny and the quality was to his usual high standard.

'Very well. As soon as the painting is complete they can be installed at the earl's chateau.' The maestro turned to his housekeeper. 'Molly, can you arrange for that carter fellow to be hired for the day and he can assist in the mounting of the doors.' He looked at Gerant. 'You know what you have to do?'

'Of course, Maestro. I have now seen the stairs where these will hang and it should only take an hour or so.'

'Good.' Shagreen nodded and started walking back to the street.

Molly gave both the artisans a broad grin and pretended to wipe her forehead with relief. They both started chuckling quietly as she hurried to catch up to the maestro.

Chapter 24
The Earl

A horse pulling a flat-bed dray with two men sitting in the front pulled up to the gatehouse. The guards had been watching the cart approach and put up their hands. Gerant hopped down and showed the guards the pass.

'Sergeant!'

This time, the sergeant was a younger man with brown hair and a trimmed beard. He appeared and checked the pass quickly and walked around the dray. 'What's in the cart?'

Gerant reached up and pulled a corner of the sacking up so that the sergeant could see the edge of the cast-iron work.

'We've finished this piece for Earl Sherrington and will install it at the chateau. They know we are coming.'

'OK, no problems, then. On your way, gentlemen.' The sergeant took a final look, switched the sacking back over the screens and disappeared up the stairs within the gatehouse archway.

'This is going to be interesting,' murmured Marcus, the carter. 'I've never been up here before.'

Gerant had met the nuggety, squat carter when he had arrived at the workshop that morning. Marcus had been hired for the day and so was very happy when he heard where they were taking the load. Between Marcus, Gerant and Ray, they placed some hessian sacking on the floor of the dray before lifting in and lying flat the two screen halves, roping them in securely before covering them with more sacking.

A similar process occurred at the main door of the chateau, except that the chief steward was not available. He had left word that they were to go directly round the back following the manicured cart path to the rear of the building, which gave access to the stairs.

'Corr, this place is flash!' was Marcus's comment, repeated several times as they had approached the chateau and led the placid horse and dray around to the rear of the building.

They parked the cart close to the stairs and Marcus gave his horse a little bit of chaff in a nose bag to keep it occupied while they worked. First, they took out the two halves of the screen and leant them up against the wall near the bottom of the stairs.

Gerant laid out the various tools he had brought with him and examined the best way to take off the wooden doors. Eventually, they came off without issue and he and Marcus laid them flat in the bottom of the dray.

He picked up the hammer and chisel. 'I'll just take down the frame and the top boards. Would you be able to throw the pieces up in the cart as we go?'

'Sure. You are the one doing the hard work, matey.'

Gerant attacked the frame and was quickly able to clear the timber away from the stone archway. He stood on the wooden crate they had brought and attacked the boards and wooden partition covering the arch above where the doors had been. He inserted the chisel into the top join and was about to strike a blow to separate it cleanly when he heard a discrete, 'Ahem.'

About halfway up the flight of stairs, a young lady had appeared and was discretely lowering herself to sit on one step, her leather shoes peeping out of the skirt of a bright yellow dress. The yellow tones of the dress complimented her copper-coloured complexion and the dark ringlets framing her face and cascading down her back. After a moment, Gerant recognised the woman as one of the three riders who had appeared when he was measuring the space the previous visit.

'Annie and I heard the noise and came to investigate. We're just going to watch from here.'

Gerant registered an older woman with short grey hair who was sitting on a chair at the top of the stairs, working on some embroidery.

He hopped off the crate and looked up at the glorious vision in yellow that was perched halfway up the stairs. 'Ah, that's no problem at all, Miss . . .'

The woman smiled briefly. 'Best to stick with my lady, or countess. Countess Tahlia, of House Sherrington.'

Well, that was a big surprise.

'Of course, my lady. Apologies for the noise and the mess.'

'Oh, this looks like fun. You need to tell me exactly what you are doing.'

And then followed a curious interplay between the two of them. Gerant finished clearing away the old wooden frame, then he and Marcus manipulated each side of the screen into the archway and marked off where the hinges would go. Then they drilled some holes into the stonework, attached metal plates for the hinge brackets, and so on. At each step he had to explain what he was doing, and, on several occasions, Lady Tahlia came down the steps to inspect the work more closely and ask more questions. Annie, who it turned out was Lady Tahlia's maid, stayed at the top of the stairs watching proceedings and continuing her embroidery. Marcus helped out where needed and often stood there shaking his head in amazement.

With the hinges anchored into the stonework, it was then a matter of lining up the screens so that each half door clicked into the hinges and could swing. That took a little bit of brute force and then some adjusting of the bolts so that the halves swung freely. Gerant also applied a little oil onto the hinges, so they moved with only the smallest noise. The final step was to drill holes in the pavers where the two halves met for the drop bolts to engage and on the edges of the corridor for when the screens were fully open.

Gerant sighed quietly with contentment and looked at the cast-iron screen doors hanging in their new location. The arched shapes followed the stone opening exactly all the way to the top of the arch. The blackened cast iron truly looked like a series of grape vines winding in and out of each other, with leaves and tiny bunches of grapes growing out of the stems. And with the oil they opened silently and with only a minimum of effort. He opened them fully and the two drop bolts fell into the holes in the paving leaving the arched frame open to its widest extent. Then, as a final check he closed one half of the screen and the drop bolt engaged into its hole with a gentle *thunk*. He was about to shut the other screen so that the latch engaged.

'Do you mind if I do that?'

Lady Tahlia had risen from her step and had an enquiring look on her face.

'Of course, my lady. It would be our honour.' Gerant was hard put not to smile as he said this. Marcus was furiously agreeing.

The young woman slowly reached the bottom of the flight, stepped through the half-opening, then gently pushed the screen door together so that the latch clicked shut with a soft clang. After a moment, she clapped her hands in delight and her face was beaming. Even Annie at the top of the stairs had stopped to watch and was nodding in agreement.

'Papa is going to be so pleased with them. I am just going to find him so he can see.'

Lady Tahlia opened the screen door again and quietly ran up the stairs and disappeared around the corner at the top. Her maid watched her go but continued with her embroidery. Gerant didn't know what to do, so he and Marcus tidied up and put the tools and other scraps of wood and metal into the dray. They had almost finished when they heard the sound of voices approaching the top of the stairs. There was a female voice, clearly Tahlia, and a quite deep, softly spoken male voice.

Down the steps came Lady Tahlia animatedly chatting to a tall, older man in a simple doublet, soft leggings and half boots. His plain but superbly tailored outfit was complimented by a distinctive silver emblem on a chain, consisting of a rearing stag depicted in green with silver spears on either side. He had the same copper complexion but his black hair, cropped short, was peppered with grey. From his clothing, facial features and demeanour, Gerant presumed this was the Earl Sherrington. Glancing quickly at Marcus, he could see the carter had made the same conclusion. Marcus had a look of quiet horror on his face and didn't know what to do, gripping strongly the last bits of cast-off wood from the old door frame.

The two reached the bottom of the stairs and Tahlia proceeded to show her father how the doors closed and how they could be kept open by engaging the drop bolts into the flooring.

'See, Papa, isn't this so much better than those old, worn-out doors? And the design is so marvellous, you almost feel you could pick those grapes!'

The earl smiled gently at his daughter's enthusiasm and nodded. Then he turned and Gerant noticed his dark brown eyes still had the remnants of warmth in their expression but had become more alert and piercing. 'And these two are?'

'Oh, Papa, they put the gates in. He was here the other day doing some measuring.' Tahlia nodded at Gerant.

The earl looked inquiringly at Gerant.

'I am Gerant, my lord. I am one of the artisans with Maestro Shagreen.'

'Um, my lord, I am just the carter . . .' Marcus looked down at the floor in embarrassment.

The earl turned his gaze back to Gerant. 'Well, Gerant, you can see that my daughter thinks this is a very fine job. At first look I tend to agree. But I would welcome you telling me a little about how they were designed and built. I presume you were involved?'

'Yes, my lord. I worked on the screens with my workmate, Raymond, to the maestro's design.'

'Hmmm. Describe for me how you took the design and converted it into this impressive structure.'

Gerant hesitated slightly.

'No, I don't need to hear everything, just give me the idea of the key steps.'

'Well, my lord, the design of vine leaves, bunches of grapes and branches is a combination of lost wax casting and traditional smithing. You can see how the parts make up the feel of grape vines intertwined with each other, but they repeat the design. We do this by using a . . .' Gerant struggled with how to explain this thought. *Ah.* '. . . using a series of master moulds. For instance, here, here and here the bunches of grapes are exactly the same, but look different because the leaves and branches are positioned in different ways.'

'Just so. I can see what you are meaning. Very clever.' Gerant could see that the earl had very quickly picked up the idea he was trying to explain.

'The branches are used to provide reinforcement to the structure of the door, while still being part of the artistic design.'

The earl pondered for a moment. 'And this was so from the beginning?'

Gerant hesitated. 'Well, I realised that changing the design slightly would mean that the strength of the actual screens could be increased. When I explained this to the maestro, he agreed.'

'Ah, so you proposed this adjustment?'

'I guess you could say so, my lord.'

'Hmm. Your explanation has given me a better understanding of how well made these screens are. My thanks.'

Gerant didn't know what to say to this, so confined himself to giving a slow nod, trying to indicate his gratitude with what the earl had said.

'It will also mean I can ask some more intelligent-sounding questions when the maestro comes to formally confirm the project has been completed. Again, my thanks to both of you and I will be passing on to the maestro that I am very happy with the finished work.'

The earl smiled gently at the two young men before gesturing to his daughter.

'Come, Tahlia. We should let these gentlemen finish. All the same, it has been a welcome distraction from court business!'

The two figures climbed the stairs and disappeared around the corner at the top of the flight.

Gerant took his tools and the sacking used to cover the screens into the workshop after Marcus had dropped him back. Ray was not at his bench, so perhaps had finished a little early. Gerant also felt that he might call a close to the day and head off. But he was going to do something he had been meaning to do for a little while. And he decided that he deserved a little treat for himself now that the screens had been completed and installed at the earl's chateau. He walked out to the street and followed it a little farther into the Florian Quarter. After another hundred yards or so he saw the building he was looking for, entering a large door with a low hum and bubble of voices emerging from within. This was the Purple Heart tavern, which Gerant had noted on a number of occasions when walking past on errands with Ray. Sveg had sometimes stopped off at the Wheatsheaf in Ashford for an ale at week's end or after a hard day's toil. Maybe he would see if this was something he might try. He certainly felt like he deserved an ale today.

Similar to all the taverns he had gone into previously, the main room in the Purple Heart was somewhat dimly lit, with a bar running down one side, some tables and a few booths along the far wall. It was late afternoon and there were a number of patrons talking quietly. Ray had said this tavern was frequented by tradesmen and artisans who worked in the quarter and was less rough and tumble than some other taverns closer to the port or market areas of The Capital. That suited Gerant fine for when he wanted to have a relaxing ale and think about a few things, not forever be worrying about fights and melees. He walked up to the bar.

'What'll it be?' asked a bartender with a brief smile. 'Ale?'

'Just a tankard, thanks.'

'Well, we have our usual, or our pale ale or our special dark ale.'

The dark ale sounded interesting and he hadn't had anything like that before. Well, in for a copper, in for a gold. 'The dark ale, thanks.'

'Right, one tankard of Black Heart. That will be five coppers.'

He took the tankard carefully over to an unoccupied booth on the far wall and sat down. Already he liked the room as there were no noisy people and there was an almost gentle ebb and flow of conversation between people standing at the bar or seated on the tables. No one seemed interested in him, apart from a quick glance his way as he walked past. He took a sip of ale. Well, that was a little different! Still cool and refreshing and a slight bitter taste, but also like raisins and a hint of the flavour like the one time he had been given chocolate to try. He could get to like this, although one ale every week was all he was allowing himself.

As he slowly kept sampling the ale, he thought about travelling north during the midsummer break and what he would need to take. *My bedroll, blanket and food, of course, and a change of clothes. It sounds like it can get cold up there, so certainly my thick coat, gloves and a cap. What else? My two throwing daggers.* The confrontation on the way to Osmount made them an absolute must. While he knew how to handle them well, one aspect was that potential attackers didn't know what they were facing. He thought of taking another longer dagger or sword or spear but dismissed that. It was quite amusing that he knew how to make high quality weapons, but had only the very basic idea of how to wield them. And he didn't have the time or want to spend coin to take lessons.

What else? An axe? Too big and heavy. Hatchet? No. Wait! He mused on this. *It will be fairly light and also be very useful for getting wood for a camp-fire. And if I have a hatchet looped onto my belt that people can see, maybe that will give them second thoughts. With a hatchet and the throwing knives that could suffice. I could even make the head out of talium steel! That will give really good strength, a sharp edge and weigh less. It will be fun to try shaping something different with talium besides swords or daggers. And I could craft the handle out of a nice wood. There's that old man at the market who sells dressed pieces of timber who might have some for sale. Something like cherry or walnut might work. This feels like a plan. Hmmm.*

As he finished his tankard, Gerant thought some more about his rapidly evolving idea. He could start working on it in the coming days. He was sure that Redman's had a hatchet or axe that he could borrow to use as a guide. And the maestro would have more projects coming along. But that would likely happen after the midsummer break. Now that the screens had been completed, he could do with a few small projects for himself. He took his empty tankard and left it on the bar, nodded to the barkeep and wandered out into the late afternoon air.

Maestro Trantor Shagreen was in his element explaining the cast-iron screens to Earl Sherrington. 'My lord, there are a number of features of the design that I wish to make you aware of.'

'Do go on, Maestro. I am particularly interested in what this represents, both visually and structurally. I see it is up to your usual superb standard.'

Excellent, Trantor thought, *this is going to go well.* He politely gestured to the earl to walk back some twenty yards along the gravelled path to the stables.

'From back here, you can see the strength of line of the stone archway where the stairs finish. We needed to match that space within the archway with similar strong features, which is why I chose cast iron. From this distance they merge together and provide a clear visual barrier you can see as you come from the stables. Clearly, the primary purpose is to protect the back of the chateau should it be needed, yet maintain the ease of access for all who use the back stairs.'

'Yes, from back here I can absolutely appreciate those concepts. Carry on.'

Trantor accompanied the earl back to the screens. 'As you approach, the solid iron barrier changes from still being made of iron but becomes a screen that allows air to flow through them. Everything will stay fresh and gentle breezes can move up the stairway and circulate into the chateau. Rain won't get through because of the stone archway and should the weather get terribly cold in winter it would be a matter of moments to hang canvas drops or similar on the inside of the screens.'

They moved back to within a few feet of the installation. 'Then, of course, my lord will see the design I have incorporated into the structure of the screens, that of a grape vine. See here, we have bunches of grapes, vine tendrils, leaves and the vine branches. This gives the impression of grapevines growing at the bottom of the stairs. It is a happy combination of artistic flair and structural integrity. You will also note that the vine branches twist and join up the screen to provide basic strength so it still functions as a barrier should it be needed. We have anchored the screens into the stone archway using strong bolts and both sides can be swung out of the way if required.'

The earl looked suitably impressed. 'I particularly like the way the branches of the vines look natural but provide the support for the screen doors at the same time. Did you have to revise the design very much to include that structural strength?'

The maestro thought about the implications of the question and decided there was little danger to it. 'A very astute observation, my lord. As with any large project like this, you are always thinking about how to improve the design. While the original version was good, I realised I could cleverly weave the branches so that it gained strength without altering the overall look and keeping the pleasing lines. So I made some small adjustments and my craftsmen were able to build something better.'

He watched the earl to see what effect this explanation had. The earl was looking at the screen and then slowly nodded and looked at him.

'Excellent, excellent. It is impressive that you are always looking to improve your designs to end up with a better outcome.'

Trantor smiled and bowed his head gently to acknowledge the compliment.

'Well, again, my congratulations on a fine job. I can see this will be in place for many years to come.' The earl's expression became a little more serious. 'I have to go for a council meeting at the palace, unfortunately. But I will have a couple of my men come around this afternoon with the coin. We agreed on 400 gold, did we not?'

Good, thought Trantor, with relief. He nodded again, positively but in a discreet manner. 'Correct, my lord.'

'There will also be a small purse containing an additional ten gold for that young fellow who works for you. When he came to install the screens, he showed some remarkable expertise for someone so young.'

'Of course, my lord. I would be happy to pass that on to him.'

'What was his name? I didn't catch it when he was here.'

'Oh, Gerant. He has only been with me for a few months and has turned out to be not too bad.'

The earl nodded and looked up the stairs and called. 'Waterford? Oh, there you are. Would you mind escorting the maestro out? We are done here.'

Later that day, the maestro took the pouches to his coin room and opened the chest, after first locking the door from the inside. The earl's men had delivered the payment and there was no need to count it: it would be 400 gold. He unwound the silken cord from around the neck of the leather pouch and dropped the ten extra gold in. Then he quickly tied the cord securely and hefted the pouch into the main part of the chest, so it lay with the other sacks of coin spread across the base. Trantor put the other trays back on top, locked the chest and left the coin room with a grim smile on his features.

Chapter 25
Ownership

Gerant was happy with the way the hatchet was looking. He gave the cherry wood handle another rub with the linseed-soaked cloth. It had been an easy matter to visit Redman's Inn and borrow a hatchet from the wood pile out the back of the tavern for a few coppers deposit. Dorian Redman had been in a good mood when Gerant had wandered up and found him in the bar room getting ready for the day's trading.

'I know where you live. Still at Mrs Lammings? Just give me a few coppers in case one of my staff ask where it has disappeared to. It's summer, so we're not needing to split much wood.'

'I'll have it back in a few days, Dorian. I just need to measure it and get the shape and angles right.'

The hatchet he had borrowed was well used and he was content to follow the profile of the handle and the general construction of the head, including the angles of the bit and how the handle shaft fitted into the head. He had got to the stage of working on the head and after quite a bit of thinking, decided to make only the bit out of talium steel. So, he had fashioned the head out of core steel and then folded over some talium edge steel on the forge once it was hot enough to fuse with the core. After carefully hammering out and quenching the bit to match the profile of the borrowed hatchet, he now had a strong steel hatchet with the blade part of the head featuring the now familiar greenish-grey surface of talium steel.

Similar to his sword and dagger blades, it had easily taken a keen edge when he had carefully worked on sharpening the hatchet with the whetstone. Gerant also liked the way how the deep cherrywood colour from the handle somehow complimented the green-tinged steel and made the hatchet very distinctive.

He checked over the new piece carefully to look for any spots he had missed in polishing and sharpening that might need some slight adjustments. No, it was all looking good. He hefted the hatchet in his right hand, and it had a nice feel and balance. A surprise thought surfaced while he was gently polishing the handle. *Hmmm. What the heck*, he thought, *I may as well have a go.* He walked away from the workshop and stood around ten feet from one of the posts in the yard near the kiln. He relaxed and after a couple of gentle breaths threw the hatchet at the post. The hatchet hit the post about six inches from where Gerant had been aiming and bounced off, dropping to the ground. *Well*, Gerant thought, *not too bad.* He had tried to throw the hatchet overhand, which was different to how he had learnt to throw daggers. Also it needed a little more finesse to get the blade to hit at the correct angle to bury itself into the post. He picked up the hatchet and walked to the mark and tried another couple of times. The second time was not much better, but on the third attempt the hatchet buried itself in the post about a foot below his aiming point. *Wow! This might even work.* And thinking more on this idea, Gerant realised that this might be a good way to pass some time on his trip. If he set up camp of a night and then practised throwing the hatchet for a few minutes, hopefully he would steadily improve. He also realised he would have to keep practising his dagger throwing, to make sure learning with the hatchet didn't affect his underhanded throwing style and accuracy. Gerant gave the hatchet another quick polish and resharpened the edge. He had already sewn in a loop of leather onto his belt, and it was just a matter of moments to carefully hitch the hatchet into the loop, where it sat comfortably on his left hip. He was very pleased with himself and what he had achieved in his day's work. He left the hatchet on his workbench and decided that he would reward himself with a tankard of ale and do some thinking about another idea he had been mulling over. He took a piece of parchment he had brought from home, grabbed a couple of scraps of paper and a pencil and walked off to the Purple Heart, gently humming to himself.

Gerant grabbed his tankard of Black Heart and found that the seat at the booth he often sat at was vacant. He plopped down and had a satisfying couple of swallows of the dark ale. He was acquiring a taste for it, but was not worried about drinking too much. For one, he had too much work to do at the workshop and, for another, it would be too much of a strain on his purse. He quickly looked around the room and saw it was not overly full and a number of quiet conversations were happening. He was starting to feel at home here and now knew the names of some of the regular staff and was happy to have a quick chat about the weather or recent happenings in The Capital or more locally in the Florian Quarter. He took out the piece of parchment he had brought and looked at the lettering on it. It was actually a copy of something Sveg had obtained many years ago when he was learning as an apprentice. On it was each letter of the alphabet, in various styles. Sveg routinely used it as a guide when he had to make any signs or to design letters made from metal. There were three styles: one with formal straight-backed lettering, one in a more informal, everyday form and the third one that Gerant was particularly interested in, having a more curling, cursive style. He mused on the two ideas for small projects that had found their way into his consciousness a few nights before as he was dropping off to sleep. It involved using a cursive letter made into a design. One idea was to use the lost wax method to make a pendant for Marion as a thank you the next time he went back to Ashford.

The other one he needed to think more on. Hence why he was sitting here, as he wouldn't be distracted by smithing tasks or Ray interrupting with questions or other work. The gentle hubbub of conversation in the tavern seemed to recede and reach a background murmur. Focusing, he recalled clearly seeing the maestro being happy to pass off a piece of fine smithing work as solely coming from his talents. Sure, he was responsible for much of the design work, but the making of these fine pieces were actually from the hands of his two artisans. Gerant had already got the sense that his work was not being appreciated enough. He knew, for instance, that

Earl Sherrington had known he had made the iron screens that were installed at his chateau, but nothing more had been said. There was also the dagger he had already made that apparently had been well regarded by Viscount Urbright. Again, Gerant had nothing to show that the dagger had been made by him, even though it was to the maestro's design. Ray didn't care a hoot about recognition for his work, only that he got paid and was largely left alone.

So what might be the solution? Gerant had got to thinking about being able to stamp a design mark on any work he made. Straight away, he had thought of a drawback where using talium steel for the blade made it very hard to impress something into the surface. But then he realised using a pure talium stamp might mean it was sufficiently hard enough to work on anything. Thinking further, that meant it would have to be a small mark, as he didn't want to use lots of talium in the making. And it would also mean that the design would have to be small and wouldn't be really noticeable, unless you knew where to look. Once he was happy with the physical aspects of the project, he had spent quite a bit of time pondering the design. He could design a symbol, but couldn't think of something that was distinctive and depicted something meaningful. So he wondered about a letter. That was why he had brought with him his copy of Sveg's parchment of letter designs. He sought inspiration, as he occasionally sipped his ale and watched people at the other tables without really seeing them. He didn't want anything formal looking, so looked at the cursive letters. *Probably 'G' for Gerant, maybe.* He couldn't decide whether it should be a capital 'G' or a small 'g'. He looked at them and still couldn't make up his mind. Looking at the small 'g', he wondered about it and suddenly a funny thought came into his mind. On one of his scraps of paper, he drew a 'g' like the primer but changed its lines and curves slightly. *Hmmm.* It was certainly a 'g' if that was what you were thinking but, looking at it slightly differently, it could also look like an 'S'.

'g' for Gerant . . .or 'S' for Shagreen . . .Wow, this might work! A mark that could be put on a blade and could mean the Shagreen workshop, but Gerant would know it was one of his pieces. The room and the quiet chatter seemed to slow down and become softer again as he thought more about this idea. After starting and then discarding some thoughts, he wondered about enclosing the letter in a circle to make it distinctive and clear-cut. He quickly drew the letter again in the cursive style and put a ring around it.

He was on to something good and thought about how to replicate the design using lost wax. Gerant took a couple of swallows of ale just as a shadow appeared on the piece of parchment and stayed. He looked up. Standing next to the table in the booth was a tall, thinnish young man with cropped blond hair and a goatee beard. He was holding a tankard and dressed in a uniform that Gerant recognised as like those he had seen up at the gatehouse.

'Anyone else sitting here? It's got busy.'

Gerant looked up and realised he had got lost in his design and not paid attention. He nodded.

'I recognise you. You came through the gatehouse a couple of times and went to Earl Sherrington's chateau. I'm Dirk, by the way. I work up there as a guard.'

Dirk slid into the booth on the other side of the table and had a couple of swallows of his ale.

'Gerant. I work for Maestro Shagreen. We did a set of iron screen doors for him and we've started doing weapons for a few. I'm a journeyman smith.'

Dirk nodded. 'I haven't seen you here before.'

'Oh, I've just started coming here as the workshop is just round the corner. It helps me to think if I have a drink at the same time.'

Gerant looked at the other young man with an enquiring look.

'Me? I often pop in here after I finish my shift. I've got a room a few blocks away. A few of us lads live in a house together. It keeps the costs down to share.' Dirk took a few more swallows and gestured with his tankard at the parchment and papers. 'This what you're working on?'

Gerant found he was enjoying the conversation. He'd initially been a little dismayed when a stranger had come up, but the other young man had been genuinely interested in talking with someone roughly his own age. 'It's a design I am going to make into a stamp I can impress into the blade of a weapon up near the hilt. Just to show where it was made and who made it.'

'Bit fancy looking, but I can still see it's an 'S'', muttered Dirk, poring over the scrap of paper.

Gerant flushed with pleasure. 'Yes. Good of you to pick up what I am trying to show.' He was also interested in talking with someone of his own age. 'So, you work up the hill there. Are you always at the gatehouse?'

Dirk put down his tankard and eased back in a relaxed pose. 'Nah, I move around a bit. Depends on the roster and where they need guards. Sometimes at the gatehouse, on patrol around The Park – that's what they call the area we have to patrol – sometimes at the palace, sometimes out in the Argent Quarter, or down to the port to escort important goods to and fro.'

'Wow. What do you like best?'

'Depends. Sometimes it's a bit boring just standing around, but other times if you are up at the palace you see some really interesting stuff, or one of the royal family goes past or something like that. Then you really stiffen up and make sure they know you are doing a good job. Sergeant says I am doing really well and could get a promotion soon.'

'Great. So you know most of the important people up there?'

'Weeell, I don't get to talk to them, but I have a fair idea of who they all are and what they do. As well as the royal family and the dukes and viscounts and lords and ladies, there are heaps of really important people in senior positions as well. The chancellor and chief steward and chief cook and head ranger and the senior lady-in-waiting and so forth.'

'You must be quite important yourself, then, knowing all that.'

Dirk took another big swallow and couldn't help puffing himself up a little. 'Don't know about that. But I'm doing an important job, I guess.'

Gerant filed away in his mind that Dirk might be a good way to find out a bit more about some of those things in the future. You never knew when you might need to try to approach these people and he already knew that you needed to know who was the right person and the correct way to try to get a meeting. He realised that Dirk had asked him something while he had been thinking about these possibilities and quickly recalled it: he had only been half-listening. 'Yes, it looks like we are going to be crafting more and more weapons, particularly daggers and swords. We have made a dagger for Viscount Urbright and I believe we will soon be making a sword for Earl Sherrington.'

Dirk's face showed how impressed he was when he heard the names. 'Very important people. But would you make blades for people like me? I can always can use a new sword or dagger.'

'Well, that might be possible if we have the time and you have the coin.'

'Oh. How much for a dagger?'

'Well, the one for the viscount I think we asked two hundred gold for.'

Dirk had been taking a long swallow from his tankard and burst into a long fit of coughing as the ale went down the wrong way. After a minute or so, the coughing subsided and he looked at Gerant with new respect, wiping his eyes to get rid of the tears from the coughing fit. 'That's, that's, two year's wages! No way I could afford that. These must be amazing blades for you to charge that much!'

'Well, I like to think so. That's why I want to put this stamp on so everyone knows where they have come from.'

Dirk nodded in understanding and asked more about the styling of the weapons and their balance and length and other details. He clearly knew his stuff. Gerant was happy to talk to him about this. It was something he missed being able to chat about. Ray was only interested in lost wax and his own work and only took a passing interest. And the maestro had even less interest apart from what he could pass off as his own. They spent a pleasurable half an hour chatting about weapons and guard work and smithing and living in The Capital. Gerant suddenly realised the strength of the daylight was starting to change. He took a last few swallows of his ale and wiped his mouth.

'Well, Dirk, I really enjoyed this. I have to head off as I live in the River Quarter and I need to do a few things before dark.'

'Likewise, matey. Would be good to share an ale next time. I'm here every other day at this sort of time, depending on when I finish.'

'I come usually on this day to wind up the week. See you next time.' Gerant gave Dirk a hand clasp as he left and wandered out. He felt good. He had progressed a couple of good ideas and worked on some drawings for the project. Hopefully he had made a new friend, or at least someone to have an ale and a chat with. And with the hatchet finished, he was almost ready to go on his journey north. There were just a few more things to plan and get ready. He walked off towards the River Quarter in the gradually failing light.

Chapter 26
A Word of Advice

Gerant sat at the kitchen table and let the noise of lunchtime conversation wash over him. After finishing his wedge of goose pie, he had listened to the plans the others had for the midsummer break. He thought of his own plans to walk north to try and obtain a tusk from one of those sea creatures and realised it sounded far-fetched. He also realised he didn't want to explain why he wanted it, so he kept silent. Molly was going to visit a friend and stay at New Town for a while; Faith was going to some of the festival events, particularly plays and theatre performances; Susie was going to Nutley where her family came from; and Donald was going to do some work for his brother-in-law, who was a carter. Ray wasn't doing anything apart from disappearing somewhere and as the conversation ebbed and flowed, Gerant got out his piece of scrap paper and continued working on his design for Marion's pendant. He was working on making the 'M' a little more curvy and vaguely registered that the conversation started to quieten down as the rest of them packed up their plates and there was some scraping of chairs. He was getting really close to what was starting to look right and what he was hoping for in the design. He kept focusing on getting the curves and thickness right. Then an excited remark intruded into his thoughts.

'Oh, how lovely. What a gorgeous design. Is that "M" for me?'

He looked up quickly, annoyed at the interruption, and kept strengthening the lines of the letter shape. 'No, it's "M" for Marion. She has done so much for me.'

There was a short, shocked silence and then he heard Molly's footsteps rapidly disappearing out of the kitchen. He realised what he had said. *Oh, fuck, you idiot,* he railed at himself in his mind.

'Well, that was not well done, my young cock,' muttered Faith, with her hands on her hips and a look of perplexed anger on her face. 'Who the hell is this Marion?'

Gerant held his head in his hands and wished that the ground would suddenly open up and swallow him. He slowly told the cook who Marion was, his voice slightly muffled as he kept looking at the table surface only inches away.

'They took me in when I was just a homeless nothing and I almost feel like she is my mother. I have very little memory of my own mother – she died when I was small – but I am sure she was just like Marion in the loving, caring way. I owe Marion so much and I thought I could give her a pendant when I go back next. It's just a small thing but I hope she will like it. I didn't even realise that Molly would think it was for her. I am such a brainless twit. What do I do, Faith?'

It was clear that Faith had lots of further questions, but she sighed and made a decision that now was not the time. She came round the table and sat down next to Gerant and took his hands and looked into his eyes.

'You poor boy. I knew only a little of your previous circumstances. Look, your heart is in the right place.' She patted his hands. 'You know she's sweet on you, don't you? That's why she was so offended.'

New understanding dawned on Gerant. His mouth softly formed a large O. 'She'll hate me now. I can't believe I said that. That's it, isn't it?'

'Gerant,' soothed Faith softly. 'All is not lost. Just tell her the truth. And tell her you care for her. She will come round. But give her a bunch of flowers when you tell her. And buy her something. Some jewellery perhaps, maybe some earrings. Stay away from a pendant.'

'But she won't want to see me when I want to explain,' wailed Gerant.

'Oh, she'll see you if you make it sound important and you are clearly sorry about it.' Faith patted his hands again. 'It'll be fine, Gerant. Just don't leave it too long, that's all.'

Gerant walked out of the kitchen and back to the workshop in a daze.

The door to the shop in the Florian Quarter closed gently and Gerant rang the tiny bell on the counter. After a few moments, a well-built but short man wearing an apron emerged from a door behind the counter. His somewhat pudgy features were unremarkable apart from very bushy eyebrows over warm-brown eyes and strands of brownish hair draped over a large bald front. He peered over some very strong glasses and a broad grin appeared on his face as he recognised the visitor.

'Well met, young Gerant. I hope those garnets and tourmalines were of sufficient quality and size for what you needed? What are you after this time? I just got a shipment of some quality peridots that have a lovely green hue to them, if you like.' Adam Purslip waited patiently, polishing his glasses softly on his tunic.

'Well, Master Purslip, I am sure we could use them for a new blade, once the person who orders it tells us his colour preference.' Gerant paused in embarrassment. 'Actually, I am here on a personal matter. I wondered if you could help me out with some jewellery I want to get. Some earrings . . .'

'Ah. Young man, that is also not a problem. We do have quite a few items I could show you. But perhaps a little more information would help me. Who is it for? What do they like? What sort of style?'

Gerant reddened even more. 'Umm, I don't actually know. About my age. Umm.' Gerant thought rapidly about what he remembered about jewellery and what sort of options there were and the cost. 'Maybe something in sterling silver. Nothing too fancy. Have you got anything with onyx or similar?'

The jeweller had been in this situation many, many times and was not the least bit perturbed. He rapidly thought through the options. 'Yes, yes, yes, yes. Are you meaning black onyx or the red form?' We got some nice red onyx not long ago and I think there are a least a couple of small teardrop styles in sterling silver.'

'Umm. Red, I think.'

'One moment while I find them.'

Without waiting, the jeweller disappeared into the back and Gerant hastily walked over to a glass display case with a few pendants, brooches and rings displayed. Most of them appeared to be way out of his price range and featured quite large gemstones in a silver or gold setting.

After a few minutes, Purslip reappeared carrying a couple of velvet-lined trays with pairs of earrings pinned within. He showed Gerant several pairs of sterling silver earrings with the banded, red stone attractively polished and set in oval tear-shaped droplets.

Gerant quickly made his decision. They were all beautiful but there was one pair where the banding on the onyx was particularly striking.

'A very wise choice, Gerant. I am sure she will love them. Someone special, obviously?' The jeweller's eyes twinkled at the young man's continuing embarrassment.

'Umm, I hope so. They will be terrific. Umm, what do they cost?'

The jeweller could see the worry that had quickly spread over the young man's face.

'Hmmm. Sterling silver and red onyx. A lovely combination but not cheap. But because I know you . . . and you and the maestro are such important customers, let's say . . . five gold.'

Purslip peered at Gerant to see what the response was. He would normally have charged double that or more, but he really liked this young man. He wondered who she was and hoped it would have the desired effect.

Gerant swallowed hard. 'That should be fine, Adam. Thank you.'

'No, thank you, young man. I will put them in a nice little velvet case. No extra charge. Good luck!'

The next day, Gerant walked with Ray to lunch, but quickly bolted his food. The others were only partly through their meal as they continued to discuss their midsummer plans. Molly had been her usual friendly self with the others, but it felt like she was deliberately ignoring him and had not responded at all to a couple of comments he had made. He looked at Faith, and she had surreptitiously nodded quietly as if to say, 'Don't worry, it will be fine'.

He quickly walked into the main part of the house and looked both ways before opening the room that Molly used as her office. Without waiting any longer, he put a folded note on the desk and walked out. If Molly found it and read it, it said:

'What I said the other day was unforgivable and I need to explain the true circumstances and why I care for you. Please meet me at the bench on the riverbank near the port bridge tomorrow before lunch.'

Gerant had laboured over the words for many hours and had actually shown Faith what he had written.

'Good work, young man. If that doesn't convince her to come, nothing will.'

Gerant sat on the bench, looked at the gently lapping water on the riverbank, and wondered again if he was just being stupid and she would, of course, not come. He had been there from mid-morning as he had no idea really what would happen and when she would show. Or not. The little sack was under the bench, and he had already checked it twenty times or more. He quickly looked along the street emerging from the River Quarter again and there was no familiar figure approaching. *Oh gods, she's not coming. You were an idiot then and you are an idiot now.* He held his head in his hands, bending over and looking at the dirt in front of the bench without really seeing it. After a few seconds, he straightened up and decided he should get back to the workshop and maybe start to carve the seal for his weapon stamp. IIe stood up about to head off, then suddenly noticed a familiar figure stalking towards him with a grim look on her face.

'This had better be good. I had to get Faith to cover for me and say I was meeting with one of our suppliers, in case the maestro is looking for me.'

'Thanks for coming, Molly. Please sit down. I have something to say to you.'

'Hummph.' Molly sat down on the bench next to Gerant with her arms crossed.

Gerant reached under the bench for the sack. He pulled out a bunch of flowers he had bought at the market that morning. 'These are for you.'

Molly couldn't help but uncross her arms and hold the posy. She smelled them contentedly.

'And this is also for you. As an apology.'

Molly's mouth mimicked a small O and she gently opened the velvet-lined box. Her O got bigger and she looked at Gerant for the first time.

'Can I tell you about Marion? You would love her: she's almost my mother.'

Molly nodded slowly. As Gerant quietly explained, a few tears started to track slowly down her cheeks. Throughout the short explanation, Molly was silent as the tears multiplied, joined up and began to flow freely.

'So, Molly, I owe her much and wanted to give her a small token. She means a lot to me.' He paused. 'But there is someone else that means a lot to me, but in a different way . . . and that is you.'

Molly started to cry properly. After a few moments, she wiped her eyes and started to smile. She reached out gently and held Gerant's cheeks in her hands.

'Oh Gerant, I am so sorry with how I reacted before. These flowers are lovely. And the earrings are gorgeous. I love them!'

They sat on the bench, holding hands, talking about all sorts of stuff. Through it all, Molly had been slowly building up to something she had long been curious about. It felt right to her that she changed subject a little.

'You've told me some things about your apprenticeship, but I know nothing of before that. Tell me about your family and where you grew up.' Molly was excited to hear at last a little bit more about Gerant's background and what made him what he was today.

It took Gerant quite a while to even start, looking into the distance and swallowing a few times.

'Look, if you don't want to, that's OK,' murmured Molly. 'Another time is fine.'

Gerant sighed. 'No, it's not that. It's just I haven't actually told anyone this before, so I almost don't know how to begin.' He swallowed again and then started talking quietly and steadily, almost as if he was narrating a story that he had heard about someone else.

'I have forgotten lots about my mam. She had browny hair and brown eyes and wasn't tall or short. She often laughed or sang when she was at home and that's what I remember most. Her name was Britt and she came from down south somewhere. She ended up in Ashford and met my dad and then things happened. As soon as I came along, Dad shot through. But Mum looked after me and she got a job serving in a grocery shop in the main street. She had to work long hours to make ends meet. She would go off to the shop early in the morning and I would spend all day playing with the kids in the street, until she came home just before dark. She would cook some dinner for us and then tell me stories of far-off lands with strange people and creatures.' Gerant stopped and sighed.

'Then one day she came home and said she wasn't feeling too well and went straight to bed. Next morning, she was still in bed and was all hot and sweaty and shaking and shivering. I ran to get Mrs Parbury, who lived next door. She took one look and got the doctor, who said Mum had a bad fever and left some medicine. We spent the next two days trying to look after her, giving her drinks of water and wiping her forehead with a damp cloth. But the heat just seemed to eat her up and she got weaker and weaker. Just at the end, she kind of woke up and stroked my cheek and whispered what a fine, young man I was. Then she fell asleep again. But next morning she didn't wake up and she was all cold and stiff.

'Mrs Parbury took me in, but I just went off and did what I felt like. After a week or so, I didn't go back and just stayed on the streets. Found a little nook to sleep in and got very cold and hungry. Then I found some other boys who also didn't have families and joined their little gang. That was all right for a while, but I almost owed it to my mam to do something more than just sneaking around, trying to find food or stealing stuff. So when the fight with the other gang happened, I just took off. I didn't know what I was looking for. I just knew I wanted to do something worthwhile. That's when I stumbled across the workshop and Sveg took me in as his apprentice. You know the rest.'

Molly listened in silence, tears gently dripping down her cheeks and nose. 'You still miss her, don't you?'

Gerant nodded silently and a series of quiet shudders shook his frame as he finally got to release some pent-up emotion after all this time.

'Oh, you poor, poor thing.' Molly reached over and brought her arms around the young man sitting next to her. She gently kissed him on the lips and continued holding him and rocking him slowly as he continued to cry quietly into her shoulder.

Chapter 27
North Haven

Gerant put the map away, swung the pack back up onto his shoulders and adjusted the straps a little. He checked his two throwing knives were safely sheathed and that the hatchet was handily looped into the belt at his waist. Then a quick scan around the open glade at the ridgetop and a look back towards The Capital sprawling several miles away across the valley and up the next ridge. He sighed as he registered the faint haze from woodsmoke carpeting the view and the occasional glint of something metallic. He almost felt he could hear the gentle rumble of hustle and bustle in the city, but it was probably just noises of the wind rustling through the trees. He made a brief farewell gesture to the vista. *See you in two weeks or so*, he thought, as he turned and continued along the road out of The Capital.

He was glad he had stopped for a quick break. Gerant had found a little brook just a short way into the trees and munched on a rock cake while he checked the map. It was not far to walk before he reached the little village named Nutley, where the road branched. Continuing straight on along the river would lead to Cobham and back to Ashford. He could have gone to Cobham and picked up the main north road there, but at Nutley was a side road that followed another smaller river to meet up with the main north road farther on. This apparently was used by most travellers heading north from The Capital and was well maintained. More importantly, it was more direct and saved travellers a day or so travel time. Given how far Gerant had to go to reach North Haven, any saving in the total distance was a real boon. He had talked to Annie one lunchtime, who came from Nutley, and apparently the side road could not be missed and was where the village tavern was. Well, it wouldn't be long before he would get there and then swing off. He hoped to make it to the main road before nightfall and find a quiet camp to bed down for the night. He had rapidly regained a regular rhythm of walking, smiling to himself as he realised it could be a bit like his smithing routine. Walk ten strides or so, take time to think about anything, then keep walking while you checked the surroundings, listening, watching the road ahead, then another ten strides to think. It was a good way to move forward steadily, combining time to think or just daydream but still being sufficiently alert to check the path ahead. Another hour or so walking and he might stop for a quick lunch that Mrs Lamming had insisted he take. At least the weather so far had been kind. He strode on, watching his surroundings gradually change and on the alert for oncoming travellers or the noises of riders or carts coming up from behind.

Two days later, Gerant stood on the outskirts of Rivernook. It looked to be crammed into the bend of a river that must flow out of the mountains to the west. He couldn't truly judge, but it looked somewhat smaller in size than Ashford. Certainly from where he was on a slope that the road traversed on its way to the town, it was mostly houses. There was no gate or wall encircling the town, so maybe it had just grown up and hadn't been part of wars or sieges in times past. There were a few larger buildings in the centre on a little knoll quite close to the river. Well, there would almost certainly be several inns or taverns here that he could spend the night. After two nights camping out a little bit away from the road, Gerant was ready to treat himself to a more comfortable place to sleep. Not that he wouldn't sleep out if he needed to, but the odd night here and there on his trip staying at an inn would be fine. He had already noticed the nip in the air after nightfall, which helped him get up promptly around dawn, have a quick bite to eat and head off. He hitched his pack a little more, adjusted his hatchet and moved off towards the town.

Not long after, he found a sprawling building at a crossroad in the town proper that, from its sign, was clearly a tavern. He looked again at the gently swinging sign on its hooks. The Parson's Nose, he read. The painting above the writing showed an overweight priest with a very hooked nose. Perhaps the priest was a well-known figure in the area. Gerant would have to ask, if he remembered. He could hear the chatter and laughter coming from the open doorway into the tavern. The outside looked OK. It certainly wasn't fancy but was reasonably well kept and not run-down or dirty looking. It was definitely worth a quick look inside before he decided.

Stepping in to a moderately sized room, he saw that the bar was actually in the middle of the open space with a counter running on each side. The collection of tables and booths were around the outer walls. Being late afternoon, there were a lot of customers here. Either this tavern was very popular, or the people of Rivernook liked their ale, or they came here to meet others and catch up on the news. *Well,* he thought, *plenty of people might mean that custom is good and it will be OK to stay the night here.* He walked up to the central bar and waited until someone noticed him. One of the barkeepers finished pouring a tankard of ale for a customer and walked over with a professional smile on his face. Gerant could see him rapidly looking over this new person, not one of his locals.

'Ah. A traveller from the south. Looking just for an ale or somewhere to stay tonight?'

'Both, actually. Heading farther north tomorrow but wouldn't mind a room. And some dinner.'

'Well, you've come to the right place. I'm Tom, the owner and we can do a room for six silver, including a meal. Ale is extra. We do have a bunkroom that you share with allcomers for a cheaper rate, but we're already full up there. There's a party of timber cutters who are using it.' He nodded over to one of the tables where a group of rough-clad men were talking among themselves and largely ignoring the other customers.

'A room is fine, thank you. OK to take my stuff up? I'll come back down for an ale.'

'I'll give you room two. Just come up to the bar here when you are ready to eat. Enjoy your stay.' The innkeeper took the coins and started to turn away.

'Oh, by the way, do you happen to know the Martinsons, who live here somewhere in the town?'

Tom scratched his head a little and then clearly remembered. 'You might be meaning old Nat and Ulla, perhaps. They have lived for years near the end of Bridge Street. A few of their grown-up kids and families live in the district.' The innkeeper frowned a little as he recalled more things. 'There was another son who married a local girl but then went south to try to find more steady work. Don't know what happened to them. Called Sam or Sven or something like that.'

'Thanks. Just someone I know mentioned them one time and said they were well known in the district.'

'Yes, lots of Martinsons around. Nat doesn't come in here very often but their place is easy to find. Maybe three houses before the river on the left on Bridge Street. Quite a big place but just the two of them knocking around inside now, I suppose.'

Gerant just nodded and didn't say anything. When the innkeeper saw this wasn't going anywhere, he moved off to serve another customer. Gerant shouldered his pack and moved out towards where he presumed the guest rooms were. He was looking forward to a quick wash and then an ale and some food. As he walked down an open corridor along one side of a small courtyard, he felt glad he had remembered to ask about Sveg's parents. He wasn't planning to go and visit, but at least if something unexpected happened up here or he was in a bit of trouble, he could go there in a crisis. A couple of times Sveg had mentioned in passing he had discussed his new apprentice with his parents, so it might be they would at least vaguely know of him. But that was as a last resort, right? It wouldn't ever get to that. Things would be fine and he would be back in The Capital in a week or so with a tusktooth and wondering why he had been concerned at all.

He reached a short corridor with doors opening off either side and opened the one with *2* on it. He heaved the pack onto the bed and looked around. Wow, the room was really small, with just a single bed, a small chest next to the bed and a chamber pot. There was a tiny bit of clear floor on the side and end of the bed. At least it was relatively clean, not that it would take the staff long to sweep and give it a quick dust. Gerant shut the door again and wandered off to find a place where he could have a quick wash. He could already taste that ale!

Although it was nearly midsummer, the trudging figure was rugged up against the biting wind blowing steadily from out of the still frozen far north. Gerant had been daydreaming a lot to try and take his mind off the cold air that pierced through all the layers he had on. On turning a corner in the road, he almost missed the hand-drawn sign. "Welcome to North Haven (¼ mile more). Visit the Icebreaker Tavern for all your needs."

Gods, he would be glad to get there and get some warmth into his bones. He started to pay more attention, keen to get a first view of North Haven. The road was essentially flat with an occasional slope up and down and gentle curves. He had been able to smell the sea for the last few hours – a salty, weedy odour on the gusty, cold breeze. There had been occasional glimpses of it on the right-hand side when there was a break in the trees or where the road climbed slightly to a small hill or rose to a knoll. You wouldn't call it a forest and the trees were not particularly tall – just enough to block the view most of the time.

A few hundred yards more and he came around a gentle curve to the right where the trees gave out to scraggly bushes and knee-high grass. He could now see the grey sea, with waves being kicked up here and there from the gusty breeze. The road arced down to the shore and met the beginning of some houses and other buildings. This must be North Haven. Gerant couldn't see much beyond the first set of structures, but he sensed this was a pretty small town. Most of the buildings had chimneys from which scuds of smoke burst out and flew quickly away on wind gusts. He reached the first of the buildings on either side of the road into the town. They all seemed to be huddled up against each other and were quite small. None of them had a second storey. They also were mostly the same shade of grey-brown, with streaks of dirt and mud along the walls. It was almost like the houses suffered from the cold and stayed as close to each other as they could for what little shared warmth they could derive. A little farther in, he could start to see boats tied up on the edge of the water, with wooden and stone piers going out, from which the various vessels were moored. No guesses for what North Haven was known for and relied upon. At the point where a number of these piers reached the land, there was an open area with heaps of wood and other building materials mounded haphazardly. Directly on the other side, where the main street appeared to start again, was a somewhat larger building with a number of chimneys from which smoke billowed in the wind. There was only one main door that he could see and very few windows, probably to keep the warmth in. A large sign pegged into the scrabbly ground proclaimed that this was the Icebreaker Tavern, known far and wide as the best tavern and inn in the northern parts. Looking around, Gerant couldn't see anything other than more houses and cottages and what looked like sheds adjacent to where the piers were. *Maybe this is all there is*, he thought. With some hesitation, he opened the heavy wooden door, stepped inside and pulled it shut before too much cold air came in after him.

The low-lit room was significantly warmer than outside, not surprising given the two large fireplaces at either end with steadily burning fires. Part way along the far wall was the bar, featuring a wooden counter atop large stones cemented together to give an imposing, solid base. A number of people were clustered at the bar, either standing or perched on high stools. Ringed around the two fireplaces were several couches and chairs where others were soaking up the warmth while they drank. There were two small windows behind the bar. Otherwise, any light in the dim space came from a few lanterns hanging at various points from the lowish ceiling. There was a clear sense of keeping things snug and warm, meaning that the two fires at each end would have the best chance of heating the room.

The gentle thud of the door and an unavoidable blast of cool air triggered a pause in the quiet conversations as the occupants of the Icebreaker all looked to see who had come in. Gerant let his eyes wander around the room. He was obviously being assessed – he sensed they pegged him for a stranger and clearly a Southerner – then the attention waned as he just stood there, not moving.

As the talk picked up again, Gerant walked up to the bar and shrugged his pack down. The barkeeper had been like all the rest in his trade and watched him come in. He was a large man with a solid build, getting a little fat now with a developing paunch. He was balding with brown shoulder-length locks and reddish tinges, and a large moustache with handlebars drooping down past his mouth. The leather tunic with short sleeves sat under a tan-coloured apron, from which muscled forearms emerged, covered in multiple tattoos swirling down to his hands. Each of his fingers had a symbol or letter tattooed on them. The man's expression was neither welcoming nor unfriendly.

'How about you leave your pack near the door. There's not heaps of room if everyone brings their stuff in.' He gestured near the door where there was an alcove with various packs, bags and other items grouped on the floor.

Gerant hesitated.

'Don't worry, no one's going to touch it. They won't get far if they did, and they all know the rules.'

The visitor went to the alcove and put his pack down against the wall but in clear sight of the bar, and came back. The barkeeper finished polishing a tankard with a piece of rag.

'Yep?'

'I'm from down south. Might want to stay for a night and will get a drink in a minute and warm up.'

The barkeeper's face showed that everyone had already worked out the newcomer was from out of town, and he picked up another empty tankard to polish while he waited to hear more.

'I've come here because I wondered whether you know of anyone who knows about fishing and hunting. I wanted to have a chat with them about a couple of things.'

The barkeeper didn't need to think for very long. He pointed over towards one of the fireplaces. 'See that old fella in the chair just to the right nursing his drink? That's Gramps, also known as Grampus, who was fishing and hunting seals and whales and other critters years before I was a kid. Doesn't do much now, but comes in here most days just to chat with folk and think about the good ol' days. He is probably your best bet.'

Gerant looked over to near the fireplace and could see the figure of an old man lounged back in a chair with a tankard in his gnarled fist, occasionally having a sip. He couldn't see too much of the man, as the chair was pulled up fairly close to the blazing fire.

'Thanks. I'll go up and have a chat. What does he drink?'

'Ale with an Icebreaker chaser.'

'OK, I'll have two of those then.'

'Call it two silver, then.'

Gerant nodded and the barkeeper turned to prepare the drinks. He tried not to show his shock at the price. It sounded like it was ale and then some stronger liquor. Also, he guessed that maybe with the isolation of North Haven and the Icebreaker being the only tavern for miles, they could charge more. Still, it would be worth it if this Gramps was able to help him with what he needed.

The barkeeper turned around and put on the counter two tankards of ale and two small glasses of a clear, slightly oily liquid. Gerant handed over two silver and picked up the drinks, walking carefully over to the fireplace so as not to spill. He placed the drinks on a nearby small table and approached the old man. Up closer, the man was wearing a comfortable, slightly threadbare woollen shirt and pants, leather boots up to his knees and a wool beanie pulled down over white hair. He gazed into the fire as he clutched his tankard. His eyes under bushy white eyebrows were red-rimmed, with a large reddish nose criss-crossed with bluish small veins and a roughly trimmed white beard. The man's hands were large, scarred and wrinkled, clearly hinting at the hard work they had undertaken over the years and the strength they had once had.

'Umm, Gramps. Hello. I wondered if you could chat to me about your experience in fishing and hunting. I brought you another drink.'

The old man turned his head and shoulders around suddenly and his gaze shifted from being vaguely watching the dancing flames to surprisingly piercing, quickly checking the young figure standing just to his right. 'Maybe. Who are you?'

'My name is Gerant. I'm from down south – from The Capital. The barkeeper said you have been fishing and catching animals from the seas for years. I just want to ask a few things and won't take up too much of your time.'

Gerant passed over the tankard and then the glass of liquor.

'Well, not doing too much at the moment, so I guess I can talk for a bit.' The old man picked up the glass, threw back the liquor in one gulp, inhaled deeply and wiped his mouth.

Gerant took that for an agreement and pulled up one of the vacant chairs. 'Do I call you Gramps or Grampus?'

'Either is fine. No one calls me by my real name. They wouldn't even know it's Abraham.'

'Ah, thank you, Gramps.'

The old man took a pull of the ale. 'So, what do you want to know?'

Gerant looked over the old man and realised he would have to show a little trust and give some details about what he was after, or this would be a very quick conversation. Perhaps he could just start off with trying to get some information and take it from there. He should at least be able to find out a bit more and if it didn't work out, maybe get a name of someone else to approach. He decided to embellish the truth a little and see what the old man told him.

'Look, I have been reading an old book about creatures in the sea and it mentions something called a tusktooth. They sound really strange, and I wondered if you knew about them or had ever seen them.'

Grampus looked at Gerant with disbelief showing on his face. 'Are you kidding me, boy? The only things that I don't know about tusktooths are things that aren't worth knowing about. I've been hunting them for forty years or more.' The expression of disbelief changed to that of quiet pride.

'Oh. Well, it sounds like I am talking to the right man, then. Are they difficult to hunt?'

The old man took another sip of ale and leant back in his chair, staring into the flames. 'Used to be quite common in these parts, but these days you don't see so many. The tooth is very valuable, as well as the hide. That meant many people started to hunt them and lots of boats were out. Only a few do now. The critters might be starting to come back a little.'

Gerant took a sip of his ale. This was starting to sound really good. Grampus really knew about this subject. The old man continued, clearly musing over old memories.

'I've hunted some big old bulls in my time. Up to fifteen or twenty feet long and a tusk maybe nine, ten feet. Have to sneak up real quiet in the boat and make a clean strike. Otherwise they might attack the boat and it will flip or roll. I remember when that happened to D'Arcy and the three of them all drowned when a big bull slammed the boat. Poor old D'Arcy. He was a good fella.' The old man held the tankard, watching the flames and sighed. 'Yup, key is to see them first before they see you and just close in until they surface and you are ready to strike. Got a few harpoons at home still sharpened. You never know when you'll need them or want to go out.'

Gerant struggled to keep the excitement out of his voice. 'I can understand why you'd want to keep all your gear. You have to make the most of your experience. What do you do if you want to head out? Do you still have a boat?'

The old man's pondering at past memories suddenly stopped and his piercing gaze locked onto Gerant's face. 'I've kept me old boat. Not big enough to go after the big, old bulls but plenty enough for the sort of tusktooths you might find today.' He paused. 'You're asking a lot more questions than just for the hell of it, matey. What are you really after?'

Grampus sat back and watched the younger man intently while he took a long pull of his ale.

Oh shit, Gerant thought, *that's it then. He is suspicious, for sure.*

Without thinking and wanting something to do, the young man grabbed the small glass and had a quick swallow. After a second, his eyes widened suddenly and he started to cough violently. The old man started chuckling and pounded Gerant on the back, none too gently.

'Easy, easy, young fella. Never had an Icebreaker before?'

Gerant's eyes watered as he smiled grimly back and shook his head, as another bout of coughing erupted. There was nothing for it but to talk plainly and see what happened. His voice was still quite shaky for a little bit and then it got stronger and returned to its normal measured tones.

'You are right, Gramps. True – I did read an old parchment about a tusktooth and using it for a special purpose. You see, I'm a smith by training and the tusktooth is a part of an old recipe you can use in making really good sword blades. So I wanted to come up north to talk with someone who knows about them. I am wanting to go out hunting for one and bring a tusk back. I have no skill in being on the water and hunting them. So I would need someone like yourself. I am willing to pay for that. And I am being really honest with you.' Gerant paused, almost not daring to go on. 'So, are you interested?'

The old man's face had become difficult to read as he listened to Gerant's explanation. 'Depends. What are you proposing?'

Gerant thought quickly. Maybe all was not lost. He'd go with the proposal he had spent the miles thinking about and see what happened. 'I still have little idea of what is possible. But maybe if you can take me out in your boat for a couple of days and we can look for tusktooths and if we find one, hunt it. I just want the tusk. Anything else you can keep. Ten gold now and ten gold after. Another five if we get one.'

The old man's gaze shifted from Gerant to stare into the fire for long seconds. Then he started to mutter. 'Haven't been out for a while, but it is all ready. Glad I checked the sails and put that patch in. We'd need two day's rations and water. We could sleep at the old hut at Sharkey's and then see if there were any in Fingal's Bay. Maybe try Chester's Reef if we had no luck at Fingal's. We could be there and back within two days if the weather holds. What else? Harpoons, plenty of line, knives, would skin it and take the hide — he doesn't want it — and some of the meat, maybe. Hmmm.'

Gramps smiled, reached across and shook Gerant's hand formally. 'There's a bit to prepare, young fella, but I am willing to do this. We can use my boat and I'll sail you there and try to find the critters. But I am past harpooning, so you would have to do that yourself.'

The old man stopped and saw what reaction that had. Gerant was silent for a few moments and then nodded slowly.

'We could push off tomorrow morning. Suit you?'

This raised a question that had been bothering Gerant since Gramps had started talking. 'I could stay here, but do you have a place? That might be easier . . .' He trailed off.

Gramps sucked in his breath a little and thought through what that might mean. 'I have me cottage but it's not flash. As long as you don't mind sleeping on the floor, you could stay, I guess.'

'I've got my own bedroll.' Gerant gestured to the alcove near to the door of the tavern.

A pause. 'Well, I don't live fancy but if you're happy with that, then it will be possible. Krug here knows how to run a good tavern, but that means you'll pay through the nose for a room. Best to save your coin, methinks.'

Gerant agreed.

'Do you want the ten gold now or can I give it to you before we go tomorrow?'

Gramps shifted in his seat, looked around, then leant over towards Gerant, speaking a little more softly.

'There are some shifty characters around here. Showing coin is like a beacon to them and they'll suddenly become interested. Later is better. Out of sight of any prying eyes.'

Gramps nodded knowingly and Gerant couldn't resist also quickly scanning the nearby customers to see if any of them were listening in. There were maybe seven or eight men bunched around the tables and leaning up against the fireplace and they all looked to be chatting away to each other. One tall, older man with crumpled clothes was in a large armchair near the fire, apparently dozing, and a small, thin, weedy man with a scar on his right cheek was reading a piece of paper intently at the next table. No, Gerant thought, it looked like their conversation had just been one of the many happening unnoticed in the tavern and everyone was looking to their own business or acquaintances. He looked back at Gramps and they started talking again. The small, weedy man continued to hold the paper in his hands; he quickly glanced up at the pair at the next table and looked away again, continuing to listen.

'I've never been in a boat before, so I don't know what that will be like. I'll just try to stay out of your way.'

Gramps nodded, as if he was expecting nothing else. 'You'll be fine. I think the weather will largely behave and we won't get much of a swell, if I'm any judge. Might yell out a thing or two or need you to pull on some rigging, but nothing fancy. I'll get you to where we need to be, but harpooning will be your job. I will tell you what to do and where to aim, but I'm not up to that sort of physical stuff anymore. If we get one, then you'll also need to do the heavy stuff, but I can do the skinning and that sort of thing.'

'Can I leave most of my pack at your place when we are out in the boat?'

'Of course. We should just take our clothes and some food and water and a few things like the harpoons and some knives. Nothing more. We won't be away for too long.' This was right in the older man's expertise, and he thought some more. 'Hmmm. It might be smart to take a few things down to the boat this afternoon, so we don't have much to carry down in the morning. Suit you?'

Gerant nodded and couldn't think of anything else that occurred to him. They could chat more on the way to wherever Gramp's place was. 'I'll just grab my pack, then.'

The old man nodded. But Gerant could tell something else was bothering him.

'Look, no offence to you, young fella, but are you going to finish your Icebreaker?'

Gerant was stunned for a second and then burst out laughing. 'Go ahead, go ahead. I'm happy just with the ale.'

As the young man walked to get his pack, Gramps quickly threw down the liquor, quietly muttering. 'Good strong liquor, that. Waste not, want not, I always say.'

The door of the Icebreaker Tavern opened and closed again. Gerant and Gramps emerged, still talking quietly. Gerant had grabbed his pack, and still had lots of questions to ask the old fellow. They walked off down the packed dirt street farther into North Haven. Not long after, the tavern door opened again and a thin, weedy figure emerged. The man had a distinctive scar on his cheek and the eye on that side was clouded. After watching the two figures disappear, he quickly darted to the left and into an alley opening off the main street.

Chapter 28
Gramps

'I've had this place for ten, twenty years or so. Just a bedroom, living room with a stove and sink, privy out the back. Not very big but haven't got a lot of stuff. Some of it is in the shack and some of it I keep on the boat.'

Gramps and Gerant continued to talk as they walked through the narrow streets of the town. The houses and cottages didn't change much and looked generally the same, with just the front door being on a different side, or a curtained window every now and again or some faded colour on door frames or wooden trim here and there. After just a few minutes, they reached a similar wooden-fronted cottage with a door on the left-hand side facing straight onto the street and a single glass window with drapes behind. Both the timber of the door, the frame and the window were the natural colour of the wood, with what Gerant guessed was some sort of oil to protect the timber. The walls were timber planks painted in what probably once was white but now was a grotty light grey from the prevailing winds blowing dirt, dust and snow. The roof was clad in wooden shingles and a stone chimney poked out, erupting a brief trickle of smoke every now and again.

Gramps turned the doorknob and opened it, walking inside after stomping some of the dirt from his boots onto a coarse mat just inside. He took them off and placed them in a small rack next to the door. He padded off and reached into the stove, gave the embers a stir and put a fresh block of wood in.

'I don't bother to lock it unless I am away for a bit,' he called behind him. 'Nothing particularly worth stealing and too much hassle.'

Gerant stomped his boots on the mat and took them off, leaving them next to Gramps's. He looked around the fairly low-ceilinged room and his first impression was how neat and uncluttered it was. There were various cupboards and chests of drawers scattered along the walls, a small table and a couple of chairs in the centre, and a rocking chair in the corner that looked well used. A small kitchen bench next to the stove and a small sink and that was about it. Everything looked like it belonged in its own place. There were very few personal trinkets that he could see – everything that Gerant noted had a purpose and was functional. There were two doors apart from the front one. One to the right was presumably the sleeping place – maybe any trinkets and memorabilia were in there – and an exterior door just to the right of the sink. That must be to the privy.

Gramps had been watching him quickly glance around and nodded in satisfaction. 'As I said, nothing fancy but it does me. Always tidy up before I go out and know where everything is. Was taught to be neat when I was at sea. You need to know exactly where everything is in case you need it in a hurry.'

The old man nodded over to one of the taller cupboards. 'Just going to get a couple of days' worth of jerky and some nuts to chew on, then we can get some harpoons out and check their edge. After that we can go down to the boat and stow most of the stuff ready for tomorrow. Best to take a few last things in the morning, rather than clomping about wasting time.'

Gerant nodded in agreement. Gramps was his type of person: thoughtful, organised, and not filling up the air with small talk that didn't mean anything.

'All right if I look at the harpoons?'

Gramps was reaching into a cupboard near the sink and didn't turn round. 'Sure, we call them irons. In that tall cupboard, in the brackets. Three should be enough, plus a lance.'

Gerant padded over. Inside the cupboard were various carefully stacked implements and at the back were some metal-tipped spears about six feet in length slotted into a wooden bracket arrangement to keep them separate and orderly. He got out three of the sort that had a short triangular head splitting into two barbs facing backwards and a smooth metal shaft joining onto a roughened wooden base. He also grabbed one with the same wooden base and a longer metal piece, maybe eight feet long. The metal head was diamond shaped at the end, and all the edges were razor sharp – this must be a lance.

Gramps saw that Gerant had grabbed the right gear and nodded. 'Sharp enough? Good, we'll attach some rope coils to them when we get to the boat. The rest of the stuff is already stored on Betsy.'

Gerant replayed this last remark in his head. 'Umm, who is Betsy?'

'Oh, that's me boat. You'll get to meet her in a little bit. Damn finest little vessel north of The Capital. I keep her looking real neat and in good order. Gives me something to do.' Gramps had stopped, looking into the distance as he remembered fond memories, caught himself, and started putting a few things in a large sack. He continued talking through the preparations.

'You'll need your bedroll to lay out on the floor here for tonight. Also take a change of clothes tomorrow in case you go in for a dunk, and your coat, gloves, hat, that sort of thing. Got any tools you want to take?'

Gerant nodded and pulled out his hatchet and the two throwing knives. Gramps inspected them quickly and then realised they were incredibly high quality and worth a closer look. He spent several minutes looking them over carefully. 'You made these yourself?'

'Yes. The knives some time ago but the hatchet fairly recently.'

The old man continued to look them over with a professional eye and looked at Gerant with new respect.

'A man would be very happy with one of these. We will definitely use the hatchet when we camp out and need some wood for a camp-fire. I have some skinning knives on the boat, but these might do just as well.'

With that Gramps disappeared through the sleeping room door for a few seconds with the sack and came out again with it a little fuller. He looked at Gerant inquiringly. 'All set to take the irons and the lance? OK, let's go and stow this stuff on Betsy.'

It was only a few minutes' away and the two conversed quietly as they walked. They reached the last row of houses and crossed some open ground before reaching the harbour wall, with the sea breaking in small wavelets against it. One of the piers intersected a break in the harbour wall and marched out into the water on regularly spaced wooden piles. Various boats were tied up on either side out to the end of the pier. Gramps stopped and pointed out some features to Gerant, who gazed about a little uncertainly, as none of the sights were familiar to him.

'Betsy is tied up on the left of this pier not far from the end. This is one of three piers. You can see the others over there, and over there. In case you missed it, there's the Icebreaker over yonder.'

Gerant followed Gramp's pointing as he tried to take it all in, and nodded thankfully when the tavern was pointed out. It looked a little different from this side, but he recognised the shape of the building and the smoke pouring out from chimneys at either end before it gusted off in the wind.

Gramps walked onto the pier, with Gerant following. Around twenty yards from the end, the older man stopped and pointed down at a boat securely tied to bollards. Gerant looked down and saw a wooden boat with a single mast, gently rocking as it nestled up against the timbers of the pier. It was about fifteen or twenty feet long. The front tapered to a rounded point, from which the bowsprit emerged. The mast was set midway but a little towards the stern and there was a small cuddy right at the rear where the tiller was housed. Similar to the cottage, various bits and pieces of equipment were all stored neatly, and looked to be in good condition – nothing appeared to be bedraggled or left untidied or in the way. Gerant saw ropes, canvas, bags and other things he had no idea what they were called or what their purpose was.

'This is Betsy. You'll get to know her over the next day or so. We'll just stow this stuff so all will be ready for an early start tomorrow.'

Gramps threw the sack he was carrying down onto the deck and clambered down a wooden ladder attached to the side of the pier that Gerant hadn't noticed. He gestured up for the harpoons and

Gerant passed them down along with the small sack. Then he carefully reversed and climbed down the ladder to the deck. Almost immediately, he experienced the strange sensation where the floor kept on gently moving with the remnants of the waves jostling up to Betsy. Gerant quickly checked that the ropes tying the boat to the pier were holding. Gramps saw his look and smiled.

'Just part of being on the sea. You'll get used to the motion here in the harbour real quick. But if we get a bit of a blow, then you probably get pretty sick for a while and chuck your guts up. Then you'll be fine.'

Gerant nodded, thankful for the warning. He hadn't realised this at all and wasn't looking forward to when they went out tomorrow, if that was what it was going to be like.

Gramps stowed the two sacks in the cuddy out of the way and uncoiled four sets of rope. He quickly spliced each end through the iron ring on the end of the harpoons and the lance, tugging them carefully to check the ropes were strongly attached. He took the four shafts with the rope trailing towards the bow and tied them securely to the frames and coiled the ropes and lashed them out of the way. Gerant carefully walked up to inspect the new location.

'See, young fella, tidied up and out of the way. But if we see a tusktooth, it is just a few seconds to release an iron. Know how to tie a secure knot? Like a clove hitch?'

Gerant nodded. Sveg had been very insistent that learning some of the common knots was part of becoming proficient in the smithy.

'So when we need to, you can lash the loose end to that iron ring there near the bow. When you throw the iron correctly and it strikes, the tusktooth is attached to the boat and can't escape. That's the idea, anyway. It's thirty feet of rope, so it won't be able to dive deep and pull us under and we can haul it in fairly quickly.'

Gerant pondered what this all meant. 'Sounds kind of straightforward. But I'll need some more hints about throwing the harpoon and what I am aiming for. Throwing the knives is no problem and I am getting pretty good with the hatchet. But no idea about this sort of stuff.'

'Once we get going tomorrow, we'll have plenty of time to talk about what to expect and what you'll need to do.' The old man's eyes narrowed a little and a slight look of suspicion crossed his face. 'These throwing knives. Good, are you? Show me.'

Gramps stood with arms folded as Gerant reached down and pulled out one of his knives and looked around.

'The ladder back up to the pier. Middle of the highest rung.' Gerant relaxed a little, straightened and the handle of the throwing knife appeared quivering halfway along the ladder rung just below the decking of the wharf. He checked to see that Gramps had seen the throw, carefully walked over, reached up and pulled the knife out. The look on Gramps's face had transformed from a little disbelief to almost grudging approval.

'You'll be fine, then. When we go out, we'll hitch an iron onto the boat, and you can practice throwing just to get the feel of things.'

'Thanks, Gramps. I would feel more comfortable having a few practices, particularly if the floor is moving and things like that.'

'Huh, shouldn't be a problem, matey. Will be harder to find a tusktooth and then sneak up quietly without it knowing. The rest is not too bad. They look fierce but don't usually attack the boat. Not like orcas or other whales. Then, you're often in trouble if you don't score a clean hit and they get riled and come after what's hurt them.

'I can tell you some stories, but let's get back to the shack. We can go past the Icebreaker on the way back and pick up a flagon of ale to whet our whistles.'

As Gramps and Gerant walked over to the tavern and disappeared inside, a cloaked figure stirred in the nook out of the wind he had been resting in and stretched. White-eye rubbed his face and had a quick nip of spirits from the small leather goatskin. It had been worth the wait to confirm the pair's plans after he had happened to overhear the chat earlier in the tavern. So old Gramps was going to go out after tusktooths with the young man from down south fairly soon. Once the boat had gone, he would check to see when they came back and then report to the boss. The reward for the information wouldn't go astray, that was for sure. White-eye checked that the pair hadn't come back out of the tavern and then quickly slipped off into the town.

Gramps pottered at the stove, talking occasionally. Gerant got the feeling that although it was directed at him to some extent, it was also Gramps's way of filling the space and he always talked to himself when he was alone in the cottage.

'This stew from yesterday will be fine reheated. I'll just put in a few more carrots and spuds to bulk it out a little.' There were sounds of chopping on a board. 'Yup, almost tastes better than yesterday. Maybe a tad more salt and another bay leaf. Then it should be ready to serve in an hour or so.' Some rummaging around in one of the cupboards near the sink. 'Hmmm. A little stale but not too bad. Will slice this thickly and toast them and they should be fine.'

Gramps wiped his hands on a spare cloth and walked over to the table where Gerant had been sitting and watching. He poured two tankards of ale from a flask and pushed one over to Gerant.

'Have one of these and turn your chair around. We can yarn a bit while we wait for dinner to be ready.' The old man padded over to the rocking chair near the stove and eased himself into it before taking a long pull on his ale. 'So, what do you want to know? Much better to ask now, rather than we get out on the boat and you have no idea or stuff things up.'

Gerant paused. 'You're right, Gramps. I've been thinking about quite a few things. Maybe I'll just start, and you can fill in as we go.'

'Happy enough with that,' replied Gramps as he settled back farther into the chair, giving it an occasional rock.

'So, tell me a little about where we are going tomorrow. I don't know this area of The Realm at all and the map I have just shows North Haven and nothing more.'

Gramps closed his eyes, rocking gently, ordering his thoughts. 'That's because there is pretty much nothing northwards of here. Really tough country and snowbound for a fair bit of the year. There are a few little groups of houses here and there where people scratch out a living hunting and fishing. The road out of North Haven is just a track and a cart could only go about another ten miles or so north. Then it just wanders up to Sharkey's and there is next to nothing after that. More of a goat track and most of the marker poles have fallen over or been used for firewood.'

'Oh, so North Haven is it? The map was right?'

'Yup.' Gramps paused in thought. 'But by sea is a little easier.'

Gerant was relieved to hear that.

'So, tomorrow . . .'

'Well, we will follow the coast. We may see some tusktooths on the way to Sharkey's. May or may not. It will depend on if they are finding feed there.'

That was one of questions Gerant had. 'This Sharkey's you mention. What is it?'

Gramps took another swallow of ale before responding. 'It's a point of land about five or six hours' sail, depending on the wind. Named after an old-timer fisherman who lived there. It's easy to spot, and there is a reasonable camping site where his shack used to be. Also, there are the remains of a little pier where we can tie Betsy up to overnight.'

Gerant's relief was obvious to Gramps.

'Nah, we won't spend the night on the water. Will stop on solid ground or anchor in close to land out of the wind. If we haven't seen any tusktooths before Sharkey's, we'll keep going the next day. There is some good cod and squid fishing in Fingal's Bay, and I have often seen tusktooths there. Unless they have been scared off by hunters, we probably will find a few there.'

That ticked off a few more of Gerant's questions. 'Thanks. But how do you hunt them? Are they dangerous?'

Gramps rocked gently for a few minutes, got up and added a new log into the stove and checked the stew. He came back to the rocking chair, collected his thoughts and continued. 'Tusktooths are pretty easy to hunt. Only the males have the tusk. They aren't ferocious when barbed, like a whale would be. No, they have got hard to hunt because everyone was after them and they have got very wary. Have to be real careful to sneak up on them. If they hear the boat, then they go to the bottom and scoot off and you won't have any idea where they have gone. They can hold their breath for a half hour or more, so no hope.'

Gerant pondered on all this. It sounded like Gramps would know where to look and be able to sail his boat to get close enough if they found some tusktooths. But there were an awful lot of things he didn't know, particularly what he would be expected to do. He had a couple of swallows of ale while he collected his thoughts.

'Ummm, if we find a tusktooth and get close enough without it seeing us, what do I have to do? I don't want to stuff things up.'

Gramps nodded in understanding and launched into another explanation. 'If we come across one, then I should be able to get us into position – had plenty of experience and practice with it. That's why a boat like Betsy is ideal. Very quiet and just eases along in the water and doesn't scare them off. No funny or loud noises and it just seems to them like a whale swimming on the surface, or such.

'Anyway, once we get almost alongside and it surfaces, your job is to throw the iron, once it is tied off to the ring, of course. Try to pin it about a foot behind the blowhole, where the barbs will work in well and cause the most damage. The main thing is to stop it from getting away and then we can haul the boat in towards it and then put in another harpoon, or better, finish it off with the lance. Then it's a matter of waiting while it dies and securing it to the side of the boat and then get to shore so we can skin it and grab the tooth and anything else we want to take.'

So many questions, Gerant thought, but he could ask some more tomorrow. There was one he needed to ask, though. 'How long will I have to get ready to throw? Will I have any warning?'

Gramps thought a little and drank some ale before responding. 'Depends. They can stay on the surface for a minute or two, but if they are feeding, they might just surface for a few seconds to take a breath and then go under to keep hunting for fish or squid. But I will holler if I think you should cast the iron, or we just have to be patient for the right opportunity. You only get one shot, normally, otherwise they spook if you miss.'

Gerant thought that there was a lot to take in and he was glad that Gramps had offered to take him out hunting. He would have had no idea, otherwise. They would have plenty of time tomorrow to keep talking, and it sounded like he would have a chance to practice throwing the harpoon, just to get used to it.

Gramps got up and checked the stew and started toasting some hunks of bread through the open door of the stove where the coals were. After a few more minutes of muttering to himself and shuffling around in front of the stove, he got out a couple of earthenware bowls, ladled out some stew into each and plopped a couple of hunks of toasted bread on top. Gerant had watched the preparations while he thought more about hunting tusktooths and turned his chair back around as Gramps brought over the gently steaming bowls.

'Here you go, young fella. Tuck into this while we keep on talking. Mind, it's pretty hot, so start off slow so you don't burn the roof of your mouth.'

Gerant slowly stirred the stew with the spoon and thought to himself how good it smelled. He cautiously took a mouthful – yes, it was hot – but then couldn't help enjoying the flavours of the stew – carrots and potatoes and a few other vegetables, some herbs and, by the taste of it, chunks of beef that had been slowly simmered to soft tenderness and little cubes of bacon or something like that. He soaked the toasted bread in the juices and sucked contentedly.

'This is amazing, Gramps! I can't remember tasting a better stew. I love it – how the meat and vegies all combine and taste so good together. But there are a couple of flavours in there that I am not all that familiar with, something extra. What are they?'

Gramps leant back in his chair and nodded with quiet satisfaction at the compliments. 'Well, you've got to let it slowly simmer for a good few hours to get the flavours to combine and for everything to become tender. One of the things you probably are tasting is using some really smoky bacon. Makes all the difference – I've got a mate who raises pigs and I get a haunch every now and again. The other thing you are probably tasting is my secret ingredient.'

Gramps was silent for a few seconds and let the suspense build. 'A touch of fermented eel paste.' The surprise on Gerant's face was clearly what he was expecting.

'Yes, fermented eel paste – an old family recipe. I usually make it in the late autumn – just a few small pots – layers of eel and some good quality lard and plenty of salt and pepper, bay leaves and sage. Then seal it up and bury it over winter and it will be good for years. You don't want to put too much in – just a small spoonful – and it just lifts the flavours something amazing. Me old grandma showed me how; she was a terrific cook.'

Gramps's gaze was unfocused as he was clearly thinking through some old memories. He gave a start, had a quick sip of ale and continued eating.

The two of them continued talking for some time about the weather and what to expect tomorrow. Gerant helped wash up the bowls and tankards. Gramps had been filling a leather sack with some water bottles and some jerky and a few apples.

'These are just for during the day as snacks or if we get held up somewhere and have to hunker down for a while. Plus some lard and a few herbs for cooking. I'll toss a line out tomorrow when we are sailing up the coast and we should have fresh fish for tomorrow night's dinner at Sharkey's.'

Gerant nodded as he wiped the bowls out and put them back in the cupboard. Gramps continued.

'We'll have everything ready to go for the morning. Best to start just after dawn after a quick bite to eat. You can put your bedroll out here on the floor. I tend to go to bed early and rise early, so I'll just take a quick piss and then head off for bed. Yell out if you need anything in the night, I'm just in the next room.'

'That all sounds good, Gramps. I'll just take a change of clothes and all I have to do is roll up the bedding in the morning and I'm set.'

A little later, Gerant lay on the bedroll with his hands linked behind his head and waited for sleep to come. He was comfortable enough and the meal was sitting very well with him. He had ducked out to the privy after Gramps and got a small sack ready for the morning to quickly grab on the way out. He lay in the dark listening to the sounds of Gramps snoring gently in the other room. It was always a little strange trying to sleep somewhere else than your usual bed; the sounds and smells were always different, and it took a little getting used to. It had been a good couple of days, though, and he was looking forward to what tomorrow would bring. He just hoped that the rocking of the boat was not too bad and he didn't spend the whole day just leaning over the side trying to chuck his guts out. With that thought, Gerant turned over and slowly drifted off, thinking about this next phase of the adventure and whether it would be successful and he would be coming back to The Capital with a tusktooth.

Chapter 29
The Cruise

Gerant awoke to quiet shuffling and noises of the stove being poked awake. He rubbed his eyes and watched Gramps briefly before silently springing up. The old man turned around and smiled.

'Just after dawn. I'm just going to toast some bread, then we can have it with butter and jam. After that we'll head off and go down to Betsy.'

Gerant nodded as he quickly rolled up his bedding, strapped it tightly and left it leaning next to the front door. He checked his sack and then sat down with Gramps to eat the plain breakfast.

'Last summer's strawberries,' mumbled Gramps through a mouthful of toast.

'Good,' Gerant mumbled back.

After quickly washing up the platters and going out to the privy, Gerant was as ready as he was going to be. Gramps nodded at the preparations and had his own couple of sacks, one with clothing and gear, and the other with some of the food and provisions.

Gerant stepped out the front door with his bedroll and sack. The sky was starting to lighten and there were a few grey clouds to the west towards the mountains but nothing more. What breeze there was also came from the west, but little more than a breath every now and again.

'I'll meet you out front in a second.'

Without waiting for a response, the old man left his sacks with Gerant, went in and shut the front door and there were sounds of some sort of bar being placed, before there were a couple of short tugs from inside. Gramps emerged from a laneway a few houses away and came up to Gerant still standing in front of the cottage.

'Don't normally bother when I am around. If I'm away for a few days, I just bar the front door from the inside and duck over the back fence. Won't stop anyone who is determined, but at least it makes it seem like it is locked.' Gramps nodded. 'All set? Right then, let's go and get Betsy ready for this little trip.'

Things with Betsy were as they had left them the previous afternoon. At least Gerant now knew to clamber down the ladder and onto the boat, before Gramps handed down their sacks and then climbed down himself.

'Just stow them out of the way in the cuddy while I get out the sails and rig them. I'll get you to help a little with bits and pieces, but largely just stay out of the way. Although I will get you to fend off until we get clear of the pier and the sail starts biting.'

Gerant nodded and put the sacks and his bedroll in the little space out of the wind that was built at the rear of the boat where the tiller was. It could hardly be called a cabin but at least there was room to store a few things and little nooks and hatches built into the side where other bits were stored away. Gerant decided to stay put there as Gramps efficiently moved about the deck of the small boat uncoiling ropes and getting what looked like a folded canvas sheet from a hatch near the mast. After a few minutes of what looked like random organising, he was ready.

'Right, I'll set this small staysail just to get going and then when we get out of the harbour, we can go for the mainsail. Here.' He handed Gerant an oar. 'Your job is to fend us off the pier and other boats until we get clear. Should be no problem but sometimes you just need to poke 'em off a bit if things get tight.'

Gramps bustled up to the mast and hauled on some ropes. What had seemed to be a folded sheet started being pulled up and Gerant could see this was a small sail. Gramps tied it off and then came over to the tiller and hauled it around a little. Then he walked up to the two cables tying Betsy to the pier and nodded in question at Gerant.

Gerant swallowed a little, grasped the oar even harder and nodded back. *Here we go*, he thought.

After that, he was too busy to think any more about this new experience. Gramps cast off the two cables.

'Fend off against the pier pilings. That's it. We need a little bit of clear water and then the tiller will bite.' Gramps adjusted the staysail and it started to fill gently with the westerly breeze. He walked over to the tiller and pulled it right over towards the pier.

'Fend again. Good.'

Even Gerant could see that the wind in the sail was pushing Betsy away from the pier and the tiller was helping as well.

'Push off Crappy's boat there.'

Gerant used the oar to fend off the next boat moored to the pier. The shove was enough to get Betsy past without touching and the combination of the sail and the tiller was starting to move the boat away from the pier and out into open water. Gramps continued to fuss, adjusting the sail as more and more wind filled it, then moved to the cuddy and straightened the tiller. Immediately the boat picked up a little speed and moved safely farther out into the harbour. Gerant still grasped the oar instinctively, but saw it looked like he wouldn't need it anymore. Looking ahead, he could see Gramps steering for the break in the harbour wall, where the open sea was.

'Not too bad for a beginner. We'll make a sailor out of you yet.' Gramps nodded towards the side. 'You can lash that oar to the strake there where the other ones are.'

Gerant didn't know what a strake was, but he could see where some other oars were lashed to the planks making up Betsy's sides. It took him only a few moments. Even in that time when he next looked up, the entrance to the harbour was that much closer and there was the occasional rock of the boat as it pushed through the water. Gerant also liked the way the breeze pushed through his hair, ruffling it gently. Importantly, his breakfast was staying where it was meant to be. So far, things were looking OK, but he was sure things might change once they got out into the sea. At least it would be something he would be able to tell Molly about when he got back. He was pretty sure Sveg had never been in a boat, so that would also be worth a tale or two whenever he returned to Ashford for a visit. He carefully walked back and squatted down, holding onto the side next to the cuddy. There he could watch Gramps and ask him about sailing his boat and how he could help out. He settled in and tried to keep his mind off the increasing little lurches that the boat occasionally made as it got closer to the open sea at the end of the harbour walls.

Gerant leant back and absorbed the noises of the wind piping gently through the rigging and the main sail, the regular gentle butting of the bow into the occasional small wavelet and smelled again contentedly the salt-laden air. They were now a couple of hours from North Haven and Gramps had changed over the staysail for the mainsail once they were well clear of the harbour. He had kept the land within sight on the left but struck out into deeper water. At first Gerant had started to feel a little queasy in the stomach. Gramps, noticing this, had suddenly got Gerant doing all sorts of jobs, like tightening the ropes (he now knew they were called halyards) to trim the sail, store away (the correct term was stow, he learnt) the staysail in the sail cupboard (locker) and a hundred other things that Gramps dreamt up. It was only after fifteen minutes where he had had no time to think that Gramps called him back to his spot just outside the cuddy.

'See, young fella, you have been too busy to even think about feeling sick. Just enjoy the motion, it's just like riding a good horse. You move with the rhythm and don't fight it.'

Gerant didn't have the heart to tell Gramps that his limited experience with horse riding had been far from pleasant, and something he only did because he needed to. Nonetheless, Gramps was right – he had been focused on loosening and then tightening the halyards and other things to get Betsy sailing well and had no time to dwell on his initial queasiness as they left the harbour. He had also enjoyed hearing some of the other words used by Gramps and other sailors. He had learnt that left was 'port' and right was 'starboard' and the front of the boat was the 'bow' and the cuddy with the tiller was at the 'stern'. When he had asked Gramps why it was port and starboard, he was told that it had always been that way and that it was fine to ask questions but not to ask stupid questions like that. *Aha*, thought Gerant, *he doesn't know the answer.*

But he kept quiet and after a minute or so asked a different question. Gramps had answered as if he had forgotten that little exchange.

A little later, Gramps suddenly pointed to starboard and smiled.

'See those critters popping up out of the water and then curling over to dive again? They're dolphins, kinda small whales. A good sign as it means there hasn't been any hunters around.'

Gerant watched the five or six dolphins for as long as he could before they slowly disappeared into the distance.

'You don't ever hunt them?'

'Nah, they're always friendly and don't do anyone harm so we leave them alone. You could eat them I guess, but it would be a lot of trouble and there are better creatures in the sea for that.'

Gerant thought about what he had just been told and that reminded him of something.

'Would now be a good time for me to practice with the harpoon? I would really like to get used to throwing it in case we meet any tusktooths.'

'Good idea, young fella. See anything unusual coming up?'

Both Gramps and Gerant craned forward. Gerant didn't quite know what he was looking for, but if they kept going in the same direction, they wouldn't hit land; it just looked like nothing more than water and small waves ahead.

'Looks clear and the wind seems steady. Could be a good time to have a bit of a lesson.'

Gramps checked where the boat was heading and lashed the tiller, then tested the halyards were tight as he moved up to the bow to where the harpoons were stored. He took out one of the harpoons and tied the end of the rope leading from the harpoon securely to the eye bolt just at the base of the bow.

'Right, always remember to secure the iron to the boat, otherwise when you throw, there's no way to reel in the tusktooth. Keep out of the way of the coil of line when you throw, otherwise you'll get caught up by the leg and might get pulled overboard.'

Gerant nodded. That all made sense.

'Then you just try to sneak up on the old tusktooth so it is just off either side of the bow, no more than ten or fifteen feet away. That's my job. Just be ready to cast and then I'll holler when you should launch. Remember to aim about a foot behind the blowhole on the top of its back.'

'But how do I practice? There are no tusktooths around.'

Gramps sighed as he struggled to keep the exasperation out of his response.

'You just have to pretend. Pick a spot about ten or fifteen feet away and aim for it. Then throw and we'll see how close you got. The main thing is to get used to the feel of the iron and what it's like to cast. We can just haul it back in and you can try again. And again. And again, until we are happy.'

So began Gerant's lesson in throwing a harpoon. After carefully standing away from the coiled line attached to the end of the harpoon, he grasped the wooden handle and hefted it a few times to judge the weight. It was quite a bit heavier than the throwing knives but not too much more than the hatchet. He looked ahead and saw a bit of weed floating in the water about fifteen feet away. A quick breath, a small mental adjustment to where he was aiming and then he threw the harpoon forward at the weed, using as smooth and powerful motion as possible. The harpoon pierced the water about two feet to the left of the weed and about three feet short.

'Going for the weed?'

Gerant nodded.

'Not too bad for a first try. Well, pull it back in and we'll coil the line up and try again.'

While Gerant pulled in the line and then the attached harpoon, Gramps quickly went back to the tiller and checked things were still tight and nothing of concern was approaching. This time Gerant aimed at a little wavelet that had just appeared ahead and got within two feet. Mainly through luck than skill, his third try was pretty close to the spot he was aiming. After about another ten tries, he was able to cast the harpoon pretty close to his goal. In his last attempt, they had come across another piece of weed and Gerant had managed to cleave it before the harpoon disappeared into the water. That was enough for him.

'I think I want to stop now. Maybe I'll rest for a bit and have another go later. I think I am getting used to the feel of it and could get pretty close.'

Gramps nodded understandingly and agreed. 'You certainly don't want to wear yourself out. But be aware – if your aim is good when you are practising, it is another matter when your heart is beating fast and you have to throw the iron at a living, breathing tusktooth. That's a whole different story.'

Gerant agreed. 'You are right, Gramps. But that's why I want to stop for now and have another go later. So I'm as ready as I can be.'

'Well, we might see some a little later, but I wouldn't be surprised if we get to Sharkey's and haven't seen any. All the same, I would be really surprised if they aren't hanging around in Fingal's Bay, which we'll get to tomorrow morning or so.'

The weather held and Gerant had no particular feelings of discomfort. He was actually enjoying being on the boat, which was totally different from anything he had experienced. The only slight disappointment was not sighting any tusktooths, but Gramps wasn't at all surprised. There were plenty of other things to do. Gramps set up some lines off the stern to catch some fish, using a little bit of jerky on the hooks. They also passed close to a cloud of seabirds squawking and diving into a circle of water. Gramps anticipated Gerant's questions.

'They are gannets and pelicans and they've found a school of fish at the surface. See how you can see the fish jumping out of the water to escape? The birds dive and feed as fast as they can. The fish will be there for five or ten minutes and then disappear, and then the birds will scoot off as well.'

Gerant watched the birds circling the pool of sea where the fish were for as long as he could see before the boat moved farther northward. He sighed and thought he had so much to learn about the sea and the creatures in it.

'Well, here's the start of dinner.'

He turned, surprised, and saw that Gramps had pulled in a wriggling, thrashing fish from one of the lines over the stern.

'Good-sized mackerel. Hope we get a few more. Pretty good eating.'

Gerant nodded but he had no idea if what Gramps had said was right. Over the course of the next hour, Gramps brought in another three mackerel that he put into a wooden bucket in the cuddy out of the way. As the afternoon progressed, they saw another pod of dolphins playing closer towards the shore, but no sign of tusktooths. Gramps was periodically muttering at the sky and even Gerant noticed some clouds starting to build up in the west and stream towards them.

'See them? We might be in for a bit of a blow. We'll get into Sharkey's alright, but maybe have a bit of wind tonight and maybe into tomorrow. Then again, we might get nothing. Hard to tell at this time of year. It wants to be calm like summer, but winter starts coming early in these northern parts.'

Gramps muttered again under his breath. 'Been doing this enough that you just can't tell. As soon as you think you know, she'll turn things around just to spite you.'

Gerant wasn't sure who 'she' was, but thought it was something he could ask about another time.

'Well, there's Sharkey's, so we can moor Betsy in nice and close in case it decides to come on for a blow.'

They looked ahead and Gerant noticed that Gramps was steering for a spit of land that jutted out from the coast. As they got closer, he could see what looked like the remains of a wooden pier on the closer side of the spit. Gramps bustled around preparing the boat and this time Gerant was able to help by hauling a little on the halyards to partly lower the sail so they started to slow. Gramps was watching over the side ever now and again and leaning against the tiller to change their direction slightly. They were approaching the remnants of the pier quickly and Gramps started rapping out instructions as he quickly looked on either side of the boat as it approached the timber structure.

'Haul down on the halyard so the sail is less. That's good, that's good. Now take it totally down. Be ready for the mooring lines and to fend off with the oar.'

Gramps looked either side and steered to miss the pier by a few yards. Then as the forward motion came off the boat, he swung the tiller towards the pier so that Betsy headed towards the pier pilings. Gerant pushed hard with the oar against the pier and then was able to loop the mooring line around the top of the pier piling and haul really hard. The boat stopped gently against the remnants of the pier and Gerant was able to wrap first one and then the other mooring line up around the pilings. He looked around as Gramps started fussing over the lines, making sure Betsy was nestled hard against the posts. The pier was only about twenty feet long and had planks missing here and there, although the posts all still looked solid. There wasn't much on the spit of land where it jutted out into the water. There were the remains of a cottage or shed overlooking the pier, where some stone walls were partly intact, but the roof had fallen in and there were no doors or windows remaining. There were also small stacks of rock and timber scattered about.

'How long has it been empty and no one living here?'

Gramps grunted as he checked the lines and got out bits and pieces from some of the lockers. 'Old Sharkey scratched out a living here for years and years. Did alright when whaling was doing well and boats stopped in here for supplies and such. It was a good place to ride out bad weather. I think he enjoyed the solitary life. Got harder and harder over time and he was getting older and not able to do as much. Then he just disappeared – no one knew what happened. Maybe he just knew his time was up and he just went off somewhere quiet and lay down and died, or had a bit of coin hidden away and just left for the south somewhere and started again.

'Anyway, people just use Sharkey's as a place to moor and stay for the night. Whoever comes leaves enough wood for the next person to start a fire and there are some emergency rations in an iron box where the rats and foxes can't get at it. There's a spring just on the other side of the point that's drinkable, even if a bit brackish.'

Gerant clambered up onto the pier and Gramps passed up some sacks, Gerant's bedroll and another one that must have been stored on the boat, some cooking gear and the bucket of mackerel. They walked up to the ruin of Sharkey's cottage and in through the open doorway and found the side where the stone walls still made a comfortable corner. The remains of past camp-fires showed where travellers tended to set up and sleep. A couple of the roof beams still arched over the corner, but the tiles or shingles had long disappeared. Gramps glanced up at the sky and sniffed.

'Doesn't smell like rain so we won't bother with rigging up a tarp over the beams. We'll be protected from the wind in here if it gets up during the night. Still not sure what it's going to do.'

He picked up the bucket of fish and took out a small filleting knife and a frying pan from one of the sacks.

'I'll go down to the water and fillet these ready for dinner. See that pile of firewood there? We can use that to get a fire going in a minute. But take that fancy hatchet of yours and go out and find some stuff that we can leave for the next visitors.'

Gerant was happy to do that as it would give him a chance to look around. He wasn't expecting that there would be much to find, but it was good to be on solid ground again, even if only for the night. He dropped his bedroll and sack against the wall and picked up his hatchet. Gramps had already walked back to near the start of the pier and was crouching down at the edge of the water working on the fish. Gerant headed off looking for suitable wood. There was the occasional bush poking above the long grass on a faint trail he followed. *I probably shouldn't be surprised that close to the hut all the wood has been collected,* he thought. After a few minutes wandering along the trails left by animals, he reached a little gully where a small rivulet gurgled towards the sea. Here he found a few stunted trees sheltering out of the wind. One of them had a dead limb that had partly snapped off about eight feet up. He clambered up to the fork and it took only a few targeted blows with the hatchet for the limb to separate and crunch down to the ground. Chopping the wood into suitable lengths took a few more minutes. He looped the hatchet on his belt and picked up the first armful and walked carefully back to Sharkey's ruin. It took several trips, but he had soon added considerably to the carefully stacked firewood within the walls. Gramps had already finished getting the fish ready and had started a small fire in the ring of stones.

'Nice work, my young friend. The next people won't be able to complain that we left them no wood! I'll just let this fire settle down a bit and then I'll cook the fish, just with some lard and a few herbs. Nothing fancy, but you can't beat fresh fish just caught. We can have it with ale. Best to save the water for when we need it.'

Gerant decided to lay out his bedding along one of the walls a little away from the fire. Gramps had already laid his bedroll out on the other side of the fire. Like most of Gramps's gear, it looked like it had been used for many years but was neat and well maintained.

He also decided to go back to the little streamlet he had found and have a quick wash. Although the water tasted a little brackish, it was good enough for a quick duck of his head and rub of his chest, arms and neck. The cold breeze on his exposed still-wet chest was bracing, but he felt the better for having done it. He jumped up and down a few times, swinging his arms to get the blood pumping and dry off a little, put his top back on and wandered back. Gramps looked up as he walked in.

'Good timing. I was about to holler. Grubs up.'

Gramps had pulled over a small log that they could both sit on next to the fire and eat. Gerant was a little cautious with the pieces of fish and then tucked in as he delighted in the flavour – something he had never had before. He should have known by now that Gramps was very proficient in cooking in his own way. He also really liked the way the beautiful flaky pieces of mackerel went so well with the ale. It did not take very long to clear his plate and then they had a couple of apples to finish off. Without being asked, Gerant took the empty plates, fry-pan and eating utensils down to rivulet and gave them a good wash. When he returned, Gramps had added a few logs to the camp-fire and had topped up the tankards of ale. He was clearly in a relaxed and contented mood, softly burping and staring off into the distance. Gerant looked up at the sky through the rafters; the light was starting to fade. He could see cloud banks marching from the west and the wind had picked up a little.

'Will the wind be too strong tomorrow to continue looking?' Gerant tried to make his question sound casual, but he was dreading the response.

'Hard to say. My instinct is we might get a stronger wind tonight based on those clouds coming over and it might shift more northerly. But it could die down around dawn and the sea should stay calm. Time will tell. There's nothing we can do about it, so we may as well just get a good night's sleep and see what tomorrow brings.

'Don't worry, young fella. Whether we come across any tusktooths is in the lap of the gods. But they seem to like Fingal's Bay as there is good food for them there. About another hour north and then the bay opens out with a little island about a half a mile off the shore. They are often in the waters around the island; it's a little bit shallower and easier hunting for squid and such.'

Gerant pondered what tomorrow would bring, staring into the flames. 'It would be good if we catch one, Gramps. All the same, I have already learnt so much and there is so much to tell the people down south. The old lady I lodge with won't be able to believe it. I don't think she has ever left The Capital!'

Gramps was nodding slowly, with his eyes closed, not paying that much attention.

'Is that a fact? Well, I've never been that far south. Takes all types, I guess . . .'

His head started to nod even more, and he started to snuffle and mumble. Gerant could see the old man was starting to fall asleep. He quickly got up and went outside. Darkness had well and truly arrived, and he had a quick piss. Coming back, he found Gramps had succumbed and was a large, blanket-covered lump on his bedroll, from which gentle snoring had already begun. Gerant got his bedding ready, gave the fire a quick check to make sure the coals were tamped down and snuggled down into his blankets. He lay listening to the wind whistling a little around the stone ruin and fell asleep dreaming that they had woken up in the morning to a howling gale from the north. Betsy crashed through an endless series of waves over six feet in height. The fifty or so tusktooths, one with a tusk over twenty feet long, continued to swim ahead, just out of harpoon range, despite Gramps's pleas for them to slow down.

Chapter 30
Tusktooth

Gerant became aware of the sounds of Gramps moving around in the ruin of Sharkey's cottage, getting the fire going. The dream was still fresh in his mind, and he quickly sat up and looked at the sky. It had that faint change from full darkness that signalled dawn was not far off. The moon was setting and partly obscured by some wispy cloud. Gramps noticed him looking and commented cheerfully.

'Well, it looks like the wind didn't really pick up much, and I think we'll have another good day of it. It's shifted slightly more from the north but that won't matter much. Just going to get a hot drink going and we can have the leftovers of the mackerel for a nice little breakfast snack. Then we should get moving so we can get to Fingal's fairly soon and see if we are in any luck. Probably a bad luck move, but I'm going to lash in a couple of harpoons and the lance. I think we're going to find one, and I'd prefer to have everything as ready as we can.'

'Morning, Gramps. I agree. My master always said it's better to prepare and then you get less surprises that way.'

Gramps nodded in agreement. 'Sensible fellow. Can't be too careful and you always forget an important step in the rush. Like that time I forgot to lash the iron to the boat and I lost my best harpoon in a beluga because I had rushed.'

Gramps stopped and relived the memory, clearly still hurting a little even now. He sighed and put the frypan on the fire with a little lard and the leftover fish. Gerant went outside to have a piss and came back in to eat some more of the delicious fish from last night. It was then a few moments to pack up the bedrolls, douse the fire and make a last check around the dilapidated cottage. The two men trooped down to the pier and piled into Betsy once more, following the same routine of setting the staysail and fending off with an oar.

It was only for the first few minutes where Gerant felt a little uneasy with the rhythmic motion of the boat and then he was fine. They set the mainsail once well past the point and headed north. They stayed closer to the coast this time and Gerant could see that the land was largely flat, with few trees or hills, although far to the west the land rose towards some distant mountains. After an hour of uneventful sailing, the land retreated as a large bay opened to the left and Gramps tacked in, following the shore from a couple of hundred yards away. He was looking ahead all the time and actually got Gerant to clew the mainsail – another term Gerant learnt – to reduce their speed a little. Gerant could also see some land rising out of the water in the bay, which he took to be the island Gramps had mentioned. It looked to be about a quarter of a mile long or thereabouts, with a few scattered trees and bushes on its slopes. There was a channel of about half a mile width between the island and the land itself.

'Does it have a name?' He gestured.

'Nope, just the Island, or maybe Finley's Island.' A pause. 'Before you ask, no, I don't know who Finley was, just always been called that.'

Gerant just nodded.

It was when they were off the island and Gerant was watching a seabird hovering and then diving into the water close to the shore of the island that he felt Gramps tense and then stand for a better look. After standing still for some seconds looking a little to the left, Gramps suddenly pulled the tiller over and motioned towards where he had been looking and held up two fingers. Gerant watched ahead and couldn't see anything noteworthy. He was beginning to doubt Gramps when a little farther to the left of where he was watching he saw one and then another smooth, sleek body emerge from the water for several seconds and then smoothly and gracefully disappear again. There was a small puff of spray that emerged from the tusktooth blowholes as they breathed, and Gerant almost imagined a distinctive *pfff* sound, although being a hundred yards or more away he was not so sure he actually heard it. Gramps beckoned agitatedly at him, and he clambered back from the bow where he had been idling. In an undertone, Gramps gave him some quick instructions.

'Two males. I'll try to ease up to the starboard of them so when you strike, they are stuck between the boat and the shore and can't dive too deep. Go up to the bow and get ready to throw the iron when I signal. You remember where to aim?'

Gerant gulped and nodded.

'Right. Hopefully they won't get panicked when Betsy eases up to them and you'll have a clear shot. But be ready. Strike true, young fella. Good luck!'

Gramps began quietly bustling with the main sail, clewing it in a little and heading a little to the right of where the tusktooths had last surfaced. Gerant quietly moved up to the bow and checked the harpoons and lance another time and made sure the lines were neatly coiled and he wouldn't step in them in the rush. Then he crouched down a little, peering ahead now and again. He wasn't sure whether the tusktooths saw much when they came out of the water each time, but he didn't want to take any chances. Just then they surfaced and Gerant got his first good look.

It was hard to judge just how big they were as the whole animal was never above the surface of the water, but based on what Gramps had said, maybe they were ten feet or a little bigger. Both of the creatures had a tusk, again hard to estimate at a quick look, but perhaps five or so feet long. The heads were quite rounded and smooth, and he couldn't see any eyes from this distance. The smooth skin across the back of the tusktooths was blotchy or spotty and in shades of grey with almost tinges of green, like their skin was made from tree bark or leaves. The tusktooths gently dipped back under the water and there were tiny ripples that spread out from the place they had disappeared. Gramps jumped up and lowered the mainsail a little more so they would gently coast up to close to where he guessed the tusktooths would next reappear. He mouthed, 'Ready?' at Gerant, who nodded back, grasping one of the harpoons and quietly stretching his arms and shoulders.

A tense minute or so went by with no sign of the tusktooths. Gramps craned left and right, muttering quietly. Gerant crouched down near the bow liked a coiled spring and rehearsed what he was going to do. Stand up quietly, wait for the right moment, pick the spot and then smoothly throw the iron. Gramps looked ahead suddenly to the left and quickly pulled the tiller over to the right. He must have spotted something, but Gerant couldn't see anything different. Then he quickly noticed a few bubbles and swirling in the water about fifteen feet or so ahead and to the left of the boat. This is it, he thought, and then his view seemed to focus in, sounds dropped away and everything slowed to the *thump, thump* of his heartbeat. One tusktooth slowly broke the surface and its arched back started to rise, the water slipping off its smooth, sleek back. *I'll go for the other one,* thought Gerant, and hefted the harpoon even tighter. Then the other tusktooth started to emerge just to the right of the first one. Gerant stood up and cocked his arm back, ready to cast. The second tusktooth slowly rose out of the water and arched over gently, the tusk and its nose starting to dip back into the water. A small *pfff* emerged from its blowhole.

'Now,' yelled Gramps, jumping up and down in excitement.

Gerant had already started his cast when the moment came and he only vaguely heard a yell as he focused on a spot of the tusktooth's back a foot from where the puff of water-laden air had emerged. An almost animal-like, 'Yaaah,' emerged from someone nearby and Gerant vaguely realised it had come from him. He smoothly but powerfully flowed into hurling the iron and watched with intense satisfaction that the head of the harpoon buried itself into the hide of the tusktooth only six inches or so from his aiming point. His feeling of elation at a strong and accurate cast suddenly altered with another thought. *What have I done?*

He could see a splash of blood erupt from the back of the tusktooth, now sporting the wooden shaft and the line and he heard almost a deep moan and a shudder in the water. The tail of the tusktooth rose rapidly out of the water and then smashed down, almost drenching Gerant in the boat. Both tusktooths rapidly disappeared under the surface, with a violent roiling in the water where they had been. The line attached to Betsy quickly disappeared over the bow with almost a hiss and then the last loop disappeared into the water and there was a large thrum as the line went taut and the end of the rope tied into the loop at the bow held. Betsy suddenly lurched forward as the tusktooth started to tow it. Further roils of water and traces of thick blood emerged on the surface ahead of the bow. Gramps bustled forward, bringing down the mainsail in a rush.

'Good cast, good cast. This thing will tow us along so the sail will just get in the way and we could end up with the wind blowing us the wrong way. We just ride this out for about a minute or so and then slowly reel him in. You'll need to use your strength to pull in the line and I'll hook it onto the cleats here.'

The boat continued to be pulled through the water by the harpooned tusktooth. At one point the wounded animal surfaced about twenty feet directly ahead, before it rapidly arched, took a breath and dove towards the bottom. Gerant could see the harpoon buried in its rounded back, with a quick slick of blood forming in those short few seconds.

'Right, Gerant, try and start pulling in the line.'

Gerant grasped the taut cable and leant back, heaving. After a few heartbeats he was slowly able to pull in about three feet, which Gramps deftly looped around two cleats anchored into the gunwale of the boat near to the harpoon anchor point. Gerant felt he wasn't actually reeling in the tusktooth, more that he was pulling the boat closer to the rapidly swimming animal. Gods, this was hard work! He was grateful for his training in the smithy and having good strength in his arms. He also naturally slipped into the breathing technique he had learnt: haul one, haul two, haul three, haul four, rest one, rest two, rest three.

Several minutes of concerted effort had resulted in twenty or so feet of line being pulled in by Gerant and Gramps had quickly wrapped it between the two cleats. Gerant looked up and realised they had been pulled forward several hundred yards. At least they were still in clear water and had not been dragged towards the island or the main shore. The tusktooth had been forced to come up for air more and more as it appeared to tire and was not able to dive so deeply because of the shortened line attached to the harpoon. Gramps thumped him on the back and yelled. It was now surfacing only a few feet ahead of the boat as it was effectively tethered to the boat which was a huge weight that could not be pulled under the water.

'Grab the lance and when it next surfaces, pierce it as close to the blowhole as you can reach. Try to hang on and keep stabbing it in if you can.'

Gerant nodded quickly. He wanted this to end as quickly as he could. He picked up the lance and got ready. The tusktooth broached the surface again just ahead and this time he thrust the lance straight at the blowhole as it emerged. He felt the lance head cut into the body before he quickly withdrew it and stabbed again. Gerant held on, trying to work the razor-sharp head into the body of the tusktooth. The animal went into a frenzy of thrashing on the surface and Gerant was hard-pressed to not be knocked over, gritting his teeth with the effort to hold onto the lance. Gramps also reached out and grabbed Gerant's hands in his own to try to add his strength. The tusktooth continued thrashing its head about and its tail flailed the water in its agony. Gerant must have hit something vital, as the shudders and agitations began to lessen, until the body convulsed a few more times and then lay still in the water, with gouts of blood continuing to erupt from the stab wounds and the head of the harpoon and lance. Gerant realised that he was quite wet from the seawater thrown up from the tusktooth's splashing and he was starting to shiver uncontrollably from the reaction to the events.

'You often feel this way after a successful hunt. I remember it took me maybe ten hunting trips before I was able to handle the excitement and danger of the chase.'

Gramps patted Gerant gently on the back, clearly sympathetic.

'Right, we can rig up the holding brackets and lash the critter to the side. Then we can go back to the island and do what we need to do. There's a little beach in a cove that we can just run the boat up onto. Just sit down to catch your breath. I'll do this bit.'

Gramps went to one of the hatches in the deck and pulled out a pair of L-shaped iron brackets that he then fitted through some iron rings on the strakes. The brackets rose up and then the arms leant out over the water. Gramps paddled with an oar so that Betsy eased up to the dead tusktooth floating in the water until the body bumped against the side of the boat. The old man leant out and passed a loop of rope over the tusk and head of the animal, and another loop over the flukes of the tail. Then he carefully tightened the ropes and lashed them to the brackets. Gerant could see that now the tusktooth was floating in the water right next to the boat, lashed to the side using the brackets. *Very neat,* he thought.

'Right, let's get that mainsail drawing again and then we'll tack back up to the island. The cove is on the other side: a nice sandy little beach. After we run Betsy ashore, there's a handy tree that we can run a block and tackle around and then use that to pull the tusktooth onto the land. It'll weigh more than a tonne, so too hard to get it on land by ourselves. Better to use our brains for this. Also much better to do it this way: we'll get wet and filthy enough without trying to skin it in the water.'

'Sure, Gramps, whatever you reckon. Biggest thing I've skinned is a rabbit, so I'll leave it up to you how you want to do it.'

'Hummph,' was all Gramps said as Gerant helped him raise the sail and check the halyards. It took them about twenty minutes to work their way back up to the island and come around the outer side. Gerant checked the lashings holding the tusktooth to the boat and they were holding. As they tacked in towards the island, he could see a lovely little beach about fifty yards long, with grey sand and some trees clustered nearby. The cove looked a little protected from the weather as the main part of the island rose quickly in a ring behind the sheltered area. A few more trees survived on the slopes above, but it was mainly covered with low shrubs, rock outcrops and long grass.

Gramps lined the boat up with the middle of the beach and stood up to watch progress.

'Just hang on. When we ground, it'll stop real quick.'

Almost as soon as he was told this, Gerant could see the water rapidly lessening in depth; he could already see the sandy bottom. Then there was a sudden sound of the keel of the boat started to grind on the sand and then a lurch as the boat stopped. Betsy had been moving forward steadily with the wind pushing on the mainsail. As Gerant leant over the side, he could see about four feet or so of the bow had ridden up on the sand, with the water gently lapping farther back. It looked firmly wedged, but he guessed that Gramps must have done this many times and it wouldn't take too much pushing to get the boat back off. The tusktooth was still lashed to the side of the boat and had beached as well, with the nose and tusk of the animal just reaching the exposed sand and most of the body lying in the shallow water. Gramps opened a locker and took out a block and a ratchet and some longer line. He carefully eased himself out of the bow onto the sand, took the block and looped it around a nearby sturdy tree of about fifteen feet high.

'Unlash the cable around the tail and pass it over.'

Gerant did as he was instructed and passed the line over to Gramps, who hooked it into the block and tackle. He then started to crank the line taut and slowly but steadily the loop around the tail tightened.

'Your turn, young fella. Just keep on working the ratchet.'

Gerant hopped out of the boat and then began steadily ratcheting the line tighter and tighter. The tail of the tusktooth started to quiver a little with each ratchet and then slowly began to inch its way around and then towards the tree. Gerant cranked steadily on, passing the rope through the ratchet and the body of the tusktooth inched farther out of the water by the tail, until it was totally lying on the sand and not immersed in any water.

'That will do. Now, I'll just grab some knives and tools and we can start the skinning. This will be a slow and pretty messy process, so what I might get you to do is start a fire. Afterwards, we can have a bit of a wash to get off the worst of the blood and gore and dry off. Don't want to be sailing back shivering and get a fever. Learnt that the hard way!'

Gramps shuddered recalling an old memory and started rummaging in one of the sacks in the cockpit. Gerant grabbed his hatchet and went off to grab some firewood. At least this bit he could do. He would follow Gramps's instructions after, but what was coming didn't sound all that inviting. It took a few minutes to find some twigs and kindling and a couple of armfuls of small branches to start a fire on the sand. He was happy with how it caught and wandered back to the tusktooth. Gramps had taken off his top and his white-haired chest and still ropy sinews in his arms were already spattered with drops of blood and flecks of tissue. He had made a long slit in the tusktooth's hide from the mouth to the flukes of the tail. He looked up at the fire and at Gerant approaching and nodded in satisfaction.

'Grab a knife and we'll just work the hide off. Kinda like peeling the skin off a melon. Just go slowly. You don't want to knick the hide and create holes. If that happens, it will be less likely to come off in one piece and won't be worth near as much.'

Gerant took his top off, took a quick drink of water from one of the water bottles and grabbed one of the knives sitting on top of a leather sack. 'OK, Gramps, what's first?'

'You hold the edge of the hide where I've already cut, and you gently pull. I'll work my knife under and ease it away from the blubber and meat if it catches. Pretend it's a big rabbit.'

Gerant couldn't imagine how this huge beast could be like skinning a rabbit, but he gently opened the initial cut near the flukes a little more with his knife so he could hold the edge of the skin and started pulling up. There was a thick layer of fat, which he guessed was what Gramps had called blubber. The meat and muscle were mostly underneath and only occasionally directly beneath the hide. Gramps carefully nicked away the blubber and flesh with his knife and they gradually worked on releasing the skin from the animal.

After twenty minutes or so they had worked their way about halfway along and now had the hide off the rear end of the animal. It had taken both of them to roll the body each time to expose more of the hide to work off. As they stopped to have a quick drink of water and put more wood on the fire, Gerant was glad he had taken his shirt off. He was now almost caked with blood and little gobs of blubber and slime from the skin. It had been unavoidable given the wrestling with the carcass. He and Gramps grinned at each other – they both looked like wild men who had been in the middle of a huge bar fight or hand-to-hand battle with knives.

Finally they managed get the hide off in one piece. The body of the tusktooth was now skinned, with the blubber and muscle exposed, apart from the flukes of the tail and just near the mouth, where the tusk emerged. They both carefully lugged the sheet of skin to the water and gave it a wash to release some of the blood and slimy secretions. Then they cradled it up to the grassy verge, laid it out with the inner side on top and then folded the hide in on itself. It took the two of them to awkwardly carry the bundle of skin and then heave it into the boat.

'We can pack it away a bit neater when we're finished but it should be fine for now. I just want to grab a little of the meat and then we'll do the tusk,' mentioned Gramps as they walked back to the carcass.

The old man honed one of the knives on a small steel and then cut into the blubber near the slightly raised back. A dark red, muscle layer was exposed and Gramps carefully cut out a piece of the flesh with the blubber attached. He trimmed it to leave a few inches of blubber on top and then carefully placed it into a wooden box he had brought from the boat. It looked like to Gerant that he had sliced out a couple of pounds of meat.

'What's that for, Gramps?'

As Gramps quickly washed the knife in the water, he explained.

'I've got a mate who is very partial to whale meat. Bit of an acquired taste, but he grew up on it and he doesn't get to have it very often now. I always try to bring a bit back if I can. The blubber layer will keep it fresh for quite a bit. We'll be back well before it starts to turn.

'Right, let's get this tusk off.' Gramps paused and picked up a small saw from the sack of tools. 'You hold the tusk while I cut.'

Gerant had a closer look at the tusk and admired the way it was almost like a horn in the way it regularly spiralled out near the animal's mouth until it reached the tip. It looked like it was about five feet long. He grasped it about a foot from the mouth in both hands. Gramps lined up the saw at the thickest part of the tusk just where it disappeared into the head of the animal and started gently sawing. Bits of dust from the bone slowly appeared as the old man worked the saw, which he occasionally puffed away. After a few minutes, the saw had cut through almost to the bottom and Gramps looked up at Gerant expectantly.

Gerant nodded back that he was ready and held the tusk steady. A few more cuts from the saw and Gerant could feel the weight starting to increase in his hands. Then, suddenly, the saw was through, and he held in his hands the complete tusktooth. He passed it over to Gramps, who examined it quickly and hefted it, feeling the weight.

'Have seen and taken bigger ones, but this is a decent size. Let's wrap it in some sacking and then we can wash and dry off a little at the fire. It's a bit of a waste to leave the rest but it would take us all day and tomorrow to take everything.'

Gerant pondered on that. He had really only needed the tusktooth ground up for the paste that the old parchment talked about. Gramps had told him that the hide was quite valuable and he would get a good price for it, once it was cured properly. And he had taken a small amount of the meat. He looked at the large carcass lying on the sand in front of him.

'What's going to happen to it, Gramps?'

The old man was sitting on the sand, carefully wiping his tools with a bit of rag. He looked up for a second and then continued cleaning the knives. 'Don't concern yourself too much, matey. This will be a huge feast for all the critters around here. There will probably be a few foxes on the island and then the hawks and sea eagles will find it pretty quick. Who knows what else will come along? But if you come back in a few weeks, there will be only the skeleton left, that's for sure.'

Gerant felt a little bit better now, as he knelt at the edge of the water and washed his hands and arms and chest. He had a few patches of blood and filth on his leggings, so he decided to take them off and rinse them in the seawater. Gramps was also rinsing off and giving his head a quick dunk. His head emerged with his hair plastered down and water dripping off his beard.

'Don't worry about your leggings. Put on your spare pair, if you brought some, and we can hang them up on a line in Betsy and they'll dry in the wind.'

Gerant hadn't brought a spare, but put his shirt back on and walked up to the fire to warm up. Gramps joined him combing his hair and beard with his fingers before putting his shirt back on. He held his gnarled fingers out to the heat and gently burped.

'I reckon we get going after we've packed up and just see how far we get. Should get well past Sharkey's by nightfall, so easier to just anchor near shore and sleep on the boat. Unless the wind drops or we hit a bit of heavy weather, we should be back home round about lunchtime tomorrow. That suit you?'

'Sure thing, Gramps. That will give me tomorrow to get things ready but then I might head off back south the day after.' Gerant thought about what he would need before he left. Nothing much, just a matter of packing everything again and he could be on his way early. There was one thing, though.

'As well as fixing you up with the balance of the coin, I thought I might go to the tavern and get a meal, some more ale and that liquor you like. It will be nice to have a little celebration when we get back to your place.'

The older man's face crinkled into a smile as he gently rubbed his hands over the fire. 'They make a really good pork pie at the Icebreaker and I certainly wouldn't say no to some more of their fine liquor.'

The two men formally shook hands.

'Deal,' murmured Gerant.

Chapter 31
Too Good to be True

Gerant tightened the line mooring Betsy to the pier at North Haven, then patted the gunwale of the boat affectionately. 'Thanks, Betsy, for a smooth ride. I really appreciate it.'

Gramps overheard the soft comment and muttered quietly in confirmation. 'Yes, always thank a lady for a good experience. You never know when they'll get you through some unexpected strife.' Then he got more businesslike. 'I'll leave the hide here on Betsy, as I need to get a big bag of salt and then start curing it. Also need to come back over the coming days and give Betsy a good tidy up and get her ready for the next trip. Not that there will be that many before winter arrives. Hmmm, I need to restitch the bottom of that staysail.'

Gerant started to throw his pack and bedroll onto the pier and carefully laid the sacking-covered tusktooth next to his gear. 'Take the harpoons and the lance?'

Gramps shook his head. 'Nah, I'll give them a look and sharpen them in the next day or so. They can stay here for now.'

Gerant was happy, as he didn't feel like taking piles of gear back to the old man's cottage. They started out with a comfortable load each and reached the neat cottage after a few minutes. It had not changed, and Gramps ducked around the back to unbar the front door. Although he had only spent one night here, it felt a little like home and he was extremely glad to lay his bedroll and pack on the floor and lean the tusktooth into a corner of the main room. The small pile of things he had not taken on the trip were as he had left them. Gramps fussed around the stove, getting some shavings and kindling to start a fire going.

'Well, I might duck down to the Icebreaker and get that dinner and the drinks. You want anything else?'

Gramps stopped blowing gently on kindling that was just starting to catch and shook his head.

'Oh, I need a few bits of fresh food for the trip down south. Where's the best place to get a few potatoes and some green stuff? And maybe a couple of apples?'

'Well, there are a few places in town, but the one I go to is Mrs McCreedy's, fairly close to the tavern. She will have those sort of things and the prices are reasonable and the quality is always good. Tell Violet that Abraham sent you.'

Gerant quickly looked at the old man, who had turned back to the stove and was carefully laying some wood on the small dancing flames. But not before he thought he noticed a little blush on the old man's cheeks. *Aha,* he thought, *that's how things are. Good for him.* He grabbed an empty sack and walked out the door, calling back. 'OK, I won't be long. No more than an hour.' He ran back after going past a few houses, as he had forgotten to get directions to Mrs McCreedy's place.

The visit to the tavern had been uneventful and he had a tasty-looking pork pie in his sack that would feed the both of them. There was also some ale in a small skin and a little flask of the Icebreaker that he would leave with Gramps. He would just stick to ale. Eventually he might enjoy stronger stuff like the liquor but for now he would pass up on it. He wandered off towards his next stop. After turning left at the first cross-street and left again, he quickly came to a neat white cottage with yellow trim on the doors and windows. Around the side opening out onto a small space was a small lean-to with baskets of fruit and vegetables and a small wooden counter on the side. He rang the small bell on the counter and within a few seconds a neatly dressed older woman with a lilac-grey dress and a white pinafore came in from the house, her grey hair in a bun.

'Good morning, young man. What can I get for you?'

'Err, good morning, Mrs McCreedy, my name is Gerant. I need just a few things for my trip south . . . Umm, Abraham sent me.'

'Oh, you know Abraham? How lovely.'

'Well, I am staying at his place tonight before I go back. He took me out fishing.'

Gerant thought he didn't need to explain what they had gone out looking for.

Mrs McCreedy's face remained friendly, but her eyes squinted a little and her voice hardened slightly.

'You can tell Abraham that he hasn't been to see me for over a week and those strawberries I have been saving for him won't last forever.'

'Happy to pass that on. I'll make sure he comes round as soon as he can.'

Gerant smiled internally and kept his face serious. The slight cloud on Mrs McCreedy's expression cleared and she was once again very pleasant.

'So Gerant, what items are you needing for your trip?'

'Oh, not much. Just a few potatoes, whatever green stuff you recommend and maybe a couple of apples if you have them.'

Mrs McCreedy walked around to the various baskets and brought back the items, commenting as she went.

'These potatoes are last season's but still eating nicely. I could give you some kale, but these little zucchini are probably better and really tasty. Hmm, Jonathans or Granny Smiths? Three Jonathans should be better.'

'There you go, young man. That will be six coppers. Do come again if you are up this way. And don't forget to tell Abraham that I am still waiting.'

A few minutes' walk and he was back outside Gramps's place. He had hardly noticed the journey as he had been thinking about preparations for tomorrow and how far we would get on the road to Rivernook. Still thinking about where to camp, he pushed open the front door and walked in. And then stopped, as he quickly took in what he was seeing. One of the chairs had been knocked over and was on the floor near the stove. Gramps was lying huddled on the floor, quietly groaning. He was holding his arm and there was blood on his forehead and staining the beard on his cheeks. A large bruise was already starting to colour across the bridge of his nose. Various bits of gear from the table were scattered on the floor. A quick glance at the corner of the room showed that the wrapped tusktooth had disappeared. He quickly threw the sack onto the table and leant down to gently turn Gramps over a little.

'Hey, old man. Are you OK? What happened? Here, let me give you some water.'

Gerant quickly spotted a waterskin and helped Gramps sit up and gently let a trickle of water fill his mouth. The old man swallowed, coughed a little and leant against Gerant, his eyes unfocused and bleary.

'Was just putting on some water for a brew. They just walked in and jumped me. Roughed me up real good and knew exactly what they were after. Just found the tusk in the corner there and gave me another going over when they left. There was nothing I could do.'

He cradled the old man gently and gave him another few sips of water. He gently felt over the old man's chest and arms and looked at his bloodied face.

'Well, looks like nothing is broken but you will be real sore for a few days. How many were there? Did you know any of them?'

The old man coughed and nodded. 'Two of them are with the Brotherhood. They're the local gang and always up to bad things. The third was that dirty White-eye. I reckon I remember he was in the tavern when you first started talking to me about going after a tusktooth, and I reckoned he must have heard enough. By cripes, when I catch up with him, he won't walk on his own legs for a while.'

'Well, Gramps, let's get you into bed and clean you up a bit. Before you rest, there's a few other things I need to find out.'

Gerant went to the door of the sleeping place and opened it and then carefully supported Gramps to stand up and hobble over to the room. It was compact and had only a few chests and cupboards and a single bed with a neat reddish woollen cover. He sat the old man on the bed and quickly got most of his clothes off. After laying the old man down, he went back out and found a basin that he filled with water and found some pieces of rag. After gently wiping down the old man's face and neck to get rid of the worst of the blood, he went back out to get a chair, one of the tankards and the flask of liquor.

'Here, Gramps, this might help with the pain a bit. I'll leave it right next to the bed for you.'

After a couple of sips of the Icebreaker, Gramps groaned quietly and lay back with his eyes closed. Gerant tucked the blanket around him. He had probably made him as comfortable as he would get. But there were a couple of things he had to ask, regardless.

'This Brotherhood gang. Do they have a place in town? I want to go and see if I can get the tusktooth back.'

Gramps opened his eyes to look at the younger man for a little, with a clearly worried expression. 'Yes, they have a compound up at the north end of town, near the road out. You can't miss it: a square building with no windows on the outside, just a guarded front door and locked gates that they can get carts through into the inside courtyard. By all means go and have a look, but I don't think you'll have any luck getting it back. If you were stupid enough to go to the door and ask for it, the best that would happen is you get beaten up, but more likely they would kill you.'

The old man sighed and shut his eyes. 'I feel really sorry for you, Gerant. We went to all that trouble and now it's gone just at the final hour.'

A growing anger had been building in Gerant about what must have happened. It was bad enough that they had taken the tusktooth, but worse was how they had treated someone who he now greatly admired and respected. Gramps was probably right that he would never get it back. But he was not going to give up straight away and would at least still see what might be possible. For all he knew, this Brotherhood group had not even taken it back to their compound and it was somewhere else. There were so many things that could have happened. At least doing this would give him something to do and not dwell on feeling hopeless and unable to do anything about it. He made up his mind.

'Gramps, I'm just going to go up there and quietly just look around. I'll be back in a few hours and give you some dinner and get you comfortable again. I probably still need to head off in the morning, but I'll set you up. I might even go and tell Mrs McCreedy about what's happened and see if she can help.'

He looked over the old man and saw that he had already fallen asleep, breathing shallowly but at least with a peaceful expression on his battered and bruised face.

Gerant watched the wooden building from the doorway across the street and focused on the alcove opening off the heavy door with the iron bracing and reinforcement. There was a cough audible from across the street and a figure in the alcove of the building shifted slightly and went back to being motionless. He watched silently for a few minutes more and then eased himself out of view from the compound door and trod silently down the laneway.

So far everything had confirmed what Gramps had told him about this Brotherhood building. The dark-stained timber building appeared to have been built around a small central courtyard. There were no doors or windows on the outside apart from the main reinforced door with the guard watching in the alcove, and the barred double gates at the back where carts could come in and out. He had now looked at the back, one side and front and there was no easy way in. As he walked carefully along the fourth side down the laneway, he thought the only way might be onto the roof and somehow drop down from there without being noticed. It looked like it was made of shingles and he was not confident that he could even get up there easily and wouldn't just crash through into a room full of thugs and that would be the end of it. He suddenly stopped, had another look and then quickly checked up and down the laneway to make sure it was empty. Then he scuttled over to the wall of the building and leant down to carefully inspect the padlock he had spotted. The building appeared to be built on wooden stumps and the planks covering the outside of the wall had been extended down to cover the open space below the floor level. A small wooden access hatch had been built so that the under-floor area could be reached and had been carefully padlocked shut. Gerant looked at the padlock: it was not a very fancy one. Although it was not rusty, it looked like it wasn't opened very often. He smiled grimly and got out a small set of picks in a scuffed leather wallet. Who would have thought that all that time spent learning about locks from The Picker when he was a kid would now be useful? As he got things ready and inserted his favourite pick into the padlock, he mused about his earlier circumstances and wondered what had happened to the boy. When he had been part of the homeless gang in Ashford, they had sometimes relied on The Picker to break into places and steal coin and other valuables. He felt the mechanism in the lock click and pushed the pick a little more. The boy's real name was Marvin, but they all just called him The Picker. He was a weedy, thin fellow with one leg a little shorter that made him limp. He probably wouldn't have lasted long in the gang except he was a magician with his tools and could open any lock. The mechanism gave a little again and he continued working the pick gently in the mechanism. So The Picker was really valuable to the group and had been able to help them out on so many occasions when they had nothing to eat or no coin to buy food. Marvin had been more than happy to teach Gerant how to pick locks and they enjoyed a quiet friendship in the rough-and-tumble life the boys had to live. There was a final click in the lock that he felt more than he heard, and the hasp sprang open. Gerant put the pick back in the wallet, checked the laneway again and worked the wooden grating open and crawled inside, dragging his sack after him. He laid the padlock on the ground and then carefully positioned the grate back over the opening.

Lying quietly in the space, he looked up in the very dim light. The wooden floor was maybe two feet above and so there was room to wriggle along without too much effort. He could hear the occasional scraping of furniture or other stuff above and the murmur of voices. He crawled carefully in the space between the wooden stumps and stopped when he could see the edge of the inner wall and daylight streaming into the courtyard. He stayed back in the gloom close to one of the thick round stumps and peered out at what he could see. There in the middle of the courtyard were the wheels of a cart. Gerant couldn't see much of the actual cart from where he lay, otherwise he might expose himself too much and be spotted. There was no horse hitched to the cart and from what he could see the gates to the courtyard were firmly barred. Just then, there were further scraping noises from above. He could see that there were some steps coming down from the building, down which two sets of legs suddenly clattered. A couple of kegs and boxes were then lifted down and placed on the ground near the cart. One set of legs jumped up into the back of the cart and the first set of legs lifted up and passed the kegs and boxes up. He could hear two male voices talking while they moved the items into the cart.

One voice spoke. 'Right, these are only going to Rivernook. So leave them up the back so they are easy to get. That box is going all the way to The Capital so it can stack up the front.'

The other voice replied. 'What else is going to The Capital? We should pack that in first.'

The first voice spoke again. 'Well, those two crates with the tapestries and the fancy clothes. And the small box of daggers. And the jewellery. And that tusktooth that just came in. I believe they want it in Pearl City for a buyer there, but it can be put on the right with the crates for The Capital next to it. It'll be wrapped up in the padding so we can lash it between the boxes and the side of the cart so it can't shift. It's worth a heap of coin.'

The second pair of legs jumped down from the cart and both sets disappeared back into the building and the talking continued in a muffled manner, which Gerant couldn't understand lying where he was under the floor. A few minutes later the two Brotherhood men brought out more goods to load into the cart, including a sacking-wrapped slender package that, even from his dim viewpoint under the flooring, Gerant recognised as the tusktooth. That disappeared into the body of the cart, presumably on the right-hand side against the crates as the voices had discussed. The cart was loaded over the next hour or so and it reached a point, based on the conversation between the two men, of being ready.

The second voice spoke. 'Well, that's it then. All ready for a start tomorrow and we should make it to the Chapter House in Rivernook after the second night. I'm looking forward to The Capital; been stuck up here in the north for too long. I need a bit more action. That little dust up with the old man wasn't much. Good on him for trying, but it was over too quick.'

The first voice responded. 'Yeah, you think with your fists too much, Knuckles. I just want a nice quiet trip down south. Don't forget we get paid for getting the goods delivered and will get kicked out if things go wrong.'

The second voice again. 'Yeah, yeah. Let's just get the last couple of things in and it all laced up. Then we can go to the

Icebreaker for a few ales knowing everything is ready for the morning.'

The first voice. 'Agreed. I hope that nice little barmaid is there tonight. She gave me a bit of a wink the other night. I think I might be onto something.'

'You're a dreamer, Sam. But let's get finished here and you can show me.'

The two thugs went back into the building, brought out a few more things that were stowed in the cart, and then one pair of legs hopped up into the cart and from the regular noises seemed to be carefully lacing up a protective canvas arrangement over the goods.

Hearing all this, Gerant started to ponder things and a germ of an idea emerged. As soon as these thugs had finished, maybe he could wait a little while and then crawl out carefully and climb into the cart and grab the tusktooth. Yes, this could work out really well. He would have to be careful and creep up as silently as he could, as there were sure to be other thugs in the compound. But it would be unlikely they would check the load in the cart again and, even if they did, he would be long gone. He was starting to plan how long he was going to wait, when there was scrabbling noises and then one of the thugs emerged with two dogs. Gerant froze in shock and peered out, his heart racing. One of the dogs was a brindled bulldog-type and the other was a similar size and build to Fang, but black and tan. The man chained the two guard dogs to each end of the cart and laid down two bowls of meat. The dogs quickly wolfed down the contents of the bowls, growling and snarling at each other. It was clear that the chains were what was preventing them from reaching and attacking each other. Gerant quietly shuddered and got the strong feeling that if something else distracted their attention, the two dogs would forget their feelings towards each other and happily attack the new threat together. *Well,* he thought, *there goes that plan.* There was no way he could get at the tusktooth while it was in the compound. He would need to think more about this. Based on what he had heard, the cart was going to head off to Rivernook in the morning and then on to The Capital. He would have to work out whether there was a way to get at the tusktooth somewhere on the road, or maybe it would be less protected at one of the other Brotherhood buildings down south. He would still leave tomorrow morning at first light, get ahead and plan something. The first step was to quietly crawl away without the guard dogs noticing. They seemed to have finished their dinner and were quietly watching each other. All the same, it wouldn't take much to attract their attention. Gerant very, very carefully started to back up towards the wooden grate on the other side of the under-floor cavity.

Arriving back at the cottage just on dusk, Gerant checked in the sleeping room and Gramps didn't appear to have shifted; he was quietly snuffling and snoring. In the couple of hours Gerant had been away, the bruising across his nose and cheeks had coloured more strongly and was a livid combination of shades of purple, greenish-grey and yellows. One eyelid had coloured up now and looked quite swollen. He quietly went out into the main area and packed, laying out his sleeping roll. Then he portioned out some of the pork pie onto a couple of plates. He sat down on the chair next to the sleeping man before he gently shook him.

'Gramps, Gramps. I'm back. I thought you might like to have something to eat.'

The old man opened one eye blearily − the other was swollen shut. 'I heard you come in. Had quite a bit of sleep. The pain's not too bad. Some of the Icebreaker helped.'

Gerant sighed with relief. 'Can you sit up a little? It might be easier to eat that way.'

He gently eased Gramps up, who let out a little hiss of pain. After that the old man was able to get more comfortable and slowly started eating the pie.

'A tankard of ale would be good, laddie.'

Gerant went out to the kitchen and brought some back in two tankards.

They talked quietly as they ate the pork pie, which Gerant found really nice. It was difficult not to just wolf it down − he hadn't realised how hungry he was − and he forced himself to have regular bites between talking to Gramps.

'You were right. That Brotherhood place was impossible to get into. The best I could do was to overhear that they have put the tusktooth in a cart and will be taking it to The Capital. So I plan to leave early and get ahead and try to work something out.'

'They didn't hear or see you?' asked the old man.

'No, I was pretty careful.' He finished his portion of pie and was pleased to see that the old man had eaten quite a bit before he pushed the remainder away. Gerant tidied up a little and saw a chamber pot in the corner, which he brought over. Gramps had managed to lay down again and appeared OK. Gerant walked to the door with the plates and tankards and turned as he thought of something else.

'I'm going to turn in myself once I have washed up. I won't disturb you in the morning   I hope you don't mind if I just head off quietly. Also, I popped in and told Mrs McCreedy. She said she would come around in the morning.'

The old man nodded and carefully pulled the blanket up. Gerant was starting to shut the door when there was a quiet call.

'Gerant? Thank you. You are a good lad.' A pause. 'I would be proud of you if you were mine.'

He gently shut the door and walked to the sink to wash the dishes. He felt his cheeks redden a little.

Chapter 32
The Rescue and Return

Gerant had spent plenty of time pondering things while he had walked down the road towards Rivernook. It had taken him some hours after leaving North Haven to work out how he could make the cart stop long enough for him to get into it undetected. He questioned himself as he strode steadily forward. What would make the cart stop? Would the thugs be suspicious when it happened? How could he creep up? Wouldn't they just see him and attack him? All these questions he gradually solved so that it looked like it might work. Then it was a matter of getting far enough ahead of the cart to find a suitable spot, but not so far ahead other travellers might clear his little 'accident'. He was starting to despair of finding a place to set things up when he came to the bridge across the stream. The late afternoon sun shone through the trees on either side of the road to Rivernook, throwing dappled shadows here and there. The road had emerged out of the grove at the top of the fold of land and gently curved down to a gurgling stream at the base of the valley. It crossed the stream over a short wooden span that arched between the clumps of elms, ashes and maples lining the water. It then worked its way through and around more clusters of trees to the township a mile or so away.

A quick scout around showed one of the elms on the edge of the water had a large limb already arching over the road. It took several minutes of chopping with the hatchet before he felt the limb starting to crack and he jumped out of the way. With a huge crash, the limb smashed into the dirt and gravel of the road about eight feet from the bridge. A cloud of dust flew up and several birds squawked in alarm before silence returned. Gerant carefully trimmed the stump of the limb so it looked like it had just split and fell across the road in the past day or so. He carefully brushed away any footprints on the road or on its edges with a switch of leaves and then went back over the bridge to find a suitable hiding spot far enough back. He settled down with a waterskin to wait and daydream, occasionally checking the road from the north.

Sometime later, he started to hear steady clops as two riders on horses appeared out of the grove and moved sedately down towards the bridge. They looked a little dusty and travel-worn. One could easily assume they were looking forward to arriving at the town in a short while. Around thirty yards farther back, a cart pulled by another two horses also emerged. The cart was also a little dusty and the canvas spanning over the arched frame protecting the tray had taken on the browny-grey tinges from the road dust. Another two men sat on the seat at the front of the cart behind the nags. One of them appeared to be fast asleep.

The horseback riders crossed the bridge and then stopped just before the large limb that had fallen across the road, blocking a way forward. One of them dismounted, handed the reins to the other and then walked forward a little and stopped, with his hands on his hips. The cart came up to the bridge and then stopped, with the driver nudging his companion awake. The first man walked forward, kicked the large limb viciously and started cursing loudly. He turned around.

'Don't just sit there, you lazy bastards! It's not going to magically move itself off the road. You! Sam. Knuckles. Put the brake on and come and help. And find the axe in the toolbox. It's too heavy even for the four of us.'

The other horseman dismounted after tying the horses' reins to one of the bridge posts and started to help the leader break off and throw to the side some of the smaller branches. One of the men on the cart jumped down and ran to the back, unlaced the canvas looped over the tray, and wriggled underneath. There was the sound of gear being shifted and then the man reappeared with an axe and walked forward to where the three others were waiting. The gentle gurgling of the stream was soon overladen with sounds of wood being chopped, as well as the cursing and heaving of branches and foliage as they were dragged away to the sides of the road.

A hooded and cloaked figure silently emerged from the trees on the near side of the bridge and approached the back of the cart once the four men were totally distracted with removing the fallen limb of the elm. In its grasp, the figure had a slender shape about five feet long wrapped in brown sacking. It pushed the shape under the unlaced canvas, took another quick look and then disappeared into the tray. If someone had been standing at the back of the cart, they may have heard a few scrapes and gentle thumps of items being moved. But the sounds of chopping and heaving by the men just ahead drowned out any of these noises. A few moments more and then the figure reappeared and quietly hopped down, reaching in to take a similar slender shape, wrapped in sacking of a similar shade, perhaps more of a rusty hue. It moved stealthily away from the wagon and disappeared back into the foliage lining the stream. After a little time, the noise of chopping ceased and there was the sound of men's voices.

Then the leader's voice. 'All right, you useless bags of shit. On the count of three. One! Two! Three! Heave . . .'

Gerant had gotten out of sight and quickly unwrapped the sacking to make sure it was the tusktooth. It was! He gently stroked the spiral horn and rewrapped it and left it with his bedroll and pack hidden well into the trees. Then he snuck back to the road and carefully climbed a tree a bit back from the bridge where he could see what was going on. It had taken the four men another fifteen minutes or so to clear the road enough for the cart to get through. After throwing the remains of the limb and smaller branches to either side, they had grouped at the cart and got out what must have been ale or liquor which they passed around. He was close enough to hear the loud voice of the leader once the skin of drink had been finished.

'Right, let's go, my merry men. We should still be able to make the Chapter House by dark. By the gods, they better have a decent meal ready.'

'And some good hard stuff to drink, as well!'

With that, two of the men climbed back onto the cart and it moved onto the bridge and past the fallen elm branches scattered on either side. The two riders took up their position about twenty yards ahead of the cart and the little convoy moved off through the glades towards the town not far ahead.

Gerant had spent the hour or so hiding in the brush near the roadside thinking about another problem he was concerned about. That was how to disguise the tusk so that no one would know he was carrying it. Having got it back, the last thing he needed was one of the Brotherhood to see him walking along with the distinctive slender shape and accost him. That would not go well, he already knew.

Now that the cart and thugs had moved off to Rivernook, he was ready to take the next step. He unwrapped the tusk and took out one of his knives with the talium edge. He sat on the ground with the tusk across his knees and carefully started to score the tusk about halfway along. The keenness of the blade certainly helped, and he was able to carve a ring around the ivory to an even depth. *Well, that seemed to work,* he thought. *Now for the difficult bit,* he mused. *I hope this works!*

He found a couple of biggish stones that he placed on the ground so that an end of the tusk was sitting of the two rocks. Gerant unlooped his hatchet and reversed it so that the poll of the hatchet head was face down. After a couple of practice little taps above the tusk, he brought the poll down smartly where he had scored the ring around the tusktooth. With a sharp snap, the tusk broke into two halves and fell onto the ground next to the stones. He started breathing again in relief. He picked up the two halves, examining them closely. It looked like the tusk had snapped exactly where he had done the scoring.

He took his bedroll and loosened the straps and laid it out. Taking the two pieces of tusk, he put them in the middle and then rolled up the bedding again and tightened the straps. He strapped the bedroll to the top of his pack and looked carefully. It looked just like it did before and no one would realise what was hidden in the middle of the bedding.

Gerant smiled contentedly and shouldered his pack and bedroll. He made a last check of his hiding spot and the only thing out of place were the two large stones. He eased his way through the bushes and undergrowth back to the road and headed off towards Rivernook. He hoped to walk for an hour past the town and find a quiet camping spot, before it got really dark. He couldn't help whistling softly as he reached the bridge and kept moving down the road towards the town.

He entered through the back laneway as he couldn't be bothered walking through the front door and hallway with all his gear. He braced himself as he turned the corner and could see into the small yard. There was no turning of a large head, no joyful yelp of recognition and no quick thunder of huge paws to rush over. *Hmm, that's a bit strange*, Gerant thought. He eased his pack off at the back door and quietly put down a small canvas bag. He walked into the kitchen area and a large set of eyes swivelled round and a gruff little bark of welcome erupted from deep in Fang's throat. Gerant had just had enough time to shut the back door before he was almost bowled over by the huge mastiff body that rocketed over from the pile of old blankets he had been lying on near the stove. After ruffling his head for a bit and giving Fang a quick hug, he brought in his gear and threw it in his room.

'Dierdre, Dierdre,' he called.

Mrs Lamming emerged from the sitting room and came forward with her knitting in her hands.

'Oh, Gerant. How lovely to see you. I hope you had a good trip.' Her look of quiet welcome turned quickly to surprise and a little confusion as her young lodger strode forward and engulfed her in a huge hug.

'There, there. We have both missed you.'

Gerant didn't know where to start. 'I have so much to tell you. So many things. I got to North Haven and met an old fisher guy and he took me out and there were seals and dolphins and other stuff.'

Gerant realised he had blurted things out like a child coming back from visiting friends and stopped, a little embarrassed. 'But first I want to take Fang down to the plot to drop something off, and then go to the Blue Moon and have a long, hot soak and then there's someone I need to see.'

Mrs Lamming was trying to take all this information in and just nodded understandingly. 'I'm sure you are very excited about your trip. How about you get the things you need to do and then we can have a long, relaxed chat. Now that you are back, how about I make you a chicken and leek pie for dinner? I got some leeks from Mr Abernathy yesterday. They looked particularly fine.'

'That sounds great.'

The older lady started to wrinkle her nose a little and then spoke up gently. 'Also, if you have any washing you need done, I would be happy to help out. Once I get the pie prepared, I will have some time to spare.'

'Umm, sorry. I'll get changed into some old clothes. I really do need to go to the bathhouse and clean up. It's been a busy few days with a lot happening.'

The day sped on rather quickly as Gerant took a walk to the plot with Fang, who almost uncharacteristically gambolled along beside him. He took that to mean he had been missed, although Mrs Lamming had clearly welcomed the company of Fang in the kitchen area of a night. He also had his bedroll strapped across his back, with its secret treasure hidden away. It had taken only a few moments to place the sacking bundle behind the garden tools leaning in the corner of the little shed at the plot. After dropping Fang back, he went to the Blue Moon bathhouse for a well-deserved and needed soak for an hour or so. He had discovered the bathhouse on one of his trips with Mrs Lamming to the market and it was only a few streets away. For a silver piece, he was able to lie quietly in a corner of the communal tub and ruminate. At that time of day there were very few customers, although it would pick up in the afternoon and early evening. He came out feeling much refreshed and his muscles relaxed. More importantly, he was clean and not obviously reeking of a week or more of journeying. He applied a touch of scent under his arms. On a whim, he had bought a small vial at a small street-side stall on the way back – the lady had told him it was cloves with a hint of musk; it smelled OK to him. And then he was ready for the next thing on his list for the day.

Gerant walked through the side gate, through the back courtyard and into the kitchen. There were some used bowls and spoons and such on the big table and a nice smell coming out from the oven but no sign of Faith. By the look of it she couldn't be far off. He walked into the main part of the house and reached the office. He stood silently at the door watching Molly writing on a piece of paper and realised how much he had been looking forward to seeing her. She had her hair tied up in a lavender-coloured scarf and was wearing some sort of waistcoat and pantaloons outfit. He knocked gently on the doorframe, and she looked up. A broad smile crossed her face and she quickly stood up and ran over into his embrace and reach up to kiss him on the lips.

'You're back. I am so glad.' She paused and then smiled quietly as she buried her head into his shoulder. 'I've missed you.'

'Me too. I've got so much to tell you.'

Her voice was slightly muffled coming from his shoulder. Molly sighed a little. 'They got back yesterday and so I have a lot to get ready. They are out visiting friends today but back for good tomorrow. How about we got up to my room and you can tell me all about it? One of the others might disturb us if we talk here.'

Gerant realised he had never been to her actual room. She shut the door of the office, and they walked up the hallway together holding hands. On the second floor, she led him towards the back of the house until they reached a plain door at the end of a dim hallway, which she opened. Inside, Gerant could see the room was fairly small, with a window overlooking the back courtyard. There was a bed in the corner and a small chest of drawers. A curtained-off area hid one of the corners of the room. Molly sat down on the bed and patted it next to her.

'Sit next to me and tell me all about it. I want to hear everything!'

So Gerant started from the beginning, and he talked quietly for nearly half an hour about his travels to North Haven, meeting Gramps and all the adventures of finding the tusk tooth, losing the tusk and then how he had managed to get it back. Molly was a good listener and only interrupted where Gerant had not mentioned something she needed to know or where she was curious about something. Or how he was feeling when something happened. One thing did surprise him early in talking about his story. He had been describing how he had reached Rivernook and started asking the innkeeper about Sveg's mother and father.

'Wait a minute, wait a minute. You found the main road again after leaving Nutley and then you got to Rivernook. What about going through Samphire township? You didn't tell me about that.'

Gerant stopped and thought back. 'Oh, is that the little town about a day's walk away? I never realised what it was called. I just went straight through. It looked OK, but I was keen to get to Rivernook before night. Should I have stopped to look around?'

He could tell Molly was not impressed. 'It just so happens, Mr Know-it-all,' she pronounced, poking him in the chest, 'that I am from Samphire and grew up there. My mother still lives there. Of course, it is a lovely town and you should have stopped.'

Gerant realised what a serious blunder he had made without knowing it. 'Well, now I know that, I will be sure to stop next time.'

He paused, a little embarrassed, and when Molly nodded, he went back to his tale. Then he described the trip back and finished up.

'So, I managed to get back without any more problems and I hid the tusktooth in a careful place, went to the bathhouse, and then came here.'

Molly clapped her hands with delight at the story, also pleased that Gerant had got back safely.

'Here, let me give you a special thank you kiss for telling me all about your travels.'

She turned to Gerant and planted her lip on his. She pressed briefly and then her lips parted, her tongue reaching into Gerant's mouth and beginning to sensuously caress. After a brief shock, Gerant returned the favour. After what seemed a lifetime, they both suddenly broke off and gasped for air, subsiding in delighted laughter as they hugged each other. Gerant reached up to her face and they had another long, passionate kiss. Molly stopped and gently stroked Gerant's face.

'Well, my darling, we should stop. Not that I don't want to keep going, but one thing could lead to another and then where would we be? I also have to finish off those orders and you need to go home to that special dinner Mrs Lamming has made for you.'

He reluctantly agreed and then realised what she had said. 'What did you call me?'

She smiled contentedly as she pulled him up from the bed so she could hug him. 'I called you darling, my darling.'

Chapter 33
The Special Paste

Gerant lay on his bed and read by lanternlight from the old parchment. He focused on the section that talked about the tusktooth and refreshed his memory by slowly reading aloud each sentence.

'The recipe uses rare ingredients that are very hard to find and are known to impart their properties of hardness. You will need a piece of the tusk from the spotted tusktooth, ground into small pieces. This creature lives in the waters of the far north and is hard to find. It will not give up its life easily. You will also need ash made from burning the wood of the hedge apple. This tree of moderate size is found in open forest in the eastern lands, often on the edge of farmland and has a large green fruit that should not be eaten. Any forester or woodcutter should be able to find a tree. While they are not common, they are also not rare. The final ingredient is clay taken from a stream bank that has a golden tinge like the newly risen sun. Mix up six parts of clay, two parts of ash from the hedge apple and two parts of the ground tusk from the spotted tusktooth. The mix is applied to the blade carefully so the paste is thicker on the spine and very sparse on the cutting edge. Be careful to then heat the blade in the forge very slowly and carefully, if possible in a darkened workshop. When the temperature of the blade changes from dull red towards bright red, the blade should be quenched in a bath of water. You will find that the hardness from the hedge apple and tusk tooth have been imparted to the blade, with the brightness from the sun-hued clay.'

Hmmm, he thought, *I will have to grind a small amount of the tusk, which should be fairly straightforward. Some of the gear at the workshop should deal with that.* The other two parts, hopefully, would be fairly easy. In the morning, he would go and see Morrison Levy and see if he could get some hedge apple wood to make into charcoal. Then to Evelyn Hanson, the potter where they got their clay from. The description of the clay sounded a little strange, but it must mean a clay that had a lot of yellow colouring in it, rather than something from a particular location. He would have to see what Evelyn said once he had outlined the issue. All of it sounded possible and then he could start to make this strange mixture and experiment on a few spare dagger blades he had lying around.

He arrived at the workshop in the morning and waved hello to Ray, who was already working away at something.

'Had a good break, Ray?' asked Gerant. 'Did anything interesting?'

Ray grunted while he kept working on a lost wax casting. 'Only went away for a few days. Then just did some stuff around here.'

Gerant wondered why he had bothered even asking and checked his bench before walking off to the wood merchant's yard. There he hit his first hitch.

'Nah, never heard of this hedge apple. Can get you any of the usual stuff, but this must be some rare kind of special tree that doesn't grow around here. Or else this hedge whatever is not what it's normally known as.'

The timber merchant had been politely welcoming when he recognised Gerant, but quickly lost interest when he realised there would be no business coming out of it.

Gerant was not hopeful but thought it was worth asking. 'Know anyone else who sells wood who might know? I don't even understand what I'm asking about, apart from it growing somewhere in the east.'

Morrison Levy paused while he thought. 'Caithcart would have no idea. Spurling might, but he largely deals with only big lots and this sounds very specialist-like. The only thing I can think of is to ask someone who knows about trees. Maybe ask the royal forester. He might be able to help.'

The timber merchant nodded as if the conversation was closed and started to turn away and get on with other tasks. Gerant understood that he would get no further assistance. That was fine. He knew a little more than when he had arrived.

He had slightly more luck when he arrived at the studio of Evelyn Hanson, the potter.

'Ah, Gerant, here you are.'

The lady was in her late forties, with brown hair tied up and a vaguely greenish gown with smears of clay randomly streaked across it here and there. She frowned.

'Was that last batch I sent to Ray OK? Or have you used it up already?'

Gerant smiled in relief. 'No, Evelyn, nothing like that. Actually, I'm here to ask about a new project I want to start working on.'

He proceeded to explain what he was after. 'I have come across an old piece of parchment that uses a recipe to be used on sword blades.' He thought of what he had read the night before. 'It speaks of using clay that has a golden colour like the sun. Have you any clay like that?'

The lady's expression continued to frown, but moved from a worried expression to one of deep thought, as she mused softly through possibilities. 'Well, if you mean clay that is an actual golden colour, I haven't heard of anything like that. If you mean a yellowish shade, then what have we got? That stuff from Smedhurst is vaguely yellow, but probably not sufficient. Medbury? Possible, but not really... What about Wadling Brook? Wadling Brook. Yes... That might work.'

The potter spoke up directly to her visitor. 'There is a clay with a yellowish hue that lines the banks of Wadling Brook, about an hour or so from here. I don't use it for pottery, as the quality of pots it throws is not as good as some others. If the colour is the most important thing, then it could be what you need. I would have to talk to my contacts and see if we could get some for you. It might take a week or so to get and I don't know what they would charge.'

'I don't need much. Maybe a few pounds worth at this stage, as I am just experimenting. Just put it on the maestro's account, if that's OK with you.'

The potter smiled understandingly. 'Glad I could help out. I'll be in touch to let you know if there are any issues. Otherwise, I just might bring it around, since we are talking only a little bit at this point.'

'You are the best, Evelyn,' thanked Gerant.

'Oh, I don't know about that, Gerant.' The potter smiled back. 'You will do the same for me if I need to ask for you to make me a tool or something in your line of work.'

He walked out of the studio well satisfied.

Later that day, Gerant had gone to the Purple Heart specifically to see if he could catch up with Dirk. He also had a few things to think about getting ready for his next batch of blades to make, as Molly had told him to find the maestro tomorrow morning to talk about a sword that Earl Sherrington had commissioned. He was only part way through a tankard of Black Heart when he looked up and saw the tall, thin man with the cropped hair and goatee arrive. He weaved through the customers and approached the bar.

'Hey, Dirk! What will you have? My treat.'

Dirk turned round at the greeting and smiled, gently rubbing his beard. 'Well, that's mighty nice of you, Gerant. Just a regular ale. I've worked up a thirst for this, that's for sure.'

Dirk grabbed the tankard when it came, and they wandered back to their usual booth. They clinked tankards.

'Ahhh, I needed that.' Dirk paused. 'Haven't seen you for a little bit. You been away?'

Gerant took a pull of his dark ale and smiled. 'Oh, went up north and did a bit of fishing. Just got back yesterday.'

Dirk was not impressed. 'Hmmph. It's alright for some. I've been working my tail off here. People just get stupid with the midsummer holiday, and we have been out and about in the town keeping the peace.' He took another couple of gulps and wiped his mouth. 'Up north, you said? Where did you go?'

'Oh, up to North Haven and then out in a boat a bit farther again.'

Dirk quietly digested the news while he finished off his tankard. 'Never been farther up that way than Rivernook. But been south to Pearl City. That's a sight! You been there?'

Gerant smiled into his tankard. He could see where this was going. 'No, Dirk, haven't been there. Only as far as Ashford.'

'Hah.'

The guard had a look of smugness now. Gerant could clearly see in Dirk's eyes Pearl City trumped North Haven and he was the better travelled of the two.

'Well, matey, feel like another one? You like dark, don't you?'

Gerant nodded and realised he hadn't yet got to the thing he wanted to ask his companion about. Dirk returned nursing two new tankards. Taking a quick sip, he started a new conversation.

'You know all the senior people that serve the royal family up the top, don't you?'

Dirk took a large swallow of his ale and his eyes narrowed. 'I wouldn't say most of them. Some we cross paths on a daily or weekly basis, but there are a whole bunch of them that stay in the palace looking after the king and queen and we don't have much to do with them.' He paused. 'Why do you ask?'

'Oh, I just need to see if I can meet someone who works up there.' Gerant decided to sort of tell the truth but embellish things a little. 'You see, on my trip I found out about a type of wood that might be really useful for some of the swordmaking I want to do. I was talking to one of our suppliers and he said that the royal forester might know more about these special trees and where they are found.'

Dirk looked slightly impressed but then a thought occurred to him. 'But swords are made of steel. What's this about a tree? Ah. You use it for a fancy hilt or something like that?'

He was clearly proud of himself for working it all out.

'Yeah, something like that, Dirk, something like that. But have you heard of this royal forester position?'

Dirk pondered a little while he sipped his ale. 'Can't say I have. Haven't come across such a person. But I'll ask my sergeant. He might know.'

'Great. Thanks, Dirk. I really appreciate it.'

Gerant decided that was about the best he could do for now and hopefully Dirk would at least be able to find out a bit more and whether this person actually existed. The wood carter had rattled off the name when he was thinking about other contacts and so it sounded real and not something he had just made up to get rid of Gerant. That would be the first step. And then if there was a royal forester, he would have to think about the best way to get to see him. Hopefully a letter of introduction from the maestro would be sufficient to get a meeting. Silently musing, he realised Dirk had said something to him.

'Sorry. What was that?'

'I was saying that I have the day off tomorrow, but I can find out after that. Need to know fast?'

'No, no, nothing urgent. Just when it suits.'

Gerant finished his tankard and stood up.

'See you next time, Dirk. I have a big day tomorrow to begin some new blades. Better head off.'

The young guard leant back with a contented sigh.

'I might have another couple of ales, yet. Might just sit back, not having to work tomorrow. Be seeing you.'

Gerant negotiated his way to the door and walked out into the early twilight. *This may work out*, he thought. That was another job to think about tomorrow. He needed to work out how to grind up a piece of the tusktooth according to what the old parchment needed. With that in mind, he headed off home.

The maestro gestured to the drawing of the sword that he had designed for the Earl Sherrington. 'I spent a good hour with the earl to learn of his preferences. He would like it to be elegant and understated, so I have designed the hilt, pommel and quillons very simply and with smoothly flowing lines. No jewels or gems, but he has given me the family crest in a small medallion to be used in the pommel. I have it here and you can collect it from me when you are ready for it. Any questions?'

The maestro watched his journeyman closely as Gerant pored over the drawing and then quickly looked at the medallion.

'The blade. The measurement here of the length from the base of the quillons to the tip. You measured this with the earl in mind?' Gerant looked expectantly at the maestro.

'Of course, of course. I measured this personally based on his reach and positioning when on guard.'

The expression on the maestro's face said that he wasn't to be taken for a fool. 'We also measured the earl's current favourite sword, and he wants this one to be one inch longer. He graciously mentioned that he is not quite so spry as what he was and a little extra reach might be useful.'

Gerant nodded and looked once more at the drawing. 'I can take this?'

A nod.

'I think I have everything I need to get started. Now it's after the break, I will have to do a kiln run to make some more talium steel. It will take me a few weeks to forge the blade with talium and for the two of us to make the hilt and put it together.'

He looked up to see what the response was and this time the maestro indicated he was happy with his proposal.

'Maestro, I want to make this a stand-out piece to come out from the Shagreen Studio. If I have time, I would like to try something that I believe will make the weapon even more effective. It has to do with the edge I can put on the sword blade and making it even sharper and keeping that edge honed. Would that be OK?'

'Of course. The earl is almost my most important client and only the best is worthy of him. If you craft something that he is totally happy with, then the orders will flow. In fact, I already have several daggers or swords that have been ordered with me. Focus on the earl's one first, mind.'

Gerant pondered over this piece of news and realised his next few months would be fully taken up. He thought about how he could phrase this without drawing a bad reaction or some sort of retort. *Ah, maybe I can broach it this way,* he thought.

'Absolutely, Maestro, we will work first on the earl's sword and give it the highest priority. Many of our kiln runs can be performed so that multiple pieces can be fashioned. Perhaps you could show me what the orders are, and I can plan ahead.'

The maestro passed over the rolled-up drawing and stood up. 'It will have to wait until tomorrow. I am due to meet with the count of Ravenswood in an hour to discuss his needs, which might mean a matched dagger and sword combination.'

'That will be good, Maestro. What time?'

The response echoed back to Gerant as the maestro was already striding down the corridor. 'Talk with Molly. She knows my movements.'

Several days later, Gerant was sitting in the Purple Heart working on the lettering for his blade stamp when Dirk plopped down across from him with a look of satisfaction on his face.

'Well, my friend, you are in luck. I talked with my sergeant, and he had heard about this royal forester fellow. Turns out he is the man responsible for watching over The Realm's forests and whatever hunting happens in them. The sergeant has met him a few times and his name is Griffin Someone-or-other. Don't remember his other name. We were about to go out on patrol, and I didn't really hear it clearly.'

Gerant sighed internally with relief. 'Hey, that's great, Dirk. I guess I owe you an ale.'

His companion smiled smugly. 'I was hoping you'd say that, matey.'

Next morning, he found Molly working away in her office area. After quickly checking no one was going to walk in, she gave him a quick peck on the cheek.

'He's got visitors for a bit, but after lunch he should be free.'

Gerant nodded and thought that would work in well.

'Oh, another thing. You know how I told you about the tusktooth? As part of that paste, I need to use charcoal from a particular type of tree. Apparently, someone who would know about these trees is the royal forester. I guess I would like a letter of introduction from the maestro if that's possible.'

He held his breath and watched Molly's face to see her reaction. She paused and thought. Then she smiled impishly.

'I guess that would be alright. Must be one of the senior positions with responsibility for all of The Realm. I could write a letter from the maestro requesting an audience and get him to sign it. He sometimes doesn't look at the letters that I get him to sign. He's usually in too much of a hurry to get to his next important meeting with Viscount So-and-So or Lady La-di-Da.'

They both laughed at the image of the maestro meeting with his next well-known client and agreed that once the letter had been signed, the journeyman smith would be able to head up the hill to The Park and seek an audience.

Gerant walked up the tailored and manicured road towards the palace. This was a part of The Park he hadn't been to, and he walked past the road leading to Earl Sherrington's chateau and then farther up the slope, looking at the new sights. At the top of the slope amidst scattered tall trees, the sprawling three- and four-storey palace emerged. The building was crafted out of white stone and many windows looked out at a courtyard with a large fountain spouting in the middle. Gerant could see there were two wings on either side of the main entrance area. He had already been told to head to the left wing and go to one of the other doors and begin asking for the royal forester there. After presenting his letter at the main door of the wing, he was successively passed from one uniformed usher to the next. Eventually he was left in a small room on the second floor and told that the royal forester would arrive shortly. After the usher had left, Gerant spent a minute or two looking around the sparsely furnished room, which had a table and two plain wooden chairs. After pacing, he realised he would just have to be patient, sat down on one of the chairs and started thinking about his next kiln run and what he would need.

The door suddenly opened and a thin, tall, clean-shaven man walked in. He was dressed in greeny-brown clothes with soft boots up to the knee. He nodded as he sat down and looked over his visitor with keen brown eyes.

'Ah, Mr Royal Forester. My name is Gerant and I have a letter of introduction.'

Gerant passed over the letter and the man quickly scanned its contents. The man had a quiet but moderately deep voice when he spoke.

'So you are wanting to speak with me. Well, I am here. But the letter doesn't say what your request is. Oh, by the way, you can call me Griff, if that helps.'

Gerant took that in and launched into his story.

'Thank you . . .Griff. I work with Maestro Shagreen and my craft is smithing and making swords and daggers. I have come across a very old parchment that talks about using charcoal from the hedge apple. I understand it is a tree that grows somewhere in the eastern parts. I was hoping you could tell whether you have heard of these trees and where they grew, so I could get some of the wood.'

The forester looked at Gerant keenly, looked at the letter again and came to a decision.

'Yes, I know of these trees. They grow in the forests a little north of here. There you go. I have a lot to get done today.'

And the man stood up and walked to the door.

Gerant's thoughts plummeted to a very low place as he realised that was the end of the meeting and he was really not really any closer than what he had been. *Damn,* he thought, *that was a waste of time.* What should he do now? It was only then that he realised the royal forester had stopped with his hand on the doorknob and was gently grinning. After he saw the look of shock on his young visitor's face, he shut the door again, walked back and sat down.

'My apologies . . .' He looked at the letter. '. . . Gerant. Sometimes all these many, many meetings get the best of me. People are usually coming to ask me to get themselves on a royal hunting party or to hunt a stag or a boar. I thought I would play a little trick on you. I hope you will forgive me.'

Gerant did not know what to say, so he just nodded.

'Yes, I do know of hedge apples, and I can think of several that I could find quickly off the road between here and Samphire.' He sighed gently and watched the young smith's face. 'Look, this could be just the excuse I am looking for to get out of the city and do what I am better at. Let's go for a bit of a jaunt. I can take you there and you can see these trees and we can also check how the woodlands are doing and how the game are coming along.'

The change in the forester's manner was quite noticeable and he had changed from the overworked, abrupt palace official to a friendly, relaxed man that you would be happy to have an ale with at your local tavern. They agreed to meet in a day or so and travel north.

'We'll need to ride, so how about I meet you with the horses at the gatehouse the day after the morrow? Bring some water and something to eat. We have about two hours' steady ride to get there and the same back.'

The forester noticed the look of alarm on the young man's face and correctly interpreted it. 'Don't worry. I'll make sure your horse is quiet. I'll see you at the gatehouse the day after tomorrow, two hours after dawn. I'll let a valet know we're done here, and they will escort you out.'

The forester smiled quietly in farewell and slipped out. Gerant headed off with the valet, realising how well this turn of events had played out. He would have to let Molly know he would be away for the day, but was sure the maestro wouldn't even care, as long as the earl's sword could still be crafted in time.

Chapter 34
Hedge Apples

Gerant waited within sight of the gatehouse and felt a little foolish just standing there with nothing to do. He had been waiting for at least half an hour, wearing comfortable clothes and soft half boots. He had his two throwing knives and the hatchet hanging from his belt, along with a couple of lengths of strong cord. In a small pouch was a small apple, some beef jerky and he had a full waterskin. He knew enough of how things worked now in The Capital to not wait too close, as then the guards would notice him and want to know why he was hanging around.

Just at that moment, the royal forester appeared through the arched entrance riding a large black horse and leading a smaller brown animal that was saddled but riderless. He nodded at the guards as he rode through, and the senior guard present gestured back in recognition. Gerant stepped out into the street and half-heartedly waved. The rider changed direction slightly and came over, before dismounting. Griff was wearing a similar outfit to what he had been wearing the other day, but this time had a bow slung over his shoulder and a quiver of arrows was strapped to the saddle of his horse.

'Ah, Gerant, well met. I am pleased you're on time. We have a bit of a ride and I want to get there well before noon.'

Griff gestured towards the saddled horse he had brought over. 'This pony should suit you fine. He's very quiet and shouldn't give you any problems. All set? Let's go then.'

Gerant quickly tied his waterskin, pouch and loops of cord to the saddle, breathed deeply a couple of times to settle himself and then swung up. After checking everything quickly and putting his feet into the stirrups and grasping the reins, he nodded to the forester. The two horsemen headed off towards The Cross at a sedate walking pace, before gradually picking up speed to a slow trot.

Reaching Nutley in good time having maintained the slow trot in between short walking spells, they had stopped briefly for a drink and a bite to eat and then were chatting while the horses ambled along the main road.

'Tell me again about why you need the charcoal from the hedge apples.'

Griff had been describing the country that they would soon reach and the type of open forest they would find. Gerant had found the way the forester talked about the trees and shrubs and the game that lived in them so interesting. He was very knowledgeable in what he talked about, and the young man picked up a lot of new things. Gerant had a strong impression that Griff could be absolutely trusted and was genuinely interested in hearing more about why the wood from the hedge apple was needed.

'When I was doing my apprenticeship, I found a book about smithing in the local bookseller's shop and almost hidden away in the back cover was an old parchment with these strange descriptions of how to craft really strong steel that makes peerless blades for daggers or swords. One of the ways is to use something called talium, which I was able to get from a mine near Osmount. It also talks about making a paste made from three ingredients, one of which is charcoal made from the hedge apple wood. I don't know why that is, but I think it must be because when you put the paste on the steel and heat it to a certain temperature, it changes the steel and gives it a stronger edge.'

Griff was silent for several moments while he thought through what Gerant had told him.

'I am not sure I can tell you much, apart from finding these trees for you. The hedge apples have an unusual fruit that I have never bothered to eat. They may even be poisonous. They also have large greeny leaves that have a waxy finish, and the wood is quite tough and yellowish. Not like cedar or oak or elm. They are not a tall tree – only medium size – and you tend to find them on their own or along the edges of larger groves.'

Gerant also didn't know why this wood and the charcoal made from it was important; he would just have to get some and take it back to try it out.

A little later, Griff turned his horse down a path that left the road just after they had crossed a small brook. It wended its way between groves of trees and open grassland studded with pockets of shrubs and clusters of small trees. Even Gerant noticed that what forest there was grew in small patches and the soil was a little sandy. Maybe that was why the trees were more open. That was another thing he could ask the forester about a later.

The path looped around a small pond in a shallow hollow and then gently rose towards a small ridge with pockets of open forest on the crest. Griff stopped and waited for Gerant to catch up before pointing to a tree about twenty feet high and just off the left of the path.

'This is one. See how it sits on its own? Wrong time of year for the fruit but you can see how the wood is quite spindly and the leaves are that distinctive green colour quite different from those others over there?'

Gerant glanced at the tree and was glad that the forester had pointed it out. Now he looked closely, it was quite different from the other types he could see. But he would have struggled to work out what made it different. At least the hedge apple was growing on its own. That would make it easy enough to cut down some branches and get some wood to take back.

The forester had been looking ahead to the ridge and spoke up. 'We can grab some wood in a little while, but we might tie the horses here for a bit. I want to go for a walk up to that rise. On another occasion I found a stag holing up there in the trees and it would be good to see if they are using it as a resting place. You can stay here while I have a quick stalk, or you can come along. As long as you can be quiet, of course.'

This might be fun, thought Gerant. *Another thing I haven't done. Although I have done my fair share of sneaking when I was in the gang,* he mused.

'I will do my best, Griff. I'll just follow behind you and try not to step on any twigs or kick stones.'

'Good. Let's tie the horses to the hedge apple. We'll only be gone for ten minutes or so, hopefully.'

The forester tied both horses up and took down his quiver of arrows and strapped it to his hip. The bow remained slung on his shoulder, but Gerant got the feeling it could be slipped off in a moment should it be needed.

'Ready?' enquired the forester quietly. 'I'll use hand signs for most things or whisper really close if I need to. The breeze is heading towards us, so we should be able to head straight up.'

Gerant nodded. He hadn't even thought about which way the wind was blowing. From the little he knew, wild animals had a keen sense of smell and hearing. So that made sense that they would keep the breeze in their face so any game wouldn't smell them. Together the pair slipped off up towards the rise, moving slowly and calmly up to and then around the scattered trees and bushes, keeping behind what cover there was. The forester was in his element and effortlessly moved forward silently, stopping every now and again to check up ahead. Gerant tried to mimic the silent glide forward and looked out especially for sticks or other things when he stepped. They worked steadily up the slope, which was covered in a line of trees with some thicker understory of bushes and shrubs intertwining underneath. When they got to within about fifty yards of the ridgeline, the forester stopped for a minute or so and carefully scanned ahead. Then he nodded and silently eased back to where Gerant was standing a few yards behind. The forester brought his mouth very close to Gerant's ear and almost seemed to breath the words.

'Can you see the stag lying down up there? Where the rowan tree is and then about eight feet to the left.'

He pointed carefully ahead. Gerant looked where the forester was pointing and could see a rowan tree with its distinctive leaflets and scattered red fruit. Looking to the left, he could see a few shrubs and bushes between the rowan and then the next tree that looked like an elm or similar. One of the shrubs must have died because the branches were still there but the leaves had fallen off. But there was no deer that he could see. He was just about to give up when there was a flicker of movement and he realised he had just seen a pair of ears swivel to focus on some sound. Then he realised that the dead bush was actually the stag's antlers, and he could then see the outline of the deer's body. He signalled to Griff he could see the stag. Then the two of them quietly turned around and carefully walked back to the horses.

'Well, that's good to know there is at least one reasonable-sized stag in this area. Might be worth making a hunting trip out here at some point. You saw it OK?'

'I couldn't see it until its ears moved. Then I could see its shape and also the antlers. That was interesting.'

The forester was satisfied. 'You didn't do too bad there. A lot of folk have no idea how to move quietly.' A pause. 'OK, let's get this timber cut and then head back. There's a place I want to check for game sign, but that won't take long.'

Gerant unhooked his hatchet and selected a couple of branches to lop off. Then he cut them into short lengths and ended up with a large armful of wood pieces. Griff divided the cut lengths into two piles, and they quickly lashed the bundles behind the saddles of both horses.

'Mind if I have a look at your hatchet? You were able to cut through the lengths with no trouble.'

Gerant handed over the hatchet and then explained how it was edged with talium steel which meant it cut through the sections deeper and with ease compared to a regular hatchet or even a full-sized axe.

Griff tested the edge and was clearly impressed. 'Hmmm. This special steel – talium, did you call it? Ever use it in arrowheads?'

This was something Gerant had never even thought about. 'How do you mean? Could you show me one of yours?'

The forester pulled out one of his arrows from the quiver and gave it to Gerant. Looking at the head, Gerant could see it had a triangular broad head, with long barbs on either side that the head tapered into.

'We call this a swallowtail and this is quite useful for hunting large game. It goes well in flight and packs a nice punch when it hits.'

Gerant carefully checked the profile and thought it would be pretty easy to make a couple to try out.

'If I can borrow this to get the shape right, it would be straightforward to make two or three heads out of talium. Then you could fit them to some shafts and try them out. I would be happy to give it a go. Give me a week and I'll see what I can do.'

'Deal.' The forester was clearly happy about this arrangement and so Gerant fed the arrow into the bundle of wood behind his saddle, out of the way.

On the way back to the main road, Griff detoured slightly to find a small stream where they tied the horses again. The forester carefully walked along the bank until he got to a place where a game trail intersected the water. Griff spent several minutes squatting at the water's edge on either side of the stream looking at prints impressed into the dirt and mud. He gave a running commentary to his companion about what he saw.

'Some sort of small birds like doves have come in for a drink all over the place. Then there are rabbit tracks and here a fox came down and wandered along the edge of the water. Ah, this is more interesting.' He pointed to some slots in the mud on the edge of the water. 'Deer. Quite big, so it may even be that stag we saw before.' He cast about a little more and then squatted on the other side where the game trail left the stream at the top of the bank. He called out. 'Want to look at this?'

Gerant splashed through the ankle-deep water and walked up to the forester.

'See this? Those tracks are a boar. He came down here. Had a sniff around. Those pellets here on the side is where he had a dump. Then he walked a bit up to that tree there and had a scratch and rolled around on the ground. See the hair on the trunk and then the crushed plants that have been flattened?'

Gerant went up to each of the signs that Griff pointed out. 'That's amazing. How do you know all that stuff?'

The forester grinned and stretched a little as he uncoiled from his squatting position. 'Years of practice. And that's what I am meant to do. The king would get rightly annoyed if I took him out hunting and we didn't find anything because I hadn't checked beforehand.'

'Well, I am still impressed.'

He's right, Gerant thought. *He is an expert in his craft, and this is his bread and butter. Like mine and being able to forge weapons or tools or whatever.* This was almost magic, though. To be able to work out what sort of animal it was and what they did, even if it was hours or days ago, was a special skill. It was something that he would be interested in learning more about, if the opportunity arose.

They walked back to the horses and mounted again and then spent an enjoyable hour or so chatting about hunting and the duties of the royal forester. In return, Gerant talked about smithing and how to forge blades, what this new paste was going to achieve and what steps the smith would go through to make the new arrowheads. He was a little surprised when he suddenly looked up and they were well into the city and not so far from the Florian Quarter. A few minutes more and they had drawn up outside the gate leading into the workshop. Griff helped carry in the bundles of hedge apple wood, which Gerant stacked near the kiln, after remembering to put the hunting arrow on his workbench. He gave the forester a quick tour of the kiln and forge area.

'Well, I had better get back. Good luck with your forging and I hope the paste works out.'

'Thanks, and I hope your hunting goes well. I'll drop some arrowheads up to you in the next week or so.'

'That would be appreciated. You don't need to try and find me when you come. Just leave them with a valet and they will make sure they get to me.'

They clasped hands briefly and the forester headed off, astride his black horse and leading the brown pony by a lead. Gerant went back to the workshop to talk with Ray and plan his next steps — particularly to start making Earl Sherrington's blade.

Gerant liked being busy and being able to fill his day. He had done several runs with the kiln and now had a good stock of talium steel of the two grades to work into blades. The long hours spent at the workshop had been a little tough by the time he got to the end of the last run. He found that to combat the tiredness of the all-night sessions that he became very focused. He tried not to snap or be rude. He just didn't have the time or energy for other stuff like long conversations. Molly had initially been concerned but then just gave him the occasional hug when they saw each other once she had understood. Even Ray had done little bits like making sure the water jug near the kiln was full and that there were bits of food around.

That had now passed, and he could work on the other projects, like burning down the hedge apple to charcoal pieces which he kept in a special sack near the forge. And the tusktooth had taken a good half-day to grind down enough to make a small pile with a consistent powdery mass with no lumps or flakes of ivory left. That went into another small sack next to the charcoal. Then Evelyn Hanson had arrived one morning with the special yellow clay wrapped up in wet hessian sacking. He had put that in another box that Ray used for his lost wax work. So now he had the three ingredients he needed to make the special paste and would be ready to try that on some spare blades very soon. Rather than use the precious talium steel, in one of the kiln runs he had just used iron and ended up with some standard-quality steel to use for testing the paste.

Then there was the list of new weapons that he had got from the maestro, a selection of daggers and two swords. It had been stressed that these were only to be commenced if it did not interfere with getting Earl Sherrington's sword completed as soon as could be managed. As Gerant had explained to the maestro, it was efficient to have several jobs going at the same time and he would be careful to only progress these other jobs when he had free time. So now with the kiln runs he had enough talium steel to make them and would just keep the bars on the shelf until there was time to work them further.

For now, he would focus on the earl's blade and the first try with the special paste. In between all that was taking Fang down to the plot whenever he felt like some weeding or getting fresh vegetables, going with Mrs Lamming to the market for food, and seeing Molly when he could and when they knew the maestro and his family were out visiting. Plus the weekly visit to the Purple Heart and a tankard of ale with Dirk, which was a good way to hear about the happenings in The Capital, which his acquaintance delighted in telling him about. Plus making some arrowheads for Griff, the royal forester. So many things to do!

Right, he thought, *enough dilly-dallying*. It was time to get the talium bars ready for the earl's blade. And perhaps try the paste tomorrow if things went well today with fusing the layers for the sword.

Gerant gently burped and he remembered the delicious pasta dish Faith had made for lunch. The forging work on the earl's blade had gone really well, and so he had been prepared to have his first go with the paste. He had read the old parchment again in his room the previous night. He wasn't quite prepared to bring it to the workshop yet. It was a bit of a crazy superstition to not do that. As if Ray would steal it and read it, or the maestro would find it and know enough to use what it said! *Huh*, he thought, *I need to get over this!* All the same, though, he would leave it at the cottage.

He started to mix up in one of Ray's wooden bowls a small amount of six parts of the yellowish clay, two parts of the carefully ground-up hedge apple charcoal and two parts of the ground tusk tooth. The old parchment had not talked particularly about the consistency of the paste, but it did mention being able to spread the paste from thick to thin on the blade surface. So maybe it was safer to mix it so it was not too hard and not too runny. Gerant added some spring water to the dry ingredients and worked up a mix that felt and looked right. He smeared the paste carefully on a steel dagger blade, making it thicker on the spine and next to nothing on the edge. It was hard to know if what he was doing was right. Gods forbid that he tried it on the sword blade he was working up for Earl Sherrington!

The next bit was to use the forge and heating the blade to the correct temperature. He appreciated trying to do it in a darkened workshop made it easier to get the temperature right, but it was not possible with the position of the forge and daylight streaming in fully on one side, so he would have to go even more slowly. He carefully positioned the dagger blade on the already cherry-red coals and started to push air in through the bellows. After gentle heating, the blade started to glow dull red, then cherry red, then it got a brighter red along all its surface.

This is right, thought Gerant. He quickly grabbed the blade with the tongs and pushed it into the barrel of water next to the forge, which emitted a huge cloud of steam. He brushed off the deposit of now-blackened paste and inspected the small blade. It was a little hard to tell, but there seemed to be a line where the paste had been that followed along around one third in from the edge. Looking more closely, it was a part of the steel, not painted on. The smoky line wandered a bit along the blade, showing where he had not been as clean as what he could have been on this first try. Maybe it would be a little easier to examine the effect of the paste and quenching once he had cleaned, polished and sharpened the blade. That should tell him whether it was an improvement and worth continuing to try again, or whether it was just a waste of time. The use of talium in the steel based on what the old parchment had said had been proved right. For that reason, Gerant had high hopes this paste would also lead to significant improvements in the type of blade it produced and specifically how keen the edge was.

He sat in the Purple Heart and occasionally had a pull of dark ale and worked on his drawing. He had on the table the three talium arrowheads he had crafted for the royal forester wrapped in a piece of sacking. They had worked out to be pretty straightforward and he was able to use a combination of straight forging and lost wax casting of the heads. Whichever way he looked, the arrowheads were similar in shape and profile to the one he had borrowed but a tiny bit lighter. He would have to see what Griff thought of them. He planned to go up to the palace complex later on his way home to the cottage and drop them off.

The thing he was struggling with was the special paste containing the tusktooth ivory, hedge apple charcoal and the yellow-tinged clay. He had found that indeed the treatment led to a clear improvement in the edge of the blade and better keenness. He was not so happy with several attempts to get the edge of the clay applied neatly, so that the final result with the almost etched line in the blade ended up being where he intended it to be. After several attempts on some steel dagger blanks, he had come up with the idea of using a flexible template to make sure the paste was applied as evenly and regularly as he could get it. One thought had led to another, and he had wondered whether making a template in a softer and more flexible metal like copper, using the lost wax technique, might work. This had offered promise, so he was currently thinking about a stencil pattern that would keep the edge of the blade largely free of clay paste and have its protective effect on the spine, yet have a pleasing design. That had started him thinking about patterns he had seen, and he thought more about his trip north and particularly being out on the boat and the pattern the waves made out in the sea. He looked at his scrap of paper where he had doodled some shapes and thought he might see if Ray could make something in copper that would work on a blade.

He would also have to see if they could craft this template so that the copper was a little thicker towards the spine area to help account for the thickness of the paste.

He held the blade up to the light and marvelled at the greenish-grey sheen once more. After some more days of preparation and finishing, Gerant had been confident enough to try the special paste applied using the copper stencil. Ray had been a little bemused at what he had wanted, but had got onto it straight away. The first try on the spare dagger blade had been serviceable. The second one was actually quite good. He had suddenly realised he had forgotten about putting in the fullers on either side of the blade and dreaded that this would interfere with the new pattern or, worse, ruin the strength and inherent structure of the piece. A quick trip to the Purple Heart to think about this over a soothing ale had made him realise that the use of talium provided more strength and lightness to the blade anyway, so the need to impress fullers on the blade was superfluous. Once he had come to that conclusion, he felt confident to try the paste on the earl's sword blade. The trick had been to take his time, as he carefully smeared on the paste within the stencil on one area, then carefully pick the stencil up, wipe it and place it on the next section of blade. Then repeat those actions until he had the paste applied on the whole length. He also knew if he wasn't happy he could just wipe it all off and start again, but the consistency of the paste meant it stuck to the blade. Then he had fired one side, repeating the process on the other side and refiring in the forge. He was now looking at the final product.

Holding the blade and squinting along it gave him the best angle to see the way the etched line in the talium steel looked like a series of waves breaking. You could only see the finish at certain angles, but he knew, regardless, it was there. He also knew from his checking with the dagger blanks that the edge of the weapon would be even sharper and easier to maintain an edge. This latest experience had proven once again the old parchment was describing a truly wonderful and long-lost art.

Enough! He would hold off polishing and sharpening the sword blade until after he had fitted and then riveted on the blade to the hilt. That had been carefully stored for a week or so. He and Ray had made the quillons, hilt and placed the medallion into the pommel ahead of time. The hilt was built up with carved sections of oak and then a sleeve of green-dyed sharkskin neatly sewn around and with twists of silvery wire intertwined to hold the grip in place. It was very elegant but understated.

There was one last thing, which he had been holding off doing. It was partly his way to confirm to himself that the blade was finished and he was content with how it had gone. Gerant reached for a very small pouch he kept on a leather thong around his neck and took out the small talium stamp and put it next to the forge. He placed the blade into the coals of the forge and gently heated the end of the blade so it only glowed a faint red colour. Placing it on the flat surface of the anvil, he then positioned the stamp onto the surface of the blade where it still glowed. He gave it two sharp raps with one of his peen hammers. *There,* he thought, leaving it to fully cool. After a drink of water, he inspected the blade. On one side of the blade near to the tang was a small ring with a single cursive letter within, etched into the surface of the talium steel. It was quite small – maybe a quarter of an inch in size and not immediately obvious unless you were looking for it. Gerant sighed in satisfaction. Now he could truly say that the sword was finished, apart from anchoring the tang into the guard and hilt assembly, followed by a final clean, polish and sharpening the edge to a razor keenness. This would take several hours and would be a good use of the afternoon.

'Well done, Ray. Good work!'

Ray turned around at the sound of his companion's voice. 'What?'

Gerant smiled. 'Oh, nothing. Just looking forward to what Faith will have made for lunch today. I'm feeling extra hungry.'

When he had wanted to tell Molly that he had the sword, she had told him the maestro and his family were off for a day visiting friends outside of The Capital. A quick wink followed, which Gerant had interpreted correctly. After returning to the workshop, he had told Ray that he was slipping out on an errand. Ray had nodded without even looking up. Returning to the mansion, it looked like the other staff had taken the opportunity to finish early and he found Molly in the office on her own. They had a quick hug and a longer kiss.

'Stop, stop. There might be one of them still around. Let's go upstairs.'

Once truly alone, it had not taken long for some pent-up feelings to emerge from both of them, with periods of hushed conversation in between longer bouts of passionate kissing. This had almost naturally meant that first Gerant's shirt had come off, then Molly's blouse. Gerant had been very keen to explore her breasts now that he could see them and cup them. He was mightily impressed with how soft they were. But how hard Molly's nipples got once he kissed and sucked on them. Then during another bout of kissing and giggling Molly's skirt had come adrift and then Gerant's pants. So now they were both naked and coiled on the bed together, hugging each other and giving each other the occasional kiss in between softly talking. Molly stroked Gerant's cheeks and talked quietly as she did so.

'Gerant, dearest, I can't afford to get pregnant and have a baby. As soon as that happens and they notice my belly growing, they would throw me out and I would have to go back to Samphire and my mam. So we can't couple, although I would dearly love to.'

Gerant didn't know what to say. This was beyond his experience. Molly gave him another kiss and she grinned mischievously.

'But there are other ways to give each other pleasure. Here, let me show you what I mean. Lie back. That's it.'

Molly started kissing Gerant's neck, then moved down to kiss his nipples and then moved lower, kissing his belly button and then lower. Gerant lay back, enjoying these strange sensations he had never felt before.

Molly kissed the top of his member and her lips gently enclosed his tip, before opening up wider and wider and starting to engulf him. Gerant closed his eyes and the road of pleasure opened within his mind as Molly started to moan in pleasure as he realised his own grunts were happening more and more frequently. In his mind he started to flap his wings and fly up into the sky, as the sensations became even more pleasurable.

Chapter 35
Scarlett's

There was a gentle knock on the door.

'Come. Ah. The earl's sword?'

Gerant placed the wrapped bundle on the maestro's desk and sat down in one of the chairs. The maestro quickly unwrapped the cloth and pulled out the sword in its custom-made sheath. He took it in and then his face started to redden slightly and his nostrils flared. Gerant recognised the signs and began the first of his carefully prepared little speeches.

'You were away for a few days when we had to make the scabbard so I was not able to get your thoughts on the design. So I thought it prudent to consult the earl himself about what he would like. In keeping with his other wishes, he wanted something rather plain but elegant, in his house's colours. Based on these thoughts, which he was rather insistent on, I am sure he will approve.'

The maestro looked over the leather scabbard dyed in a moss green, with the throat and chape worked in sterling silver and silver wire criss-crossing in a regular pattern in between. He calmed down somewhat when he heard the explanation and that the earl had been consulted. 'Hmmm. Next time check with me first.'

The older man gripped the sword and pulled it smoothly from the scabbard and laid the sheath on his desk. Gerant thought he saw approval and fascination on the Maestro's features, before they were quickly masked.

'I like the way how my design for the hilt and the gems and decoration set off this greenish tinge on the blade. And it feels very light but incredibly strong. You need to tell me again about the process sometime, just so I understand it better.'

And be able to pass it off as your own work, thought Gerant savagely.

In examining the edge and surface of the polished steel, the maestro noticed something different.

'This regular, flowing thing like a watermark on the steel. This is new. What is its purpose?'

'The talium steel gives the blade the usual green-grey cast, strength, lightness and flexibility. I have now worked out that applying a special paste to the blade and heating it in the forge gives it added strength, changes the steel in some way and makes the edge even sharper and more resilient.'

Gerant stopped there to see what effect his rehearsed words had.

'This so-called special paste. Tell me about it.'

'I used an old recipe that has three special ingredients that when mixed somehow changes the metal in a way I don't understand. But I was able to apply the paste using a stencil we made to give it that regular pattern.'

'What are the ingredients?'

Gerant started explaining but was quickly interrupted.

'Actually don't tell me. I'll just say it is a long-lost recipe and the details of what it contains must remain a secret known only within the studio.'

The Maestro marvelled at the way the blade had the almost hidden pattern embedded in its surface that hinted at its incredible hardness and strength. About to put the sword down, he noticed something else, which he peered at more closely. On one side of the blade where it emerged from the grip, there was a small punch mark on the highly polished and buffed surface. It was a circle about a quarter inch in size, within which lay a single letter in a flowing, cursive design. The Maestro traced the shape of the letter in his mind and then guessed what it depicted.

'And this?' The maestro pointed to the design stamped into the blade surface.

Gerant paused for a moment. *So he had noticed it*, he realised, rapidly going through the words he had rehearsed to himself earlier.

'I thought it appropriate to indicate this work has come out of the Shagreen Studio. So I chose a design that shows this. In this way, anyone can see this is an authentic work of high quality that will increase in its desirability and value.'

The maestro pondered on this as he gently stroked his trimmed beard.

'A nice touch to show where this was made. That cursive and flowing 'S' is elegant, and there is no doubt it depicts a piece that has come the Shagreen studio. I can see this will only enhance the value of the pieces, as people clamour more and more for Shagreen works. Continue to add this on any future work.'

Gerant smiled and looked down, before formally nodding.

The fencing master saluted the earl with his sword, panting gently and chuckling as he wiped his face and neck with a towel and stripped off the wickerwork breastplate used for protection.

'Well met, my lord. I thought you had me several times. I have never seen you fight so intensely and move so quickly.'

The earl also smiled as he too stripped off his breastplate. 'Agreed, Parvo. There were openings in your defence that were suddenly there, and I froze not expecting them. Then by the time I got over my shock, you had recovered. I think it has to be this new sword. I feel twenty years younger wielding it.'

The earl moved the new blade from Maestro Shagreen to and fro in the morning light and examined again the surface. He was convinced the green tinge to the steel had something to do with how light and strong it felt. And the subtle, regular markings down the blade that must be part of the structure of the steel. He had noticed he could cut, thrust and parry so much faster than normal. And the strength when he had parried the sword master had surprised them both.

He also fingered the stamped symbol on one side of the steel surface near the end of the grip and the quillons. The design was rendered in a cursive letter, which the maestro had said was an 'S'.

He could see that. Then he peered a little more closely. *Or it could be a different letter*, he mused to himself. *Hmmm.*

After a quick wash and change of clothes back at the chateau, the earl went looking for his daughter and found her seated in the grove reading a book. Annie, her maidservant, was sitting companionably on another bench working on some embroidery. Tahlia looked up at the sound of soft approaching footsteps and smiled.

'Papa.'

'Tahlia.'

The earl sat down next to his daughter. 'I wondered if you could cast your mind back to when we got the iron screens put in on the back stairs. Remind me what that young fellow's name is who works with Maestro Shagreen.'

Tahlia paused while she thought. 'Well, Papa, I only saw him a couple of times but I think his name was Gerant. Why?'

The earl was silent for a few heartbeats. 'No particular reason. I had in my head his name started with 'S'. But that explains something I was wondering about. Thank you. It would have bothered me otherwise.'

Tahlia watched her father disappear back up the path, shrugged her shoulders and went back to her book.

Gerant was working away at his bench near the forge, trying to juggle what the next projects would be. With the earl's sword completed, he was ready to start on some daggers and then the matched sword and dagger for the count of Ravenswood. He was absorbed in working out the items he would need and vaguely registered the very small sounds of someone approaching. He quickly looked up with a look of worry and then broke into a grin as he recognised the royal forester. He clasped hands with Griff.

The forester spoke softly. 'I hope I didn't startle you. You look so intent on your work.'

'No, no. I am very pleased to see you. I was only thinking about my next set of projects.' Gerant suddenly had a horrible thought. 'The arrowheads. They were OK? Or were they a waste of time for you?'

'On the contrary. Let's go out into the yard.' The forester nodded at Ray working away at his bench and gestured out to where the kiln was.

They sat on the bench next to each other and Griff quietly told Gerant what had happened.

'I fitted the new heads to some spare shafts I had and went down to the archery range. I tried them from fifty yards up to two hundred. They were true in flight and landed on the target as expected. What was surprising was that they were consistently a hand's width higher. Now, my skill is pretty good, and this happened every time, so I can only conclude that the arrows fly lighter than normal, and it is easy enough to aim a little lower before release.'

Gerant nodded without really understanding the details about shooting. But he was not surprised about the lightness, which he had seen in using talium steel now for some time. He told Griff about what he had found when forging blades and the forester agreed that this might be the explanation.

'Then I decided to take the new arrows on a hunt. After an hour or so we found a stag and I put a shot up, remembering to aim a hand's width lower than normal. I'll have to take you on a hunt one time.'

'Oh, that would be fabulous, Griff.'

'What normally happens even if you get a clean heart shot is that the deer will leap up and may even bound away for ten or twenty feet before it collapses. With this new arrow, it was a good heart shot.' The forester paused. 'Essentially the stag started to leap after the arrow hit it, but all it did was just fall to the ground. When we got up to it, I swear the arrow had punched in maybe an extra three or four inches.' The memory of the hunt was enough that the forester still shook his head in wonder.

'My young friend, you need to be very careful. If word gets out, these talium arrowheads will be highly desirable and well-off folk would pay very good money to get them. They are going to be very useful for hunting big game – and for other purposes, no doubt.' Griff sighed and looked over at Gerant sitting next to him on the bench. 'You might be forced into making these at the expense of anything else. Another word of warning. The royal arrowmaker is very skilled at his craft. He is protective of his position and doesn't put up with any competition for his wares. There have been others in the past that thought they could do better, and things ended up very poorly and they weren't able to work again. You understand?'

Gerant had been in The Capital long enough to understand how cut-throat some businesses were. He recalled the conversation with Sveg about one of the main reasons for staying in Ashford and not venturing into smithing in the main city.

'I do understand, Griff. I just wanted to see if I could pay you back in some way for taking me to where the hedge apple trees were. Thanks for the advice and the warning. It's good to know that they are as good as what I hoped. But I really want to focus on swords and daggers and such.'

The forester patted his companion's shoulder, then stood up. 'Then let's keep this little secret between ourselves. They will just put it down to my skill with the bow and I will only use them occasionally on a prize stag or boar. That should mean no one will find out the real reason.

'Stay safe, Gerant. You have a very promising future in front of you and please come and visit me if I can be of any help.'

They had a quick clasp of hands and then the royal forester padded off towards the street as quietly as he had arrived. *Whoa*, thought Gerant, as he slowly wandered back to his workbench. He had plenty of things to think about and was glad Griff had given him such a timely warning. Another reason to keep quiet about the wonderful properties of talium steel and not go around boasting about his skill and what he could craft. He went back to checking the measurements for the count's sword, which was a little shorter than the earl's. From what the maestro had told him, the count was quite stocky. Well, he had the correct numbers, so could start to work on a blade. Ray had already begun on the lost wax castings for the hilt assembly for both the sword and dagger, which had been specified to be identical in design and decorations. Gerant quickly lost himself in his work, working in companionable silence with his fellow artisan at the workbench nearby.

The large room was brightly illuminated with groups of lanterns placed strategically above the seven or eight tables of various sizes scattered throughout the room. Conversation ebbed and flowed in a steady background pulse, occasionally punctuated by a sudden raucous shout of laughter or exclamations. Parties of card players were seated at the gaming tables, some overseen by a member of staff dealing out cards, taking in or paying out gaming chips. Other tables had groups of clients drinking and chatting, including one larger table of eight or so who were clearly enjoying themselves and from which the loudest sounds of chatting and conversation came from.

Hislop stood discretely near the bar and surveyed the room again, satisfied with how things were going and pleased it seemed to be a good afternoon for the club. The manager was dressed in the gold and green outfit that all Scarlett's staff wore, with a few extra decorations to distinguish him as a senior person. He watched as one of his waiting staff, the young red-headed girl with the pleasing figure, took another bottle of bubbles over to the large table in the corner. Maestro Shagreen and his cronies were clearly very relaxed with what they had already drunk and Shagreen had that flushed cast to his face and eyes that were unnaturally large with the effects of the alcohol. He must be telling another of his stories, resulting in a burst of laughter from this listeners and slaps on the back at the end. Glancing around, it looked like the nearby gaming tables were going well, based on the subtle looks and signals from the staff working their table. Drinks and snacks were being brought over regularly. They were somewhat more intense and quiet, focused on the cards, with occasional looks of annoyance at the outbursts from the Shagreen table. But it all seemed under control and not developing into a situation where he would have to intervene, smile to everyone and calm them down. That was what he was paid the extra coin for. It was his ability to appear to be on the side of everyone and be understanding of all points of view. He would go in and say it was all a terrible misunderstanding and drinks were on the house and what was all the fuss about anyway? That said, he decided he would go on a slow circuit of the room and greet the people at each table, many of whom he knew by name – just to make sure everything would continue to go smoothly. He started off towards the first table, a professional smile already set on his carefully set features.

'Ah, Mr Foxham. How lovely to see you again. Are the cards falling well for you? Good, good. Always a pleasure to see you.' He moved on to the next table.

The five men carefully looked at the pair of cards Wallington had dealt.

Urbright nonchalantly picked his two cards up and looked at them quickly, so as not to allow the other players to get a peek. A Ten of Clubs and the King of Hearts. He put them back on the table and pushed forward two gold-coloured tokens. While he waited for the others to put in their initial stake, he continued to listen to the conversation coming from the table close at hand where that loud-mouthed Shagreen was holding court with his acquaintances. Normally he would have got Hislop to have chucked them out as being too noisy. Nevertheless, he couldn't help but be interested in the subject being discussed, so he was happy to bide his time. It was making it hard to hear things and still keep up in the game. So be it. It looked like Wallington was about to deal the three community cards face up in the centre of the table. He continued to eavesdrop, not that it was hard to do with the loudness of the voices.

'So tell me again about this talium stuff, Shagreen. Everyone is talking about the fine quality of the blades you are making.'

The maestro grinned at Mainwaring, who had asked the question. 'Well, my dear fellow,' he drawled loudly, 'it is according to an ancient parchment that means adding this to the steel gives it a special slight greenish sheen. And makes it stronger, lighter and sharper, of course.'

Mainwaring was clearly impressed. 'So you found this old parchment? What a find!'

Mainwaring chortled to himself as he swallowed another mouthful of the excellent red that Shagreen had provided for the table.

'Huh!' snorted Shagreen's wife. 'It was that new artisan fellow Trantor now has who found it! Such a disappointment . . .'

Shagreen's expression changed instantly from those of a drink-flushed, man of the moment to a hard, furious stare at his wife for having blurted out that little secret. She could feel his anger and almost cowered in response.

'Catherine, that was unfortunate. We'll talk afterwards about this.'

Shagreen thought for a minute. Well, it was out there now. Hopefully there was little damage done. He glanced around the table quickly and they were all just clearly curious, with no knowing or accusatory looks he could discern. He decided it was probably more damaging to try and cover it up than continuing with the story. Besides, he was enjoying the company, and it was a long time since he had felt this relaxed and expansive.

'Sadly, it was the new smith I have working for me. He tried it on a dagger and I could immediately see how valuable it was and that I could build up a huge market for the blades. I should get all the credit for it. So I took it, of course.'

Loud exclamations of 'Oh, well done, well done!', 'The least you could do!' and 'Only to be expected', rang out from the other members at the table.

Count Dodsworth was also a little bleary-eyed with the excellent wine, his face flushed. 'So what about this new process that you've used on Sherrington's sword? He told me just the other day how impressive it is.'

The maestro leant into his colleagues a little, confining himself to a loud hissing whisper. Before he started, he looked around the room again and saw the usual spread of other groups chatting at tables or three or four groups of card players. They all seemed to be busy looking at their cards or talking to each other. No one appeared to be looking up and listening.

'Well, this smith came up with the mixture and it works even better on the talium steel. He tells me you smear it on and heat the blade and it is remarkable how effective it is. Cuts like a razor!'

'What's in the paste?' gestured Dodsworth, trying to keep his focus on the equally flushed face of his friend Shagreen.

'Well, that's a secret. I should really find out what it is, but I just say it is three special ingredients and only a few people know what they are. I think the earl naturally assumed I knew and wasn't at liberty to tell him. So I'll just use that ploy and everyone will think it comes from me. People are so gullible, sometimes.'

Trantor paused to receive the congratulations of the group and made sure the glasses were filled again. He loved the way they all saw things the way he did. He was in a very expansive mood given the delight the earl had shown, along with the significant purse of coin that came with the completed sword. And the orders for new blades that were starting to rush in. This was going to work out extremely well and he could already tell that he would soon be able to knock back some of the approaches from some of the lesser nobles and those with less influence. He loved being in a position of power like this. He gazed with fondness at Cathy next to him, who was looking radiant in that new off-white dress with the lilac trim, that set off her carefully arranged blond ringlets. She saw his gaze and gave him a quick peck on the cheek before murmuring in his ear, 'My clever husband.'

Viscount Urbright tried to keep his attention on the current hand without much success. *So, the maestro has a very talented smith working for him, and that's the reason why my dagger is so magnificent. Hmmm.* Shagreen obviously had no idea of the details but was milking the success for all it was worth. Urbright wondered how many people knew this. Probably not many, if any at all. He mused how he could use this to his advantage.

'Urbright. Urbright! Pay attention. It's your call.'

'Ah, my apologies. Was thinking about something else.'

He checked the new community card dealt and grimaced as he realised he couldn't make anything useful with the two cards he held. 'Fold.'

Out of the hand now, he continued to listen in to the loud talk at the next table.

The conversation continued to follow the increased standing of the maestro's studio. One of the wives piped up.

'So, Cathy, this new artisan that makes these blades. What's he like?'

'I can happily say I have never met the chap.'

There were some pretend gasps.

'As with all the staff working for my husband, they know where their place is, and they are lucky to work for such a well-respected studio. I am sure he is as competent as he should be, and Trantor always looks after his staff.'

Cathy looked on her husband with unadulterated admiration and he gallantly picked up her hand and kissed it to the applause of the table. At that point, the manager at Scarlett's arrived at the table and gently clapped with his smile fixed on a beaming face.

'So good to see you all. What a lovely group who are having such a wonderful time! I have merely come to tell you that your table in the dining room is now ready, and we would be delighted if you could wander through. No rush, of course. We have another couple of bottles of complimentary wines and bubbles ready for discerning tastes. And Chef tells me that the duck with cherries is particularly fine today.'

Hislop looked over at Maestro Shagreen with the beginnings of a concerned frown on his face. 'Of course, I am ahead of myself. Would that suit you, maestro?'

'Ah, you always anticipate me, Hislop. My darling, will you accompany me?'

A flushed Trantor Shagreen gestured to his darling wife. She rose graciously and the couple led off the others to the next room, happily chatting and calling to each other in loud voices.

Viscount Urbright pondered more on what he had heard. *Shagreen obviously has no idea of the details of this new steel and making these amazing blades. It's all bluff! Now, what to do with this? This is better than gold in the right ears. I need to think long and hard and talk to someone with particular influence. A few discrete words to Earl Kilvington or Lord Astor might be of benefit. Hmmm.* He reviewed his two cards and what was in the middle.

'Check.' He pushed over three counters. 'And raise.' He pushed over another five.

Wallington grimaced at his cards again. 'Fold.'

There was only Urbright and Shickleham still in the hand. Count Thorburn was dealer but had folded early.

'All done?' Thorburn queried, looking at both Urbright and Shickleham.

Urbright leaned back with narrowed eyes and affected a calmness that he didn't feel. Shickleham's expression gave away he thought he was on a good hand, and he leant forward in expectation.

'Show.'

Shickleham turned his pair of cards over.

'Two pairs! Huh!' Urbright could see his opponent had two Sevens in his hand and a pair of Tens were in the community set of five.

Urbright quickly turned over his two in front of him.

'Three of a kind.' He had another Ten in his hand.

A quick burst of emotion and disappointment from Shickleham and admiration from the others. Thorburn summed the feeling up.

'The luck of the devil, Urbright. I swear you weren't actually paying any attention to the cards. How do you do it?'

As he reached over to pull the healthy pile of counters toward him, Urbright smiled mysteriously. 'Oh, years of playing, Thorburn. Second nature to me.'

This winning hand confirmed things. He would contact Kilvington and Astor in the morning and see what the best approach would be. He looked around for anyone in a Scarlett's uniform and raised his hand for another glass of wine.

Chapter 36
Ousting of the Maestro

Gerant was feeling really good about the amount of productive and interesting work he had in front of him for at least two months. He looked again at the two bars of talium steel he had forged for the blades needed for the count of Ravenswood. It was still too early to recognise them for the glistening, slender, greenish-grey profile they would become. In his mind's eye, he could see the hidden forms in the blunt, roughed-out blocks and that he would have to go looking for within the metal. He was starting to really appreciate Sveg's long-given advice about feeling the work within the metal and almost caressing it out in the many processes linked to the forge and the anvil. That was what he felt as he lifted them up to the light and squinted along the surfaces. These were the moments that he almost felt connected to the larger beings or gods, and he was but a small part of bringing some form of beauty into the world.

So he was a little surprised when Ray suddenly got up and muttered, 'Coming?'

Looking at the light streaming into the workshop, he realised it was midday or thereabouts and time for lunch with the other staff.

He quickly packed up his drawing and yelled, 'Be right with you', at the rapidly disappearing figure. *Nothing gets in the way of Ray's meal*, he mused, as he hurried to catch up.

It was the usual post-lunch chatter of interest across the table. It had been one of his favourites that Faith made every now and again. The bacon and bean soup had been served with plenty of freshly baked crusty bread and lashings of salty butter. Donald was having a lively argument with Ray about the benefits or otherwise of growing your own tomatoes or making do with what you could get at the market stall. Gerant had some very nice tomato bushes starting to harvest well at the plot and Mrs Lamming was starting to bottle up batches of chutney and other preserves. So he was interested to hear what came up in the back and forth between the two. He was just about make his own point about the joys of growing your own produce when there was a gentle clapping by Molly at the end of the table. She had her usual cheery half-smile on her lips but somehow portrayed a more serious note.

'Just to let you know that the maestro is in a filthy mood. Please, for your own sake, avoid the good rooms and stay in the back of the house. I am sure it will blow over, but you all know how angry he can get. The least thing might set him off.'

'Got out of the wrong side of bed this morning, did he?' Donald smirked.

Molly shook her head gently, her face becoming even more serious. 'If only. He received an official document from the palace. He didn't show me what it said but his face went to thunder as he was reading it. He has an audience with the royal chancellor tomorrow morning to set things right. That's all I know.'

Molly got up, smiled quickly at Gerant, then left the table and disappeared into the house. As he helped the others pack up lunch, there were murmurings of what had been sent from the palace, but no one had any firm ideas. Ray, as usual, put his dishes in the pile to be washed and then wandered back to the workshop. Gerant trailed behind, thinking further. Molly was clearly a little concerned. He might try to find her tomorrow and ask of more news about the maestro's appointment at the palace. There was nothing he could do about it. So, he put those thoughts away and brought to his mind's eye again the blades for the Ravenswood project and getting the forge ready for a big push of work in the morning.

Trantor Shagreen paced up and down in the large salon room that a palace usher had brought him to.

The uniformed flunky in burgundy and gold had murmured discretely before gently closing the double doors. 'The royal chancellor will be with you in a few moments, sir. Please take a seat, if you please.'

Trantor nodded distractedly, refused to sit at any of the carefully placed sofas or padded chairs and continued to grasp the royal missive with the multiple seals and ornate writing. He was dressed in his best velvet doublet and half boots. His hair and beard had been carefully trimmed and he presented an absolutely elegant but imposing figure. *It has to be a terrible mistake,* he thought for the umpteenth time. He looked down with unseeing eyes at the unfolded parchment and glanced about at the immaculate wood panelling lining the walls, the marble fireplace with a small fire chuckling merrily in the grate and the large paintings of members of the royal family festooning the walls at regular intervals.

Just then the doors opened and in filed an elderly, somewhat stooped older man with greying hair and a goatee beard, wearing a doublet of a deep blue with purplish shading and soft leather shoes. His rheumy eyes alighted on the pacing figure in front of him as he grasped a couple of beribboned parchments. A palace guard in a burgundy and gold uniform closed the double doors and took up a position on one of the walls. He had various paraphernalia placed at points across his uniform coat, along with a sword in a well-adorned scabbard on one hip and a dagger on the other. As soon as he took up position in front of one of the bookcases, his face adopted a blank expression with his eyes looking straight ahead into the distance.

'Ah, so sorry for the wait, Maestro. Pressures of palace business, I am afraid. Come, come. Sit here and you can tell me what troubles you.'

The rheumy, reddened eyes watched the tall figure that had stopped pacing and Duke Astonborough patted a sofa across from a small round table, before sinking into an identical sofa on the other side.

Shagreen stalked over and perched on the edge of the sofa, leaning forward, his eyes boring into the duke's eyes. The duke's expression remained unchanged as he smiled back weakly at the other man, his own eyes remaining directed at Shagreen but somewhat unfocused.

'My lord. There seems to be a major misunderstanding here at the very least. I received this letter, if you will, stating that my appointment as one of the artisans of The Realm has been suspended pending an enquiry. This letter . . .' Shagreen jabbed at the offending piece of parchment. 'This letter states there is evidence that I am not fit to be in that role. What utter nonsense. A pack of lies. I have a good mind to . . .'

Shagreen stopped himself at the last moment. The duke's expression had changed from being welcoming and affable to a look of understanding and concern.

'My dear chap. I have been made aware of this missive. Not of my doing, of course. But we must let things run their course. I am sure there is nothing to worry about.'

The duke picked up a piece of parchment he had carried in, glanced at it briefly and put it on the small table in front of him.

'But my lord, there is nothing in this notification that mentions anything about what I have done. Or what I haven't done. It must be a set of total fabrications. I have a right to defend myself against them, if only I knew what they were or who has made them.'

The large man's voice had got progressively louder and louder as he expressed his feelings about the situation and his frustration at not being able to find out anything.

The duke was frowning and looking slightly alarmed at the ranting taking place across the table from him. The guard had ceased being bored and had stopped staring into the distance, now watching the exchange with interest. So far he hadn't moved, apart from standing up a little straighter in front of the bookcase, about ten paces away from the pair seated on the sofas.

'Steady there, steady. All that will come out in the inquiry. You will have an opportunity to counter whatever allegations have been made then. You can't rush these things.'

'But that could be weeks, yet. In the meantime, all my clients will hear of it and cancel their orders and no one will come looking to take on new projects. It will be a disaster.'

The older man shook his head sadly. 'Quite, quite. Nothing to be done. These things take their own good time to conclude.'

The maestro realised he wasn't going to get anywhere with that particular approach. He tried another. 'My lord, at least give me a sense of who has laid these claims or what the allegations are.'

Duke Astonborough couldn't help but quickly glance at the parchment on the small table in front of him, before looking away. Shagreen saw the look.

'Of course, it would be improper for me to tell you that. I need to maintain my independence in this matter and, as I said, I had nothing to do with this.'

'But from the sounds of things, you do know who brought these clearly false claims?'

The maestro watched the duke's face intently and the older man couldn't help rapidly glancing down again at the table in front of him.

'I can't tell you that, Maestro. That remains a protected piece of information at this point.'

Aha, thought Shagreen, *it's on the parchment. How dare he? I'm going to have a look.*

'We'll see about that', muttered Shagreen, as he quickly grabbed for the square of parchment with its closely packed writing sitting on the table in front of the duke.

'Hah!' He started quickly scanning the parchment feverously.

It took a moment for the royal chancellor to react. 'Oh, I say! That's privileged information and confidential. Give that back immediately!' He reached over the table and tried to grab the parchment off the other man, who reacted by moving it out of reach as he continued to read.

The guard had been observing the conversation with interest. He now started to stride over to the pair with a look of shock and a little alarm spreading on his face. Duke Astonborough now stood and came around the small table, the look of gentle sympathy now replaced with a reddening on his cheeks and a look of righteous indignation and a little anger.

'Stop immediately. This is beyond the pale! How dare you. This is highly irregular and must cease.'

The duke made another grab for the parchment and this time was successful. He leant back with a look of triumph. The maestro's features were a mixture of stubbornness about not giving up the parchment and fury about what he was starting to read. He jerked the parchment towards him again and there was a loud ripping sound as the piece split in two halves. Both men were instantaneously thrown back to various degrees. The maestro was perched on the sofa and rocked against the padded back and then leant forward again holding in both hands the piece of ripped parchment, a look of competitive anger changing instantly to dismay.

The duke was not so fortunate. The initial look of triumph on his face changed to rampant shock and fear as he suddenly careened backward holding his part of the parchment. He experienced the sudden change of trying to wrestle the parchment off the other man to no resistance at all as the piece had suddenly ripped. His body was not able to adjust, and his feet did not even plant as he flew backwards, with his knees crumpling and he landed heavily on his bottom. His chest and shoulders continued moving backwards even as he folded, and his head hit the polished floorboards with a resounding thud. The duke's body did not move from its slumped position on the floor, with a slim trickle of blood already beginning to flow from somewhere on the back of his head where it had cracked with stunning force into the wooden surface.

Shagreen's face had instantly paled as the shock and enormity of what had happened sunk in. The guard had reached two or three paces away when the parchment had ripped and had been closing the distance quickly. He couldn't help but stop as the duke hurtled backward and his head smashed against the floor. The guard couldn't believe what he had just seen. His features matched the paleness shown on the maestro's face and he clearly was battling to understand what he had just witnessed. The maestro rapidly stood erect and looked around wildly. The guard's training kicked in. He fumbled for the silver whistle on its special lanyard on the left of his uniform coat, found it and brought it to his mouth before drawing breath. The beginnings of an alarm call started as he expelled the first part of the air held in his lungs. Then his eyes went wide with surprise. The sound from the whistle subsided rather quickly and the whistle dropped suddenly from the guard's now wide-open mouth. His eyes looked desperately at Shagreen, then looked down at his dagger which had suddenly appeared in his belly, before becoming more and more unfocused.

Trantor held the guard by the shoulder, one hand working the dagger even more into the other man's stomach. After a few seconds, the guard's knees started to give, and Trantor almost gently helped him collapse to the floor. The guard fell in an untidy heap. Shagreen quickly pulled the body behind one of the sofas and hoped the rapidly growing pool of blood would not be noticed straight away. He was shocked at what he had just done. Instinct had taken over. He had needed to stop the guard from sounding the alarm and had used the one weapon he could easily see: the guard's dagger. The guard had been concentrating on finding his whistle and had not even noticed the other man rapidly close, grab his dagger out of its sheath and stab upwards into his belly. The maestro gave his clothes a quick dusting off and then thought to check the duke. The bleeding from the back of the head had not grown much more and when he carefully rolled the older man onto his back, the duke gave a reedy groan. *He is still out*, thought Shagreen, *but alive.* The maestro quickly stalked to the double doors of the audience room, carefully opened one side and peered out into the corridor. Everything had remained quiet and he could see no one. After a quick check of what he could see, he edged out, gently shutting the door. As calmly as he could, he began walking away down the corridor.

In the bustling hubbub of The Capital, a green, enclosed carriage pulled by two matched greys wheeled up the stone-clad two-storey Shagreen residence. The coachman pulled on the brake and spoke quietly to the horses as the maestro jumped down and headed to the arched front doorway.

'We'll be no more than ten, fifteen minutes. Then off.'

The maestro yelled this back at the coachman just as he disappeared into the house. The driver muttered to himself. 'Whatever. You're payin'.' Then he settled down into his cloak, closed his eyes and ignored the clutter and bustle of the street noises.

The imposing figure of Trantor Shagreen stalked into the entrance lobby, paused a moment before looking up the staircase and down the hallway towards the back of the house.

'Catherine! Catherine! Madeline! Brock!' A pause. 'Molly! Molly!'

His shouts echoed throughout the house, initially to silence. Then a door opened down the hallway and Molly appeared, walking forward with a worried expression on her features.

'Right. Major change of plan. Find Catherine and the children. Tell them they can pack two bags each. No more. And tell my wife to pack all her jewellery and finery. They need to be ready to leave in ten minutes.'

Molly digested this unexpected news and could only nod.

'I am going to grab some important documents from my study. You need to find the small handcart that Donald uses and bring it here. We'll need it to load the coin and valuables from the coin chest.'

Molly's face had become pale, and her blue eyes had somehow taken on a greyish tinge with the shock.

'I want you back here in five minutes. Now move! Go and find Catherine!'

The young woman almost wilted at the forceful verbal explosion from the maestro and ran off towards the staircase. Trantor looked wild-eyed at the fleeing figure and then rushed into his study, slamming the door in his hurry.

Chapter 37
A Stop Gap

Gerant was making good progress on ordering materials and preparing for his next few weeks' of work. There seemed to be a thousand details to think about and he found it easiest to write down a list of jobs and stock he would need ahead of time. Sveg had sometimes done it when it was a complicated job. Just at the moment with – he counted them in his head – eight sets of blades to be forged and made, he had to be very organised. The last thing he needed was to forget to order polished stones or gems from Adam Purslip or run out of charcoal from Levy and then have to wait a day or two, or even longer if they could not be supplied. That would be a disaster and he would have to suffer the ire of the maestro for it. And probably fair enough, too. Hence the list on his sheet of paper. He had also found with recent experience that it was easier to do this kind of planning work away from the workshop. He was sitting in the tavern sipping occasionally from his tankard of Black Heart as he worked away. Perhaps it was his training as a smith where he was able to concentrate on the work at hand and not find the steady chatter and noises of a busy tavern in any way distracting. It was only when he took a short break every now and again and scanned the bustling bar from his usual booth that he noticed the noise and smoke and yells and shifting sounds and sights.

No, this all looked sensible. He would make a quick trip to the jeweller to order things for the hilts that Ray would start to cast. They had sufficient clay for the lost wax and firewood stocks were adequate at least for a few more weeks. He finished his tankard. Dirk hadn't come in for their regular drink and chat. It was perhaps a little early for him – he would still be working up the hill. Well, he would take his workings back to the workshop and head off home. He needed to put in a good hour at the plot before dark. He left his tankard at the bar where they would find it, nodded briefly to Phil the bartender and walked out of the swinging doors.

Gerant wandered back to the workshop, looking over his list. His feet knew the way and he subconsciously navigated around people coming in the other direction, a pile of steaming horse dung and a couple of wooden staves strewn on the street. In his mind, he realised he had reached the gateway at the entrance to the workshop, so he was greatly shocked and almost jumped back in alarm when a firm hand suddenly pressed against his chest and prevented him from moving forward.

'Not so fast. This place is closed. No entry allowed.'

Still holding his list, Gerant looked up at a tall, hulking man in a uniform he recognised was similar to the one Dirk always wore. The man had an officious look on his face, closely cropped blackish hair and hadn't shaved for a few days. The guard had a pike that was around eight feet long and some sort of large cutlass sheathed at his waist.

This was absurd! What was happening? A swirl of panicked thoughts went through his mind. *It must be some mistake.* 'But I work here! This is Maestro Shagreen's workshop. I only went down to the tavern for a quick ale and am dropping this back.'

He looked around the guard and saw a similarly dressed figure poking around the workshop, looking for something.

'Just following orders, me lad. There is a royal warrant out to detain this maestro fella. All his property and belongings have been seized. So you can't go in.' The guard had a look of smugness on his face as he said this.

Gerant didn't know what to do. It looked like there was no way he could talk his way in. Then he had an idea.

'Wait. Ray can vouch for me. Ray also works here, and he knows me, of course. Where's Ray?' He peered around the hulking guard, trying to see some sign of his colleague in the workshop beyond.

'If you are meaning that other fella, as soon as we explained the situation, he packed his gear and bolted. That was a little while ago.'

Typical of Ray, he thought. Then he latched onto something the guard had said. 'Can I grab my stuff? It's in there.' He nodded towards the workshop.

'There was only that fella living there in the back room. All the rest of it is confiscated as special evidence. So, no. Push off, we have our own work to do here.'

The talk at the gate had drawn the other guard from the workshop, who was older and clearly a bit more senior. He walked up and smiled sympathetically. 'Sorry, lad, Larry's right. We are here to lock everything up and seal it and the rest of the detachment are at the house doing the same. If there's something particular that is yours, you will have to see the captain about that. Maybe wait a few days and try then.'

Both guards watched the figure almost stumble away down the street, before the older of the pair returned to the workshop to continue checking through things. Larry remained on duty at the gate, occasionally watching as people wandered past. Some of the neighbours discussed in hushed voices why guards were at the workshop and what might have happened to Ray and Gerant.

Gerant walked along the main street of the Florian Quarter, not really paying attention where he walked. Several times he had bumped into others without noticing and had to utter a quick 'Sorry' before moving on. *What had happened? The guard said they were confiscating everything. What about his tools? Oh . . . what if they found the talium buried under the pavers near the privy? Gods, at least they wouldn't know what it was. But how was he going to check it was still there when everything was locked up?* After several minutes of panicked thought, he recognised he was standing across the street from the maestro's mansion. He looked and could immediately see more of the uniformed guards standing on either side of the front door, calmly gesturing officiously at onlookers to stop gawking and move on. A steady stream of guards shuffled through, carrying bits of furniture, boxes and sacks out of the main doorway or emerging from the side gate from the back of the house. They heaved their loads onto a large flat-bed cart positioned strategically on the street outside the mansion, guarded by two other hefty, uniformed figures.

'Gerant, Gerant. Over here!'

He turned and noticed Molly feverishly waving at him from across the street. He ran over and buried his girl in a fierce hug as she burst out crying and sobbing.

'Oh, it was terrible. He came back from the palace in a frightful hurry. They just packed up some bags and he took all the coin and they rushed off. Then about half an hour later the guards arrived, and they have confiscated everything. We were allowed to grab a few of our own belongings and then we were all thrown out.'

Gerant looked down and saw two large bags that Molly had sitting on the ground next to her.

'But what happened? I came back to the workshop and the guards were already there. They said Ray had grabbed his things and disappeared. I just don't understand.'

In the course of the next few minutes, between sobs and tears, Molly related what she knew. 'The lieutenant was understanding but had to follow orders. Apparently there was a major incident up at the palace when the maestro visited the royal chancellor. Something about a guard being stabbed and the chancellor attacked. There is a warrant out for the maestro's capture and all his property has been confiscated by The Realm. They are looking everywhere for him!'

Gerant thought on that for a bit. 'Molly, I know the maestro has a temper, but I can't believe this. It has to be a big mistake.'

Molly sniffed and then her mood hardened. 'Well, you weren't here, and it was terrible with lots of shouting and foot stomping. We had no idea what was happening, and we were just grateful that we could get our stuff and they didn't confiscate it.'

Gerant tried to understand what Molly and the other staff had experienced and could not begin to guess what it had been like. 'So you've got all your stuff?'

'Most of it. There are a few things that I have left that mean little to me. The main thing is that I've got quite a bit of coin saved away for a rainy day. Things are finished here, though.'

Gerant grappled with these thoughts and the large question looming in the background. 'Molly, what are you going to do now?' He thought further. *And what about me?*

'I've had time to think about things while I was waiting to see if you'd turn up.' Molly gulped deeply and gave Gerant another hug. 'I'm going to go back to Samphire for a bit and stay with my mam. I want to go up to The Cross and book a seat on the coach north for tomorrow. Can we go up there?'

Gerant's mind was in a new set of whirling panic. He blurted out one question after another as his mind sifted through what Molly had said. 'You're leaving? But what about us? Is that it? Why don't you stay with me? It will be easy to find other positions, won't it? Won't it?' His voice took on a degree of desperation.

Molly took his hands in hers and looked steadily into Gerant's eyes. 'Look, my love, I have made up my mind. No, we are not finished. But I can't stay here in The Capital. I want to have a think for a bit and make sure Mam's OK and work out what to do next. I have enough coin for that.'

'But you could stay here and we could be together,' wailed Gerant.

'I could. But what does the future hold? You need to find new work and I am not the sort of girl that is happy to sit at home and cook meals and talk nicely when my man gets home each day. I would go mad!' Molly looked at him with firm determination as she said this. 'We can make this work. I want to. But you also need to get things sorted and be back on your feet. Then we can work out how to be together again.'

Molly stroked his cheeks tenderly before looking a little more mischievously at him. 'About tonight. Would I be able to stay with you? I have the coach to catch in the morning, but before then?'

Gerant accepted the peace offering and nodded enthusiastically.

'Great. I can get to meet Mrs Lamming and we can spend the night talking and planning. And whatever else needs doing . . .'

The trek back to Mrs Lamming's had been uneventful. Gerant had shouldered both bags and found it somewhat challenging to carry them and hold hands with Molly at the same time.

'Look after the green one, especially. It has all my savings in it apart from a little for the next few days.' Molly answered Gerant's question that was on his lips. 'I packed some clothes tightly around the pouch so the coin wouldn't clink.'

They had made it to The Cross and Molly negotiated a ticket on the coach leaving the next day for Rivernook and travelling through Samphire. It left mid-morning and would get to Samphire around sunset. Then they went on to the cottage. Gerant led Molly around the back and Fang gambolled like a huge puppy when he saw who had arrived with Gerant. Molly ruffled his ears and then looked at Gerant expectantly. They walked into the kitchen and Molly sat down at the table. Gerant went off to find Dierdre. He found her in the front room busily knitting away.

'Hello, Dierdre.'

'Oh, Gerant, you're home a little early. I'll get dinner on directly.'

Gerant paused. 'That's not why I am home.'

Dierdre put down her knitting and waited expectantly.

'Would it be OK if Molly stayed here this evening? She is catching a coach back home tomorrow but needs a bed for tonight.'

Mrs Lamming smiled delightedly. 'That would be lovely. I have so much looked forward to meeting her and now I shall! I can set up a bed here. Or will she be sleeping . . .'

Despite her friendly and welcoming personality, Dierdre Lamming had been young once and knew how things were. Gerant reddened.

'Oh, in my room. No need to go to any trouble.'

Dierdre matter-of-factly nodded and put away her knitting. 'So, when do I get to meet this young lady?'

'Umm, she's waiting in the kitchen.'

'Oh, wonderful! Well, young man, what are we waiting for?', she continued, as she headed out of the room.

'So, you must be Molly. I have heard so much about you from Gerant.'

The raven-haired young woman turned at the sound of the voice and saw the smiling, older lady with white hair tied up and a dark dress under a carefully tied apron. A somewhat sheepish Gerant was standing behind her. Molly's expression broke into a sudden warm smile, and she walked forward to give the old lady a big hug.

'And you must be Mrs Lamming. I am so pleased to meet you at last. May I call you Dierdre?'

For the next twenty minutes or so while the kettle was on and a hot drink brewing, Gerant perched on one of the chairs, marvelling at the two women chattering back and forth. It was almost like they had always known each other, and he was just an interested onlooker. He couldn't help but start thinking about his own circumstances and what he was going to do. He guessed he could find some sort of smithing work fairly easily in The Capital but would have to look into it. Maybe a first step would be to visit Hamish Wheelwright and ask his advice. Hamish had his finger on the pulse with selling metals and crafting them and would have some good suggestions. He wanted to avoid having to go back to Ashford in disgrace. Not that it was his fault. And Sveg and Marion would be very supportive and understanding. That said, he would always feel he had let Sveg down in some way. So that was to be avoided, except as a last resort.

He suddenly registered that the two women had stopped chatting and were looking at him expectedly.

'I said, Gerant,' Dierdre explained, 'that I need to get dinner going and Molly has offered to help. Why don't you take Fang with you to the plot and grab some beans. And if there are any of the apples left, we can make them into a tart.'

Gerant realised his presence was not needed. Dierdre and Molly were already enjoying their own company after such a short time. It was a good reason to stay out of the way and to take Fang for a walk. He grabbed a small bag and whistled for Fang as he marvelled at how the conversation between the two continued without missing a beat, interspersed with sounds of chopping and the rattling of dishes and pans.

Later that evening, Molly snuggled into Gerant's shoulder in the bed. 'Dierdre is lovely. Such a sweet, loving soul. You know she depends on you a lot?'

He hadn't thought about it in that light. After a moment thinking about it, he agreed.

'I'm going to see tomorrow if Hamish Wheelwright knows of any openings for a smith. Hopefully I can find something quickly.'

He paused and plucked up the courage to ask again. 'You haven't changed your mind? You're going back to Samphire for a bit?'

Molly sighed. 'I don't think I have a choice. I would just fret staying here with nothing to do. Having had to look after the maestro's brats and manage their schooling, I wondered about teaching kids to do their letters and such. As far as I know, no one has been doing that in Samphire since old Godfrey passed, so I might be able to do that. I need to talk to Mam first.'

They both talked quietly for another hour or so, discussing events and options for the future and what they could do.

'Enough, Gerant. I am talked out.'

He was happy to stop too. His mind was a whirl of things to ponder on and it had been a huge and eventful day that neither of them had anticipated.

'Happy to go off to sleep?'

'Almost. There's one more thing I want to do.'

'Oh. What's that?'

'This, my darling.'

Chapter 38
Change in the Air

He lay back, enjoying the quietly slumbering shape cuddled next to him in the pre-dawn period. He could get used to this, he thought. As things were, however, he had only a few short hours to make the most of it. At least their whispered conversations the previous evening had made it clear that Molly was not abandoning him. Things would have to wait until circumstances sorted themselves out. Either she would find something worthwhile, perhaps in the schooling line of things in Samphire, or Molly would come back to The Capital if suitable jobs could be found here. She had made it very clear that Gerant was now part of her life, and it was a matter of finding something that suited them both.

'We're partners in this, my love. Agreed?'

He could only think to kiss her longingly in response.

He hugged her at this memory, and she murmured fondly without waking. Well, it was another big day to contemplate. The hardest thing would be seeing her off on the coach. Gerant snuggled closer to her form and tried to get another hour or so of sleep.

They held each other intensely one last time. Molly's bags had been loaded onto the coach and the other travellers were also having their final farewells.

'As soon as I am settled and know what I am doing, I'll somehow send word to you. By then you should have a better idea of your own prospects and we can work something out.'

Gerant nodded. 'I'll do the same . . . my love.' The words sounded strange to him as soon as he said them, but they had a nice ring to them.

'Last caaalll,' rang out from the coachman as he checked the bindings on the luggage and climbed back up onto the driver's seat.

'Well, this is it. I adore you and I will miss you terribly. But it won't be forever, my love.'

Molly was engulfed in a huge hug, and they held each other, gently rocking for what seemed hours.

'We need to leave, Miss.' The coachman leant down and was gently watching the young couple.

Molly nodded with tears in her eyes and hopped up into the side door of the coach. One of the coach people at The Cross closed the doors and rattled them briefly before patting the side of the coach with his hand. He looked up at the driver. 'All good. On your way.'

The coachman nodded and clicked to the horses, who leant into the harness and the coach headed off down the main thoroughfare on its long journey north. The last Gerant saw of Molly was her head suddenly appearing out of the side window, looking back and waving furiously. A few seconds later her head withdrew, and the coach worked round a slight bend in the road and disappeared.

Gerant was in a very black mood as he walked back to the cottage. At one point he bumped into a large, well-built man with a handful of papers hurrying in the other direction. The papers fell out of the man's grasp, and he was about to burst out in protest when he noticed the burning dark brown eyes and frowning features of the young man who had walked straight into him. No words were exchanged. The larger man thought better of saying something and quickly bent to gather his documents. The younger man hardly noticed as he continued to walk somewhat aimlessly down the street farther into the River Quarter.

Back at the cottage, Gerant found Dierdre cleaning up in the kitchen.

'Just heading down to the plot for an hour or so,' he muttered. 'Come on, Fang.'

'All right, Gerant. See you in a short while.' Mrs Lamming responded without turning round from her tidying up, so didn't see the intense frown that her lodger still had on his face.

After two hours of solid attack on the somewhat unyielding earth at the plot, Gerant felt pleasantly exhausted. He had dug the beds at a furious pace, deliberately trying to beat out his frustrations. Each step forward he had imagined the particular instances that had led to Molly leaving and the shovel had buried itself into the soil with an angry grunt and with the full force of his pent-up energy. He had reached the end of one bed and the next bed met the same punishment. He calmed down enough to weed the beds containing the beans and tomato bushes without leaving a path of destruction through the carefully spaced plants, Hoeing the beds of carrots and potatoes had also helped, although by that stage he had become a little more resigned and was able to maintain his anger at a more manageable level.

'That will have to do. Come on, Fang. Let's go back.'

The large dog had just slumped down near the small shed and was happy to watch his companion as he worked up and down the beds. He, at least, was his usual unruffled self.

Returning to the cottage, Gerant lay on his bed feeling a little spent. He decided he might head up to the Blue Moon and have a long, hot soak.

It was then he heard a loud knocking and Dierdre hesitantly approaching the front door. A short silence ensued before the old lady called out in a tremulous voice.

'Gerant? There are some gentlemen to see you. They wouldn't say what they wanted.'

He quickly got up and passed Mrs Lamming in the hall, looking a little apprehensive. *I wonder what this is about?*

Approaching the door, he could see two men, one blond and the other brown-haired, waiting impatiently. They were in similar brownish leggings and tunics with green trim. If it was a uniform, it was one that he did not recognise.

'You Gerant? Worked for Maestro Shagreen?' This was from the blond man.

'Yeeesss.' He felt he needed to be careful here.

'Good. We are from Viscount Urbright.'

He passed over an official-looking note on a piece of parchment. 'He would like to see you and discuss a proposal.' A pause. 'Like today.'

Gerant quickly scanned over the note. It stated that the Viscount Urbright had a business proposition to make and would have time to meet him that afternoon. He was to present himself at the viscount's official residence in The Park and the matter would be revealed to him. *Very odd*, he thought. But at least it would be worth going and hearing what was on offer. He had not got any further in his thinking apart from going to see Hamish, so that could wait. He had no idea what this proposition might be.

'I could be there in three hours.' That would give him enough time to go up to the Blue Moon and then put on his best outfit.

'Very good. We will tell the viscount he should expect you in three hours. Don't be late. He is a very important and busy man.'

Gerant nodded and the two men immediately left. He shut the door and found Dierdre in the kitchen preparing some food. She looked up with concern showing on her face.

'Don't worry, Dierdre. I just have to meet someone later to discuss something. It is a bit of a mystery what he wants. Sorry if they gave you a fright.'

The older woman looked instantly relieved. 'Goodness me! I thought for a minute you were in trouble.'

She paused for a few moments. 'I am just starting to get dinner prepared. You will be back for that?'

'Absolutely. I just need to go up and had a good wash and then go off to meet this Viscount Urbright. I can't imagine it will take long. After all, he is such a busy and important man.'

Dierdre clearly agreed with him and didn't realise that Gerant was merely parroting the last bit based on what the men had implied. He smiled, secretly amused, and grabbed a couple of things before heading off for a long soak at the Blue Moon.

A neat and very clean Gerant in his best dark brown doublet, matching tights and half boots waited in a small but tastefully decorated room in the mansion of Viscount Urbright. Knowing the routine, he had arrived at the main gatehouse and presented his letter of invitation and had been waved through after a brief inspection. Reaching the central fountain with the palace in the distance, he had noted Earl Sherrington's chateau peeking through the trees on the left. This time he took the carefully trimmed and maintained avenue to the right and soon reached a series of two- or three-storey stone mansions clustered in a loose group, with hedges in between and their own neat gardens. The second one on the right had been the one he was looking for. Again, he gave a quick explanation for the purpose of his visit to the neatly dressed woman who came to the door when he pulled the polished brass bell. He was then shown into this small salon on the second floor.

Gerant was still looking at the various paintings and pieces of furniture when the viscount came through the door.

'Ah, you must be Gerant. So good of you to come. You'll join me in some mulled wine? Excellent. I have a proposal for you to consider.'

Gerant eagerly looked at the viscount, who he had not met previously. Urbright had a similar copper-coloured skin, dark brown eyes, black curly locks and a facial resemblance to his cousin. He was quite lithe and tall, although there were a few hints that he enjoyed his privileged status and the best of wines and food – the whites of his eyes had that slightly yellowish tinge and he had the faint beginnings of a belly that exercise was struggling to keep in check. Nonetheless, his outfit was superbly tailored, and he was clearly partial to jewellery, with rings on most fingers, gold chains around his neck, piercings in his ears and nose.

Urbright poured two tankards of a gently steaming liquid placed on a side table and brought them over to a couple of sofas. 'You found the place all right?'

'Indeed, my lord. I have been to Earl Sherrington's chateau on a couple of occasions so knew the general layout of The Park.'

'Ah yes. I have seen Sherrington's sword. Most impressive, but a little too plain for my taste. Yet the workmanship is superb.' A pause. 'That's why I asked you here.'

Gerant took a sip of the mulled wine and decided not to say anything. It might be best to see how this played out.

Urbright was playing with one of his rings as he started to speak. 'You will be aware that Maestro Shagreen was involved in a very serious incident at the palace the royal chancellor was accosted.' He stopped and looked at Gerant, who slowly nodded.

'The Palace had no alternative but to seize all the property and assets once it became clear Shagreen had managed to leave The Capital. He is still being sought. So far he has managed to elude capture.'

Gerant nodded again. This was news to him. Although he often had found the maestro difficult to deal with, he was secretly glad he had got away. Based on what Molly had told him, there was more to this than first glance. He decided to play along to see what emerged. 'I had no inkling, my lord, of any of this. I had just ducked out on a quick errand and when I came back to the workshop, some soldiers had taken possession of it.'

'Yes, they were following my . . .' Viscount Urbright coughed discretely as he realised what he had started to say. '. . . following the instructions of The Realm to take possession of everything before an inquiry is held. The disappearance of Shagreen is a clear admission of guilt and so the house has already been sold off to the highest bidder. The workshop and all its goods was also to be sold.' The viscount paused. 'I was able to acquire it. That's where you come in.' Urbright took a sip from his tankard and patiently waited for Gerant to say something.

'My lord, I am but a humble metalsmith.' Gerant couldn't believe he had just said that! *Oh well,* he thought, *I may as well play this out to the end.* 'The workshop is well set up to make weapons and such. Are you proposing to use this for yourself?'

A flare of the nostrils and almost a look of shock crossed the viscount's face. 'What a bizarre idea! No, I know you were the one who made the various daggers and swords for Shagreen – he just took all the coin and the credit. No, I am proposing you continue to use the workshop but work for me.'

Aha, thought Gerant. *Now we get to the truth of the matter and I can start to see how this has happened.* He decided to continue to play the innocent tradesman. 'That would be extremely generous, my lord. But what would I do? I can make you a certain number of blades and then you will have more than sufficient for your needs. I would not want to waste your lordship's time.'

'Oh, don't you worry about that, Maestro Gerant. First, I need a matching sword to go with the dagger you have already crafted for me. Then, there are all my friends and acquaintances who are all very keen to have weapons made for them. My very good friend Viscount Joffrey has been most put out that his order for a matching dagger and sword is still to be made. You would have more than enough work, believe me.'

Maestro Gerant! It sounds a little odd, but I could get used to that, he thought. But he would keep up the pretence of feigned confusion for one more question.

A further look of concern crossed the young smith's face. 'But who would pay? These weapons are not cheap to craft. They take several weeks and lots of materials to make. And I need to eat and pay for my lodgings.'

The viscount smiled easily and patted Gerant on the knee as they sat on the couch. 'Don't worry, that will be all taken care of by my bursar. All materials and costs in making the swords and such will be paid by him once you show him receipts. Purchase of the blades will be a private arrangement between my contacts and me. And because you are a skilled artisan, you will be paid five gold pieces a week to cover your living expenses.'

Gerant couldn't keep his mouth from opening in surprise. This was many times what he had been getting from the maestro. *Five gold! A week!* He would hardly know what to do with that steady amount of coin. Any doubts he had about working for Viscount Urbright vanished in a moment. He hadn't seriously been concerned about not having enough to do. As well as any blades to be made, he wanted to spend time looking into his old parchment. The instructions about the talium had been correct, and the paste to allow a keener edge had also worked out. That left the almost far-fetched magical effects that could be put onto a dagger or sword. He would have to spend a lot of time thinking whether this was worth pursuing and read a lot before he would even think about trying it. This new arrangement could be just what he needed. He could even try it on the viscount's sword and see if it worked. If it failed or just didn't work and the sword was damaged in some way, he would just make a replacement. And the viscount would cover all the costs!

'That is very generous of you, my lord. I would be delighted to accept. Is there a trial period?'

From the look on the viscount's face, Gerant could see that hadn't been thought about. 'Very sensible. Let's see how things go for three months, shall we? Good, I'll take you down to Waldron and leave you with him to sort out all the little details.' The viscount stood up and unsheathed a dagger he was wearing on his hip. 'Oh, I should tell you the first item is to make me a matching sword for this. You recognise it?'

Gerant nodded. 'I made this a few months ago. Would you like the same design for the hilt and quillons? As he said this, Gerant suddenly wondered whether Ray had taken the lost wax castings when he cleared out. *Probably not, knowing Ray. But better to not promise too much.* 'I am certain we kept the drawings, so it should be very straightforward. I will have to measure your reach and see your stance to have it customised to meet your lordship's needs? When would be appropriate for you?'

The two men walked down the broad staircase to the ground floor and towards the back of the mansion. 'Oh, I will be either here in the late morning or down at Scarlett's having my daily practice with Parvo or playing cards. It might be easiest to do any measurements there, in the fencing gallery.'

Gerant realised that there were already lots of things to get ready for. He would have to arrange to get more garnets and tourmalines from Adam Purslip and stain some more stingray leather. Also, to check whether there was any of that braided wire left. He almost bumped into the viscount who had stopped after opening the door to a small room filled with books and piles of paper and parchment. Inside there was a somewhat overweight man with greying hair, a pair of spectacles perched on his nose. He looked up with pursed lips and a look of annoyance, until he recognised the viscount.

'Ah, my lord.'

'Waldron, this is Gerant, who has agreed to work for me fashioning weapons and will be based at the new workshop. This is as we have already discussed. Take him through the arrangements and what is expected.'

The viscount nodded briefly to Gerant and departed. *These sort of details were things that he left to others*, the young smith thought.

Waldron gave Gerant a brief glance, pointed to the one seat on the other side of the desk and reached into a pile of papers, consulting one quickly and scrawling a quick note. 'I look after all the viscount's affairs and would appreciate that you pay attention to how this will work. I will pay all bills to do with running the workshop, provided they can be fully justified. No invoice or receipt, then no payment. You will have to pick up the expense in that case. Second, bills are paid at the end of the month. Most suppliers prefer it that way. Best to check beforehand, mind. Third, for your wage, you will receive ten gold pieces every second week. You will have to come here to get the coin and sign a receipt to say you have received them. You are expected to work normal hours and days. Any time off will have to be put to me in writing and I will consider it.'

Gerant struggled to take in all the details, but they seemed to be reasonable. Clearly, based on the piles of papers and ledgers in the room, Waldron expected everything to be written down, otherwise it did not exist in his world. 'That all appears to be acceptable.'

Waldron nodded, then continued. 'You start tomorrow, and I believe the viscount has already discussed your first piece of work? Good. You will also need this.' He ferreted around in one of the drawers in the desk and pulled out a short chain on which two keys were hung.

Gerant did not recognise it. 'These are?'

'The workshop property has been padlocked to protect the viscount's new acquisition. Also, I have installed a key to the entry of the workshop building. You will need them to get access. Always make sure you lock up when you leave, particularly at the end of a day. I will be coming around every now and again to check that things are as they should be.'

Gerant nodded and took the keys. He decided not to mention to the bursar that anyone could just jump over the padlocked gate or could access the workshop through the open spaces between the wooden posts near the forge, bypassing the locked door to the workshop itself. *Whatever makes the man happy*, he thought, as he left the viscount's mansion. He mused whether Waldron was physically capable of walking that distance to the workshop and then guessed he would take a cart. If he ever came, which Gerant also doubted as well.

Chapter 39
The Fourth Skill

It felt like any other day in many respects, but strange all the same. Gerant left the cottage with a small bag containing some lunch and walked his usual route to the workshop. He arrived at the gateway between the two buildings, behind which the workshop was laid out. It all looked exactly the same, apart from the large chain and padlock closing off the two halves of the gate, along with an official-looking piece of parchment and a wax seal affixed to one of the gateposts. The notice stated that the property and equipment had been confiscated by The Realm and no one was to enter, upon pain of immediate arrest. He glanced around and no one appeared to be watching as he removed the parchment. The bursar had not mentioned the document, but he assumed it was not in force now that the viscount had bought the workshop and was wanting Gerant to start working there again. A quick jiggle with the key and the padlock clicked open. He walked to the closed workshop door and used the second key to open it.

He spent the next ten minutes or so touching all the tools and gear, which had all been moved a little, when the guards would have been searching the workshop. Most importantly, he levered up the flagstones near the privy. The small sack of talium was undisturbed, which was a weight off his mind. It would take a day or so to get everything back to its normal place and to get the forge fired up.

And to visit the various suppliers he used and explain the new arrangements. He was relieved those aspects would not appreciably change, as he was not comfortable having to do all the payments himself. It would be the same system, just that instead of letting Molly know, he would have to take any orders and receipts to Waldron. Having had more time to think, part of the new system would be that he would have to do all the lost wax casting himself. He was pretty confident it would go fine, as he had watched Ray closely over the previous months. He would still use Ray's bench for lost wax work, as all the special tools and materials needed were neatly arranged near there. Obviously, a major difference was the absence of Ray. He walked over to the door of the basic room Ray had lived in. Ray had always been neat and hadn't had many personal belongings. Gerant wondered where he was now. He had never found out from Molly where Ray came from. Perhaps she hadn't even known.

Standing in the doorway, he could see a small sink and some shelves making up a small area for preparing food, a small square table and a chair. There was a bed in the corner with a couple of shelves above and a small chest of drawers. The privy was out the back in the corner near the kiln. That was all — just a few items of furniture and blankets on the bed and a couple of pots and pans near the sink. Not much to show for however long Ray had lived here.

Gerant sighed as he shut the door to the room. He had no plans to move in here and live at the workshop. His arrangement with Mrs Lamming was far too comfortable and he would have felt bad for not being around to help Dierdre out with some of the heavier work. Also, five gold a week said he could absolutely stay where he was. No, he might use this room to boil up a hot drink and use the table to do some of the design work away from the dirt and dust of the forge. He would have to visit Adam Purslip, Morrison Levy and Evelyn Hanson to let them know the new arrangements. It was time to start a list. He might also see if Hamish Wheelwright was around to make sure he could still access the iron ore from down south. He put on his leather apron and started to tidy up and get the forge ready for working again the next morning.

Gerant gave the viscount's sword another quick polish and sheathed it. It had taken him a few days to get back into the swing of smithing, let alone having to work on his own. There were more things to think about, particularly working with lost wax, which had its own set of materials to use and order before they ran out. Previously Ray had looked after that and now it fell to Gerant to make sure he hadn't missed anything. And there wasn't a fellow artisan at the next bench to ask about a step in the technique, or what type of material to order or just chat about the weather.

Luckily, their suppliers had been happy to continue with a valued customer, even if payment came from a different source. Each of them also knew exactly the materials that he and Ray preferred, so there was no change in the quality when Gerant went looking for clay, or gems or charcoal or other things like pieces of leather. He had a hole in his heart with Molly heading back home and he spent long periods thinking about how he could get to see her or at least visit Samphire and go looking for her. He hadn't heard anything since she had left. He needed to be patient – it was only a few weeks. Already it was starting to feel much longer than that. One of the things that hadn't changed was his regular drink with Dirk, which he looked forward to more and more. They often didn't talk much and just quietly sipped ale, watching the other patrons at the Purple Heart. It was a growing bond of friendship that didn't need words. Gerant didn't even know exactly where Dirk lodged. It was enough to know that on the same afternoon every week Dirk would be there ready to share a tankard of ale and sit and chat as the urge took them.

All said, things at the workshop were going well. He had borrowed Urbright's dagger to make sure he was able to match the decorations on the hilt and quillons and also make a suitable sheath that featured the same design of stones and metal wire overlaying the dyed burgundy leather. He had also done a couple of kiln runs to prepare more talium steel bars for the various blades the count had told him had been ordered by his colleagues. He wrapped the two weapons in their sheaths in a square of sackcloth and chained shut the gate onto the street as he left. It was time to make a visit to the viscount. Hopefully he was still at his residence, although he may already be at Scarlett's, given the time of day. Well, it would be a nice walk and he could finish a little early and do some digging at the plot afterwards.

'Ah, Maestro Gerant. You were lucky to find me still here. I was about to go to Scarlett's. Today's luncheon is going to be roast lamb, which is one of my favourites.'

Gerant chose not to make any comment in response. He had already learnt to stick to what he needed to say and resisted the urge that other people seemed to follow of agreeing furiously with a member of the gentry and whatever they said. The one point he had decided to not dispute was the title of maestro that Urbright had settled on using. Gerant was careful not to use it with other people and suspected that the viscount only used it because he was employing a master artisan of the first order.

'My lord, here is your dagger and I have your matching sword.' He laid the bundle on the table and unwrapped the two weapons.

Urbright clapped his hands in delight and went straight for the sword and withdrew it from its scabbard. The slender, steely green-grey of the talium blade was a contrast to the ornately fashioned hilt. The viscount hefted it and moved it back and forth, admiring the edge. 'So light! And deadly, as well.' He stood up and practised some rapid thrusts and swipes. The sword made almost venomous hisses as it rapidly cleaved through the air.

'Ha, and ha and ha!' The viscount danced around Gerant, thrusting and cutting at the seated figure of the smith, stopping a foot or so from impaling him. Gerant froze, not daring to move a muscle.

'Ah, gods. This is fabulous. It's made my day already. Wait until they see it down at Scarlett's. They will be so envious.' Urbright's face was flushed from the sudden exertion and the delight at having a new toy. 'You will have to excuse me. Must rush.' The viscount quickly grasped Gerant's hand in thanks, grabbed the empty sword sheath and the dagger and rapidly left.

'You are welcome, my lord,' replied Gerant, to the now empty room. He sighed to himself. At least he now had plenty of time to go to the plot and do some weeding. And then he might go to the tavern and read over the old parchment again. With the viscount's sword completed, he might think over the last section of the instructions and decide whether he was courageous enough, or silly enough, to see if these incantations would work. The conversation with Sveg several years ago still resonated in his mind.

'I wonder who this smith was. The last couple of lores appear to be more in the arts of magic and wizardry than smithing. The first two lores made some sense to me as a master of smithing, but the third one about the tusk tooth and then these spells to change how a weapon behaves is fantasy!'

He sat in the usual booth of the Purple Heart and laid out the old parchment on the table, being careful not to spill ale on it. Today was not a day when he would expect Dirk, so he wasn't keeping half an eye on the door into the tavern and slowly followed the faded writing carefully.

'This power is a great gift to someone who is given the enchanted blade, the ring or pendant and the secret Word of Power. That is why the Words of Power are the opposite of each other, and mayhap will bring some sort of balance to those who choose to impart these spells and their use.'

He sat back thinking, watching some men sitting on stools at the bar without really paying particular attention to them. *Hmmm.* A way to make a blade even more powerful by being able to fight faster or stronger. On the other hand, to somehow be able to make a sword feel slower or make it more brittle and likely to snap. Gerant couldn't understand how these things could happen and the parchment didn't go into much detail. He could see why Sveg thought this must be fantasy and a figment of someone's imagination. He had heard about witches and wizards and the like but had never met any or was not even sure if they had real magical powers and abilities. When he had brought up the subject once with Sveg, the smith had also not known much. 'Certain people are born with a power to cast spells and make things appear and disappear and the like, but it is all beyond me. I believe that the king has a royal mage who is supposed to be trained in the magical arts, but I have never seen him or experienced anything magic myself. Best to just get on with what you can control yourself, Gerant, and leave that fancy mysterious stuff to others who would like to believe in it.' It was pretty clear from Sveg's comments what he thought of it all.

Thinking more, Gerant wondered if it would be worth finding Griffin and asking him if there was such a royal mage, or even Viscount Urbright might know. The more he thought on that, the more he decided it would be too difficult to explain why he was asking and was half expecting that they would think him a fool who believed children's tales. Perhaps the best thing would be to make an attempt at following the writings in the old parchment and see what happened. The steps involved were fairly easy to follow. He needed a gem of the right sort in a ring or pendant, which he could easily get from Adam Purslip, and then make a paste to smear on the pommel. If it looked like nothing had happened, then he could just give the ring or whatever back to Purslip and wipe off the paste. No one would know any different, apart from himself. He would certainly make sure he read out the words in the workshop with the gate chained shut so he wouldn't be interrupted and have to explain why he was chanting strange lines. That was a quick way to lose any standing he had as an artisan, that was for sure!

Should I try? He mulled this over while he had a sip or two of ale. *Well, why not?* Only his pride would take a hit if it didn't. He would just have to see if he could borrow an old blade from the viscount to test. He read the parchment again and decided on trying one of them. Maybe he would choose Fast. What did he need for that? First, an emerald. Well, not cheap, but he could see if Adam was willing to let Urbright pay a deposit in case he needed to return it, or maybe even Urbright already had a suitable ring or jewel. The anise seeds. He recalled there was a merchant in the market where they went shopping that sold various herbs and spices. That should be easy. The parchment didn't say what other things the paste needed, but he might just make it in water and a little lard and see what happened. He finished his ale, and carefully folding up the parchment, he put it up his sleeve and walked back to the workshop. He would get the things in the morning and then have the bits and pieces ready. It shouldn't take long before he had an answer, and he could fit it around getting the various daggers and swords worked up.

Gerant sat at his bench in the workshop and looked over his preparations. He had written out the strange verse on a scrap piece of paper. Next to it was a sword that Urbright had given him, plus a gold ring with a small emerald set in the crown. The conversation with the viscount earlier had been a little troubling. It had started off well, when Gerant had found Urbright eating a sweet bun and a hot drink in a room with breakfast laid out and sunlight streaming in through the windows.

'Ah, Maestro Gerant. Help yourself to breakfast. No? I have to tell you my new sword is even better than I had hoped. If anything, my swordcraft will be much improved. I gave Parvo a stern workout, let me tell you. Now what can I help you with? Need more commissions? More materials? Just see Waldron.'

Gerant paused a moment. 'Actually, my lord, I have a rather strange request. I am keen to try something I have found in an ancient work on sword smithing, and would like to borrow an old sword of yours to try something out.'

'Absolutely no issue there. You can have one that I don't need now I have this superb example you have crafted. I'll get it in a minute. Was there anything else?'

Yes, my lord, could I borrow an emerald ring or some other jewellery with an emerald in it?' He waited with his breath held.

The viscount had been about to take a sip from his hot drink and stopped, intrigued. 'What a strange request. What do you need it for?'

'It's a little hard to explain. There might be a way to impart additional powers to a blade for a short period. For that I need a few things, including an emerald. It will not be damaged, and I will be able to return it in a day or two. And the sword.'

'You say it will impart even more power. How intriguing. It sounds like some sort of magic.'

'So it would seem, my lord. It may or may not work, but there is little harm in trying.'

'Well, I am sure I have an emerald ring somewhere. I will go looking for it and bring my old blade as well.' Urbright paused, clearly thinking on something that had occurred to him. His face hardened a little. 'A condition is that you only try this new power on my blades and for my use.'

Gerant was more than happy to agree to that.

'And I am reminded that you will be starting to make some blades for my friends. They should be of your usual excellent quality, but perhaps slightly less excellent than mine.'

This was a turn in the conversation that Gerant hadn't expected. It didn't take him long to realise he didn't like what the viscount was hinting about.

The young smith's face took on a serious, almost grim cast. 'My lord, I appreciate your support and patronage in making the best blades I can. I have made you a sword that you have just now praised in its workmanship. To ask me to somehow craft something that is less than my best is to not consider how I am trained to work. And not considering my reputation as an artisan.' He paused. 'Or to consider your reputation. How do you think Viscount Joffrey would feel when he gets his long-awaited pair, and they are not quite as good as what he was led to believe? How will you deal with that, my lord? Instead, Joffrey will thank you profusely for allowing him to obtain such fine weapons. I ask you to think on that, my lord.'

Urbright's face flushed, listening to this upstart tradesman, then as the logic of the explanation took effect, calmed down somewhat.

'Of course, of course, you are quite right. Do perform at your best and we will both gain the rewards. But I do insist this new trick is only to be for me.'

Gerant smiled secretly and gave the viscount a short bow to cover his amusement. 'Of course, my lord, I had no other intention. First we need to see if it works, of course.'

Gerant chuckled to himself as he recalled that earlier conversation. As a backup, he had also gone to the jeweller, Adam Purslip, and the jeweller had a variety of rings that would have been suitable.

'Whenever you need anything like that, Gerant, I am more than happy to either bill for the full cost or borrow for a day, on the understanding that it comes straight back if you don't require it. After all, I know where you work.' He peered over his strong glasses and nodded in agreement as he quietly arranged some of the trays of rings he had been showing Gerant.

Regarding the anise seeds, it had been extremely straightforward. A quick trip to the market had meant going up to the stall with the sign on which was written, 'Nathaniel's finest herbs and spices. The best in The Realm.' He had approached the tall, slim man with black locks and a scar from forehead to chin who looked rather threatening until he spoke in a gentle, lilting voice.

'How can I help you, young sir? You know what you want? Ah, anise. This year's crop is from a delightful grower just this side of Mortensville. How much do you need?'

Gerant had walked away with a small paper sack of seeds, which he guessed was enough to make a handful of paste suitable to coat a sword pommel. He had done a quick grind in the mortar and pestle that Dierdre had in her kitchen at the cottage. Mixing up the ground seeds into a paste with some water and lard took a few moments when he got to the workshop and it was ready. He checked again he had everything he needed – the sword, the scrap of paper with the words written down, the emerald ring and the anise seed paste. He walked out to the gate and closed the halves, looped the chain through and put the padlock on.

Returning to his bench, he read the parchment again. It said you had to wear the gem, so he put the viscount's emerald ring on. They must have a similar finger size, as it fitted snugly. He then smeared on a layer of paste on the pommel, which was a slightly flattened metal casting of a crown. He was not sure how thick it had to be, so he added enough to cover the crown on both sides. *Well, here goes,* he thought, as he picked up the sword and held it in both hands. Feeling a little foolish, he read out the lines he had written in a slow, firm voice, trying to use as serious a tone as he could manage and not stumble over any of the words.

> 'To weave and carve the very air,
> No eyes can follow this deathly dance.
> This blade is now beyond compare,
> It sings like in a lethal trance.'

As he completed the verse, the emerald ring flashed bright green suddenly and the pommel of the sword glowed for a second or two with a greenish tinge before fading again. As he looked at the pommel, he saw that the paste had somehow dried, and he was able to brush all the bits off the sword. Well, something had happened! He looked at the ring on his finger and it looked the same. But it had flashed brightly for a moment. And the pommel had glowed with the same sort of green hue and then returned in moments back to its normal colour. Gerant had thought quite a bit about the next step. Part of the problem was trying to show the words in the verse had done something. All he could think of was to try wielding the sword to get a feel and then say the Word of Power and try again to see if there was a difference. Having never had any training in sword fighting, he just held the blade in his right hand and swiped a few times in the air. Well, this was the viscount's old blade and was well-put together and balanced. The steel was of reasonable quality and under normal circumstances Gerant would have said it was well crafted. With his recent experience and skills in using talium and the paste, he could make a blade far better that was stronger and lighter. The sword certainly swung sweetly, and he was able to pretend to lunge and change direction fairly easily.

Now it was time to see if the verse had done anything or this was all a big waste of time and effort. He held the blade and said clearly, 'Fast.' Almost immediately the viscount's ring on his finger flashed bright again and the pommel of the sword almost throbbed with a green colour before returning to its normal steely hue. Gerant then tried a few swipes and lunges through the air. *Wow!* Somehow the sword had become lighter, and he was able to swing faster and lunge forward more rapidly. It was almost as if the blade knew what he was thinking of doing and was able to anticipate him making a move. A feeling of elation stole over him, and he danced around slashing and prodding the air as he laughed and chuckled to himself.

'It works!' he cried to no one in particular. He could not see any difference in the sword but somehow he was able to wield it better. He continued pirouetting around the workshop striking at imaginary enemies and uttering cries of 'Huh!', 'Take that' and 'Die, you fiend!'

Suddenly the pommel on the sword gave off another throb of green and straight away the blade returned to its previous weight. He could still cut and thrust his imaginary foes, but he had lost that edge in speed and dexterity that he had been able to use just a few seconds ago. Gerant realised how foolish he must have looked – like a little boy with a new toy – and doubled over in laughter. He put the viscount's sword on the workbench, sheathed it, then took off the emerald ring and put it in the small pouch around his neck where he kept his special stamp. According to the parchment, the magic would not work again until tomorrow, so he would go before mid-morning and catch the viscount at home and show him. It would be interesting to see whether it worked for Urbright. At least now Gerant was feeling slightly more confident that this fourth ancient technique might be as useful and valuable as the first three he had tried. So, he packed away the gear and got on with his other tasks for new daggers and swords. First up was to do some clay moulds for new lost wax casting. This would be the first time he had attempted this without Ray's help and guidance. He wasn't particularly worried, but it was always slightly different when you did it all on your own, at least the initial try. He laid out the equipment he would need on Ray's old bench, becoming quickly immersed in carefully carving a new wax template for a dagger hilt and quillons based on a detailed drawing he had made.

'My lord, I have finished with your old blade and have something to show you.' Gerant paused and then continued. 'Do you have somewhere you practice here, or do you always do it at Scarlett's?'

He had come at an hour where he hoped the viscount had not left and was lucky enough to have caught him still at the residence.

'True, I do most of it at Scarlett's, often with Parvo, but there is a small area on the terrace with a dummy set up. Come.'

As they walked downstairs, Urbright unsheathed his old weapon and examined it closely. 'It looks and feels the same.'

'Ah, I will have to explain and then I hope you will like the effect.'

By then they had come to a small courtyard tucked into a corner of the mansion, where there was an old and somewhat bedraggled torso shape made of wood padded with some sort of stuffing material and covered with heavy canvas before being belted and sewn. It was clear the figure had taken years of punishment and had been repaired many times, with bits of stuffing poking out of the canvas in a few places. Gerant had been thinking of the easiest way to explain the new power and had decided to not go too deeply into details, as he really had little idea of how it worked himself.

'My lord, the ancient parchment I have in my possession allows someone to put on a blade an enchantment using a Word of Power. In this case, the word is "Fast", which allows the swordsman the ability to wield the blade with even more speed and dexterity. It is really rather straightforward. You put on this ring of yours, which I borrowed. Then all you have to do is say the word, "Fast", and the sword will magically become easier and lighter to handle. The effect will only happen when you say the Word of Power and will last for a minute or two. The ancient parchment says a short while, so I am not sure how long that is, but best to assume it will not last very long.'

The viscount took all this in with eagerness and was ready to begin straight away.

Gerant interrupted. 'A moment, my lord. Perhaps you can do a few practice moves with the sword first, then say the Word of Power, and then try again to experience if it handles better. Here is your ring again.'

Gerant passed over the emerald ring, which the viscount put on.

'Now, have a practice.'

Urbright followed one of the drills that he had clearly been taught, spinning, cutting and thrusting at the stuffed figure.

'Hmmm. Not a patch on my new blade. It is sufficient, but hardly has the ease, lightness and strength of the one you made for me.'

Gerant flushed with pleasure and nodded.

'Now say the word "Fast". Watch the ring and also the hilt of the sword.'

The viscount readied himself and clearly said 'Fast'. There was a brief bright flash from the ring and the hilt of the sword briefly glowed green.

'Now try the same exercises, My lord.'

Urbright pirouetted, cut and thrust at the dummy, noticeably faster and more deftly. He did not stop but began a more complicated series of feints, thrusts and movements, landing many cuts and blows within a few seconds. He suddenly stopped and looked at Gerant with a look of astonishment and wonder. 'It feels lighter and almost understands what I am wanting to do and where I want to strike. Amazing. Truly amazing.' He performed another longer group of manoeuvres, each time lightly dancing around the stuffed mannequin and planting cuts and stabs into it with greater ease and fluidity. He stopped, panting a little and was examining the sword to try and determine what was different when the hilt glowed green again briefly.

The viscount looked at the young smith with genuine respect and asked in a hushed tone, 'What is this magic?'

Gerant chose his words carefully. 'I don't truly understand it, my lord. Only that when you say the Word of Power, the weapon takes on extra properties of lightness and being able to be wielded easier and with more dexterity. I must find out more about how this magic achieves these effects.' He paused. 'But you need to be mindful that you can only use it once per day, and the magical effects only last for a few minutes.'

The other man was clearly thinking through the possibilities. 'Even for a short time, this would be of enormous benefit. Almost no one could touch me in ability. Even Parvo would struggle, and he is almost the best in The Realm! That said, it would be sensible to know how long the effect lasts. It would be rather unfortunate if you misjudged things, expecting it to still work.' He chucked to himself. 'Hmmm . . . Think what my new sword will be like when it has this magical ability bestowed on it. You can do that now, can't you, Maestro?'

Gerant paused. 'I believe so, my lord. The teachings do not say whether I can use the same ring to bestow the power. Safer to use a new ring. Do you have another emerald ring, my lord?'

'No, but that is easily fixed. I will go to my favourite jeweller straight away and order one. I should have it in a day or two and then how long do you need?'

Gerant had also got caught up in the excitement of the demonstration. 'Only a few hours my lord. I would only need to borrow your new weapon and the ring for a morning and return them soon after. I am quite confident in that.'

The viscount clapped the other man on the back as they walked back into the mansion. 'This deserves a celebratory drink. Parvo and the others will be so jealous and amazed! Don't forget this little secret needs to stay between you and me. We can't have everyone having this little ability, can we?'

Gerant heard this and a small alarm bell rang quietly in his mind. Given what he had seen just now, he chose to ignore it, basking in the warm emotions he felt about a productive and successful morning.

Chapter 40
The Calling Out

He continued to polish Viscount Joffrey's dagger, enjoying the way it glinted in the morning light. The citrine and yellow garnets set into the quillons and around the pommel were a nice contrast to the honed talium steel blade with its subtle grey-green highlights. The matching sword was coming along well, with the blade finished. Gerant had taken Maestro Shagreen's original design and made everything slightly larger for the sword compared with the dagger, yet maintaining the decorative features. The lost wax castings were sitting on Ray's old bench waiting for a final sand and polish before the decorative stones were added. Then he had to cut and fit the dyed sharkskin for the grip and use the decorative wire to finish everything off.

The sword for the count of Ravenswood was also progressing. Luckily for Gerant, he had already been given the design by Maestro Shagreen in the week before his ill-fated visit to the palace to plead with the royal chancellor. Gerant still did not know for sure what had happened. There had been hints here and there from the viscount in unguarded moments, but nothing definite. Dirk also had not heard anything, meaning that Shagreen was still at large and had not been caught. *Good luck to him,* thought Gerant.

And now this new project. The viscount had summoned Gerant just the other day to say how fabulous his new sword had behaved when the Word of Power had been cast on it.

'I am unstoppable now. I can dance around and strike wherever I wish! Even Parvo has said my swordcraft is far improved and he has been teaching me some new, complex thrusts and parries that he only shows to the very best of his students.'

Gerant had been pleased the incantation on the blade had worked and just nodded in feigned admiration. Then Urbright had mentioned that a sister of his had seen the cast-iron screen at the earl of Sherrington's chateau. It emerged that the countess of Bannerfield had been inspired and wanted something made of cast iron by the same craftsman.

'Something in the garden. I wasn't paying too much attention. Mitzi can rabbit on so much. But you need to go to see her. I said you would. The Bannerfields are in the last place back towards the fountain.'

The next morning Gerant had put on his best doublet and presented himself yet again at the gatehouse leading to The Park. By now, the guards were thoroughly used to him coming and going and just waved him through. He approached the first chateau in the group of large houses near Viscount Urbright's residence and walked up to the imposing two-storey sandstone building. After explaining the purpose of his visit, Gerant was shown into a large sunny room at the back of the house and told to wait. Within a few minutes, the door opened and a slender woman in her thirties walked in, her dark hair framing her face and falling to her shoulders. She had the brown eyes and copper-hued skin of the family and looked at her visitor with undisguised interest and pleasure. Her purple silken dress flowed from her hips and the tight fit around the bodice area accentuated her feminine curves.

'Ah, my brother's fabulous artisan. You must be Maestro Gerant. I am the Countess of Bannerfield, but everyone just calls me Mitzi.'

Gerant was struck by the beauty and feminine charm of the visage in front of him.

'Thank you, my lady.'

There was a pause. 'No, just call me Mitzi.'

Another pause. '. . . Mitzi.'

'See, that wasn't so hard, was it?' Mitzi smiled and grabbed Gerant's hand. 'Come. I want to show you what I am thinking about. I am sure Ferdinand wasn't listening when I described it to him.' From that, Gerant assumed she was referring to her brother. He filed that little nugget away and was almost dragged by the countess through an outside door into the carefully laid-out and tended garden.

'Tahlia showed me the screen you made, and I thought it was gorgeous. Then when I asked Manfred about it, he mentioned you.'

Gerant was feeling quite uneasy with the way that the countess was talking so familiarly to him. It was not how he had been led to expect when talking with the upper class. That aside, he was also struggling a little with who she was meaning.

'Tahlia?' he enquired.

'Oh, you've met her. The Countess Sherrington.'

'And Manfred?' Gerant couldn't remember if he had ever heard the name of the chief steward at the chateau.

'Oh, how funny.' Mitzi clapped in delight at the confused look on Gerant's face. 'Of course, you would know him as the Earl of Sherrington. He's family, so I always just call him Manfred.'

Gerant nodded politely as his mouth made a silent 'O'. He also filed away this other nugget of information to ponder at another time.

'Here we are.' They had reached a small section of carefully manicured grass with a hedge along two sides and a drooping willow tree in one corner. Gerant looked back from where they had come and the mansion was about fifty yards away, with parts of the garden intervening. In the centre of the lawn space was a small round garden bed with some sort of flowers blooming.

'I want to get rid of this bed and put a round gazebo there, where we can have little picnics out in the garden. I was thinking something made of that metal stuff with some garden seats inside. And a little roof on top in case it rains.' The countess paused. 'You know what a gazebo is, don't you?'

Gerant thought he may as well be honest. 'Ah, I am not familiar with them. Perhaps you could describe what you are wanting while I take some measurements.' He was not ready to call the countess by her first name just yet. He opened the leather satchel he had brought and got out a pencil, a length of tape and some pieces of paper.

He then spent the next half an hour or so following the countess of Bannerfield around the outside of the garden bed while she described with lots of hand waving and gestures what she had envisioned in her mind. A series of questions from Gerant clarified a number of things and he now knew what was required. He looked at his sketch and could see that, based on their conversation, the garden bed would be covered over with stone pavers to provide a solid base. He had drawn an open-sided structure with six cast-iron pillars rising about fifteen feet, with sections of open screen up to waist height joining the pillars. More screen pieces were drawn at a height of about ten feet, before a solid roof of iron sheet closed over the top of the structure. He had also drawn a couple of cast-iron benches with wooden slats inside the gazebo. He showed his rough sketch to the countess, who pored over it with her head almost touching that of the young artisan.

'Oh this is perfect. I can see it in my mind already.'

Gerant hurriedly pulled back slightly and put the sketch into his satchel, all the time keeping a half-smile fixed on his face. 'Of course, this is only a quick attempt so I have some measurements and can go back to the workshop and draw up some more detailed plans for you to approve.' He thought through some other aspects to consider. 'I will also think on a design for the sections of cast-iron screen. The earl's screen featured grape vines, but I wondered about something still with a plant theme but different.' He thought quickly of what might work. 'Perhaps roses.'

Mitzi clapped her hands with delight. 'Oh, that would be perfect! I am so happy about this. When will the drawings be ready?'

A few moments of thought and then another matter occurred to him. 'Perhaps in a couple of weeks, my lady. And because this is not something I am doing for the viscount, we will need to talk about price.'

'Oh, don't worry about that. Maybe you can just tell me when you have the drawings done. I can't wait for them to be ready. Two weeks? That will be perfect!'

As they walked back to the mansion, with the countess chattering delightedly about the design, Gerant shook his head in wonder. What an interesting experience! This would give him something else to work on in the coming month or two, along with the daggers and swords. It would also mean more things to plan for. He could see he would be very busy for quite some time yet. He nodded occasionally to the countess and murmured an appropriate reply as he continued to think ahead as they headed back into the house.

Clunk! Gerant and Dirk toasted each other with their tankards of ale and each took a satisfying swallow. Gerant had brought along some drawings he had been working on while he waited for Dirk to arrive. He had made some good progress on changing the count of Ravenswood's hilt and the quillons so they were a little less decorated and had smoother curved lines. He had also been working on the design for a climbing rose vine to use for the gazebo project.

'Looks like you are making lots of things,' gestured Dirk at the drawings.

'Yes, I've got a bit on. Most of it for Viscount Urbright's friends but a large project for his sister, the countess of Bannerfield.'

'Haven't seen her, but have heard plenty of things about her and about the count.'

Gerant decided not to ask.

'But I do need to tell you about what I heard about Urbright's latest adventure. It's all over The Park and many of the lads are talking about it. Things got very heated at Scarlett's the other day, by all reports.'

'Oh, really?' Gerant pretended to be interested and was really thinking about the next things he needed to do at the workshop. But he paid attention when he started to take in what Dirk was saying quietly against the bubbling chatter of other conversations in the Purple Heart.

'We only heard about it after, so none of us were there. You know about Scarlett's and they have the sword practice salon and then a big room where people can gamble and play cards? Well, apparently Urbright was playing his usual session of cards and things were not going well for him. One fellow was doing really well, and the others were also muttering. This fellow scooped the pot again and Urbright must have had enough and accused this fellow of cheating. Not surprisingly, the man was offended and

Urbright refused to apologise. So the only thing left was to cross swords about it and settle the matter that way.'

Dirk stopped for a swallow of ale before he continued. 'They went to the fencing salon later that day and had it out. All official-like with seconds and a doctor handy and people there to witness it all. More like a crowd of interested onlookers, methinks. Anyway, this fellow is a handy swordfighter and things are pretty even, but all of a sudden Urbright starts fighting really fast and dangerous-like. He caught the other fellow in the chest with his blade and he collapsed and that was the end of the fight. Apparently, the doctor rushed forward to try to stop the bleeding and they took him away. He's not doing well, from what we hear. I thought you might want to hear about it because you are doing that stuff for Urbright.'

Gerant's mind reeled as he took in the details of what Dirk had related. The duel had been even and then suddenly the viscount had started winning and fighting much better. And then his opponent had been stabbed and now was in a serious way. He shuddered as he thought what the outcome of the fight meant. *The Word of Power! It had to be!* He gulped down some ale as his mind tried to wrestle with what must have happened. This was terrible. He knew the viscount was very handy in a fight, but he had not ever considered that one of his swords would be used to fight unfairly. He reached a decision, his eyes blazing.

'Dirk, I need you to do me a favour. Would you be able to find out ahead of time if there is another duel involving the viscount?'

Dirk had never seen his friend with such an impassioned and almost angry look on his face. He was normally so quiet and thoughtful. 'Uh, sure, Gerant. My sergeant normally hears about these things well in advance, particularly since Scarlett's sometimes get us to come and keep the peace at these sorts of events. Why do you need to be there?'

'It's too complicated to explain. It's just that Viscount Urbright is using one of my blades. I'll drop whatever I'm doing and get there as soon as you tell me. Come to the workshop if you find out anything.'

'Steady, steady, my man. Don't get too worked up. That might be the only duel he's in. They don't happen very often, and even less so at Scarlett's.'

Gerant took another sip of ale. 'If there is anything I've learnt, this sounds like the first but won't be the last.' He forced himself to stop thinking about what must have happened and deliberately changed the topic of conversation. 'So, what other news was there from your shift or up at The Park?'

It was getting on for dusk at Scarlett's, with the lanterns lit and the curtains pulled to. The regulars had been ensconced at cards for most of the afternoon. Shickleham was starting to feel a bit peckish and thought after another few hands they could break for an early dinner and then push on afterwards. He looked at his cards again and pushed forward another two gold tokens. 'And two.'

Urbright didn't need to look. 'Fold.'

Cordner spoke. 'And another two.'

Wallington hummed and hawed a little, looking at his cards and staring at the ceiling. 'Fold.'

Shickleham pushed forward another two tokens. 'I'll go another two.'

Cordner waited a few moments, seemingly thinking, and made his decision. 'Ballocks. I'll go three.'

Cordner showed his cards and then Shickleham. 'Pair of Jacks.'

'Ah, my pair of Queens beats that.'

'Dammit!' muttered Cordner as Shickleham raked the chips towards him.

Urbright looked at the small pile of chips in front of him. He had experienced a shocking run this afternoon, with a series of terrible hands that he had folded on. When he been dealt a half-decent one and put down a decent wager, one of the others had a better hand. Even the couple of times he had tried to bluff it out, he had come unstuck. Oh well, his luck might turn very soon. He looked around for one of the uniformed Scarlett's staff and raised his finger. The older man with balding grey hair in a green-and-gold tunic who had been bringing drinks and snacks on occasion came over and leant down discretely behind the viscount.

'How can I help you, my lord?'

'Can you get me another hundred gold in chips, my good fellow? I am about to run out.'

'Of course, my lord. I will just check with the manager.' The staff member quietly withdrew and went to look for his superior.

A few minutes later, the manager appeared. Hislop was wearing his more-adorned uniform in the Scarlett green and gold, with his carefully groomed brown hair and professional smile as always affixed to his face.

'Ah, gentlemen, I hope your game is going well for you. A reminder that we will have dinner available in the dining room within the next half hour or so. Please reserve your place.' He bent down to speak quietly with Viscount Urbright. 'A word in private if you don't mind, my lord.' He gestured to a corner. 'Gentlemen, perhaps you could have a drink break while I chat with the viscount. It should only take a minute.'

The manager and Urbright walked over to an area away from the tables, where they could talk a little more discretely.

'My lord, Vincent has told me you are wanting another hundred gold's worth of chips on credit.'

Urbright was looked dismissively at the manager. 'What of it?'

'Well, you see, we have a house rule that we lend only one hundred gold in a single day. You have, of course, already received a hundred but an hour or so ago. So unfortunately, we won't be able to extend your credit.' Hislop could see the rapidly darkening features of the viscount and rushed on in his most soothing voice possible. 'This is in no way a reflection of your standing in the community and that you are good for the advance. It's just a long-standing rule that was in place years before I started here and one I cannot waiver. I'm sure you understand, my lord.'

A very angry client almost hissed at the manager. 'No, I don't understand at all, Hislop. I have been coming here for a long time and this has never happened. Ever. You know I will have it tomorrow, so what is the problem?'

'I am really sorry, my lord. But these are the house rules. I can only suggest that you finish up for today and come and have a complimentary dinner in the dining room at Scarlett's expense.' The manager paused in thought. 'I am sure your luck will be so much better tomorrow, if I am any judge.'

The viscount was fuming, his hands gripping into fists and then opening randomly as he couldn't believe what this jumped-up useless servant was saying.

'Hmmph. We'll see about that.' And Urbright stalked back to the table and sat down in his chair. He rapidly rifled through the three or four gold chips he had left and reached a decision. The others had been watching with interest the byplay between the two, although they had not been able to hear any of the talk. They watched Urbright, who had come back in a foul mood.

'Gentlemen, as you know my luck has been dreadful tonight and now Scarlett's are refusing to allow me to keep playing. Would you be able to advance me a hundred chips, say, and I'll make good tomorrow? You know I am good for it, just that I don't normally carry that much coin on me.' Urbright looked at his playing partners, totally expecting them to agree and that he could continue playing.

Count Thorburn was the first to respond. 'Of course, Urbright, could happen to anybody. Don't carry that much coin on me either.'

Wallington and Shickleham also followed suit and muttered agreement. Urbright looked at Cordner, who was playing with the piles of chips in front of his place, a growing frown on his face.

'Actually, Urbright, I don't agree. You either have the coin on you or you have to bail out and stop playing. All of us have to play by those rules, so why should you be any different?' Cordner was clearly wanting to get something off his chest and continued in a measured and quite aggressive manner. 'I am a successful businessman and have earnt my position by working very hard and appreciate the value of the coin I have earned. I know how to manage it and don't spend beyond my means and make sure I stop if I don't have the coin on me.' Cordner jiggled his pockets so that there was a clink of coin to make his point. 'I am a little tired of people like yourself who have never had to earn their keep and just expect to be given their privileges and get everything on credit.' A pause. 'So the answer is no, as far as I am concerned.'

The viscount had listened to Cordner expound his views in silence, with a look that reminded the others of a viper coiled and about to strike.

'That is a rather unfortunate view that you have put, Cordner. It certainly sounds to me that you are doubting my word and that I have problems with coming up with the coin. I have clearly said I will have it for you tomorrow and you have chosen not to believe me. I am afraid you have stained my character with what you have said and implied and I will have to ask for satisfaction.'

Urbright leant back with a knowing smile on his face. Cordner had gone pale. He realised what Urbright had said and then a furious look took over.

'By the gods, I am not going to back down on this. You lot are all the same. Name it. Your choice.'

The viscount almost appeared apologetic as he stated the terms. 'It will have to be a duel by swords. Let's have it in the salon here. Perhaps two hours after noon the day after tomorrow. I presume you know how to fight?'

Cordner responded with lips held tight. 'Of course. I'll be there. I will let you know who my second will be. I am sure Scarlett's can organise the rest.'

'Mine will be Count Permilway. We will see you there. I'm sure there will be plenty of others who want to watch. I must be off now. My dinner awaits.'

Urbright stood up and bowed to the others before moving off towards the dining room. Stunned silence remained at the table. Shickleham, Wallington and Thorburn had totally forgotten the cards. Cordner was quietly playing with his chips as he tried to digest what had just happened, and the peril he had just landed himself into.

Gerant admired the swirling pattern on the talium steel after he had applied and heated it on the forge with the paste made according to the old parchment. This was Viscount Joffrey's blade. He was getting more adept at applying it so he ended up with the smooth wave pattern he had settled on. As he slowly angled the blade to catch the morning light, he heard the latch on the gate to the street click. He put the blade down on his workbench near the forge and looked out to see who had come to call. The tall young man with blond hair and beard in his guard uniform approached through the open workshop door. It was Dirk.

Gerant smiled in delight. 'What a nice surprise! I normally only see you at the Purple Heart. Glad you found the workshop.'

Dirk grinned and looked around with interest. 'Can't stay. Need to get back before my sergeant misses me. You wanted to know if I found out about another duel. Well, I have. Sergeant told me just now.' He proceeded to relate to Gerant about another sword fight involving Viscount Urbright the next day at Scarlett's. 'Don't know much more than that. Two hours after noon. I imagine there might be a bit of a crowd come along to watch. You going?'

Gerant thought quickly and then nodded. 'I need to see what happens. Thanks, Dirk. I really appreciate you taking the time to come and tell me. Do you know who the opponent is?'

Dirk's brow furrowed as he thought. 'Not really. Some merchant fellow by the name of Cordner. Quite well off, apparently. Was playing cards with the viscount and there was a disagreement about lending money. One thing led to another, and the viscount called him out.'

'Hmmm,' was all Gerant could think to say. This was going down the same path as the other duel. That was why he wanted to go. He was sure the Urbright was gaining an extra advantage by using the "Fast" Word of Power. All the same, he would see for himself. He would be needing to watch out for the warning signs. *No need to tell Dirk about the real reason,* he thought.

'Thanks, Dirk. Let's still do our regular ale in a couple of days.'

'Right oh. Best that I be getting back. See you in a bit.' The young guard gave a quick wave and a smile and headed back out to the street.

Gerant thought about tomorrow. He knew where Scarlett's was after going to measure his patron there for his new weapon. There shouldn't be an issue with him turning up and wanting to watch. He would make up some excuse about being there to keep a check of the viscount's sword, which was partly true anyway. All the same, he might try and keep in the background so he wouldn't be recognised. He would have to wear his cloak with the hood pulled over his face. Hopefully that outfit wouldn't look too out of place. He mused on how the fight would go as he continued to work on the new sword for Joffrey.

Chapter 41
The Word of Power

He looked about one more time and decided everything was looking ready and they could commence in a few minutes. Enderby took his role as adjudicator and master of ceremonies very seriously. This was the second of these duels held at Scarlett's that he had officiated in recent weeks. They did not happen at all for many months and then there was a spate of the things one after another. *Maybe it was the weather,* he thought. He was glad that he had his main work at the tailoring shop to keep him in coin. These little events that Scarlett's got him in to oversee were a nice little addition to his purse. He checked his outfit and grooming again very quickly. He had shaved and trimmed his moustache carefully when he got up and his black pants with a burnt-orange long-sleeved shirt and black waistcoat were freshly washed and sitting well. He glanced around the fencing salon at Scarlett's once more and ticked off the details. The floor had been carefully cleaned and polished, a rope circle where the duel would take place laid out, with the spectators and onlookers clustered around the exterior of the circle. It looked like there were about thirty or so people who had come to watch from various groups – clear supporters of either duellist, regulars of Scarlett's and others who had heard of the duel. A variety of people really, mostly men and a couple of women, dressed in various outfits – doublets, working clothes, even that young man in a brown cloak with the hood pulled over his face; the women in dresses and carefully groomed as if going to an important function. The room was well lit from the wall of windows lining one side of the salon and the multiple lamps hanging down from the lofty ceiling. It all looked good. He went up to Doctor Aarons to check he was ready. The doctor was going through his bag of dressings, bandages and instruments one last time.

'All prepared, Doctor?'

The older man who nodded confidently was wearing a doublet and trousers that were a little worn and had seen better days. 'Of course, Enderby. I will be ready for whatever happens. If there are any straightforward injuries, I should be able to patch them up. More than that, we'll have to get them to the infirmary as soon as we can. Whatever the outcome, I'll deal with it.'

The adjudicator nodded and then called over the two seconds for the duel. 'Permilway, your man's ready?' A nod. 'Hamilton?'

'Yes, he's as ready as he'll ever be.'

'Good. I will just go through the formalities here and then I will announce the duel to the onlookers. You have both discussed the chance of a reconciliation and that the accusation can be withdrawn and an apology given?' He looked at both seconds. 'I am really only asking for form's sake.' Both seconds muttered that there had been no backing down by either party.

'So, to business. I have inspected both weapons and they are in order. Once I have announced the duel, I will call both opponents into the ring. After I have asked them to be on guard and I have left the fighting area, the duel can begin. Of course, the fight is to continue until one or other of the opponents is so injured that they cannot continue. Or one of them yields. Doctor Aarons is here if either of them is injured badly and he will do what he can. If it's just a flesh wound, they are expected to continue. Is all that clear, gentlemen?' He paused as both Permilway and Hamilton nodded. 'Then I wish both your principals the best of luck and the one with the favour of the gods and in the right will be successful. Please go back to them and have them be ready when I call them forward.'

Alexander Enderby checked once again that everything looked as it should and strode into the centre of the rope ring. He clapped his hands, looking around at the various onlookers lining the open area of flooring before he spoke out in his best performing voice.

'Good afternoon, gentlemen. And ladies.' He bowed discretely to the two women present in the crowd. 'We are here to bear witness to a serious disagreement between my Lord Viscount Urbright on the one hand and that of Master Samuel Cordner on the other. I have gone through all the preparations with the gentlemen's seconds and both principals are ready. Also I have confirmed that there have been no last minute changes of mind and an apology will suffice.' Enderby paused dramatically so that all watching got drawn into the theatre and the significance of what he had just said. He looked around the salon catching the excitement building, then continued. 'This will be a duel by swords to decide which of these two gentlemen are favoured by the gods. It will continue until one or the other is not able to proceed: I will leave you to understand what that means. Before we begin, I need to tell you of a few things.' He paused and drew breath.

'First, I am Alexander Enderby. I will be the adjudicator for this duel and here to make sure it is conducted with the highest standards so there is no doubt it was held with proper accord and levity. Second, the opponents can use all the space enclosed within the ring of rope laid upon the floor of this salon. Please make sure you keep well back to allow them to fight without impediment. And third, please be quiet and stay still. Both Urbright and Cordner will need their full wits to acquit themselves well without any distractions. So no cheering, talking or other noises, moving about or making sudden gestures. The various guards stationed around the salon are here to make sure of this. Well, we will commence very soon, so please find your places and be ready.'

Enderby walked over to each of the two parties standing apart from each other and spoke to each in turn. 'Seconds, give your charges any last-minute advice or instructions and then I will call the opponents over to the circle. After a brief announcement, we will commence.'

The onlookers had been finding a suitable place around the ring and some were quietly conversing with their neighbours. He walked to the centre of the circle and clapped his hands again to draw attention. Everyone looked expectantly at him.

'Can the two opponents come forward and stand at opposite sides of me, please.'

Urbright and Cordner approached the ring, careful to avoid looking at each other and making sure they did not cross paths. The viscount was dressed in dark, well-fitted pants tucked into soft suede half boots and a white, ruffled shirt, carefully tailored to conform to his tall, slimmish build. He had a lilac sash tied to his waist as a splash of colour, and his dark curls were carefully groomed. He had a number of rings on either hand, and a golden chain was around his neck. He gazed around at the crowd and seemed secretly amused at something. Cordner's grey, shoulder-length locks were tied with a leather thong at the back. He also had dark pants and a white shirt, in his case unadorned. He was quite stocky and of medium height and tending to a little weight, contrasting to that of his opponent's more athletic build. He watched Enderby with a particular focus – a small frown on his features.

'Are you ready to commence?' A small nod from each opponent. 'Then, I will shortly retire from the ring. I will ask you to salute your opponent, to then take guard, and then you may commence. Is that clear?' Again, there was a small nod from both men. Urbright looked almost bored with the proceedings whereas Cordner maintained his intense expression directed at the adjudicator.

Enderby moved to the outside of the rope circle where a place had been kept for him, next to Doctor Aarons and the two seconds close by. 'All right, gentlemen. Salute.' This was almost the first time both men had looked directly at each other. They both made an elegant bow, with their swords extended out to the side. 'On guard.' Both took up the traditionally favoured stance, across the circle from each other. 'And begin!'

What was most interesting to the onlookers was the attitude of 'If I must' displayed by both opponents when the adjudicator had directed them to salute each other. Urbright had executed the bow with clearly displayed pretence and lack of feeling. Cordner had bowed appropriately but one got the sense he had only recently practised the move and it was not second nature to him. Both duellists adopted the position with their swords held out in front of them at an upwards angle, their knees carefully bent and their other arm bent up behind them to provide balance. Nothing happened for a few moments and then Urbright almost languidly shuffled forward towards his opponent, until their sword tips were around a foot apart. Cordner watched all this carefully, mindful of a sudden attack or shifting of posture. Each of them carefully held their swords pointed towards the other, maintaining their defensive posture while the blade points circled around each other distractingly and without clear purpose.

After a few moments of feeling each other out, Cordner suddenly stepped back and stretched his arms a little and shook his head a few times, loosening up, while carefully watching his opponent. Then he took a step forward again and re-engaged. This time, after a few blade circles, Urbright suddenly stepped forward, beat on Cordner's blade and feinted to the right. Cordner had been watching intently, his eyes widened as he saw the possible blow come in and reacted swiftly for such a well-built man. He parried the feint, disengaged and remained on guard. The two opponents slowly circled each other, grunting and hissing as they searched for openings, occasionally feinting and with a ringing sound of the blades striking each other with little effect. To the onlookers, it was clear that both men were still feeling each other out and had yet to attempt a serious blow. Cordner took a deep breath, tensed slightly and pushed forward, swinging his blade to the left of Urbright's chest, which was successfully parried. Then a swing to the right side, also parried. The older man immediately swung at Urbright's head, which caused the viscount to shift his head instinctively to the right as he again parried the blade with a slick metallic sound. This time Cordner put a bit of strength into the thrust, which was met with Urbright's blade, sliding down towards the hilt. With a flick of his wrist, Urbright disengaged before stepping back half a pace and circling around to the right. Cordner hissed a little in frustration that none of his blows had got close to getting through. Urbright had a half-smile on his lips as if the whole contest was a little beneath him, but his brown eyes were very focused and intense as he watched for openings and tried to out-think his opponent. The two men engaged in a swift dalliance with the blades clashing and rapid changes in wrist position, further feeling each other out. Then without warning, Urbright suddenly lunged at Cordner's neck. As soon as Urbright had started to move, the older man had begun to step back quickly. Cordner was able to parry and then riposte with a quick lunge to the chest. But Urbright had anticipated the move and was able to parry Cordner's lunge successfully with a short flick on the end that caught the sleeve of Cordner's shirt and made a small rip. Instantly, Cordner jumped away and checked he had not been cut, then moved to the right with a growing frown on his features.

The two men continued to circle, with Cordner hissing with a quick exhalation of breath as he cut to Urbright's chest and then the head again. Both were parried and then Urbright feinted with a cut to the chest, which Cordner reacted to without their blades touching. After a short pause with both men in the defensive position, Cordner tried to lead with a horizontal cut to the waist which he changed mid-swing to a lunge. As before, Urbright had anticipated the move and took a half-step back while deflecting the incoming blade with a strong parry. Those experienced onlookers had already decided that the two men were somewhat matched, but Urbright might have a slight advantage in speed and attacks. It was probably only the cloaked and hooded figure standing behind the first ring of spectators who noticed Urbright quietly speak a single word and saw a brief greenish flash from a ring on his left hand.

It appeared that Urbright had had enough and started to go on the offensive. He tried various feints at Cordner that were increasingly rapid and vicious. Cordner managed to just position for a parry each time. Oddly, he seemed to have hardened his resolve and he attacked in a series of short swings and cuts at Urbright's chest, hips and neck. The crisp clang of the blades rang out as the viscount almost languidly blocked each of Cordner's thrusts and cuts. Then Urbright's face changed to one of intent as he riposted after the last parry blocking his opponent's blade and thrust forward at Cordner's left shoulder blade. The onlookers gasped in unison as the older man was concentrating on getting his blows through and had not anticipated a counter. But it was a feint! Urbright stopped short of following through his thrust and disengaged briefly and started circling his opponent to the left, his sword gently weaving in the air as he maintained his guarded stance.

Cordner was breathing heavily after his series of attacks. He became more resolved as he realised Urbright might have started to play with him a little. This became even more evident as Urbright changed his stance to give his opponent more of a look at his chest. Cordner did not need any more invitation and stepped forward with a grim and determined cast to his features. His opponent's right side looked less-well guarded and Urbright was favouring his left-hand side. Perhaps he was starting to feel the effects of the duel or was cramping up a little. The older man stepped forward rapidly and cut directly at Urbright's neck, which had become more exposed in the circling. Urbright reacted with horror on his face and parried just in time. This heartened Cordner and he immediately stayed on the offensive and made a strong round cut towards Ubright's waist. The taller man had been expecting the move and his face took on a look of triumph and intense concentration. He ducked under the round cut of Cordner's blade, his left hand reaching to the ground to steady his sudden drop in position. Cordner's swing met only air and he followed through, surprise and horror starting to register on his face as he fought to maintain balance. With incredible speed and agility, Urbright rose up, the point of his blade reaching up through Cordner's swing and out to Cordner's unprotected chest. Almost in slow motion, the razor-sharp point entered the ribcage of his opponent and tore into the lungs and other vital organs before emerging in a bloody eruption out of Cordner's back, just below the left shoulder. Urbright's upthrust smoothly changed to a rapid disengage and with a horrible grinding and sucking sound his blade withdrew from Cordner's chest. He swiftly stepped back a pace and came on guard, intently watching his opponent.

Samuel Cordner had managed to keep his balance after his last missed strike but had had no chance to defend himself from the sudden lunge from his opponent which had come from a completely unexpected direction. He stood slightly swaying, his blade still held in his right hand, a look of shock on his face. Blood suddenly erupted from his mouth and pulsed from his lips as they soundlessly mouthed words. His eyes became unfocused and he slowly, almost gently, bent over and then collapsed onto the ground. Those watching suddenly released their breath and there was a collective eruption of sound – shouts, roars, screams and other cries. Viscount

Urbright slowly raised his blade in front of his face in salute, a smug look of satisfaction on his features, before he turned his back and pushed his way through the circle of onlookers.

Doctor Aarons rushed forward to the slumped figure on the ground and eased Cordner onto his back. He spoke quietly to the man on the ground and grasped his jaw, turning the man's face this way and that and pulling open the eyelids. It took but a moment for him to make his judgement and his gaze reached out grimly towards where Enderby was standing. Aarons shook his head. The adjudicator didn't need any foresight to understand the gesture. The doctor wiped some of the blood off the dead man's lips and chin with a cloth he took from his bag and gently closed the man's eyelids.

Chapter 42
The Final Duel

As Gerant walked in The Park getting closer to the Urbright mansion, he mulled over what he had witnessed the afternoon before and what he had decided to do. *It's not too late to turn around and pretend nothing happened,* he thought to himself. *I could just ignore things and keep on making blades and never use the Words of Power again on a sword. No, Gerant,* he thought, *what Urbright was doing was wrong and if he had known in time, then that Cordner fellow may not have died.* So that was why he was going to the mansion and doing what he could. There was no possibility that he could convince the viscount to not use the Word of Power, or go back to using his old blade. No, he had spent most of the night awake thinking through some possibilities and this was the only one that he believed might work. It was fraught with danger and risk, and he would have to go through a pretence to achieve his aim. *So be it,* he thought, *no backing away now.*

'Ah, Maestro. How wonderful to see you! You heard about my achievements? Your blade is performing so well. All my friends are so envious. I am a handy swordsman, regardless, of course.'

Gerant blushed and muttered, 'I did hear something, my lord, but I tend to keep myself busy in the workshop.'

'Well, never mind.' A pause while the viscount languidly reached for a pastry on a silver platter and took a sip of drink. 'If you are not here to congratulate me, to what do I owe this visit?'

'Ah, my lord, I have been working on Viscount Joffrey's pieces and particularly the hilt and quillons.'

'Very good, very good. I am sure he will be pleased.' Urbright raised his eyebrows, waiting for the smith to get to the point.

'I have now discovered a better way of affixing the jewels to the sword so there is no chance they can come out if the sword is dropped or takes a pummelling. I used it on Joffrey's blade and am very satisfied.' Gerant marshalled his thoughts and then explained. 'Which leads me to wonder whether I could use the same technique on your blade, my lord. It would take hardly any time to check yours and make the adjustments. A matter of a few hours. Would that be possible, my lord?' Gerant held his breath, watching the viscount's reaction.

Urbright toyed with another of the pastries on the tray before he replied. 'It would have to be only for a couple of hours, no more. I have a practice bout with Parvo most days and who knows what else will come up. I am really getting quite attached to the blade you made me, Maestro. I almost go to bed with it, you know.'

'Of course, my lord, I totally understand. I will be as quick as I can. Would tomorrow suit?'

'Well, my session with Parvo is in the afternoon, so perhaps after that. Come to Scarlett's in the late afternoon and we will have finished. I have a game of cards organised for afterwards. Come and find me there. You'll have it back to me the next morning, mind.'

Gerant nodded his thanks. 'I'll be there, my lord. In the late afternoon. My thanks.'

Urbright signalled his agreement with a lazy wave of his hand and selected another pastry. He watched the young smith walk out through the salon door and gently close it.

He gave one final rub of Viscount Joffrey's sword and held it up to the light admiring the subtle wave-like patterns on the talium steel, before placing it in its sheath next to the matching dagger. Gerant guessed that would be an interesting task for tomorrow. Delivering the finished weapons to the client was something he was now getting used to, particularly the bits where they were clearly impressed and delighted with the completed blades. The only time he had met the man was when he had done a quick measurement check of Joffrey's stance and arm reach, done rather hurriedly at Scarlett's. The viscount was about to start a card game and was quite jittery about the whole process and wanting it to be over. Gerant had quickly decided that the man in front of him with watery eyes, well-developed belly and wobbling chins was no swordsman and more comfortable gorging at the dining table or playing cards with his crony friends. The matching dagger and sword would be merely worn as a status symbol and probably never unsheathed in anger or in the practice gallery. Oh well, Gerant had thought, as he had quickly measured Viscount Joffrey's arm span and height of his sword hand when on guard. There was some arrangement between the two viscounts about payment and Gerant was only required to provide the blades as part of his employ with Urbright. When he had approached Waldron, the bursar, to collect his fortnightly payment, the man had been deliberately vague.

'I have the details here somewhere.' Waldron had pretended to look in various piles of papers on his desk. 'Ask me another time when I am less busy.'

Gerant knew that Waldron would know exactly where the piece of paper with the details would be on his desk and was not willing to discuss the matter further. That was alright, Gerant surmised. He was very happy with the quality of the work he had put into it. He would have to find out where Viscount Joffrey lived up in The Park. Or maybe he was one of the growing number of well-off gentry who were living in large houses lining the main streets of the Argent Quarter. Dirk might know, but he was now well known by sight at the gatehouse leading to The Park and the guards there would be happy to oblige with the information.

Just then, he heard the gate at the street front click shut. He wondered who it could be. He had shared an ale with Dirk yesterday and so it was unlikely to be him. Having just been thinking of Waldron, perhaps it was the long-promised visit of the bursar to check on Viscount Urbright's investment in the workshop. He almost fell off his stool at the workbench when through the workshop door emerged Mitzi, the Countess of Bannerfield. The strikingly featured woman was dressed in a black travelling cloak underneath which a flowing green skirt peeked, with matching black boots and leather gloves. On her head was perched a small hunting cap with some feathers artfully arranged at a jaunty angle. As she saw the young smith quickly stand up and approach her, a broad smile broke out across her face. She walked forward, her hand outstretched in welcome.

'Ah, Gerant. This is where you hide! I had to ask that odious bookkeeper fellow who works for Urbright where your studio was. And here I am! I wanted to see your latest plans for my garden feature.'

Gerant had turned a bright red as he struggled to marshal his thoughts. 'A very good morning to you, my lady . . . Mitzi. What a true surprise. The, ummm, drawings are certainly coming along. Let me go and get them.'

'Of course, Gerant, take your time. Then you can show me around this delightful little area. I am so interested in what you do here.' The countess slowly pulled her gloves off as she looked around before placing them on Gerant's workbench. Gerant scuttled off quickly to the small inside area where the drawings were. *Shit, shit, shit. They are still far from ready.*

The two of them pored over the series of drawings of the garden gazebo, which were further along than what Gerant had remembered. He showed the countess the overall structure with pillars rising up to the roofed cupola and then the detail work of the cast-iron panels showing the rambling rose stems intertwining with each other across each section.

'So, I have some more hours' work to finalise the drawings and then to work out all the supplies and materials I will need, which will affect how long it will take to build and the final cost.'

Mitzi looked up from intently examining the drawings, where their heads had almost met several times. Her face showed delight at what she could see portrayed on the large pieces of paper and she clapped her hands excitedly.

'This is going to be wonderful. I can't wait to have little garden parties in the gazebo with my friends.' Her face took on a more calculating look. 'I would like you to bring the final drawings to me next week. I want to look over them even more carefully. So I think it would be best if you come to dinner and we can spend as long as we need checking over them.'

Gerant didn't know what to think at that proposal. 'Of course, I could have them ready in a week. But dinner? What would my lord think? Does he know about what I am making for you?'

Mitzi scoffed and burst out in gentle laughter. 'Bannerfield? He has no idea. Anyway, he is away on his yearly hunting trip and so it will be just you and me. If we need to spend more time after dinner, you can of course stay the night. That would be easiest.'

Gerant's mind was a swirling maelstrom of strange emotions and conflicting thoughts. This was something he had never, never considered and it held some confronting ideas. He realised that there might be a great deal of peril at play here. 'Mitzi . . . my lady. I would be delighted to bring the plans and thank you for the offer of dinner. I would be happy to accept, but after that I should be on my way.'

The countess had been watching the stream of emotions play over the young smith's face. She smiled gently and put her hand on top of Gerant's resting on the workbench.

'My sweet, sweet Gerant. I can understand your reluctance. But you need to know that Bannerfield and I have a very commonsense arrangement. I turn my eyes the other way when he regularly has a fling with some young woman or pretty little servant girl he has come across. He then has to ignore the occasional little dalliances I have with fetching young fellows like yourself. So don't worry, nothing will come of it. We will just have a lovely evening.'

Mitzi was very matter-of-fact. Gerant was still reeling with the consequences and now he had the added suggestion that he was only a plaything to amuse the admittedly very attractive woman in front of him. This was even more reason to keep things simple and straightforward.

'Thank you again, Mitzi, for the offer. I would be delighted to come for dinner and show you the final plans. But I will leave thereafter. There will be many more times when I need to consult with you and then construct the gazebo for you. I think we should leave it like that, for now.'

The countess sighed gently and smiled at some memory, picked up her gloves and carefully put them on. 'Well, Gerant. We can have a lovely dinner next week and then you can build my lovely gazebo in the coming little while. I shall have to be content with that. For now. I don't give up that easily, you know,' she said as she winked at the younger man.

They walked out to the street. Gerant couldn't recall what they talked about. His mind was in a flurry of conflicting emotions and thoughts. As they passed through the gate to the workshop, Mitzi reached over and gave Gerant a gentle kiss on the cheek. 'Goodbye for now, my young friend. See you next week. And bring a good appetite!'

The countess crossed over to the carriage that had been waiting patiently for her and the coachman hurried down to hand her up. She waved goodbye to Gerant as the coachman manoeuvred carefully into the middle of the street and headed off towards The Park. Gerant automatically walked back to the gate and pulled through the chain and clicked the padlock shut. His thoughts were still swirling about with no sense or reason. Perhaps it would be best to head to the riverbank and sit contemplating the water gently flowing past as he tried to come to terms with what was happening. The most difficult thing was he had no one to talk to about the countess of Bannerfield and what she appeared to want, far beyond the commission for the gazebo in her garden. Dirk would have no idea, and he did not even spend a second thinking about discussing it with Dierdre. Molly would have known exactly what to do. She would probably have come along for the dinner and that would have solved everything. But she was miles away and he had not heard anything from Samphire yet. He had worried every now and then that things had not gone well with Molly's trip back home. He had even started writing a note telling her of his feelings for her and asking how she was going, but had given up as he couldn't get the words to his liking. Then the new projects with the viscount had totally taken over his life, particularly as there was only himself to do all the little things needed to end up with the completed piece of work. And now on top of everything, there was the huge peril of becoming Mitzi's plaything. So he would just take some time and think through what to do. And what not to do. Gerant checked both ways and wandered off down the street, heading towards the River Greenthorn.

Urbright leant back briefly, shut his eyes and then focused again on the cards he had in his hand. *My luck is with me, tonight*, he thought. Now is not the time to be hesitant. He grunted to himself and pushed forward another ten chips. 'And ten.'

The others looked up in surprise. Either Urbright had a very solid hand, or he was pulling a massive bluff.

'Fold.' A pause. 'I'm out.' Both Thorburn and Shadcroft thought their hands were not good enough. Wallington had folded when he had seen his cards.

That left Kravensleigh. The count took another look at his cards, hesitated a moment and then pushed forward a matching ten chips. 'Call.'

Shadcroft had dealt, so it was Urbright who turned over his cards first. He revealed the Ace of Hearts and Ace of Clubs. 'Three aces.' There was the Ace of Diamonds in the community cards.

A deep sigh and a curse from Kravensleigh. 'Two pairs: Tens and Kings. I thought I had you there, Urbright. Your luck tonight is extraordinary.'

Viscount Urbright chose only to smile at Kravensleigh as he reached over and pulled the healthy pile of chips over to nestle with the significant mound in front of him. He looked behind and furiously waved at one of the Scarlett's staff for another bottle of wine.

'This one is on me, gentlemen. You are dealing the next hand, aren't you, Wallington? Let's take a short break. I really am finding this vintage rather fine, don't you think?'

A few hands later, Kravensleigh was dealer and had shuffled the deck absent-mindedly before giving out two cards to each of the five players, including himself. All had put forward two chips to start the hand. Then he dealt out three community cards in the middle of the table. They all leant in to learn what sort of hand they could build and continued staring at the three cards sitting innocently on the cloth surface of the table. Wallington was the first to say anything.

'That can't be right. There are two Aces of Hearts. How can that be?'

Each of the players thought through the consequences.

Shadcroft was perplexed, with his face showing a range of emotions. He slowly talked through what he was thinking. 'We all came here to play and are using one of Scarlett's standard decks. Perhaps the deck was not put together properly, which is possible. Or the other possibility is that one of us has been using this to his own advantage and substituting cards.'

A furious count of Kravensleigh looked around each of his fellow players and settled on Viscount Urbright who was looking as shocked as anyone. 'And which of us has been on an infernally good run of luck tonight? Who has benefited the most?'

Urbright's face changed instantly from shock to white anger as he registered what Kravensleigh had implied.

'Steady on, Kravensleigh,' interjected Thorburn. 'We have no proof and that is a very serious thought. You surely don't mean it!'

'Perhaps we can hear what our dear Urbright thinks,' muttered Kravensleigh through clenched teeth.

It was clear that Urbright was incensed with what had been said. 'I am as shocked as you are. A very sordid trick. But to somehow suggest that I am the one that is cheating is a disgusting allegation.' He stood up and looked at Kravensleigh directly across the table. 'You will need to withdraw that sleight on me and my play or there will be consequences.'

'Oh really?' drawled Kravensleigh, also now standing.

The entire gaming room at Scarlett's had seen the altercation and was watching what happened with breaths held. Even though they had not seen the start of it, the two men angrily addressing each other across the table was enough to indicate something dreadful had happened. The two men were of similar ages, height and build. Only those at the table knew where the conversation was headed.

Urbright gave a tight smile. 'Well, I demand satisfaction from you. You have besmirched my reputation and have called me a cheat!'

Kravensleigh smiled back. 'I actually didn't call you a cheat, but I am happy to do so now. Upstairs in the fencing salon? Swords? Perhaps in the morning. Not tomorrow but the day after. That will give you time to put in plenty of practice. You will need it, my lord.'

Urbright nodded and spat out, 'Agreed. You will also need all the practice you can get. Permilway will call on your second tomorrow.' The viscount scooped up the large pile of chips and threw them into a cloth bag before stalking off and out of Scarlett's.

Those in the gaming room were quickly told of the accusation and that a duel would occur in two days' time. It promised to be a very popular event, as Urbright had plenty of followers, while others found his mannerisms and behaviour quite offensive. He was known to be a gifted swordsman with an amazing new blade. Even more interesting was that Count Kravensleigh was also an extremely skilled fighter. He regularly won or was placed in the annual tournaments held in The Capital and was an opponent to be feared. No wonder he had not backed down; he would be confident of winning. Scarlett's continued to make a tidy profit as more of its guests stayed at the club and discussed the forthcoming event with much enthusiasm and excitement.

The morning light streamed into the fencing salon at Scarlett's through the wall of windows lining one side of the gallery. Enderby had decided that there was no need for lanterns. In many respects it was much more desirable if there was sufficient natural light for any contest, be it as a practice bout or, as was the case today, of a much more serious nature. There was more than the usual hubbub of onlookers for the duel to begin in a few minutes. A veritable crowd of expectant spectators was here to witness one of the highest standard of fights in recent years. Hislop from downstairs had been initially keen to charge an entrance fee for the duel once he knew how many people were to be expected. At first Enderby had not believed his ears. He had been quick to point out what was at stake and it was horribly bad taste to make coin out of a fight to the death. Regardless, many of those who had come would migrate down to the main part of the club to have refreshments and something to eat afterwards.

All the preparations seemed in hand. At opposite sides of the ring, the two parties had gathered and were endeavouring to ignore the hustle and bustle of the room. The two opponents looked ready. Urbright was in his customary fitted pants and ruffled shirt, this time with a burgundy-coloured sash. Kravensleigh always favoured a plain costume, with grey trousers and an unadorned cream-coloured shirt. Both men looked extremely lithe and flexible during their warm-up exercises, and they gave nothing away. Enderby quickly surveyed the crowd pressed up against each other in layers around the roped circle. It was the usual mix, with a number of women, amateur bladesmen and club members. Parvo, the fencing master, was standing at the back with his arms folded. Also here was Earl Sherrington and some other senior members of the court. From what he had heard, Sherrington was not here for moral support. Perhaps it was because a relation of his was involved. Or maybe just because the standard of the duel was likely to be of a very good quality. He made a mental point to seek out the earl afterwards and strike up a conversation and see where the talk went. Well, it was time to begin. He had already talked with both parties, and they were ready. It remained only for him to do his usual introduction. He strode into the centre of the circle and clapped his hands loudly to draw attention. After a few moments, there was a series of shushing noises from parts of the crowd and the noise of conversation died down to an expectant silence. He began his well-rehearsed preamble.

'My lords, my ladies, gentlemen and women. One and all! Welcome to Scarlett's to witness the duel of honour between the Viscount Urbright and Count Kravensleigh. This is a most serious encounter and one that I ask you to maintain an appropriate level of discretion and, above all, silence. There will be no calling out, words of insult or encouragement, and please keep still to allow the combatants to concentrate. I am your adjudicator and master of ceremonies. This is a large crowd and we have a number of extra guards at all points in the room who will quickly throw out anyone who infringes on the ring or disrupts the duel in any way.' Enderby paused before continuing. 'Gentlemen and ladies, be under no pretence that one of these combatants will be favoured by the gods and that it is a fight to the death, until one is too injured to continue, or until one of them yields.' There were several gasps from the onlookers. 'We have our good Doctor Aarons to take care of any wounds. I have already spoken to both parties and they are ready to commence.'

This time he looked at either side of the ring and called out. 'Gentlemen, are you ready? Please approach.'

Urbright and Kravensleigh eased their way forward through the onlookers and reached the edge of the circle on the opposite side of the adjudicator before loosening up a little and then falling still, with their swords held loosely in front of them. Enderby nodded to each of them in turn and then stepped out of the rope circle and positioned himself behind the small table that had been placed just outside the rope a similar distance from the two combatants.

'Gentlemen! Salute.' A pause. 'On guard.' Another pause. 'And begin.'

Both men had performed almost perfunctory bows with their swords and then swiftly went on guard and started to circle slowly, swords half-extended, blades slightly weaving in the air almost like snake tongues sampling the air for danger. Urbright smoothly shuffled forward a few half-steps, watching Kravensleigh's eyes intently. Without any warning, the count almost sinuously advanced directly at Urbright, the blades dancing and then ringing together as first Urbright countered and then Kravensleigh deflected a riposte from his opponent. The onlookers could almost feel the respect emanating from the two experienced bladesmen. There was no need to pretend to get a sense of what they were facing; they knew they were up against a deadly opponent and there was no soft-footing required to establish that.

Almost without a pause there erupted a furious exchange of thrusts and cuts, each desperately countered by either man as they darted around each other, the circle a whirling ring of deadly steel and constantly shifting bodies. The action occurred at such a pace that the onlookers struggled to keep up, as first Urbright and then Kravensleigh launched attack, fierce parry and then counterattack. There was a stark hiss from Kravensleigh and a quick grunt from Urbright during one prolonged exchange, and then they broke apart and separated to opposite sides of the rope ring, chests heaving with effort and examining their wounds. It was only then that there was a collective gasp from the spectators as they realised that both men had been cut in the exchange: it had occurred so fast that no one had seen it happen in the moment. Kravensleigh had almost entirely parried a rapid cut to the head by his opponent, apart from a final vicious little flick that Urbright had ended the cut with. Urbright's blade had just nicked his opponent's left cheek as he reacted by swaying his face away as Kravensleigh's parry took effect and blocked the main part of the stroke. Urbright had been cut on the back of his left hand near his wrist as he parried a series of lunges from Kravensleigh aimed at his chest. His sword arm and blade had parried his opponent's lunges, but it had been a case of coordinating both his arms to meet each attack. His free hand had been momentarily caught by the point of Kravensleigh's blade in the series of moves by his opponent.

The count pulled a small cloth out of his trousers and tried to wipe away some of the blood starting to slowly course down his cheek. Urbright sucked rapidly at the small wound on his wrist as he looked with fury at his opponent. Doctor Aarons grabbed up his bag from the table and began to move, but stopped at the restraining hand from Enderby, the adjudicator. It appeared that neither swordsman was willing to stop for medical treatment and were about to re-engage in the duel.

As the two combatants came back on guard and started to circle each other warily, those watching Urbright saw him murmur a single word and there was a muted flash coming from his left hand that was partly obscured by the flounce of his shirt cuff. Kravensleigh swiftly slid forward and there was another round of attacks, feints, parries and ripostes. The two men were still searching for an opening, but Urbright now had the upper hand. He was moving smoother and a little quicker than before and was anticipating his opponent's intentions almost as soon as they began. The viscount commenced a vicious sequence of feints, cuts and lunges at Kravensleigh's chest, neck and head. The count managed to counter them – often at the last moment – some by having to rapidly jump back little half-steps to move out of range of Urbright's questing blade. Both paused momentarily, chests heaving, a look of concern and worry appearing on Kravensleigh's face as he realised his opponent was pressing to find an opening and end the fight. There didn't appear much he could do. Then Urbright swung at Kravensleigh's right shoulder in a somewhat slow swing. This time his opponent was ready and parried strongly. As soon as the blades met as part of Kravensleigh's parry, Urbright disengaged, sunk down quickly so he was almost crouching, his body stabilised with his left hand splayed on the ground. Without a break he rapidly unfolded forward, his blade tip reaching up past Kravensleigh's sword towards the unprotected neck of his opponent. This was the same tactic that had successfully ended the duel with Cordner! The count registered the unexpected move and started to parry, realising too late that he would not be able to block in time. All he could do was fling himself back as quickly as possible, trying to maintain a semblance of balance. Urbright's blade cut the air only a finger's breadth away from Kravensleigh's chin as he fought to keep his footing. Urbright hissed in frustration and circled ominously to the right, looking for fresh openings.

A figure wearing a brown cloak and hood had found a position immediately behind the spectators lining the rope circle, with a good view of the duelling ring. They had watched the preliminaries with interest and gazed intently as the two swordsmen began the fight. They particularly watched Urbright closely as he circled, advanced and stepped back from Kravensleigh in the deadly dance. The figure was one of the few who saw Urbright speak softly a single word and the muted gleam of green flash from the viscount's left hand. They watched even more closely as Urbright started to summon extra skill and speed and almost managed to skewer Kravensleigh with the crouch and lunge manoeuvre. At that point the figure themselves quietly spoke a single word – 'Slow' – and from their left hand there was a brief flash of crimson from a ring they were wearing. The figure continued to watch very closely the progress of Viscount Urbright as the duel continued, both combatants now panting noticeably and watching each other with wild eyes as the contest reached a critical stage where the continuous exertion was starting to take effect.

To give himself a little more time, Kravensleigh engaged in a sequence of feints and half-thrusts at Urbright. His opponent suddenly appeared to be having trouble reading his body movements, and he had struggled to react with his sword and was late meeting some of the possible attacks. After that sequence of moves, they both moved apart and Kragensleigh studied the viscount carefully. He was a little perplexed and could not understand the sudden change in momentum. Urbright shook his head in bewilderment and glanced briefly at his blade. Kravensleigh slid forward and tried a fairly regular cut at Urbright's waist. He watched as Urbright reacted and started to position to parry, but was rather slow and only just blocked the cut. They broke apart again and started circling. Something had happened. A look of desperation appeared on Urbright's face, and he suddenly ran straight at Kravensleigh and leapt into the air as he got within a few feet of his opponent. His sword arm arched over, and he thrust straight at Kravensleigh's forehead. The unexpectedness of the unusual attack had meant his opponent was a little slow to react. But Kravensleigh saw what was happening and his training took over, swiftly throwing up his blade parallel to the ground and at the level of his nose. As soon as he felt Urbright's point touch his blade, he pushed up with all his might and ducked, his opponent's blade passing over his head with a few inches to spare. There was a distinct metallic sliding sound as the parry took effect and Kravensleigh backed away swiftly and tried to regroup, a look of shock on his face of how close his opponent had been to getting through with a fatal thrust. A collective gasp erupted from the crowd of onlookers as they took in the extraordinary attack by Urbright and the last-ditch parry and defence by his opponent.

A look of absolute determination came over Kravensleigh and he pressed forward. The attack when it came was easily read and rather slow. Kravensleigh shaped to attack with a cut to the left shoulder of Urbright. Compared to many of the previous attacks it was forewarned and Urbright reacted to it. He reacted well and he was able to parry successfully and the two swords clanged and then Kravensleigh disengaged. He did not move back and suddenly, all his speed and effort were put into a quick thrust to the right shoulder of his opponent. In contrast to the previous cut, this was viciously quick and Urbright's eyes widened suddenly in shock as he struggled to parry. His sword hand moved agonisingly slowly towards the correct line to parry, and it looked like he would make it just in time. Then he suddenly realised this was a feint and that Kravensleigh had changed the line of his thrust mid-move – he was actually going for the left. Urbright registered this and his sword arm started to adjust. But he was not fast enough! By the time he had made some movement, Kragensleigh's blade had slipped through. Urbright froze for several heartbeats. The point of his opponent's blade was resting on his rapidly pulsing neck and any sudden shift would mean Kravensleigh would ram the point home under his chin. Several more heartbeats.

Through clenched teeth, the darker-skinned man reluctantly muttered. 'Yield. I yield!'

There were a few more heartbeats where neither swordsman moved and then Kravensleigh burst out with a visceral 'Hah!', lowered his blade and stalked off to his party standing on the edge of the rope circle. Urbright slumped in defeat. A few more heartbeats and then there was a clear exhale of pent-up breath from the crowd during the climax and then a great swelling of noise, yelling, laughter and cheering as everyone reacted to the end of the fight. A number of them rushed forward into the fighting ring and the room changed into a roiling mess of people milling around, many shouting at the top of their voices. Doctor Aarons gathered up his bag of equipment and pushed his way through the figures to deal with the two swordsmen, who had both taken nasty cuts.

Chapter 43
Time to Go

In the midst of all the swirling groups of spectators in the fencing salon, the figure in the brown cloak with the hood masking their features quietly eased itself around various groups and reached the main door from the salon that led back into Scarlett's. The figure started to reach for the knob on the salon exit and began to pull the door open. Another hand reached out and grasped the figure's arm at the wrist, stopping the door from opening any farther.

'A moment, Gerant. I would value having a quick chat, if we could. Perhaps in the garden, where we won't be disturbed.' Earl Sherrington looked down at the hooded figure who had suddenly tensed at the contact. The hood hid much of the face of the individual, but enough for the earl to see that the young smith was shocked at being recognised.

'Ah, my lord. I guess so.'

'Good. Follow me.' The earl opened the door, and the two men left the salon that was still a shifting cauldron of figures talking loudly and reacting to what they had just witnessed.

The garden at the back of Scarlett's was not known to many of the patrons and was a leftover from when the building had originally been a family home. It consisted of a few trimmed flowers, bushes and shrubs and a couple of ornamental trees around ten feet high. A wooden bench was positioned at one edge of a curving pebbled path that led to an iron gate set into a brick wall marking the boundary of the property. Earl Sherrington sat on the seat next to Gerant, who had pulled down his hood now that they were alone as it felt somehow disrespectful to keep it up in the presence of the older, titled man. There was silence between the two for some moments. Then the earl spoke softly but firmly, beginning to formulate what was on his mind.

'I came here as I had been hearing very disturbing rumours of Urbright running up large debts on the gaming tables. Even worse, of being accused of cheating at cards and being called out. Naturally, he has denied everything and sought satisfaction from his accusers by letting the decision be decided by a duel. Twice he has bested his opponents, severely injuring the first and killing the second. This third time has resulted in him yielding, which was just as well as he was about to get skewered. What is interesting to me is that he is using a sword that you crafted. You are a superb craftsman of weapons and Urbright is better than average at wielding a weapon. All the same, that leads me to wonder: why are you here? I observed some odd things happen during the duel and I need to get to the bottom of this. Speak up, Gerant. We are beyond pussyfooting around the issue. I will be as candid with you as I hope you will be with me.'

Gerant listened carefully to the earl, with his eyes downcast, dreading where this conversation appeared to be going. He sighed as he realised he was in very deep water. But the earl said he should be honest, and the earl would be honest in return. Did he trust him? He hardly knew the man and they moved in very different circles. But the one time he had met him, he had shown he was a very smart fellow who treated people the way he found them. He sighed again. Well, there was nothing much he could do, and it was looking more and more like he would need all the help he could get.

'My lord, you are correct. The viscount's blade is one of mine, with many of the features you have in your own sword. He has employed me to craft weapons for him and his close friends. I wanted to try something I have learnt about, which involved imparting a magical effect on a blade. I did this on the viscount's sword and it imparted even greater speed and power when used. I then heard that the viscount was using the magical effect in these duels to become an even better fighter. All with my blade!' He stopped and gulped. He could not help but again feel angered at what had happened, and his words became more passionate. 'This is wrong! If you are the best man in a swordfight, then well and good, but to use magic to beat someone is unfair. And I gave him that ability. I felt I needed to stop that. So that's what I did. Maybe I shouldn't have, but I could not sleep knowing I had done nothing.'

The earl took all this in and pondered for several moments. Then he reached out to Gerant's wrist in a brief grip before relaxing. 'I don't know exactly what you did, Gerant, and I don't want to know the details. I can understand your feelings and I would probably also feel the same if these things were in my control.'

It was the earl's turn to sigh deeply. 'There are other elements that I need to consider. I agree that what Urbright has done is wrong, but on the other hand he is family. If this scandal gets too much further, then it could seriously compromise our position as one of the leading families in The Realm and could affect us for years. As head of the family, I need to prevent that. So Urbright will have to leave straight away for the family estate and keep his head down for some time while I repair any damage to our family's position.'

Gerant was interested in this point of view and could sympathise with the complicated set of events and situation the earl would have to deal with. He nodded in agreement, for what it was worth.

'Which leads us to you, Gerant.'

The young man felt very small as he wondered what the earl was going to say.

'Urbright is an interesting fellow. Nothing is ever his fault and the current situation where he finds himself bested in a duel and therefore at fault and guilty of cheating will be a new experience for him. So, he will be looking for someone to take the blame. Who could that be? It won't be his sword-fighting ability – that is without question – so it must be the sword that has let him down. And who made the sword for him?'

The earl didn't bother answering the question he had put in a musing tone. 'So he will come after you, Gerant, as the source of all his issues. Rightly or wrongly, it doesn't matter.' He sighed again. 'He won't do it himself. That's not his style. He will send his men. If they find you, the best case is they detain you on a trumped-up charge. Or more likely you will suffer a sudden accident. Or maybe just disappear, never to be heard of again.' The earl finished up his summary of what would happen and looked at Gerant directly, calmly and certainly with no anger or frustration showing on his features.

'You need to disappear, before they can find you. You don't have very much time, so go and grab a few necessary things and clear out. Stay at your peril. Go somewhere away from here and keep out of sight for six months, a year or however long it takes. When you think it is safe, send word to me and we will work out what we can do to try and rectify this unfortunate set of affairs. You are a good fellow, Gerant, but you are caught up in matters that are far beyond your experience or what you should have to deal with. Leave it up to me to find the best path to maintain my family's standing but also make sure you aren't an innocent victim. But go, Gerant. Don't delay. That's the best advice I can give you.'

The earl's eyes and sombre expression bored into Gerant's. 'Will you do that?'

Gerant was a swirl of panicky and conflicting thoughts as he tried to grasp what the earl had said. It was all too fast, but what the older man was suggesting made a lot of sense. Doing nothing was clearly not a good choice and now he was being sent down a path where he had very few options.

'Thank you, my lord. I don't think I have any say in this. I'll grab what I need and leave. And if things work out, I'll get in touch. It will probably be a note that I'll leave at your chateau. Just something plainly written with no name attached. Perhaps asking how the screen is going. But you will know it is from me.'

The older man nodded in agreement. There was an awkward pause as each of them were alone with their thoughts. Then the earl quickly reached out and grasped Gerant's hand in a strong and heartfelt grip.

'I look forward to seeing you in time and I want to do you right if I can.' A pause. 'Now go, before it is too late. See that gate? Go out that way, so no one sees you. My blessing, Gerant, for what it's worth.'

The young man nodded, feeling rather strange with the rush of emotions he was feeling and nodded. He pulled the hood of his cloak back over his face and quickly walked to the gate, opening it with a gentle squeak before slipping through and disappearing into the narrow alleyway at the back of the property.

Earl Sherrington remained on the bench, his fists clenching and unclenching as he collected his thoughts. He sighed, stood up and walked towards the doorway into Scarlett's, muttering as he did so. 'Well, Sherrington, let's talk to this toe-rag of mine and work out what we are going to do.' He opened the door, where the bluster of animated conversation burst out into the quiet space of the garden.

The old lady sighed and after a few more moments, gently clucked the horse to get it moving. It was well trained and the small two-wheeled cart it was pulling started smoothly and the horse matched the slow pace of the lady as she shuffled along at its head, holding the reins in her hands. The cart had a canvas tarpaulin stretched over the load. Various lumps and vague shapes under the tarpaulin suggested it was a mix of boxes, bags and other pieces of equipment. A burlap sack of something loose peeped out at the end of the tarpaulin where it was lashed to the end posts that rose in the back corners of the cart.

She had only got fifty or so yards farther down the road when there was a thundering of hooves behind her.

'Old lady, halt! Pull up!'

A group of three men on lathered horses were approaching rapidly. She stopped and they clattered past before halting in a loose pile of swearing men and jittery horses. They returned, loosely surrounding the woman, the horse and cart.

The woman peered mildly at the sudden arrivals and waited for them to speak. The men were wearing some sort of similar style of clothes – russet brown with green trim – a blond and two with brown hair, one whose flowing hair and moustache was streaked with grey. He might be the leader, mused the old woman. It was he who spoke first.

'Where have you come from?'

'New Town. I was at the little market there.'

'And where are you going?'

'To Nutley. Where I live.'

One of the other men – the blond fellow – interrupted. 'Have you seen a man, medium height and build, brown hair? He would either be walking or on horseback. Answers to the name of Gerant.'

The old lady considered, frowning a little. 'No, no one like that has gone past me.'

The other brown-haired man burst out in exasperation. 'See, I told you he would have gone to the port and would look for a boat to get away in. Come on! We might still be in time!'

With that, the two younger men wheeled their horses and clattered off at a steady canter. The older leader waited, looking over the old lady in front of him and at the horse and cart. He was not yet convinced. Something was a little odd. 'Is this horse yours?'

'No, he belongs to a neighbour. He lets me take him on occasion when I have stuff to move. I have been visiting my daughter in New Town for a few weeks and couldn't carry all this by myself.'

'What's the horse's name?'

'Corporal.' The horse pricked up its ears and looked around as it heard its name called.

'Hmmm. What's in that sack?'

'Grain for my milking cow. I got it at the market in New Town. Any extra milk I sell in the village for a little coin.'

The man digested what the old lady said and then reached down with a dagger and slashed the hessian sack poking out from the edge of the tarpaulin. A small dribble of wheat immediately spilled out where the cut had been made. The man looked at the wheat and looked at the woman and then quickly wheeled round and took off back to The Capital to chase down his two men.

The old lady's features went from gently polite and unassuming to a look of pure venom as she hawked and spitted in the direction of the rapidly disappearing horsemen. 'Maggots!'

The sound of receding hoofbeats had all but disappeared when two figures emerged quietly from the roadside vegetation – a young man and a large brindled dog. Gerant approached the lady and had one last look back at the now empty road to The Capital.

'Did it go OK, Vera? I could see some of it from the bushes but couldn't hear anything. I'm glad we saw them coming with time to spare and had the story worked out.'

Vera spat again. Then her face lost its angry look and became once again that of a gentle, old soul that everyone would like to have living next door. 'They asked me about where I had come from and where I was going. Then the leader looked like he didn't believe me and asked about Corporal and what was in the sack there. The filth wanted to check so he slashed it and then just rode off.'

The young man took all that in and it added up with what he had seen. He checked the sack and only a little of the wheat had spilled out. 'Well, my thanks and I am glad things didn't go too badly. I will tie up the sack so we don't lose any more.' He had a thought and checked the lashings of the tarpaulin. 'They didn't look underneath?'

'No, only the sack.'

He sighed with relief. It would have been all up if they had checked the contents of the cart and realised it didn't belong to an old woman visiting her daughter. But they hadn't and so it was all OK. He quickly looked at Fang. The large dog had shown very little interest and had quickly flopped down on the road near Corporal and was just waiting for something to happen.

'Right. it will just take me a few moments to just tie up this sack and then we can be on our way again. Let's get you to Nutley and your place and I'll take the grain in for you.' He remembered something and reached into a small sack almost hidden under his tunic and fastened to his belt.

'Here, Vera. The gold piece I promised . . . plus another to make up for the grain and to express my thanks for helping me out.' He passed them over to the old lady and closed her palm over the coins.

Vera smiled contentedly and hid the two gold away in a pocket in her skirt. 'Ah, you are a kind young man. What did you say your name was again?'

'Oh.' A pause. 'Gareth.'

'My thanks to you, Gareth. They said another name for who they were looking for, so you should be out of danger.' She paused in thought for a few moments. 'I baked yesterday, so I have some cake left. We can have a bite to eat when we get to the cottage. You sure you won't stay?'

The young man, who might have been known as Gareth, laughed and shook his head at the thought. 'I am rather tempted,

Vera, but I do need to keep going. Still a bit of travel to get to where I am heading, so I might press on, if that's all the same to you. But I would like to try your cake and maybe a hot drink.'

The dagger tear in the sack of wheat was quickly tied off and then the old lady, her new companion and the two animals headed off at a gentle pace on the road pointing north.

Chapter 44
Full Circle

One-two-three-four-five-six-seven. The smith paused and looked about. It would only be a few more hours and then the day would close in and evening would begin. It had threatened rain, still smelled of moisture in the air but the clouds suggested it might hold off until dark. Another seven blows on the faintly glowing axe head. Then a break. He looked up with pleasure at the new sign swinging gently above the entrance to the workshop. It read: 'Gareth Hartung. Samphire's master smith and artisan.' He was well satisfied with the bold but cursive writing and the symbols of an anvil, crossed hammers and a sword.

As he was about to take the axe head out of the coals again, he took a further look and noted the small figure across the street watching from the doorway of the house over the way. He made another series of blows, paused, then looked up. The figure had not moved. The smith put down his ball-peen hammer and thrust the axe head back in the glowing coals to reheat.

He pulled one of the stools out from under the work bench and placed it handy to the forge. He pitched his voice enough to carry, yet not be loud enough to be threatening in any way. 'Hey. Why don't you come over here and sit on this stool? It's a lot easier to see what's going on up close than from over there.'

The figure considered the proposal for a few seconds and then stood up and almost ran over and plonked on the stool, with wide eyes. The young girl was maybe up to his chest in height, with bluish eyes, a snub nose and freckles. Her blond hair was plaited into two braids hanging down her back. She was dressed in a simple shift-like dress and was in bare feet.

The smith smiled and spoke more quietly. 'See, this is much better. What's your name? Mine is . . . Gareth.'

The girl looked at him with almost frightening intensity. 'Sally. But most people call me Sal.'

'Nice to meet you, Sal.' He had a thought as he worked out how old she probably was. 'Do you go to school?'

'Yes. At Mistress Molly's. I'm learning my letters and she says I am doing really good.'

That solved one thing. He would ask Molly about one of her pupils once he had finished up and headed for home.

'Live around here?'

'Next street. Mam says I can do what I like after schooling as long as I am home before dark.'

The smith considered this. 'Well then, we have an hour or so.'

'I can also come tomorrow. And the next day.'

He pondered that. 'That sounds good. Let's see how you like it. I am making an axe head for a fellow who is one of the wood cutters. He needs a really good axe or two. This one is . . . is a special type of steel that will make it really light and strong.'

The smith paused and saw that Sal was watching him talk with that same combination of intensity and concentration. 'You could help out with working the bellows. Would you be able to do that?'

Sal nodded fervently and hopped off the stool, ready to do whatever the smith instructed.

'Great! Maybe stand here.'

Gerant briefly paused as he recalled a long-cherished memory from the past, before he almost shook himself back to the present. 'All set? This is what you need to do.'

A fruitful half hour or so had been spent with Sal before Gerant decided to call it a day. He didn't want to wear out Sal too much. Her interest and enthusiasm had never waned, as he watched her happy face and flashes of excitement and understanding. This was coupled with chatter about all manner of things, including what they were working on. In many respects, she reminded him of Bree at a similar age.

'That was fun. See you tomorrow!', was all the acknowledgement Gerant got before Sal ran off home, singing loudly to herself.

Gerant sighed contentedly, a warm glow in his heart. It was only then that he noticed another figure quietly watching him from the corner of the next building. Molly saw his glance, smiled broadly, and wandered over.

'I thought you would be finishing about now and that we could go over to the plot and pick some beans to have with last night's leftovers. Then I saw you had a little apprentice and I stopped to watch. Sal is a bright button, isn't she?' Molly reached up and kissed Gerant, cuddling up to him.

'Yes,' responded Gerant, returning the cuddle. 'One thing led to another. Who knows how this might end.' He paused. 'She reminds me a little of someone else I know... Which reminds me, with midsummer break coming up, are you still OK that we head down to Ashford to see my folks?'

'Absolutely, Gerant. That would be wonderful. I am so keen to finally meet them. Let's work it all out while we pick those beans.'

Gerant quickly packed the last things away, tamped down the forge and the pair wandered off, holding hands.

noli oblivisci unde venias